WO

Deep Waters

Books by Kate Charles

Evil Intent
Secret Sins
Deep Waters

Deep Waters

Kate Charles

First published in Great Britain in 2009 by
Allison & Busby Limited
13 Charlotte Mews
London W1T 4EJ
www.allisonandbusby.com

First published in the US in 2009
by Poisoned Pen Press.

A CIP catalogue record for this book is available from
the British Library.

10 9 8 7 6 5 4 3 2 1

13-ISBN 978-0-7490-0710-2

Published by arrangement with Poisoned Pen Press, USA.

The paper used for this Allison & Busby publication
has been produced from trees that have been legally sourced
from well-managed and credibly certified forests.

Printed and bound in Great Britain by
MPG Books Ltd, Bodmin, Cornwall

For my dearest Rory—
thirty-five years and counting

Acknowledgments

Grateful thanks are due to numerous people:

Deborah Crombie, Marcia Talley and Suzanne Clackson, for editorial advice and creative input.

HM Coroner Dr. William Dolman, Dr. James Cullen, the Rev. Sharon Jones, the Rev. Ann Barge, the Rev. Mary-Lou Toop, the Rev. Sylvia Turner, for technical expertise and information.

Westcott House and Dyffryn Farm, for creative spaces.

Kat, Paula and Louise, for Jodee's hair.

Chapter One

About three o'clock on a March morning, Callie Anson thought the world must be coming to an end. It was the wind that woke her, slamming against the sash window of the bedroom as though it was trying to break and enter. Above her head the roof timbers creaked and groaned, then came the sound of a sliding slate, followed by a crash.

Callie was torn between the temptation to get out of bed to look out of the window and the urge to pull the duvet over her head and pretend it wasn't happening. Cowardice won out over curiosity, aided by the common-sense realisation that it was dark outside and she wouldn't be able to see much anyway.

Then there was a scratching sound at the bedroom door, frantic and persistent.

'Oh, Bella!' In an instant Callie was out of bed, opening the door to admit a black and white cocker spaniel. 'Come on, girl. You must be terrified.' She scooped the trembling dog up in her arms and carried her to the bed. 'It's okay,' she soothed, getting back under the duvet and stroking Bella's soft ears. 'I won't let it hurt you.'

As another slate and then two more crashed to the ground, Callie wished she felt as confident as she sounded. But then, that was pretty much the story of her life.

'I don't know.' The young man shook his head as he surveyed the wreckage which surrounded the church hall: smashed slates and broken branches. He tipped his head back and squinted towards the roof. 'Yer've lost a fair few of them slates, see? And it's too high up for a ladder. Goner need scaffolding, innit?'

'Scaffolding!' That, reflected Callie, sounded serious. And expensive.

'It'll cost yer,' he echoed her thoughts. 'Got insurance, have yer?'

'Oh, the church has insurance.'

The young man gave her a suspicious look. 'Yer live in a church?'

'This is the church hall—I live upstairs. The church is over there.' Callie pointed towards the nearby Victorian edifice, its roof miraculously intact. That, at least, was a blessing. The churchyard was going to need some clean-up, with all of those branches down, but it appeared that the building itself hadn't sustained any significant damage.

Likewise the vicarage, standing stolidly next door. No, the church hall had taken the brunt of the storm, and once it had lost one roof slate, a whole army of its fellows had followed.

The wind, though it had lost the edge of its savagery, was still blowing in frigid gusts. Callie shivered, while the young man crossed his arms across his chest and tucked his hands in his armpits. 'Any chance of a cuppa?' he suggested hopefully.

'Of course.'

That she could manage: dispensing cups of tea was one of her specialities, rain or shine. It was something curates, if they were at all clever, mastered in the first week of their job.

Callie led the way up the stairs to her flat. Ignoring the fancy hot drinks machine her brother had bought her, she filled the kettle and switched it on. Some good sturdy PG Tips was what was needed here, not poncy cappuccino or espresso.

She brought two mugs back into the sitting room to find that the young man had shed his donkey jacket and was on the sofa, stroking Bella. Above his faded jeans he wore a t-shirt which revealed a surprisingly thin, wiry physique. His skinny upper arms were encircled with some sort of tattoos, like celtic torc armbands. 'Nice dog,' he said.

'Thanks.' Callie smiled. 'She's called Bella.'

'I'm Derek, by the way. Derek Long.'

'Callie Anson.' She put one of the mugs on the table in front of him. 'Three sugars, like you said.'

'Brilliant.'

How, she wondered, could he be so thin if he took three sugars in his tea? And what about his teeth? What she'd seen of them didn't look particularly attractive; her own teeth hurt, just thinking about it.

Derek picked up the mug, blew on its steaming surface, then took a gulp. 'Perfec,' he pronounced.

She drank her own tea, feeling she needed the warmth and comfort it provided after her foray outside.

'Can I ask yer a question?' Derek was looking at her over the rim of his mug. Looking, she perceived, in the vicinity of her clerical collar.

'Of course.'

'Are yer a vicar?'

Callie smiled. 'No, not exactly. I'm a curate.'

'What's that, then?'

Ah, she thought, the mysteries of the Church of England hierarchy. How could she explain it without boring this young man to tears? Bishops, archdeacons, deans, canons, vicars, rectors: even the faithful weren't always clear what it all meant. 'I suppose a curate is sort of like a junior vicar,' she said. 'The vicar—Brian—is my boss.'

'Curate sounds more like a junior doctor.' He grinned.

Callie laughed. 'I suppose it does.'

'So y're like…religious? Or somefink like that?'

How was she supposed to answer? She thought about it for a moment, then said carefully, 'Well, I work for the Church. I believe in God, if that's what you mean.'

Derek Long shook his head. 'The Church,' he said. 'I don't get it. I mean, like, y're not bad lookink. If yer don't mind me sayin'. Why would yer waste yer life on the bloomin' Church?'

She turned the question back on him. 'You're not a church-goer, then?'

'Me? Nah.' Again he shook his head. 'I mean, like, why would I go to bloomin' church? On a Sunday mornink? Not bloody likely. Not after I been down the pub on a Saturday night, like. I'm not goink nowhere on Sunday mornink.'

And this conversation wasn't going anywhere either, Callie decided. She didn't want to come across as prim and pious, and she knew that nothing she said would persuade this young man that church had anything to offer him. So she sipped her tea for a moment, then changed the subject. 'About the roof,' she said. 'It's bad?'

'It's bad, all right,' Derek replied promptly. 'To be honest, like, I fink it's past mendin'.'

'Past mending?' That sounded alarming. 'You mean you can't fix it?'

Derek ran a hand over his head—which wasn't quite shaved, but cropped very close to the scalp. 'Best to have a new roof.'

Well, Callie told herself philosophically, the insurance would take care of it. Brian would moan about all the paperwork, but it couldn't be helped. 'Will you be able to do it right away?' she asked. 'Or as soon as we can sort out the insurance?'

He shook his head. 'Not a chance.'

'But—'

'There's a waitink list, like. For the scaffolding, innit?'

Callie fortified herself with a gulp of tea. 'Then how soon?'

'Month. Six weeks, mebbe. Two months, outside.'

Two months! Callie envisioned the spring rains which were yet to come and remembered the gaping holes in the roof above her head. 'Can you do something temporary? Put some plastic over the holes so the rain doesn't come in?'

Derek fondled Bella's ears. 'Yeah. I can, like, use some poly-fene sheetink. But,' he added, as if it were an insignificant detail, 'yer won't be able to live here.'

Not be able to live in her flat—for up to two months? Callie sank back in her chair. 'But...but...where am I supposed to live?'

Derek Long shrugged.

Where on earth was she going to live? Even if the insurance would pay for it, which seemed unlikely, Callie couldn't just go off and live in a hotel for two months. She had a dog, for one thing. And she needed to be in, or at least close to, the parish. Close to the church.

She'd better talk to Brian, and soon. Maybe he would know of a parishioner with an empty flat, or someone with a spare room who wouldn't mind a well-behaved dog—not to mention a well-behaved curate—moving in.

Jane Stanford was feeling a bit out of sorts. It wasn't anything she could put her finger on, but she just wasn't at her best. She'd spent the morning at the ironing board, which she usually didn't mind at all; on this occasion, though, her lower back ached.

A possible symptom of pregnancy, Jane was aware. *If only.* But Jane knew that—in spite of her efforts—she wasn't pregnant. She'd used one of her supply of testing kits just a few days ago, and the results were negative. Again. Not this month. Maybe soon, but not yet.

A baby girl—that was what she wanted. She'd wanted it for a very long time, since not long after she'd given birth to twin boys over eighteen years before, but the hard facts of vicarage budgeting had meant that it was out of the question to have another baby. Out of the question until just a few months ago, when an unexpected legacy had given their finances a boost, and Jane had confided her long-deferred hopes to Brian, hoping it wasn't too late.

She was, she hated to admit to herself, on the wrong side of forty, when conception could by no means be taken for granted. When she'd had the twins, all those years ago, it had been so easy. Now she was doing everything it said in the book—charting her temperature to pinpoint the moment of ovulation, taking lots of vitamin supplements, even losing a bit of weight—yet nothing had happened.

Jane straightened up, arching her shoulders to ease the strain. Perhaps, she told herself, the back ache was because she hadn't slept very well. There had been a tremendous storm in the night, battering the vicarage windows with a frightening savagery. Brian, bless him, had managed to sleep through it, but Jane hadn't been so lucky. She'd lain awake for what seemed like hours, hoping the walls and roof would withstand the onslaught.

And while Jane was ironing, transforming crumpled lumps of white fabric into crisp, snowy surplice and alb, Brian had spent much of the morning in his study with his curate, Callie Anson.

There was something about Callie Anson that got on Jane's nerves. She admitted it to herself, though she wasn't sure why it was so. In theory, Jane didn't have any strong objections to women in the clergy, nor could she come up with any valid theological arguments against women's ordination. She didn't really think that Callie had designs on Brian or would ever, consciously or unconsciously, inflict damage on their marriage. Callie wasn't rude or patronising to Jane as 'just the vicar's wife'; on the contrary, she was always pleasant and polite. She was a perfectly acceptable young woman, attractive and bright and hard-working. Jane just…didn't like her.

She'd tried very hard to keep her feelings about Callie from Brian. After all, she knew how irrational they were, and she didn't want Brian to think she was some sort of jealous shrew. Still, she wasn't sure how successful she'd been until that day at lunch-time.

Lunch was vegetable soup, made with the dregs from the vegetable drawer of the fridge and a few sprouty potatoes she'd found at the back of the larder. Still, Brian ate it without complaint, and while eating he dropped his bomb-shell.

'The church hall really took a hit from that storm last night,' he said. 'I suppose we were quite lucky that the church and the vicarage weren't damaged as well.'

'Damaged?'

'The roof,' said Brian. 'Lost quite a few slates. Apparently the whole roof will have to be replaced. It's not even safe for habitation. The roofing chap told Callie she'll have to move out.'

Jane didn't have a premonition of what was coming. 'Oh, poor Callie,' she said with as much sincerity as she could muster.

'I told her she could stay here at the vicarage,' said Brian. 'Just for a month or two. You don't mind, do you, Janey?'

A month. Or *two*. Jane stared at her husband as though he'd taken leave of his senses. Which, it would seem, he had done.

'We have all this space here, especially with the boys away,' he went on. 'The guest room is made up, isn't it? Callie won't be any trouble.'

'But she has a *dog*.'

Brian shrugged. 'Oh, that won't be a problem. Bella's a quiet little thing, and we have a big garden. It's not as if you're allergic to dogs.'

Allergic to dogs. That was hardly the point. 'But...isn't there anywhere else she can go?' Jane managed. 'An hotel?'

'You said it yourself, Janey,' Brian said with infuriating patience. 'She has a dog. She can't stay in an hotel with a dog.'

'How about her mother's?'

He shook his head. 'Her mother lives in Kensington. Callie needs to be in the parish.'

'Surely there are people in the parish...' Jane looked down into her soup bowl, struggling to keep her voice even. 'Can't you ask round, Brian? I can think of several people. Elderly ladies on their own in big houses, like Mildred Channing, or Hilary Dalton?'

He raised his eyebrows and gave her a quizzical look. 'I'd almost think you didn't *want* her here, Janey. This is the logical place for her to stay. You must see that.'

Jane swallowed hard. She had one last argument in her arsenal and now was the time to bring it out. 'What about the... the money?'

'Money? What do you mean?'

Of course, thought Jane, Brian never worried about little things like money. It was up to her—and always had been—to eke out his stipend till the end of each month, to pay the bills and put food on the table. 'Her meals,' Jane said baldly. 'Am I expected to feed her out of my housekeeping money?'

Brian grinned, clearly pleased with himself. 'This is the best thing about it, Janey. I rang the EIO. The insurance company. They'll pay to put Callie's belongings in store. And they'll pay *us*. There will be a weekly cheque coming in for her accommodation!'

That, realised Jane, was it. She may as well give up and accept it.

◇◇◇

The storm had passed, bringing behind it unseasonably warm temperatures and sunshine. It was, in short, too nice a day for Mark Lombardi to eat his lunch in the police station canteen. Instead he picked up a sandwich and headed for his favourite green space.

Newcomers to London were always surprised at how much green space was to be found in the nation's capitol city. Mark, as a London native, took for granted the vast expanses of Hyde Park, to the south of the station, Regents Park, to the north-east, and the more modest Paddington Green, round the corner. But there were smaller green spaces as well, tucked away in unexpected places—tiny squares, little parks, churchyards. Some time ago Mark had discovered one of the latter just a short walk from the station: a secluded churchyard with a bench where he could sit and eat his sandwich in peace and feel a million miles away from the bustle of London.

And sitting in a churchyard, even if it wasn't *her* churchyard, somehow made him feel closer to Callie: more a part of the world she lived in. Thinking about Callie, imagining what she was doing at any given moment, was something Mark did a great deal of these days, wherever he was.

If anyone had told Mark Lombardi, six months ago, how much his life could change in half a year, he wouldn't really have believed them.

All it had taken was that trip to Venice to visit his grandmother. On the way back to London, he'd been seated next to an engaging young woman with shiny brown bobbed hair, and they'd talked for the entire flight as if they'd known each other for years. That's how it had started; by the time they'd landed he knew that he wanted to see Callie Anson again. And again and again.

Mark wondered, not for the first time, about the vagaries of fate. What if the woman at the airline check-in had assigned him a different seat that day? What if Callie hadn't commented on the Italian newspaper he was reading, and drawn him into conversation? So many variables…And yet there was such an inevitability about it, looking at it from the perspective of the present. Here, now, sitting in this churchyard, he could not imagine his life without Callie in it. She was woven into the fabric of his thoughts, day and night; they saw each other most evenings, and in between they spoke on the phone. She was even—miracle of miracles—accepted by *la famigilia Lombardi*, that formidable institution which pretty much governed his life.

He still couldn't believe that Mamma liked Callie. He'd been so prepared for the opposite that he'd delayed their meeting for months. After all, he had been programmed for his entire thirty-one years to bring home a nice Italian girl, with all that implied. And Callie wasn't just an Anglo: she was an Anglican. An Anglican in Holy Orders, at that.

To Mark's astonishment, Mamma had taken it all in her stride. Callie had won her over without even trying. And where Mamma led, Pappa followed. Pappa thought Callie was wonderful.

It was a mystery.

Mark took a bite out of his cheese and pickle sandwich and looked at the clump of daffodils near the church porch. They were a bit battered in the wake of the storm, but still held their yellow heads upright.

Rather like his sister Serena, he thought. The events of the last few months had been horrendous for her. Yet she had carried on, head held high, as if nothing had changed. Mamma and Pappa hadn't known—hadn't even suspected—that she was heartbroken, bearing the burden of her husband Joe's infidelity.

She had—in the throes of her anguish—confided in Mark. It had shaken him pretty badly as well. He had known Joe di Stefano for most of his life, and his sister's marriage had always seemed rock-solid to him, the exemplar of all that marriage should be.

Marriage. That brought Mark's thoughts round to his good friend Neville—Detective Inspector Neville Stewart.

If Mark's life had changed in six months, Neville's had altered beyond recognition. From being a confirmed and carefree bachelor, he had transformed into a married man. And it had been even more of a shock to Mark than it had to Neville.

Neville had played his cards so close to his chest that Mark had had no idea what was going on. Yes, he knew that Neville was seeing someone, early on when Mark himself was getting to know Callie. But his absorption with his own new relationship had blunted his curiosity, and within a few weeks Neville had told him, in his taciturn way, that things were over between himself and Triona. Neville had never been comfortable talking about emotions, about things of the heart; he often kidded Mark about his Mediterranean temperament, wearing his heart on his sleeve.

Suddenly, then, just before Christmas: an engagement. Neville had told him over a drink at their favourite pub. 'Seems I'm getting married,' he'd said casually, halfway through his first pint of Guinness.

Mark could only stare at him. 'Married? But who to?'

'Triona O'Neil. Will you be my best man?'

'I'd be honoured. But…'

Eventually he'd pried it out of Neville. He and Triona had lived together for a few months, some years earlier. Their breakup had been painful; Neville had really never got over her. Then they met again by chance, were drawn together briefly, and split again.

'But I finally realised,' Neville said, looking down into his Guinness, 'that I didn't want to live without her. It was like…a lightbulb going on over my thick head. Difficult as it is to be with her, being without her is worse. Much worse.'

He had proposed to her, he confessed, at the top of the London Eye. He'd done it properly, going down on his knees.

'And she said yes?' Mark surmised.

She'd said yes—or at least maybe, at that point. And that wasn't all she'd said.

'I'm going to be a dad,' Neville told him, pulling a bemused face.

Triona had broken the news to him immediately after her provisional acceptance of his proposal: the one time they'd slept together, there had been consequences which neither of them had expected. She'd known about it for weeks but hadn't been planning to tell him.

'It's not like I wouldn't have figured it out eventually,' Neville said wryly. 'But she didn't want me to feel like I had to marry her. Even after I proposed, and she told me about the baby, she said that if it made any difference to the way I felt, then we'd call it off there and then.'

Mark raised his eyebrows. 'And how *do* you feel about it?'

There was a long pause while Neville emptied his glass. 'It scares the crap out of me,' he said frankly. 'I just never thought… I never really thought about having kids. I know that sounds stupid. But it's like…being old or something. A wife is one thing. But a kid?' He shook his head. 'I'm still getting my head round it, to tell you the truth.'

That sounded a bit worrisome to Mark. 'You need to be sure,' he said. 'You shouldn't marry her if you're not sure—about the whole package.'

'That's what Triona said.' Neville stood up, ready to go to the bar to get the next round. 'So we're not rushing into anything. We're going to wait a couple of months, to give me time to get used to the idea. But I *am* going to marry her, mate,' he added firmly. 'So you can start working on your speech now.'

The wedding had taken place the previous weekend, and now Neville was on his honeymoon. Mark thought about it as he finished his sandwich.

It had been a small wedding, held at a posh hotel in the City. Neville had cleaned up well, looking positively handsome in his hired dinner jacket. And Triona, her bump unabashedly visible beneath her gown of clingy, creamy bias-cut satin, was a radiant bride. The guest list was limited to a few friends on either side: Triona's solicitor pals, and Neville's police colleagues. Mark was best man, and Callie's great friend Frances Cherry was Triona's attendant.

No family—not on either side. That seemed the strangest thing of all to Mark. He couldn't imagine a wedding without family. If it had been *his* wedding, it would have been awash with them, streaming in from near and far. Nonna—his grandmother—would have come from Venice, and no doubt other Italian relations as well.

Nonetheless the wedding had moved Mark deeply. As the couple said their vows he watched Neville's face, and his friend looked as if he'd won the lottery and inherited a brewery on the same day. And Triona, when the ring was slipped on her finger, glowed with a transcendent beauty which was partly to do with motherhood and all to do with love.

It made Mark want to rush to Callie's side, throw himself at her feet, and beg her to marry him. During the wedding breakfast, as she sat beside him looking as lovely as he'd ever seen her, the urge was powerful.

So why hadn't he done it?

Mark still wasn't entirely sure. It was partly to do with a failure of imagination. Their wedding: what would it be like? Yes, there would be family there, in abundance. But that in itself would be an issue rife with possibilities for problems. His ardently Roman Catholic family would take a dim view of a wedding held in an Anglican church. Yet that wasn't just a possibility—it was a certainty. Callie was an ordained clergywoman, within a few months of being a priest. It was who she *was*, not a mere religious preference. Her wedding should by rights take place in her own church. What would his family make of that?

Even more than that, though, he had been constrained by something Serena had said to him on the evening he'd introduced Callie to the family, just before Christmas. He and his sister had had a heart-to-heart talk in the kitchen over the washing-up.

'What do you think?' Mark had asked her; he knew that she knew the answer he wanted.

'She's lovely,' said Serena. 'Very nice, Marco.' If her voice conveyed a bit less enthusiasm than her words, at least the words were the right ones.

'I really love her,' he confided. He wouldn't have told his mother that, but he felt comfortable saying it to Serena.

'You haven't…?'

'Asked her to marry me? Not yet,' Mark admitted. 'I'm working up to it, though.'

Serena didn't look at him, but she laid a damp hand on his sleeve. 'Don't rush into anything,' she said in a flat voice. 'I mean it, Marco. You may think she's the one, the right person—'

'She *is*,' he interrupted. 'I'm sure of it. I've never felt this way about anyone before.'

'Give it time,' Serena said. 'If she's the right one, you won't lose anything by waiting. And if not…well, it's better to find that out before you commit yourself.' She swallowed. 'You think you know someone, but it takes time. Lots of time.'

Mark realised she was talking about Joe, was talking out of her own pain. He shouldn't have expected her to be over the moon about his happiness with Callie.

And yet…there was something in what Serena said. If it was right, then what was the rush? Callie wasn't going anywhere, and as his feelings for her—their feelings for each other—deepened even further, there would come a time when the next step would present itself as inevitable.

Mark's churchyard reverie was interrupted by the jangling of his phone. Callie.

'*Cara mia*,' he greeted her, a smile in his voice.

'I just wanted to let you know, Marco. There's a change of plan for this evening.'

'Well, Bella,' said Callie. 'I suppose this is it.' Home, for the next few weeks.

Home. If you could call it that. Callie looked round the room, trying hard to find something homely about it.

It wasn't a small room: that was one thing in its favour. High ceiling, plenty of floor space. The high ceiling, though, meant that there was all the more of the drab, depressing wallpaper on view. And as for the floor space...

The floor was covered with not one but two patterned carpets, joining somewhere near the wardrobe. The carpets were equally threadbare, equally hideous—one a bilious shade of green, with large swirls of a darker green, and the other a floral design, featuring overblown pink roses on a dreary grey background. The Stanfords' last vicarage must have had smaller rooms, Callie guessed, with none of its carpets large enough to make the transition to this current Victorian monstrosity. Either of those carpets would have been ugly enough on their own; together they were truly sick-making.

Unsurprisingly, none of the furniture matched either. There was a frameless double bed, covered with a dingy white candlewick spread, a dark oak wardrobe, a lighter oak chest of drawers, and a pine bedside table. Blessedly there was also a wash basin attached to the wall in the corner, its pipe-work concealed by a frilled and gathered skirt.

Callie looked at the books on the bedside table. Thoughtfully provided? On the whole, she doubted it: they seemed a random collection of old paperback novels—from some long-ago church jumble sale, or left behind by previous guests—mingled with an assortment of other tomes. There was a cookery book, a chemistry text book, and a battered children's picture book. She was glad she'd thought to bring along her own reading material.

Unfortunately, though, there was no reading lamp on the bedside table. The room's only illumination came from the window, and above—from the single dim bulb dangling from the middle of the ceiling, shrouded in an ugly fringed shade. Evidently people were not meant to read in this room.

Bella jumped up on the bed and flopped down, seemingly impervious to her depressing surroundings.

'Oh, Bella,' Callie said. She realised she should probably get the dog off of the candlewick bedspread, but she didn't have the heart. Instead she sat on the edge of the bed and stroked Bella's ears.

What had she done? What had she committed herself—and Bella—to?

She hadn't had many other options, and when Brian had suggested it, she'd overcome her reservations about living under Jane's roof for maybe two months, and had accepted his offer.

At least, she told herself philosophically, the new arrangements would put on hold the fraught question of sleeping with Mark Lombardi. It certainly wasn't going to happen here, at All Saints' vicarage. And maybe that was no bad thing, to remove that particular issue from the equation for a while.

Chapter Two

For once in his miserable life, Neville Stewart counted himself a happy man. A contented one, even.

He was, after all, on his honeymoon. In Spain, where the sun shone every day instead of maybe once a fortnight. With the woman he adored and had finally realised he didn't want to live without.

She was next to him now, in a large and comfortable bed, sleeping soundly in the early hours of a Spanish morning.

Neville himself was awake. They'd spent so much of the last week in bed that he seemed to have caught up with his chronic sleep deficit. Maybe, he thought, that was one reason why he felt so good. The honeymoon hadn't just been about sun, sea and sex—though there had been plenty of those, and not necessarily in that order. Sleep had also been on the menu, along with all the wonderful food they'd consumed.

Triona seemed to need even more sleep than he did—probably because of the pregnancy.

Neville played with a strand of Triona's long black hair, twisting a curl round his finger. Triona, in her everyday life as a staid solicitor, usually tamed her hair by wearing it scraped into a knot at the back of her neck, but on honeymoon she'd not bothered, letting it go wild much of the time and otherwise just pulling it back with a scrunchie or piling it on top of her head. He'd always loved her hair, which seemed to him to have a life of its own. When he'd first known her, when they'd first been lovers so many years ago, she'd kept it short and curly. It had been sexy then; now it was erotic in the extreme.

As was everything else about her. Whatever else he may have thought about her unexpected pregnancy—whatever his unspoken and unexplored ambivalence about becoming a father—Neville found the changes in Triona's body deeply, irresistibly erotic. The gentle swell of her belly, the astonishing enlargement of her breasts: he couldn't get enough of her. And the hormones of pregnancy meant that she was equally hungry for him.

They'd been on honeymoon for nearly a week, with just over a week to go. In ten days he'd have to be back at his desk, and Triona would return to her office in the City, continuing to work until it was time to go on maternity leave.

Living…where? That was the one fraught question. Neville had his grotty flat in Shepherds Bush, where he'd been for years; it had been good enough for Triona once, but it certainly wouldn't do for her now. Her posh City pad was tiny, really only suitable for the workaholic singleton she had been until a few months ago.

Triona wanted to find a house—a family house. That, in Neville's mind, meant the suburbs. He couldn't imagine himself stuck in the suburbs, with a long commute into work. And London was so damnably expensive these days that it would have to be quite a way out. Even with Triona's respectable salary they couldn't afford anything very convenient.

But it would have to be done. The baby would be there before the end of summer.

Neville ran his hand over Triona's tummy and she stirred in her sleep. 'Hey,' he murmured in her ear. 'Are you awake?'

Her eyes, heavy-lidded, opened just a slit. 'No, I'm not.' Triona pushed his hand away. 'Let me sleep, okay?'

He supposed he could wait. They weren't going anywhere, and she was certainly worth waiting for. Maybe he'd go back to sleep himself for a bit.

The question of sleep, though, suddenly became academic. Neville's mobile phone, on the bedside table, bleated out a few notes in a minor key which told him before he even looked at it that the call was from work.

Unbelieving, he reached for the phone and squinted at the screen. 'Evans,' he grunted. 'What the hell does Evans want? Doesn't the bloody man know I'm on my honeymoon?'

'Don't answer it,' Triona said sharply, raising her head from the pillow. 'Just don't answer it.'

By now she should have known him better. Neville punched the green button. 'Yes?'

It was, without a doubt, the most uncomfortable bed Callie had ever slept in. It was soft, for a start, and lumpy as well. There was a deep indentation—a trough, to put not too fine a point on it—in the centre of the bed, towards which she inevitably rolled and where she stayed for the whole of the night. Though it was a double bed, it would have been almost impossible for two people to share it without each clinging to opposite edges of the mattress.

Through the long and miserable night, Callie's mind threw up a succession of unanswerable questions.

How long had Brian and Jane had this bed, she wondered, and where had they obtained it? Had they bought it new, at the beginning of their marriage, and worn it out themselves, or was it a family heirloom? Had it already been through a succession of owners before it came to reside at All Saints' Vicarage?

Did Jane and Brian have any idea how uncomfortable it was? If they'd used and discarded it, perhaps they did know—and just didn't care that their guests would wake up in the morning feeling worse than when they'd retired at night. Assuming, that is, they could sleep at all.

There was only one place for a bed like this, more like a mediaeval torture device than a place for rest and refreshment: a landfill somewhere.

Should she mention it to Jane? If Jane were, for instance, to ask how she'd slept?

Not jolly likely, Callie decided. She was on shaky enough ground as it was. Brian might have insisted on her coming here to stay, but Callie could tell that Jane wasn't keen. Dinner last night had been frosty, to say the least, in spite of Brian's heedless chatter.

And unfortunately it was obvious that Jane was not a dog person. How anyone could resist Bella's charms was beyond Callie's imagination, but Jane managed it very well. She insisted that Bella be banned from the public rooms of the house and confined to Callie's bedroom. So Bella, accustomed to sleeping in Callie's kitchen, was unsettled as well, her bed now tucked into the corner of the guest room. She whimpered occasionally through the night, further interrupting Callie's intermittent periods of sleep.

How could this arrangement possibly work for the weeks it was going to take to get her roof sorted? When she had to be out during the day—and she certainly wasn't planning to spend any more time than necessary in this dreary room—what was Bella meant to do? How could her poor dog survive?

If every night was going to be as sleepless as this one, how could Callie herself survive?

As the first finger of morning light poked between the ill-fitting curtains, Callie groaned and buried her face in the pillow.

At least there was no rush this morning. This was her day off; she could remain in this dreadful bed for as long as she liked—or as long as she could bear it.

◇◇◇

Mark Lombardi rarely saw his flatmate, Geoff Brownlow. They both worked long hours, and most of Mark's evenings, when he wasn't working, were spent with Callie. He and Geoff weren't friends by anyone's definition: they'd never been down to the pub for a drink together, or engaged in anything but the most superficial of conversations. Their flat-share was a business arrangement—the result of a newspaper advert—which happened to work very well for both of them, most of the time. Both

Mark and Geoff were tidy by nature, so there was no conflict on that front. Once in a while they both needed the shower or the kitchen at the same time, but they were civilised about it and had never argued. For Mark, it was worth the occasional delayed shower to be on his own, out of his parents' house. He knew that he could never afford the flat on his own; Geoff's presence was a small price to pay for that freedom.

So it was, Mark recognised, a most uncharacteristic thing he'd done the night before.

Callie had cancelled their evening together. He'd been planning, as was customary, to go to her flat after work. It was his turn to cook—of the two of them he was by far the more accomplished and confident cook—so he'd already bought the ingredients for dinner. But Callie's flat had suffered storm damage and was off limits, that night and for some weeks to come, and her move into the vicarage left them without a place to be together. In any case, she'd felt strongly that the first night she would need to settle in to her temporary home and have a meal with Brian and Jane.

As a result, Mark had gone home with his food—home to his flat. And Geoff had come in from work a few minutes later. On impulse, Mark had made the offer. 'I have rather a lot of food here,' he'd said. 'If you don't have plans…'

Geoff didn't have plans. So Mark cooked the sort of dinner he'd grown up with and had been taught by his mother to pre-pare to perfection: heaps of glistening pasta, followed by tender braised steaks and crisp vegetables, ending with a melt-in-the-mouth pudding, all accompanied with a nice bottle of wine.

Afterwards Geoff produced an almost-full bottle of a fine single malt whisky, and they settled down for the rest of the evening.

And Mark did most of the talking. He told Geoff about Callie: how they'd met, how he felt about her. How he was trying to take things slowly, let them develop in their own time. How that process was now interrupted by Callie's forced removal to the vicarage.

'It won't be easy for you to sleep with her there,' Geoff observed, refilling their glasses.

'We're not…I mean, we haven't got to that point yet,' admitted Mark.

'You're not sleeping with her?' Geoff's look of incredulity was replaced by one of dawning comprehension. 'Oh, I get it. She's a priest. So she won't because it's against her religion or something.'

'Not exactly.' Technically, Callie wasn't a priest yet—that wouldn't happen for a few months—though that wasn't what Mark meant. How could he tell this virtual stranger that *he* was the one holding back, not Callie? Not that he didn't want to, desperately. But there was something about the fact that she was in Holy Orders…

When Mark woke the next morning, a little the worse for the whisky, it was with a slight feeling of embarrassment that he had opened his heart to Geoff that way. He could blame the whisky for loosening his tongue, but the fact was that he'd needed to talk to someone. In any other circumstances he would have gone to Serena, the person with whom he'd always shared his feelings; at the moment that just wasn't possible. And Neville wasn't around. Anyway, he knew what Neville would say: just stop being such a bloody fool and shag her.

So instead he'd bared his soul to Geoff, his flatmate. The person he had to live with, even if he didn't see him very often. How stupid was that?

He certainly didn't feel like facing him now, with his head throbbing and a rather unpleasant taste in his mouth.

Fortunately Mark didn't have a very early start this morning. He wasn't going straight to the police station; he was going to accompany someone to court at the Old Bailey.

He could use a couple of paracetamol—or some strong coffee. But he could hear Geoff in the kitchen. The coffee could wait.

'Yes, Sir. Yes. I understand. But—' Neville grimaced at Triona, who was sitting up in bed glaring at him, miming dramatic throat-cutting gestures. NO, she mouthed. N - O.

Neville made a heroic effort. 'I'm on my honeymoon, Sir. Just halfway through…' He listened to the voice on the other end, then sighed. 'Yes. I see.'

With a withering look, Triona got up and went into the bathroom, slamming the door behind her.

After a few more minutes of a largely one-sided conversation, Neville pressed the button to terminate the call, threw the phone on the bed, and followed Triona to the bathroom. He tapped on the door. 'Darling,' he said in as conciliatory a tone as he could manage. 'We need to talk.'

She flung the door open. 'Don't you "darling" me. I know what you're going to say.'

'You don't.'

'You're going back to work, Neville. I'm not stupid. I've figured that much out.'

'God, Triona. Let me explain.'

'Explain?' She crossed her arms over her chest. 'What part of "honeymoon" do you and that bloody man not understand?'

Neville took a deep breath. 'Listen, Triona. This isn't an ordinary case. It's a dead baby.' He knew he wasn't playing fair, but the bald statement had the desired effect.

'Oh.' Her eyes widened, her arms dropped to cradle her bump instinctively, protectively, and all the fight had gone out of her voice. 'What happened to it?'

'That's what Evans wants me to find out.' Neville took her arm and guided her to a nearby chair. 'Sit down, darling. I'll tell you everything I know.'

She sank into the chair, unprotesting, while Neville perched on the edge of the bed, knee-to-knee with her.

'This is a high profile case, to say the least,' he explained. 'It's Jodee and Chazz. Their baby.'

Triona stared at him blankly. 'Who the hell are Jodee and Chazz?'

How, Neville wondered, could anyone in the civilised world ask a question like that? But Triona wasn't like most of the people in the civilised world: she didn't read newspapers, she didn't even own a telly. It never ceased to amaze him, the way she managed to travel through life without absorbing so much of the minutiae in which other people revelled. Her obliviousness to popular culture was, he realised, one of the things that made her so special, one of the things he found so endearing about her.

'They're only the most famous couple on the planet,' he said. It was a slight exaggeration, perhaps, but not that much of one. He couldn't actually think of another pair who had, within the past few months, been the subject of more column inches of tabloid verbiage. Not even Posh and Becks.

Jodee and Chazz. Where to begin?

'You know about the programme "twentyfour/seven"?' Neville ventured.

Triona shrugged. 'Well, yes,' she admitted. 'The programme where a bunch of thick people get shut up in a house together with the cameras running. I've heard of it. A few people at work were hooked on it last summer.'

'Jodee and Chazz were a couple of those thick people,' he said. 'They fell in love. And…let's just say that they didn't make any effort to hide their attraction to each other from the rest of the world. Or what they did about it, either.'

She narrowed her eyes. 'You mean they…'

'Yes. Live. On camera.'

'Ugh.' Triona shuddered. 'And you wonder why I don't have a telly.'

'I didn't see it myself,' Neville assured her. 'But millions of others did.' He grinned. 'Usually, on these programmes, it's a question of "will they/won't they?". But with Jodee and Chazz it was more a question of when. And how often. Apparently they were at it like rabbits, all hours of the day and night. Mostly in the hot tub.'

'So their baby…'

He nodded. 'You've got it in one. The baby was, according to the tabloids, the first to be conceived on live telly, in front of the camera.'

Triona's hands went to her bump. 'How horrible. Didn't people complain? About public decency?'

'Thousands. The more complaints there were, the better for the ratings.'

'It's all so…cynical.'

'And that was just the beginning,' he continued. 'Morning sickness. Jodee suffered from it terribly. The watching world saw her throw up, over and over again.'

'I can relate to that,' Triona said feelingly. 'Though I'm glad no one was watching.'

He'd missed that stage, Neville realised with a pang. While she was experiencing morning sickness, he hadn't even known she was pregnant. That was something he didn't want to dwell on.

'Anyway,' he went on, 'the baby was born a couple of months ago.'

'On telly?'

'Thankfully, no. We were denied that pleasure,' he said ironically, 'because they'd done a deal with one of those celebrity magazines. The birth was a photo exclusive. A big cover story. Though,' he added, 'someone in the delivery room apparently shot a bootleg video on their camera phone and put it up on YouTube. It's been viewed by millions of people.'

Triona lowered her head for a moment, her eyes closed, then straightened up and looked at him levelly. 'So what's happened? To the baby?' He could tell that she was struggling to keep control of her voice.

'That's what we need to find out. Evans said that she was discovered dead in her cot early this morning. The doctor was called in, of course, and he notified the police.' Neville pressed his fingertips together and looked at them rather than at his wife; he was surprised at how her distress was affecting him. 'It's being treated as a suspicious death. Evans says there's no evidence so far that it's anything other than cot death, but we can't afford to cut any corners with this one.'

'Yes,' she said. 'I understand that.'

'The world will be, quite literally, watching.'

'But why,' Triona added, with a bit of her old spirit, 'does it have to be *you*? DI Neville Stewart, and no one else? Doesn't Evans have someone there who's *not* on his honeymoon?'

He shrugged. 'He says he doesn't trust anyone else. There will be quite a lot of involvement with the media, obviously, and I've had experience with that sort of thing before.' Neville admitted to himself, though he wasn't going to say it to Triona, that he was just a bit flattered by Evans' confidence in him. 'I mean, can you imagine what a disaster someone like Sid Cowley would be?'

Triona chose not to speculate on that; instead she changed the subject to the practicalities. 'Our plans,' she said. 'We can't just leave. What about our non-refundable aeroplane tickets?'

'Evans said it will be taken care of. We're just to go to the airport, and everything will be sorted.'

'Not everything,' Triona said quietly. She got up and went to the window, pulled back the curtain—'beach view', just as the brochure had promised—and stood with her back to Neville. 'I wish you wouldn't,' she said, in a voice that was little more than a whisper.

'I'll make it up to you,' he heard himself saying. 'Another time. We'll come back.'

She turned to face him; her voice sharpened. 'And how would things be different? How could I be sure the same thing wouldn't happen again?'

Neville shrugged, then sighed. He knew there was no answer he could give Triona that would satisfy her, and it was all his fault. Was this how it was going to be from now on? Twenty minutes ago, he'd been deliriously happy. He should have known it couldn't last.

◇◇◇

Mixing wine and spirits—not to mention a healthy dose of confession—had not been a good idea.

Once he'd heard Geoff leave the flat, Mark got up and went in search of paracetamol. The packet wasn't in its usual place in the bathroom cabinet; he found it sitting on the edge of the basin, which indicated to him that perhaps Geoff was also suffering more than a bit. It certainly wasn't like tidy Geoff to neglect to put something away.

Mark downed a couple of tablets, then took a long shower.

'Coffee,' he said to himself, then 'Serena'.

Mark made pretty good coffee himself, but next to his mother, Serena made the best coffee in the world. A cup of her concentrated caffeine would quickly sort him out.

If he left soon, he would have time to call in and see her before he was due in court. She should be at home this time of the morning—after getting Chiara off to school, and before going to La Venezia, the family restaurant, to supervise the lunch shift. He had a good excuse, apart from the coffee: he needed to have a word with her about Chiara's birthday.

Chiara, his younger niece, would be thirteen tomorrow. A teenager! Not a little girl any longer.

Mark reflected on this as he walked from the flat—conveniently located off High Holborn—through Holborn and Clerkenwell to the di Stefanos' house. How ancient it made him feel: he so clearly remembered himself, as a teenager, holding the tiny baby when she was just a few hours old.

He wondered how Serena felt about her baby reaching such a milestone, especially with all the other things that were going on in her life.

Serena wasn't likely to tell him. Close as they were, she kept her feelings to herself—apart from the extraordinary occasion when, under exceptional stress, she'd poured out to him her heartbreak over her husband's infidelity.

When he was about halfway there Mark rang ahead on his mobile to let Serena know he was coming, so when he arrived she answered the door promptly.

'The coffee's nearly ready,' she said with a smile, kissing him on both cheeks.

'Not a moment too soon.'

They went through to the cosy kitchen and Mark pulled a chair up to the table while Serena poured the coffee. 'Not at work this morning?' she asked.

'Court,' he said. 'The Old Bailey. I'm meeting someone there in about an hour. An old case from last year.'

His sister nodded. Mark's job as a Family Liaison Officer often involved long-term contact with bereaved families, and that meant accompanying them to court to provide moral support during trials.

Mark accepted the coffee gratefully and took a long, appreciative sip. 'Thanks, Serena. You're wonderful.'

She produced a rather brittle smile. 'I'm glad someone thinks so.' Then she shook her head and frowned. 'Sorry, Marco. I shouldn't have said that. It's not fair to dump on you.'

'Dump on me all you like.' There wasn't anyone else for her to let off steam to, he knew: she had to keep the girls from finding out that anything was wrong. Not to mention *i genitori*, their parents. Mark could only imagine the strain it must be on Serena.

'That's not why you came,' she said, decisively changing the subject. 'You wanted to talk about Chiara's birthday?'

'I just wondered what the plans are. Since it's on a Saturday.' Saturday was inevitably the busiest day of the week in the restaurant trade, so Mark assumed that Serena, as front-of-house manager of La Venezia, would be tied up at lunch time as well as in the evening.

Serena shrugged. 'We'll have to celebrate it on Sunday.' Sunday was the one day of the week that La Venezia didn't open its doors, and it was traditionally a big family day for the Lombardis and di Stefanos. 'With *la famiglia*, at lunch. And I've told Chiara that she can invite a few of her friends round later in the afternoon, for some cake. Mamma's baking it.'

'Is Angelina coming?' Chiara's older sister was at university in Birmingham.

'I doubt it. Term's not over yet. Though,' Serena added, 'she might just surprise us and turn up.'

Mark finished off the small, strong cup of coffee and held the empty cup out for a refill. 'What I really need to know is what I should get her. For a present. Something she'd really like.'

Serena twisted her mouth in a wry smile as she poured out the last of the coffee, then got up to start another pot. 'It used to be so easy, didn't it? Dolls, stuffed toys, coloured pencils and boxes of watercolours. Socks with cute animals on them, and hair ribbons.'

'But those things are too babyish for a teenager?'

She sighed. 'These days it's all pop singers and earrings.'

'Chiara doesn't have pierced ears, does she?' Mark frowned, trying to remember. His niece had always worn her hair long, over her ears, so he hadn't particularly noticed.

'Not yet. But she's wild to have them done. So we're going to pay for that, and we've bought her some nice gold earrings.'

'I suppose I could get her some earrings as well?' He'd need Callie's help, Mark realised; he wouldn't have the first idea what sort of jewellery would be suitable. 'Or is there an album she really wants?'

Serena wrapped her hands round her own coffee cup and looked thoughtful. 'She keeps talking about the new album by that singer Karma.'

'Karma who?'

'Just Karma.' Serena shook her head. 'I'm sure you've heard of her, Marco. She won the last "Junior Idol" competition. Chiara thinks she's wonderful.'

'Vaguely,' Mark admitted. He was not a follower of "Junior Idol". 'Well, that does sound like a good idea, then. If that's what she wants.'

'It would make her very happy.'

'Consider it done.' That, realised Mark, would make his life much easier—he could just walk into any record shop and ask for it. 'I'd like to give it to her on her actual birthday, though. If I come round tomorrow evening, will she be here?'

Serena got up and retrieved the coffee pot from the hob, topping up Mark's cup. 'Absolutely. Saturday night is "Junior

Idol" night. Wild horses wouldn't drag Chiara away from the telly on a Saturday night.'

'I suppose I'd better time my visit so I don't interrupt.' He laughed.

'It's not a joke, Marco. Fortunately for me, I'm never here on a Saturday night. Joe has that pleasure. But interrupting "Junior Idol"—well, I wouldn't suggest it. Not if you want to remain her favourite uncle.'

Chapter Three

Lilith Noone, a reporter with the *Daily Globe*, found out about the death of Jodee and Chazz's baby at about the same time and in the same way as the rest of the press. But she had, she felt, a natural advantage over the competition.

She knew Jodee and Chazz.

At first she had known them in the same way as everyone else did: on the outside looking in, via the live television cameras. Lilith was no voyeur; her interest in the couple and their romance was a professional one, spawning many column inches of verbiage in every issue of the *Daily Globe* over a number of months.

It was true, she acknowledged, that the *Daily Globe*'s position as self-appointed upholder of the nation's moral standards meant that those early stories had taken a somewhat censorious tone, while revealing everything the watching public longed to know. That, in Lilith's mind, was the beauty of the *Daily Globe*: they could have their cake and eat it. They could draw in readers with titillating headlines—'Naughty Romps' and 'Hot Tub Hotties'— and revel in the most salacious, prurient details, as long as moral outrage was expressed at the end of it. There was a real art to it; Lilith liked to think it was an art at which she excelled.

And everything had changed when the show was over, when the cameras were no longer focused on the couple's hot tub antics. The baby was on the way, a wedding was planned, and suddenly Jodee and Chazz were exemplars of family values—and therefore the new darlings of the *Daily Globe*. The stories became no less frequent, but now they were fawning in tone. Lilith had met them face-to-face and interviewed them on a number of occasions; she'd even snagged an invitation to their wedding, the only journalist—apart from the sponsoring celebrity magazine—to be so honoured. She prided herself that she had been invited as a friend rather than as a member of the press.

So when the shocking news that their adored baby was dead appeared on the wire, Lilith felt confident in picking up the phone and ringing Jodee's private mobile number.

She wouldn't have been surprised if Jodee herself didn't take the call; she was undoubtedly in shock. But Jodee did answer, her unmistakable Geordie voice much fainter than usual. She sounded tearful, dazed, though not displeased to hear from Lilith.

'I heard. I can't believe it,' Lilith said. 'Oh, you poor things. Can I come to see you?'

Jodee didn't wait to confer with Chazz. 'Yeah, come,' she said. 'We're at home.'

Within seconds Lilith was on her way out of the door.

Callie might not need to get up early on her day off, but that didn't mean her dog didn't have certain physical needs, first thing in the morning. So Callie had a quick wash in the handbasin, pulled on a pair of jeans and a fleece, and clipped Bella's lead to her collar.

The little dog was more than ready to go out, wriggling with excitement.

'Let's be quiet,' Callie whispered. 'We don't want to disturb Brian and Jane.'

There was no sign of either one of them as they went along the corridor and down the stairs. Taking Bella into the back garden would have meant going through the kitchen, where the Stanfords were probably breakfasting, so instead Callie checked that she had the house key she'd been issued, and headed for the front door.

Outside it was cool and damp, as if it had rained in the night and might very well rain again. 'Let's go to the park,' she said to Bella, and set off in the direction of Hyde Park.

Hyde Park was Bella's favourite place to walk, full of new smells to explore every day. There were always other dogs there as well, to be met and greeted as they trotted along with their owners. By now Callie knew quite a few of the other habitual dog-walkers by sight; often they nodded or exchanged a few words on the weather.

'How about that storm the other night?' said the owner of a friendly black lab, a middle-aged man who was usually out this time of the morning. Bella was wagging her tail, engaging in ritual sniffs with the lab. 'Worst I've seen in years.'

'It was bad,' Callie agreed as the dogs parted and they went on their way.

Bad. And its after-effects were even worse. She realised that she was going to have to re-think her plans for her day off.

She'd intended to spend the morning at her computer, catching up with e-mail and other paperwork. Then, after lunch, she would do some grocery shopping at the local shops and the nearby Tesco Express.

The computer wouldn't be a problem, as she'd moved it to her temporary quarters and could set it up on one of the folding tables from the church hall. But there was no real reason to do much shopping; after all, she wasn't going to be cooking. Not tonight or any time soon. Jane had made it perfectly clear that, as a guest in the house, Callie would have her meals with the family and would not be expected, or indeed permitted, to use the kitchen.

No shopping, then. And a free afternoon. With a sigh, Callie accepted her fate: it was too long since she'd been to see her mother. She'd managed to avoid a visit for over a fortnight, excusing herself with pressures of the job, and her mother was starting to make pointed comments. Maybe she could get her brother Peter to go with her; it was always better with two.

◇◇◇

Improbably, Jodee and Chazz lived in Bayswater, in an elegant Georgian townhouse which faced onto a square just off Sussex Gardens. It wasn't the sort of address that one might have expected for a young pair who had achieved instant celebrity— and instant riches—but Lilith knew the reason for it, and indeed had written about it at some length in one of her pieces about the couple.

Though Jodee was a northern lass, Chazz was a Londoner by birth. He had grown up on a council estate in Westbourne Green, raised by a single mum who'd worked for years as a daily cleaning lady in one of the Georgian townhouses of Bayswater. He'd lived his childhood against a background of tales about her wealthy employer and her wonderful house. 'I'll buy you one of them houses one day, mum,' Chazz had promised his mother throughout his childhood.

And he'd been as good as his word. When he emerged as the winner of 'twentyfour/seven', flush with prize money and the promise of a lucrative modelling career, even before he married Jodee, he'd bought the house and they'd all moved in together.

So it was Chazz's mother, Brenda Betts, who opened the door to Lilith. Lilith had known Brenda even longer than she'd known Jodee and Chazz; she had interviewed her while the pair were still ensconced in the 'twentyfour/seven' house. She liked Brenda, whom she'd found sensible and open.

In the split second before Brenda Betts dissolved in tears and threw herself in Lilith's arms, Lilith took in her appearance. Brenda had changed in very subtle ways since their first acquaintance. She was by no means ostentatious, but her formerly shapeless hair had been restyled in a fashionable cut, the grey threads exchanged for golden highlights, and her clothing no longer came from a High Street chain store—or a charity shop. The result was that she looked a good twenty years younger. Lilith put the change down to two things: the money, of course, and Brenda's new daughter-in-law. Jodee was nothing if not style-conscious, and that must surely have rubbed off on Brenda, living under the same roof.

'Oh, Brenda.' Lilith hugged her with ready sympathy. She wasn't really a huggy sort of person, but Lilith knew that there were times when it was a professional necessity. 'What a terrible, terrible thing.'

'She was such a tiny scrap,' Brenda sobbed on her shoulder. 'Not even two months old.' Brenda's common accent hadn't changed, Lilith observed; it would take more than an infusion of ready cash to effect that transformation.

After the hug had gone on for as long as Lilith deemed appropriate, she extricated herself deftly. 'Jodee said I could come,' she stated.

'Come in. They'll be glad to see you. But they sent me in case it was…someone else.'

'Has anyone else been here?'

'Some reporters. Photographers, of course. A television crew. I sent them all packing. Told them to have some respect. They'll be back, of course.' Brenda wiped her eyes with a tissue. 'Before that, the police.'

The police! Of course, Lilith told herself, it would be a police matter. A baby dying at home, in unexplained circumstances…

'All them forensic people. Made a mess, tramping all over the house.' Brenda, the ex-cleaner, still house-proud in the midst of unimaginable tragedy.

She led Lilith to a room she'd been in before: a room dominated by an enormous plasma television screen fixed to the longest wall. On past visits the television had been playing videos of 'twentyfour/seven'; now it was switched off, a blank black presence on the wall. Apart from the television, the room was minimally furnished with a white leather three-piece suite and a coffee table scattered with fashion magazines and celebrity gossip weeklies, most of which featured Jodee—with or without Chazz and/or the baby—on the cover. It was always easy to spot Jodee on a magazine because of her hair, even though its style was now emulated by countless thousands of teenaged girls across the country. The cut was asymmetrical, with one side chopped off well above the ear and the other side curving down to her chin. The colour could best be described as a duality: a platinum layer underneath, her pale fringe peeking out under a black top layer as if she were wearing a dark cap.

Chazz was hunched on the edge of the sofa, staring blankly into space. He didn't even raise his head at the entrance of his mother and Lilith. Jodee, on the other hand, paced the room, moaning like a wild animal.

She looked a bit like a wild animal as well, Lilith observed. Her eyes were panda-like, the mascara smeared round them in streaky dark circles. Her trademark hair, usually so carefully styled, was in disarray, dark and light layers carelessly inter-mingled. She and Chazz were both dressed in clubbing clothes; in her case, that consisted of skin-tight leopard-print capri pants and a halter top. Somewhere along the line she'd kicked off her stiletto shoes and paced in her bare feet.

'Oh, God, Lilith!' Jodee wailed. 'Oh, me poor Muffin!'

Lilith prepared herself for another hug, even holding out her arms. But Jodee ignored the invitation and instead threw herself on the floor, beating her fists on the white carpet. 'God, God, God!' she screamed.

'Exclusive Interview'. The words danced in Lilith's head, infi-nitely alluring. She had access to Jodee and Chazz—the nation's most famous bereaved parents—when no one else did. She was going to make the most of it. But it was going to be hard work; she had no doubt about that.

The defendant had pleaded guilty; there was to be no trial. It hadn't been expected, but it was a relief to all concerned, not least to Mark. He hadn't been looking forward to re-living a particularly brutal murder in the company of the bereaved family, and the trial could have gone on for days if not weeks.

The prisoner was going down for a very long time; Mark, though, was now a free man. He came out of the courtroom with the victim's family, stood by them outside of the Old Bailey as the press fired questions at them, escorted them to their car and said goodbye.

He looked at his watch. No one was expecting him at the police station for the rest of the day, so he would have time to find a record shop and get Chiara's Karma CD. He might even have a chance to see Callie. It was her day off; perhaps they could meet up and have lunch together before he went on to work. He'd give her a ring straightaway and see if she was available.

Mark stopped in a doorway and switched his phone on. There was an immediate indication that he'd missed a call and there was a message waiting.

He recognised the number. Work, not Callie. Mark sighed and punched a button to listen to the message.

He was to ring DCS Evans immediately, the message said. That didn't sound very promising.

Mark's pessimism was well placed. Evans' secretary put him through straightaway, and Evans tersely explained what was required of him.

'It's going to be a high-profile case,' he said. 'The press are already on to it. Jodee and Chazz are huge, you know.'

'Jodee and Chazz?'

Evans sighed. 'I don't get it, myself. But the wife…Mrs Evans… she loves them. She can't get enough of "twentyfour/seven".'

Mark was aware of 'twentyfour/seven'; he'd heard of Jodee and Chazz and knew something of their notoriety. But he couldn't help asking. 'Don't any of these people have last names?'

That raised a weary chuckle from Evans. 'As a matter of fact they do. In this case it's Betts. Fairly unglamorous, I suppose. And it seems to be a mark of celebrity status not to *need* a last name.'

Elvis. Madonna. Somehow, reflected Mark, Jodee and Chazz didn't have quite the same iconic ring.

'Anyway, no time to waste. You need to go to their place ASAP. It may take a while for DI Stewart to get there.'

Neville! 'But he's on his honeymoon!' Mark protested.

Evans snorted. 'Not any more, he's not.'

They really weren't taking any chances with this one, then. What the American cop shows which Mark watched sometimes, with guilty pleasure, called a 'red ball'. Mark made a half-hearted attempt to get out of it. 'Wouldn't Yolanda Fish be better than me, Sir?'

'DC Fish? We're talking about a dead baby here, Sergeant Lombardi. Think about it.'

Mark thought about it. Yolanda Fish, ex-midwife. Tender-hearted in the extreme. She took her cases very much to heart, got involved with the families as if they were her own. Usually that was a great strength; Mark could see that in this instance it would be asking too much of her. She wouldn't be able to maintain any objectivity around young parents who had just lost their baby.

And maintaining objectivity, while remaining sympathetic and helpful, was what the job of a Family Liaison Officer was all about.

Mark didn't need to ask why the police were involved in this very private, yet potentially highly public, tragedy. A baby was dead. It could have been an unpreventable cot death, just one of those inexplicable things that happened all too frequently to families round the world.

Or it might have been something else.

If it *was* something else, Neville and his colleagues, including the pathologist and the coroner, would get to the bottom of it. But not without pain for a great number of people.

Mark sighed. He wasn't going to get out of this one, it was clear. Jodee and Chazz: at least that might raise his street cred with Chiara. Though, as a fond uncle, he hoped that her mother hadn't allowed her to watch their much-publicised frolics in the hot tub…

The other good thing was that the celebrity couple's home was a mere stone's-throw from Callie, just round the corner from All Saints' Church and vicarage. If this case extended for a few days, he might have one or two opportunities to see her.

On the way to the Central Line Tube station, he gave her a quick call, mobile to mobile.

Callie sounded glum. 'My mother,' she said. 'I'm going to have lunch with her. Peter's coming too, so maybe it won't be so bad.'

Mark had met Callie's mother—though just once, at a stilted dinner party—so he was in a position to sympathise. And he'd heard a great deal about Laura Anson's unrelenting negativity, her self-absorption, from Callie. 'Poor you,' he said. 'But if you're going past a record store at some point, maybe you could do me a favour.'

'What do you need?'

'Chiara's birthday tomorrow. Apparently she wants the latest album by Karma.'

'Karma who?' Callie queried.

Mark chuckled. 'Well might you ask. Just Karma, apparently. Doesn't it make you feel old, *Cara mia*?'

◇◇◇

By the time Neville Stewart arrived at the Betts' Bayswater mansion, he was not in the best of moods.

His idyllic honeymoon had been cut short, and that wasn't the worst of it. Triona hadn't spoken to him on the flight back to Luton, so things were only going to go downhill after this. What a way to start married life.

There had been a police car waiting for him at the airport. He'd had to put Triona in a taxi, along with their luggage, and go straight to Bayswater. Bloody Bayswater—just about the last place on earth he wanted to be at that moment.

Neville's mood wasn't improved by the knot of tabloid journalists and photographers clogging the pavement in front of the house. At the sight of the police car, and him emerging from it, they all surged towards him with eager faces, and he knew that they viewed him as little more than a momentary diversion from the boredom of the stake-out. 'No comment,' he said tersely, shouldering his way to the door.

He was, at least, relieved and grateful to find Mark Lombardi on site. 'Doing your usual hand-holding/tea-making job, I see,' he said when Mark opened the door to him.

Mark looked hurt, and as he stepped inside Neville instantly repented his sharp tongue.

'I think my job involves a bit more than that,' Mark said stiffly.

'Sorry, mate. I'm just so royally pissed off to be here.'

'I'm not surprised. Your honeymoon…'

Neville didn't want to talk about his honeymoon. Not now. 'Fill me in, then,' he said. 'Before I meet them. What are they like?'

'Distraught, obviously.' Mark lowered his voice, though they were not likely to be overheard. 'Not coping very well.'

'But what are they *like*? I don't think I've ever met a real celebrity before.'

Mark scratched his cheek. 'Well, Jodee seems very…I suppose brittle is the word. A bit manic. And at the moment she's not looking as glam as her photos,' he added. 'I suppose that's to be expected.'

'What about Chazz?'

'Quiet,' Mark said carefully. 'Not much to say. Polite, but… like he's not really *there* somehow.'

From what Neville had heard and read about Chazz, the winner of 'twentyfour/seven' wasn't reputed to be the sharpest knife in the drawer. The public had loved him for his sweet nature—and his looks, of course—rather than his brains.

Mark hesitated for a second. 'And he's beautiful.'

'Beautiful?' That seemed an odd word to use. Handsome, maybe. Attractive. Good looking. 'Well fit', or some other such current slang.

'You'll see,' said Mark.

Neville did see, though he considered himself far more of an expert in female pulchritude than masculine beauty. Beautiful was the only word for it. The shape of his face, the perfectly symmetrical alignment of his features, the extraordinary eyes…When Chazz was on 'twentyfour/seven' his head had been shaved; now his hair had grown out in soft curls. It was a face that Neville now realised he'd seen on hundreds of billboards and adverts—most recently at airports. Selling perfume, selling clothing.

'This is Detective Inspector Stewart,' Mark announced by way of introduction.

'I'll need to ask you a few questions,' Neville said to the space between pacing Jodee and seated Chazz. His voice was as apologetic as he could manage, given his resentment towards the disruption to his life. It wasn't their fault, he reminded himself.

'But why?' Jodee turned a ravaged face to him, only half seeming to take him in. 'It's like you think we killed her. I mean, can't you just like leave us alone? All of you?'

Mark intervened with a conciliatory gesture in her direction. 'I did explain. We have to find out—'

'Our Muffin!' Jodee keened. 'Why would we kill her?'

'No one thinks you killed your baby,' Neville stated, perhaps more loudly and forcefully than he'd intended. What he needed now was a bit of co-operation from the bereaved parents, not a load of resistance to being questioned. Maybe he would have to explain it to them in words of one syllable. 'We need to find out what happened to her,' he said. 'For you, as well as for us.'

Chazz spoke for the first time, so quietly that Neville strained to hear. 'They took her away,' he said. He crossed his arms across his chest, almost as though he were cradling a baby. 'And her things.'

'Her bedding!' Jodee added shrilly. 'The police took it all! And it didn't half cost a pretty penny, like, that bedding. It came from Paris, not bloody Mothercare!' Her words ended on a wail; she covered her face with her hands and sobbed.

This wasn't going well. Neville looked towards Mark and caught his eye; Mark shrugged helplessly.

But it was as though Jodee's last outburst had released something in her. After a moment of noisy tears she lowered her hands and looked properly at Neville for the first time. 'I understand,' she said. 'You're trying to help.'

Thank God for that. 'Yes,' he confirmed. 'We're trying to help.' Maybe now they could start getting somewhere.

◇◇◇

While Neville led Jodee and Chazz though all of the requisite questions, Mark escaped to the kitchen to make a fresh pot of tea. With any luck, he thought, they'd have this all sorted quickly. The pathologist would perform the post-mortem, as a matter of some urgency, and it would almost certainly show that the baby's death was unfortunate but not suspicious. Cot death. Sudden infant death: SIDS, that's what the death certificate would say. That great catch-all which meant that the pathologist and the coroner didn't really know why Muffin Angel Betts had died at the age of less than two months.

The press would have a field day, of course. No matter what the pathologist found and the coroner decided, the media would make their own judgements and freely pass them on to the avid public. If they decided to spin it against Jodee and Chazz and make them the scapegoats, there was so much they could accomplish with innuendo, falling well short of libel but equally damaging. They could suggest—subtly, of course—that Muffin had been neglected, underfed or overfed, allowed to sleep on her stomach, swaddled in too many blankets. Or, perhaps more likely, they could go all out with sympathy for the celebrity parents, so cruelly deprived of their beloved baby.

There was one consolation, Mark reflected. Life for Jodee and Chazz would never be the same again, but the media would soon move on to the next sensation. Maybe Karma would meet a new—preferably unsuitable—man, or some fresh face would win 'Junior Idol'. In any case, the public's appetite for celebrity gossip would shortly find something else to feast on.

Neville's involvement with the case could be fairly short-lived—perhaps not much more than twenty-four hours or so. Once the post-mortem had been performed, and the paper-work completed, he could sign off on it and even resume his honeymoon.

But would he, Mark, be able to walk away quite so quickly? He wasn't sure.

Chazz's mother was at the kitchen table, Mark discovered, nursing a cup of coffee. She looked up as Mark came in.

'Coffee's there, if you want.' She gestured towards a jar of instant granules.

'I'm going to make some tea,' he said, brandishing the empty pot.

'Whatever.'

Mark hadn't quite decided what to make of Brenda Betts. On the whole, he was inclined to view her as a good thing. Although she was clearly grieving herself, she was easier to deal with than the taciturn Chazz or the hysterical Jodee.

The phone rang. Brenda didn't even raise her head from her coffee.

'You're not…?'

'Press,' Brenda stated. 'Lilith said not to answer.'

Mark was startled. 'Lilith *Noone!*'

'She was here earlier.'

'You let her in?' he asked incredulously.

Brenda raised the ghost of a smug smile. 'Lilith is a friend of the family.'

'Friend' was not a word Mark would ever have imagined in the same sentence as Lilith Noone's name. She was bad news on a legendary scale.

'Jodee gave her an exclusive interview. For tomorrow's *Globe.*'

Wait till Neville found out, Mark thought. He'd go ballistic. If there was one person Neville couldn't bear, it was Lilith Noone, with her self-righteous posturing and underhand tactics. Just as well that Lilith had gone by the time they arrived. No doubt she was already labouring away on her front-page exclusive.

The subject of Lilith was best left unexplored, he decided. The phone was still ringing. 'Maybe it's not the press,' he suggested. 'It could be family. Jodee's parents, maybe?'

Brenda shook her head. 'Not likely. Jodee already spoke to her mum. She wasn't much interested.'

'Not interested?'

The phone stopped ringing and Brenda took a gulp of coffee before replying. 'They don't get on. Not for years. Jodee never knew her dad. Her mum's got a boyfriend—a "partner", she calls him—and a couple of little kiddies herself. Jodee don't like her mum's boyfriend—she's never made no secret of that.'

'That's a shame.'

Brenda shrugged. 'One of them things, innit? Families are funny.'

Weren't they just, thought Mark, nodding in agreement.

The kettle boiled and he turned away to make the tea. 'What about...Chazz's dad?' he asked. It was potentially a delicate question, but he didn't really have much to lose. If Brenda Betts didn't think it was appropriate, she'd probably tell him so.

But she didn't seem to mind. With another shrug, she said, 'Gone. Buggered off, to put not too fine a point on it. When I was in hospital, having the twins.'

'Twins?'

'Chazz and his sister Di. All them years ago.' She swirled the dregs of coffee in her mug. 'Any water left in that kettle?'

'Yes, of course.' Mark took the mug from her, rinsed it out, and spooned in some instant granules.

'He said he'd stand by me when I fell pregnant. We got married.' Brenda's voice was weary, not emotional; this was all ancient history. 'But he hadn't bargained on twins. If it had been just one, he might have stuck it out. Maybe, I don't know.'

Mark handed her the coffee wordlessly.

'He came to see me in hospital, after,' she went on. 'Brought me a manky bunch of flowers. Half dead—probably got them off a skip or out of a rubbish bin, if I know him. Kissed me, kissed the babies. And that's the last I ever saw of bloody Kev Betts. Good riddance to him, I say.'

'But it must have been very difficult for you, with two babies.'

She blew on the coffee, took a tentative sip, stirred in a spoon-ful of sugar from the bowl on the table, and shrugged yet again. 'Oh, it was. Me mum helped all she could, of course. Couldn't have managed without her. I had to work all the hours God gave. Cleaning. I'd drop the twins off with Mum first thing, then collect them in the evening. But they didn't turn out too bad, for all that,' she added. 'At least they learned the value of hard work.'

'Your daughter,' Mark said. 'Di? Where is she?'

'Oh, she's done well for herself. She always said she didn't want to be a cleaner like her mum. So she got proper qualifications, like. Nursing. She loves it.' She favoured Mark with a proud, motherly smile. 'Chazz said he'd give her money so she could quit her job, but she wouldn't take it. Not a penny.'

'Chazz hasn't done too badly, then.' He didn't mean it flippantly, but realised as soon as the words were out of his mouth that it probably sounded that way.

'My Chazz was a hard worker before that "twentyfour/seven" lark,' his mother said sharply. 'As soon as he left school, he got a job with a removal company. You might not think it to look at him, but Chazz is dead strong.'

'Yes, I'm sure he is.'

'He was lucky to win that show,' Brenda allowed, 'and lucky that all them modelling jobs have come his way since. I mean, he is a good-looking lad and all, if I say it myself. But if he had to go back to humping furniture about for them removal people, he could do it. My Chazz is a good lad,' she added firmly. 'Good to me, good to Jodee and the baby.'

At those words, her face crumpled, as if she'd managed to forget about Muffin for a few minutes and had only just remembered her.

Mark made an immediate effort to distract her. 'What about Jodee?' he asked, perhaps unwisely. 'How do you get on with her?'

Brenda mastered her trembling lip. 'Jodee is like a daughter to me,' she stated. 'Ask her—she'd tell you the same. Close, like family should be. Not like that useless mum of hers.'

'It must be great for them to have you living with them, to help out with...' Mark had been about to say 'babysitting', but changed it at the last moment to a limp '...everything.'

'I do keep the place clean,' she admitted, looking round the spotless kitchen with pride. 'Mind, we could afford help. But it keeps me out of mischief.'

Then, to Mark's astonishment, a whole range of emotions played over Brenda's face. She dropped her mug, splashing herself and the table with hot coffee, put her hands over her face and sobbed. 'It weren't my fault,' she wailed. 'It weren't nobody's fault! Di said, and she's a nurse. Di said it wouldn't have made no difference. Muffin would of died, even if someone had been at home!'

Chapter Four

'Did I tell you that Maddie Fleming has a new grandchild? *Another* grandchild?' The emphasis in Laura Anson's voice was unmistakable.

Callie risked a quick look at her brother, expecting a roll of the eyes in her direction, but his eyes were wide, fixed on their mother's face. She recognised the act of will involved. 'You did mention it,' Callie said, trying not to sound defensive.

'Another boy. That makes three grandchildren. *So far.'*

'How nice for Maddie,' Peter said brightly.

'It was Celia's first, of course. I imagine she'll have at least one more. Celia always struck me as such a *maternal* sort of girl.' Laura played with her salad, turning it over with her fork, and addressed her next remark—a question, in fact—to Peter. 'You remember Celia, don't you?'

Callie held her breath, but Peter was on his best behaviour. 'Of course,' he said.

'Such a lovely girl. That luncheon party a few years ago—remember?'

'Yes, I remember,' Peter confirmed. There was just the merest trace of irony in his voice; Callie heard it because she knew him so well, but trusted that their mother was typically oblivious.

Laura, characteristically, didn't leave it at that. 'I did think that the two of you would have made such a nice couple. She's interested in the arts, and she's very presentable. Knows how to dress. And as I said, so maternal. Married just a year, and a baby already.'

Callie feared that Peter had now been pushed far enough. As he opened his mouth, she created a diversion by dropping her fork. It hit her plate with a clank, then bounced on to the floor.

Frowning, Laura turned her attention to her daughter. 'I hope that fork was *clean*,' she said sharply. 'The carpet's just been cleaned.'

'I'm sorry.' Callie's voice was suitably meek and contrite.

'You've always been clumsy, Caroline. I don't know where you got it from—certainly not from me.'

Caroline. Laura always called her by her full name when she was more than usually peeved with her daughter. Or her son, or her life in general.

Why, thought Callie, did she and Peter put up with it? Why did they subject themselves, periodically, to the torture of being with a woman who didn't seem to like them much? Who never approved of anything they did, or ever had a positive word to say?

She'd been worse since her husband died, a few years back—an act for which, perversely, she blamed him. Laura Anson hadn't forgiven him for getting cancer, succumbing to it and leaving her on her own, and her bitterness poisoned everything in her life, including her relationship with her children.

Not that she'd ever been an easy mother. Not even when their father was alive. She'd always had the ability to see only what she wanted to see and ignore the things she disapproved of.

Peter's decision to pursue a career as a freelance musician rather than follow his father into the Civil Service, for one thing. And then there was the small matter of his homosexuality. Laura Anson refused to believe in it, no matter how many times it was explained to her that Peter was not interested in being paired up with the daughters of her friends. That he was not going to marry a suitable girl, or give her grandchildren. She continued to be convinced that he just hadn't met the right girl yet, and it remained her duty to push females of an appropriate age and social status in his direction until the situation corrected itself.

Callie had disappointed Laura Anson by leaving the Civil Service for the Church, and she hadn't exactly done a great deal to please her mother in the grandchildren department, either. She'd be thirty in a few months, with no sign of settling down. No grandchildren on the horizon. And what if things continued to progress with Marco? 'That policeman,' her mother called him dismissively; he was obviously not the sort of son-in-law Laura Anson had in mind for the father of her future grandchildren.

Peter looked at his watch. 'Callie,' he said pointedly, 'didn't you mention that you had an appointment this afternoon? For an...urm...eye test?'

'Oh, yes.' Good old Peter, thought Callie as she pushed her chair back from the table. 'That's right. We'd better think about going.'

'Eye test?' Laura Anson frowned. 'Is there something wrong with your eyes, Caroline? I hope you haven't inherited your father's short-sightedness. It got worse when he was in his thirties, you know. And you're—'

'Almost thirty,' Callie finished for her. 'Yes, Mother. I know.'

◇◇◇

'Tell me, Stewart. Tell me it's all straightforward,' commanded DCS Evans wearily. 'Cot death, pure and simple.'

They were in Evans' corner office; Evans was sitting at his desk and Neville was standing. He'd not yet been invited to sit, and reckoned that the invitation might not come at all. Evans, he was positive, was not going to like what he had to tell him.

'I wish I could, Sir,' said Neville. Evans' quick intake of breath seemed to suck all the oxygen from the room, so Neville went on hastily. 'It probably is. I'm sure we'll find that it is, in the end. But there are just a few...issues.'

'Issues?' Evans raised his massive caterpillar-like eyebrows almost to his hairline.

'Of course we don't know what forensics will turn up. Or the post-mortem, for that matter. But there may be a case to be made for...' He hesitated and chose his words with care. 'Parental neglect, perhaps.'

Neville didn't think it was possible for Evans' eyebrows to go any higher; he was wrong. 'Neglect? What are you trying to say, Stewart?'

'It's just something that the baby's grandmother, Mrs Betts, said to DS Lombardi,' Neville explained. 'She said that Muffin would have died, even if someone had been at home.'

The pitch and volume of Evans' voice went up a notch. 'Meaning…?'

'DS Lombardi asked her what she meant, of course. And it turns out that the baby was left at home on her own. Purely an accident, she said.'

'How could it be an accident?' growled Evans. 'Either you leave the baby, or you don't.'

Neville shifted his weight from one leg to the other. 'She did explain, Sir. She said that the parents—Jodee and Chazz—went out to a club, assuming that she—Mrs Betts—was sleeping in the room next to the baby as usual. But she'd gone out without telling them.'

'So the baby—Muffin; what a ridiculous name for a child—was alone in the house when she died? That's what you're telling me?'

'That's it exactly, Sir.'

Evans closed his eyes and exhaled in a gusty sigh. Neville waited, feeling it better to say no more until required to do so.

'Good God,' said Evans at last.

'Yes, Sir.'

◇◇◇

Before they'd even made it round the corner from their mother's, Peter was dealing with the experience in the best possible way: with humour. He was a gifted mimic, and with years of practice he had their mother down to a T. 'Oh, *dear* Celia Fleming,' he drawled. 'She would have made such a good wife for you. She would have warmed your slippers by the fire every night, and lit your pipe for you. And shagged you senseless, of course.'

'Oh, don't!' Callie laughed.

But Peter was only just warming up. 'Not that shagging is a *good* thing, necessarily,' he went on in his mother's voice. 'Except for the purposes of procreation.'

Callie got a fit of the giggles and had to stop walking.

He stopped as well. 'Grandchildren, you know,' he trilled. 'Sorry to say, it's the only way.' Then, as Callie's giggles showed no signs of abating, Peter continued in his own voice. 'Seriously, Sis. Can you imagine our parents in bed?'

'Don't even go there,' she warned him.

'It's a wonder to me that they had two children.'

Callie put up her hand. 'Do you mind if we change the subject?'

'I'm not finished with Celia Fleming, actually.' Peter pictured the young woman in question, her thin face burned into his memory from that long-ago luncheon party. 'What a miserable cow she was. I mean, even if I was interested in girls, I would have run a mile from that one.'

'Mum just never gets it,' said Callie, stating the obvious.

'It's the bloody grandchildren thing,' Peter said gloomily. 'She's so desperate to have them. Though I can't see why—she'd be just as horrible to them as she is to us. They would be too noisy, too active, too badly behaved, never dutiful or appreciative enough.'

'It's competition,' Callie said. 'With her friends. They all have grandchildren, and she just can't compete when the photos come out and they start on the boring stories. It's *her* problem, and she keeps trying to make it *our* problem.'

He grinned and took her arm, leading her towards Kensington High Street. 'Well, we've escaped for today. What shall we do now, Sis?'

'I have an errand to run for Marco,' Callie said, smiling as she usually did when she mentioned his name. 'I need to find a CD. Have you heard of someone called Karma? A singer or something?'

'Have I heard of Karma?' Peter shook his head in disbelief; his sister's ignorance on matters of cutting-edge popular culture never failed to shock him. 'She's only the hottest thing on the charts right now. Next thing I know, you'll be telling me you don't watch "Junior Idol".'

'Well, excuse me.' Callie's huffiness was exaggerated for effect. 'That's why I keep *you* around. So I don't have to fill my head with such ephemeral rubbish.'

'It's popular culture, Sis. The lifeblood of our society.' For him, as a young gay man in London, that was no exaggeration but a statement of pure truth.

They were passing a row of shops; one of them was a news-agent, with a sandwich board out front inked with the latest headline. 'Jodee and Chazz—Tragic Baby Death,' he read aloud as they approached. 'Oh, my God.'

'How sad,' said Callie.

'You *do* know who Jodee and Chazz are, then?' he tested her, stopping to buy a paper.

'They were on "twentyfour/seven",' she said. 'Everybody knows that. Not that I ever watched it,' she added.

Peter glanced over a rack of magazines facing the pavement and pointed to several in succession. 'That's Jodee and the baby,' he said. 'And this one is just Jodee, and those two are Jodee and Chazz. Chazz,' he sighed. 'Lovely, lovely Chazz.'

'You fancy him?'

'Doesn't everyone?' Peter gave a soulful sigh. 'I mean, have you ever seen a more gorgeous man?'

Frances Cherry, hospital chaplain, had spent the afternoon in the wards. She'd said a prayer with an elderly lady who was just about to go into theatre for a serious operation and was trying to put a brave face on things; later Frances had returned to make sure everything had gone well, finding the patient groggy but grateful. She'd also talked to a few anxious families and made an effort to jolly up patients who were frightened, in pain, or just plain bored.

It never ceased to surprise Frances how many of the latter there were at any given time. Fear she could understand; pain she could empathise with. But boredom was an insidious enemy, afflicting people in strange ways. It came out in the form of stroppiness as often as it was demonstrated in lethargy. Bored patients were the ones who made life hell for the nursing staff, complaining about the food and demanding all sorts of attention. Frances was adept at identifying those people and always did what she could to alleviate their tedium and take a bit of the strain off the staff.

This afternoon, with the promise of spring just outside of the windows, Frances observed a high level of boredom in the wards. Tea time was approaching, but not quickly enough. And when tea finally arrived, it was variously judged to be too hot, too cold, too milky, too strong.

Frances was ready for a cup herself, and ready to sit down for a few minutes. She wasn't due to go home for a couple of hours, and she needed a break. So she headed for the cafe, where the tea was arguably better than in the wards.

She went through the line and got a pot of lapsang, which she reckoned would keep her going for the remainder of the afternoon, and after a momentary hesitation she added a packet of shortbread biscuits to her tray, telling herself that her blood sugar could do with a boost.

Everyone seemed to have decided that it was time for tea, and the cafe was crowded. Frances would have preferred a table on her own—she felt she'd earned a few minutes of solitude—but was willing to settle for an unoccupied chair. She spotted one and made her way to it, glancing at the man at the table for his consent to share, as protocol demanded. He was hunched over a cup of coffee, not looking at her, so she had to verbalise her request. 'Do you mind?' she said, inclining her head towards the empty chair.

The man looked up, and Frances nearly dropped her tray. It was Neville Stewart. Detective Inspector Neville Stewart, whose wedding she had witnessed less than a week ago.

'Go ahead,' he said. 'Have a seat.'

Frances blurted the first thing that came into her head. 'But… but you're on your honeymoon!'

'Make that past tense.' Neville lowered his head again and stared into his coffee cup. 'The honeymoon's over.'

Frances' history with Neville Stewart was decidedly negative; she had first met him in a professional capacity—*his* profession, not hers. He had questioned her, suspected her, and eventually arrested her on suspicion of murder. Apart from that, he had made her friend Triona miserable, impregnating her and then deserting her. When he and Triona reconciled, Frances had tried to see the man's good side, and had even served as Triona's attendant at the wedding. But she remained unconvinced. In her mind, Neville Stewart was not a nice person, or someone she would voluntarily spend time with.

Here, though, was a man in distress. Not the confident, bullying Neville Stewart who had bombarded her with so many outrageous questions, nor the ebullient man who had married Triona last Saturday. This Neville Stewart looked beaten, broken, exhausted. His skin had a grey cast and his cheeks were unshaven; his eyes were bloodshot. Frances' heart went out to him, as a fellow human being and as a priest.

Frances sat down and put her small hand over his. 'Tell me what's wrong,' she said quietly.

'I've just come from the mortuary.' Neville's voice was shaking.

Callie parted from her brother after leaving the CD shop, the Karma album safely in her bag. She said goodbye to him with some reluctance; he had certainly cheered her up, as he almost always did, and she was feeling better about life in general and her situation at the vicarage in particular. 'After all,' he'd said airily, 'you put up with having me under your roof for…it must have been a couple of weeks, at least. If you could survive that, Sis, a few weeks with a dragon of a vicar's wife should be a piece of cake!'

And Jane wasn't *really* a dragon, Callie told herself on the Tube back to Bayswater. She was a perfectly nice person who just didn't happen to like Callie a great deal. That much was clear, even if the reasons for that antipathy were far from fathomable. Callie wasn't the sort of person who could ask Jane outright why she didn't like her, in spite of Peter's counsels on the subject. 'Just confront the old cow,' he'd urged. 'Ask her what her problem is. After all, it's *her* problem, not yours.'

Callie knew she wouldn't follow Peter's advice, but she did stop at a corner shop and buy a box of chocolates for Jane: an appeasement for whatever sins she had unknowingly committed in her dealings with her.

She let herself in with the key she'd been issued and fixed a smile on her face—just in case—as she headed for the bottom of the stairs.

It was Brian who intercepted her, putting his head out of his study door, wearing a slightly anxious expression. 'Oh, Callie,' he said. 'I believe that Jane would like a word. She's in the kitchen, I think.'

'Oh. All right. Thanks, Brian.' Callie changed course and went to the back of the house, her heart thudding apprehensively.

The ironing board was set up in the middle of the kitchen. Jane stood over it, iron in hand, attacking a crumpled surplice with a determined scowl. The scowl deepened as Callie came through the door.

'Brian said you wanted me?'

Jane didn't waste time on preliminary niceties. 'It's that dog,' she stated.

'Bella?'

'What other dog would I be talking about?' Jane snapped. 'It hasn't stopped carrying on since you left!'

'Carrying on?' Callie echoed faintly.

'Whining. Howling, even!'

She'd left Bella closed in her room, reasoning that Bella was used to being alone in the flat during the day and that this shouldn't really be any different. Apparently, though, Bella wasn't any more comfortable about being in the vicarage than Callie was. 'Oh, I'm so sorry,' Callie apologised. 'I thought she'd be okay.'

Jane wasn't mollified. 'It just won't do,' she said. 'I told Brian. We can't have a dog carrying on like that all day. Day in, day out. And suppose it's…made a mess in the guest room?'

Callie hadn't even thought of *that*. Bella had good bladder control; surely she wouldn't have disgraced herself to that extent…

'It won't do,' Jane repeated. 'That dog will have to go. It will just have to go in kennels, if no one else will take it.' *You* can stay—on sufferance, her eyes told Callie. She set the iron down on the ironing board and crossed her arms across her chest. 'Brian checked with the insurance company. They'll pay. For kennels. I told him that I want that dog out of my house. By tomorrow. At the latest.'

◇◇◇

A human being. Neville Stewart!

Frances couldn't believe she was actually feeling sorry for him. That, she reflected as she made her way back to her office, was what happened when someone opened their heart to you, and you allowed yourself to be equally open to their pain.

No wonder he looked terrible. Called back from his honeymoon, plunged into the tragedy of a baby's death. And then to be expected to attend the actual post-mortem—to watch the pathologist put his scalpel into that tiny body…

On top of it all, he wasn't in the least sure how things stood with his new wife—with Triona. She'd been pretty angry when the honeymoon had been cut short, he'd confided. He knew—who better?—what a fiery temper she had, and he didn't blame her for exercising it on this occasion. But he didn't know what to do about it, or even where to find her, when he was eventually free to go to her. She wasn't answering her mobile. Not to him, anyway.

Even if he hadn't begged Frances to contact Triona on his behalf, she would have felt compelled to ring her friend. Neville Stewart aside, she cared about what happened to Triona, whom she'd first known years ago, during the long struggle for women's ordination to the priesthood. Triona had been a young Irish firebrand, training for a career in law, standing shoulder-to-shoulder with the women who knew they were called to be priests but who were blocked at every turn by the fossilised element of the Church's hierarchy. Eventually the women had succeeded, of course, yet not before they'd done some fairly extreme things; like the Suffragettes before them, they'd occasionally risked personal safety and come pretty close to the edges of the law. Triona had promised Frances that she would be there for her if ever she needed a lawyer, neither of them dreaming under what circumstances that call would finally come.

In her office, Frances took a moment to compose herself before picking up the phone. Neville had written down Triona's mobile number for her; she smoothed the slip of paper out on her desk and breathed deeply, praying that she would know what to say. The last thing she wanted to do was to get in the middle of a domestic misunderstanding, and she certainly had no wish to take Neville Stewart's side against his wife. No: she needed to be available to Triona. As a friend.

Poor, poor Triona. Frances punched in the number, willing Triona to answer.

She did, but only after several rings.

'Triona? It's Frances.'

'Frances.' Triona's voice was flat; it sounded hoarse, as if she had a cold—or had been crying.

'How…are you?'

Triona gave a harsh laugh. 'The honeymoon is over. Really over. How do you *think* I am?'

'Do you want to talk about it?'

'What's to talk about? My husband'—she laughed again—'chose his job over me. And it won't be the last time. I can see the way it will be from now on. Why should I put myself through this? I might as well just admit I made a mistake and walk away from it right now.'

Frances was appalled. She'd expected Triona to be hurt, angry. But talking about her marriage being over before it had even properly begun…this was more than a marital misunderstanding.

And there was a baby involved as well. 'Triona. Where are you?' she asked.

'My flat. Where else? Certainly not that tip that Neville calls home.'

'You need to talk to Neville,' Frances stated.

'I don't *need* to talk to him. I don't *want* to talk to him.' Her voice broke on a sob. 'Oh, God. I've just realised. He'll come looking for me. Eventually. When he's run out of excuses to keep away.'

That, Frances knew, wasn't fair. Triona hadn't been answering his calls; that meant she knew he was trying to reach her.

'I can't stay here,' Triona went on, almost to herself. 'He'll find me. I don't want to see him.'

'Then—' Frances began.

'Where can I go? He'll find me here. And he has a key.'

'But you can't just hide from him.' That would solve nothing, Frances was sure; it would just prolong the pain for both of them.

Triona ignored her. 'Do you have a spare room? Can I stay with you, Frances?'

'With *me*?'

'That big vicarage. You must have a spare room.'

Well, reflected Frances, at least it would give her a chance to speak to Triona face-to-face. She could make her see, somehow, that it was way too soon to give up on her marriage. She could encourage her to talk to Neville, to look at things from his point of view. 'All right,' she said. 'You can stay with Graham and me.' For a few days, anyway. Surely Triona would cool off, see reason, realise that all marriages required work and that her baby needed a father.

'I'll take a taxi,' said Triona. 'I'll be there within the hour.'

Frances sighed as she put the phone down. She'd better get home, then, make sure the guest room was made up, and prepare her husband Graham for the invasion.

Callie sat in the middle of the uncomfortable bed, holding Bella tightly. She felt like Dorothy in 'The Wizard of Oz', clinging to Toto in the face of Miss Gulch's determination to take him away. 'You're not going into kennels,' she whispered into the dog's ear. 'I promise.'

But what else could she do? Jane was not going to be talked round, and Brian seemed to be taking his wife's side on this one. And in spite of the recent storm, being scooped up by a tornado didn't seem a likely scenario.

She looked round the dreary room, wishing she could be transported to Oz. Even the Wicked Witch of the West would hold no terrors for someone who had faced Jane Stanford over her ironing board.

Where could poor Bella go? Who could give her a temporary home?

Callie's mother, of course, was an impossibility: Elvira Gulch would be a better custodian for a dog than Laura Anson, who wouldn't consider it under any circumstances anyway.

If things had been different, Peter might have taken her. He got on well with Bella. But Peter—as of this afternoon, anyway—was still living with Jason, and Jason had a cat: a large, fluffy and very spoiled cat who would brook no competition from any other creature, especially not a dog.

With Peter, of course, there was always the possibility of a change of circumstances. Peter's boyfriends were usually in the picture for a very short while, in spite of his persistent optimism, each time, that this would be *the* one. He'd been with Jason for over three months now, which was surely a record for Peter. He was probably due for another painful bust-up. Callie hoped not; Peter seemed very happy with Jason, and a bust-up wouldn't happen quickly enough to do her any good.

Tomorrow. At the latest. Bella had to go.

Callie continued down her mental list. Marco. Another impossibility, with his long hours and his flatmate.

But what, she suddenly thought with a spurt of excitement, about someone in Marco's family? His sister, for instance? His niece? Chiara was thirteen tomorrow—surely of an age to look after a dog for a few weeks.

She reached for her mobile and rang Marco's number, glad for an excuse to hear his voice.

Unfortunately it wasn't a good time; he was still working, and sounded distracted. 'Can I ring you this evening, *Cara mia*?'

'It's important,' Callie said, and explained her dilemma as quickly and non-emotionally as she could. 'I know you can't take her. But I was wondering about Serena,' she concluded. 'Just for a few weeks?'

Marco's reply was immediate. 'Serena's allergic to dogs and cats.'

'Oh,' she said forlornly. That was her last hope gone, then.

'What about Frances?' suggested Marco. 'She doesn't have a cat, does she? I know she's busy, but—'

'Frances! Why didn't I think of that?'

Frances. Her friend, her mentor. Not far away in Notting Hill. Callie could visit Bella there and even give her walks.

'Oh, please,' she breathed as she rang Frances' number. Please let her be in. Please let her say yes.

She was in, and she answered after three rings, sounding a bit breathless.

Callie explained her dilemma. 'I'd be so grateful if you could have her,' she finished. 'Though of course I'll understand if you can't. If Graham is allergic, or you don't feel you could take her on for some reason.'

On the other end of the phone Frances laughed, and her voice sounded bemused. 'Sure, Callie. Why not?' she said. 'The more, the merrier.'

Chapter Five

Lilith Noone was up early on Saturday morning, and in spite of the spring drizzle she walked to the newsagent for the papers. She could have checked them online, but for someone who had grown up in the journalism business—her father and his father before him had owned a provincial newspaper—it just wasn't the same. She loved the feel of crisp newsprint; the smell of newspaper ink was like a drug to her. So this was part of the ritual, especially on days when she knew that one of her own stories would be in print.

Not just in print on this occasion: front page news. Exclusive. She picked up a copy of the *Globe* from the top of a tall stack and feasted her eyes on the by-line. Lilith tended to be assigned to feature stuff rather than breaking news, so an appearance on the tabloid's front page was rare indeed.

Jodee and Chazz had not emerged from their house all day on Friday, denying gathered photographers the opportunity for photos of them in distress; like the other papers the *Globe* had had to fall back on a file photo of the couple in happier times, emerging from the maternity hospital with baby Muffin swathed in a pink fleece blanket. The headline read simply 'Jodee and Chazz: Baby Tragedy', and the subhead said 'Our reporter Lilith Noone speaks exclusively to the bereaved parents'.

Lilith breathed deeply, her chest literally swelling with pride. For a moment she savoured the sensation, then moved on to the other papers, collecting quite a stack of them in her arms. Almost all of them featured Jodee and Chazz on the front page, but none of the others had anything in the least original, let alone exclusive. The higher-toned papers focused on the medical aspect of the tragedy, quoting experts on SIDS, while the tabloids rehashed the public romance. Lilith would take them home and digest them at her leisure, saving the best for last.

World exclusive. Lilith Noone, the only member of the press who had talked to Jodee and Chazz. Face to face.

◇◇◇

Neville Stewart, too, was at a local newsagent's shop quite early. He needed to find out what the papers were saying about the case; for one thing, DCS Evans would want to know, and Evans' admirable secretary, who would usually take care of this side of things, didn't work on a Saturday. Furthermore, Neville had a strong feeling that before the day was over, he would be facing the press himself. As soon as the post-mortem results were available, Evans would want to call a news conference, and Neville would be the one taking the questions. It was important for him to be prepared.

Too bad it was Saturday. The Saturday papers were cumbersome things, engorged with special supplements and adverts, and these days with free DVDs and other rubbish. Neville stopped at the nearest bin and dumped all of the extraneous bits, retaining only the front page sections of each paper. These he carried to the nearest greasy spoon cafe, where he took over a booth, spread out the papers, and ordered a cup of coffee.

Most of the papers, he discovered, had very little information to go on. The only one which did was the *Globe*; that accursed woman Lilith Noone seemed to have wormed her way in to talk to Jodee and Chazz, and she provided an eyewitness account of their distress. It was a heart-wrenching story, dripping with sympathy. And what the other tabloids lacked in factual content, they more than made up for in the emotive language of grief. Muffin's death was a 'tragedy'; her parents were variously 'agonised', 'heartbroken', 'anguished', 'desolated', and 'gutted'.

If the lack of hard facts had sent the tabloid journalists scurrying to their thesauruses, it seemed to have sent the mainstream journalists to their medical dictionaries. As he sipped the strong, bitter coffee, Neville learned more about SIDS than he'd been able to discover from the taciturn pathologist. He learned that though SIDS was the commonly used descriptor for cot death, the actual medical term was SUDI, or 'sudden unexplained death in infancy'. And although there was no medical consensus about what caused SIDS, there did seem to be a number of risk factors which might or might not be relevant in this particular case, including the sort of bedding used and the position of the sleeping baby. Even the mother's prenatal use of alcohol or cigarettes could be implicated, as well as premature birth, low birth weight and failure to breast-feed.

Whatever the factors involved, SIDS seemed to be an indiscriminate killer of babies, and their parents were not held culpable.

Unless…

Unless there was something else. Some unnatural intervention. A pillow held over the baby's face to stop it crying, or…

Or neglect. A baby dying alone, its parents in dereliction of their duty of care.

Neville realised that none of the papers—not even the *Globe*—had mentioned anything about the potential complication he'd shared with Evans: the fact that Muffin had seemingly died alone in an empty house. That was a huge relief.

It might not have made any difference. As the baby's grandmother had said to Mark Lombardi, Muffin probably would have died anyway.

If the pathologist—and the coroner—found that Muffin Angel Betts' death was a straightforward case of SIDS, then Neville's part in it would be over. Case closed.

He could go home and forget about it.

Yeah, right.

Home.

That brought him, inevitably, to the thing he had been avoiding thinking about.

His wife. Triona.

He didn't even know where she was. She wasn't at her flat or at his. She wasn't answering his calls.

Where the hell was she?

◇◇◇

Mark woke on Saturday morning to the enticing smell of coffee. Geoff was up, then, and at home.

He wasn't at all sure about the shape his own day would have. He was determined to deliver Chiara's birthday present at some point, and that meant that he would get to see Callie. Whether she came with him or not—and Mark hoped that she would—she had the CD in her possession.

Mark was missing Callie. It had been less than three days since he'd seen her, but it felt to him much longer than that. He didn't usually discuss his cases with her; now, though, he wanted to talk to her about Muffin Betts.

This wasn't like other cases, and he was finding it profoundly disturbing.

The role of a Family Liaison Officer was a delicate and sensitive one at the best of times, requiring a special set of skills. Mark liked to think that he usually achieved the proper balance between empathy and objectivity that the job demanded, conveying warmth and caring to the family while never forgetting that he was there among them as a police officer, not as a counsellor or a social worker.

Part of the problem with this case was that they weren't at all sure what they were dealing with. It wasn't the usual homicide, clearly defined, and that changed things. Mark had never worked a case involving SIDS before; he had no idea at what point his own involvement would end. If it were ruled, by the coroner, to be a non-suspicious death in which the police need not take an interest, could he just walk away from people with whom he had already engaged?

And at the end of the day this was about a dead baby. He hadn't seen Muffin Betts; the body had been removed before he arrived. But he'd seen her in his dreams—still, white, like a tiny wax doll—and that had been bad enough.

Mark looked at his bedside alarm clock. Callie would be at Morning Prayer, so ringing her would have to wait.

He needed to talk to a sane human being; fortunately there was one close at hand. Yanking on his dressing gown, he headed for the lounge, forgetting that twenty-four hours earlier he'd gone to great lengths to avoid Geoff. Quite a lot had happened in that twenty-four hours.

Geoff was in weekend mode, sprawled on the sofa surrounded by bits of the Saturday papers, a mug of coffee in one hand. He looked up from the papers and raised the mug in Mark's direction. 'I made a pot,' he said. 'Help yourself.'

'Good man.' Mark went through to the kitchen, retrieved a mug from the draining rack, and poured himself a cup, filling it close to the brim then taking a sip. It almost burned his mouth, but it was worth it.

He carried the mug back into the lounge and sat down across from Geoff. Suddenly his awkwardness of the previous morning returned; apart from the whisky-fuelled confidences of the other night, he had no history of intimacy with this man. Mark blew on his coffee and sipped it carefully.

'Well,' said Geoff, raising his head from the papers. 'This is really something, this story about Jodee and Chazz. Poor sods, eh? I never thought I'd say that.'

Mark's stomach lurched sickeningly as the coffee hit it.

'It says the police are involved,' Geoff went on. 'SIDS, see? They have to treat it like a suspicious death until they know for sure that it wasn't. Suspicious, I mean.'

'I know,' Mark said quietly.

Geoff stared at him, comprehension dawning. 'You…you're involved in this?'

'Afraid so.' Now he *didn't* want to talk about it. Didn't want to trivialise it, engage in flippant banter.

'You actually met them? What are they like, then? Jodee and Chazz?'

Mark never would have suspected his flatmate of an interest in celebrity gossip. He chose his words with care. 'They're like any parents who have found their baby dead in its cot. Gutted.'

He wasn't sure how he would describe them, actually. Jodee's grief had been theatrical, almost operatic, in its expression, while Chazz—less demonstrative by nature—had been more understated but clearly no less devastated. There was no doubt in his mind that their anguish was real.

Geoff was looking at him, waiting.

Mark heard his mobile phone ring, faintly, from the bedside table where he'd left it. 'I'd better get that,' he said, and made his escape with his coffee.

He was hoping for Callie; instead it was Neville Stewart.

'Listen, mate,' Neville said. 'I don't know what your plans are, but you need to get back over there as soon as you can.' He didn't need to explain where 'over there' was, but he did go on to tell him why: the pathologist was rushing through the post-mortem results and the report would be available by that afternoon. The coroner would then decide what the next steps—if any—would be. And Neville had already had a call from Brenda Betts to tell him that they were virtual prisoners in their home; the press were out in their numbers, and had been joined by the paparazzi. 'It's getting ugly,' Neville said. 'They need you.'

Back at her flat, Lilith savoured the moment: not just the papers, now adding to the clutter in her habitually untidy sitting room, but an e-mail from the editor of the *Globe*. A congratulatory e-mail from the legendary Rob Gardiner-Smith. She'd never had one of those before. Sitting in front of the screen of her computer, she grinned in a most uncharacteristic manner.

Grinning wasn't Lilith's style. Lilith was elegant, well-groomed, a cut above the average tabloid journalist. Lilith knew how important appearance was in achieving the results she wanted, and that included control of her facial expressions. But there were moments, in the privacy of her own flat…

The phone rang. She looked at the caller display; it was not a number she recognised. 'Lilith Noone speaking,' she said.

'Ah, good. You're not an easy woman to track down.' The voice—female—at the other end chuckled.

That, Lilith could have informed her caller, was quite deliberate. In her line of work, the last thing she needed was a stream of phone calls from people with a grievance against her. She'd been ex-directory for years, and gave out her number only to people with a legitimate reason to ring her. Her curiosity was piqued. 'And you are…?' she asked.

'Addie McLean. Editor of *HotStuff* magazine.'

HotStuff! The ultimate celebrity gossip magazine. Addie McLean was a legend in that world; she'd left a safe job at *Hello!* to start a publication that was altogether more incendiary. *HotStuff* went where other gossip mags never dared to tread, and as a result they were constantly in court on libel charges. It was all good publicity, Addie McLean had been quoted as saying more than once. Everyone knew about *HotStuff*; celebrities dreaded seeing their names in it almost as much as they feared *not* being in it.

'Oh,' said Lilith, unusually at a loss for words.

'I enjoyed your story in today's *Globe*,' said Addie McLean. 'It was a good piece of work.'

'Thank you.' Lilith's chest swelled as she took a deep breath.

'And I was wondering whether you ever do any free-lance work? Does your editor allow it?'

It had never come up before, but Lilith didn't want to admit that. 'I don't think it's a problem,' she improvised.

'I'd really like to commission a piece from you. Jodee and Chazz, of course. Since you seem to have an inside track there. Would you be interested?'

Would she be interested? Did the woman think she was dim-witted? 'Yes, of course.'

'It's the funeral I'm keen on,' Addie McLean went on. 'Muffin's funeral. You'll be going?'

Lilith hadn't even thought about the funeral, but of course that would be the big set-piece. She should be covering it for the *Globe*. That didn't mean, though, that she couldn't write a piece for *HotStuff* as well, did it? Find a different angle?

'Yes, I'll be going.' With any luck, not just as a member of the press but as a family friend. Just like the wedding.

'Good. Then are we agreed? You'll cover the funeral for *HotStuff*?'

She'd square it with her editor somehow. Rob wasn't totally unreasonable. It would be all right. This wasn't something she could say no to, after all. 'Yes,' said Lilith firmly. 'I'd be delighted to do that.'

Putting the phone down, she performed another act that would have surprised people who knew her: Lilith punched the air with her fist and uttered one loud syllable. 'Yesssssss!'

Callie had been hoping to hear from Marco; she had so much to tell him, and she was still carrying around the CD for Chiara's birthday.

When he rang, though, he was focused. 'Listen, Callie,' he said. 'I'm afraid I've sort of landed you in it. With Jodee and Chazz.'

'What? Me?'

'The funeral,' he said. 'One of my jobs is to help people with funeral arrangements.'

'Yes,' said Callie. She knew that; Marco had mentioned it before. It was one way he could offer practical assistance to the families he was dealing with. 'But what does that have to do with me?'

'They live in your parish.'

Jodee and Chazz. Her parishioners. She was silent as the implications of that sank in.

Marco went on, 'They'd like to see you. This afternoon. To talk about the funeral.'

'But it's Brian they should be talking to. He's the vicar.' And he'd have kittens if she got involved in this without his permission.

'It's Brian's day off, isn't it?' Marco pointed out.

Brian's Saturdays were sacrosanct, fiercely protected by Jane. If the church burnt down on a Saturday afternoon, Brian wouldn't know about it until the Sunday morning unless he happened to look out of the window of the vicarage.

Callie tried again. 'But can't it wait a day or two? The funeral surely won't be happening for a while. Brian could come, say, first thing Monday morning.'

'Jodee wants *you*.' Marco sighed apologetically. 'I told her about you, *Cara mia*. I suppose my enthusiasm carried me away. And she really likes the idea of having a woman take the funeral. She wants *you*, not Brian. Not "some old vicar geezer", she said, to be precise.'

Brian would go spare. Not to mention Jane. Celebrities in his parish, by-passing him in defiance of all protocol. And Callie landed squarely in the middle of it.

'She's in a bad way,' he added. 'And Chazz, too. They could really use someone to talk to.'

She tried once more. 'But *Brian*—'

'Please, Callie.'

That simple appeal, and the emotion behind it, convinced her. People in her parish needed her. Brian might not like it, but he'd have to deal with it. 'The parishioners come first': how many times had Brian said those words to her, whether he meant them or not?

'Yes, all right,' she capitulated. 'I'll come.'

'You won't be able to miss the house,' Marco said, with a hint of a smile in his voice. 'It's the one with the crowd out front.'

'Crowd?'

'The press,' he amplified. 'Dozens of them. And television cameras. Not that they've had anything much to film. Until you get here, that is.'

'Oh, brilliant.' That was all she needed: for Brian to see her on the evening news.

◇◇◇

The news conference had already been scheduled and announced: it would be held at three p.m. on Saturday. Neville had taken the decision to schedule it after talking to Mark, who had been unsuccessful in dispersing the press from in front of the Betts' Bayswater town house.

'I asked them to leave, but they weren't having it,' Mark told him by phone. 'Maybe if we can give them a time for the news conference, they'll settle down a bit.'

'And if we hold it here, in the briefing room at the station…' Neville added. Then they'd have no choice but to leave the Betts family alone, at least for a bit.

So three o'clock it would be. The trouble was that by lunch time there was still no preliminary pathology report, and the pathologist wasn't answering his phone. Neither was the coroner, though Neville eventually managed to reach the coroner's deputy, who reported—unhelpfully—that the coroner was away for the weekend. On a romantic country get-away with his wife, apparently; that news did nothing to help Neville's mood.

It was nearly two when the pathologist turned up at Neville's office, in person, with a sheaf of papers.

Dr Colin Tompkins was, in Neville's experience, a man of few words, but those words he chose to utter were carefully considered and not to be ignored.

'First of all, as I explained to you yesterday, this is only a preliminary report,' he said, skipping the polite small talk. 'The results of all of the specialist tests—toxicology, microbiology and so forth—will take weeks to come through.'

'I understand.'

'But I did find something…unusual. And I wanted to be sure of this before I spoke with you,' he went on. 'I've been over everything twice, at least.'

Neville didn't like the sound of that. 'Go on,' he said.

Dr Tompkins spread the papers out in front of Neville, on the very small bit of his desk that was clear of clutter. His movements were precise; his hands were surgeon's—or musician's—hands, with long, tapering fingers.

'Hairline fracture,' he said, pointing at an x-ray. 'Here, in the neck.'

Oh, God. That was something Neville definitely didn't want to hear. 'So…she was murdered? Is that what you're saying?'

The pathologist shook his head. 'No. What I'm saying is that there is strong evidence that Muffin Angel Betts was shaken, hard, at some point in her life. Not immediately before death. Possibly a week or two before. That injury might or might not have contributed to her death.'

'Bloody hell,' said Neville.

'Without that fracture, it most likely would have been pretty straightforward. As straightforward as SUDI—sudden death in infancy—can be. Pending the results of the other tests, of course. And that will take a few weeks. With it, though…who knows?' Dr Tompkins shrugged. 'It's up to the coroner to say.'

The bloody coroner, who was off somewhere shagging his wife. Neville thanked Dr Tompkins, snatched up the papers, and went in search of DCS Evans.

Unusually for a Saturday, Evans was in the building. Neville found him in his office, unprotected by his secretary.

'Not good news, Sir,' Neville greeted him, terse as Dr Tompkins.

Evans squinted his piggy eyes at the x-ray as Neville reported the pathologist's findings, concluding, 'I'm afraid it's not straightforward, as we hoped it would be.'

'Bugger. So there *will* be an inquest,' Evans extrapolated.

Neville nodded reluctantly. 'The coroner is…unavailable…today. And his deputy is unwilling to commit himself. He's a new bloke—didn't want to take the decision himself. But I can't imagine that the coroner won't order one, under the circumstances.'

Evans leaned back in his chair. 'So, Stewart. What are you going to tell the press?'

'I haven't drafted my statement yet, obviously. I came straight to you. What do you suggest, Sir?' he asked diplomatically.

'Something as vague as possible.' Evans stroked his massive chin. 'You could say that the post-mortem examination was "inconclusive", and that an inquest will be opened this week.'

'They're sure to ask whether the death is being treated as suspicious,' Neville stated.

'Don't give a yes or no answer to that one—don't let them pin you down. Just something like "nothing has been ruled out". You'll know what to say.'

Neville wished he were as confident of that as Evans seemed to be. He wished, in fact, that Evans would take the damned press conference himself. But Evans, profoundly untelegenic with his prognathous jaw and his enormous eyebrows, liked to stay in the background. Less charitably, he preferred to put someone else in the firing line.

'What about that…other matter, Sir?' Neville asked.

'You mean the fact that she was home alone?' Evans scowled. 'For God's sake, man, don't mention that. It will probably come out eventually, at the inquest. But *we're* certainly not going to tell them.'

'And as far as the family goes?'

'They're going to have a few questions to answer,' Evans acknowledged. 'Talk to the FLO. DS Lombardi, isn't it?'

'Yes, Sir.'

'He'll be the best one to do it. Maybe not straightaway, if the parents are still hysterical. I doubt he'd get anything out of them just yet. But tell him to keep his ears open. If one of them has been shaking that baby, he'll be the person to get to the bottom of it.'

Well, thought Neville, that was something to be thankful for. He might have to face the fearsome press, but at least he wouldn't have to ask Jodee and Chazz whether they'd killed their baby.

When Callie went into Jodee and Chazz's townhouse, she'd had to fight her way through the press gathered on the pavement, but by the time she and Mark came out, a couple of hours later, the pavement was clear of all but the odd oblivious pedestrian.

'News conference,' Mark said. 'Neville's holding it in the briefing room at the station. No one's going to miss that.'

Callie had psyched herself up for the cameras; now she was aware that she was shaking with emotion. 'Oh, Marco,' she said, her voice wobbly.

He turned to her, looking concerned. 'Are you all right?'

'No. I'm not.'

More than anything she wanted to go home—back to her cosy flat. She wanted to make a pot of tea, light a fire, curl up on the sofa with Bella—and Marco. She did *not* want to go to the vicarage, to that horrible room. To Jane's accusing eyes and pursed lips.

'I think you need a drink,' Marco said.

She shook her head. 'Not a drink, no. I just need…' What *did* she need? 'To be with you,' she finished. 'Can we go somewhere? Where we can just talk?'

'How about the church?'

The church. Not perfect, but it would do. Brian wouldn't be there, Jane wouldn't be there. With any luck, no one else would, either.

She allowed him to lead her there, a protective arm round her shoulders. All Saints' Church, a mere three minutes' walk away, was unlocked; it was empty of people. Though the day had been overcast, the sun had been trying to fight its way out and as they entered the church a shaft of afternoon sun escaped the cloud cover and streamed through the stained glass of the west window, illuminating dust motes in the air and creating coloured pools on the stone flags of the floor.

A sign?

Marco steered her towards a pew. 'Not here,' Callie said. 'The Lady Chapel.'

The Lady Chapel, at the southeast corner of the building, was more secluded and private than the nave. Separated from the nave by a carved wooden screen, it was the smaller space in which weekday services were held. The fixed pews had been removed in favour of more flexible seating—chairs which could be shifted about as needed. The rogue beam of sunlight hadn't penetrated here; in the dim half-light, Callie felt sufficiently shielded from potential public view to move closer to Marco, to put her arms round him and rest her head on his shoulder.

'What's the matter, *Cara mia*?' he asked, hugging her close. 'That was…horrible.'

It wasn't as if she'd never counselled bereaved parishioners before. Brian considered it part of her training to do her share of pre-funeral visits, talking to people who had just lost loved ones, providing practical advice, trying to glean enough information about the deceased to cobble together a halfway decent sermon for the funeral. Sometimes she'd even known the people in question—church-goers in whose lives she had already become involved and about whom she cared personally. More often they were people like Jodee and Chazz, residents of the parish who were entitled by law to take advantage of the three-fold public services of their parish church: hatch, match, and dispatch. Baptisms, weddings, funerals.

Like Jodee and Chazz, but…*not* like them.

It wasn't their fame that set them apart. That had nothing to do with it, as far as Callie was concerned.

No. This was the first time she'd dealt, up close and personal, with the death of a baby. And she'd found it impossible to keep her feelings out of it.

It was her job to be professional, neutral, sympathetic but not involved. To provide the bereaved with reassurance and information. To help them choose a few hymns, talk through the form the service would take, give them advice about local funeral directors. To listen, if they wanted to talk about their loss, and supply tissues if they needed to cry.

But…a *baby*. A tiny baby, not even two months old.

They'd showed her photos, from the pre-natal scan to the first birth photos to the most recent pictures of little Muffin, dressed all in pink.

The parents were raw, hurting. Reeling in disbelief that this tiny, precious creature had been taken from them.

And all she'd wanted to do was…cry.

She'd managed to hold it together, just. She hadn't broken down in front of them. She'd given them the information they needed, expressed sympathy, agreed to take the funeral herself if that was what they wanted.

'But you were brilliant,' Marco said. 'The things you said—they were exactly right. Exactly what they needed to hear.'

'I was…useless.'

He tightened his arms round her. 'You weren't. You did your job, *Cara mia*. I was proud of you.'

'And you…' It was the first time she'd actually seen Marco at work, and she'd been impressed. His job was every bit as difficult as hers, Callie realised. In some ways, even more difficult: she was allowed to be sympathetic, and so was he, but he had to keep it in balance with the information-seeking functions of a police officer.

Surely, *surely* he couldn't suspect that those poor, heartbroken people had in any way knowingly contributed to the death of their baby?

'I've never worked on a SIDS case before,' he admitted. 'It's really grim.'

'Do you have to go back there?' Callie hoped he would say no. It had been less than three days since she'd seen him but it seemed like weeks.

'Not today. They need some time on their own.'

'So do we,' Callie murmured into his shoulder, suddenly shy.

Marco stroked her hair; she shivered, then felt herself go hot all over. She wanted him to kiss her and not stop for a very long time. But they were in church, where someone could walk in at any moment.

'Well, I have a little plan,' he said. 'We need to go to Serena's, to deliver Chiara's present.'

'It's in my bag,' she remembered.

'Then, *Cara mia*, after that, we'll go somewhere for a meal. Just the two of us.'

'I'd like that,' Callie said. 'Very much.'

Chapter Six

Before they could carry out their plans, though, Callie had to go back to the vicarage to change out of her clericals and to wrap Chiara's present. Mark, too, wanted to change clothes and smarten up a bit. They arranged to meet up in an hour or so.

Letting herself into the vicarage with her key, Callie heard the sound of the television coming from the sitting room and crept up the stairs to her room. It seemed even bleaker without Bella there to greet her. She looked over at the space in the corner where Bella's bed had been, her eyes prickling with tears, missing her dog. Trying not to think about it, she quickly located her favourite jumper, one she'd had from Peter for Christmas.

Once she'd changed, she got out the CD and realised that she had nothing with which to wrap it. There wasn't time to go out and buy a sheet of wrapping paper, so she was going to have to throw herself on Jane's mercy.

'Come in!' Brian called out to Callie's tentative tap on the sitting room door.

The Stanfords were side-by-side on their ugly old brown Dralon sofa, watching an ancient black-and-white film, drinking cups of tea. 'Sorry to bother you,' said Callie.

'Would you like some tea?' Brian indicated the pot on the coffee table. 'We can get another cup.'

'Thanks, but I won't.'

'Then take a seat. The film is nearly over, but it's a good one. Cary Grant. The one where—'

Jane cut him off. 'Was there something particular you wanted?'

Callie held up the CD. 'I need a bit of wrapping paper and some sellotape. If it isn't too much trouble.'

Jane's long-suffering sigh told Callie that it was indeed too much trouble, but that she considered it part of the lot of a vicar's wife to put up with such things. 'Come with me,' Jane instructed, getting up and heading towards the kitchen.

'Sellotape,' she said, as she retrieved it from a drawer an slapped it on the countertop. 'I suppose you'll need scissors as well?'

'Yes, thanks.'

The scissors joined the sellotape, then Jane pulled out a deep drawer and Callie got a glimpse of folded and stacked pieces of wrapping paper, crammed in almost to overflowing. 'Is there a particular occasion?' Jane asked. 'Birthday? Wedding? New baby?'

'Birthday. For a teenage girl.'

Jane leafed through the paper and pulled a square out, holding it up as if to judge the size. 'This should do,' she said briskly.

It was pink, decorated with flowers and 'Happy Birthday' inscriptions. It was also creased and had fragments of sellotape on the edges. 'It's…been used?' Callie ventured.

'Of course. I never buy new wrapping paper.' Jane looked smug rather than defensive. 'Waste not, want not. You just cut off the edges and no one can tell the difference.'

'Uh…thanks.' Callie took the paper from her. 'I really appreciate it.'

She wrapped the package quickly at the kitchen table, under Jane's watchful eye. Was Jane afraid that she was going to pocket her scissors or the roll of sellotape?

'The dog is gone?' Jane asked.

'Yes. To my friend Frances' house.' Again Callie's eyes prickled; she didn't trust herself to say any more.

It had been a painful parting, that morning. She knew that Frances and Graham would take good care of Bella, give her her meals on time and let her out in the garden at regular intervals to do her business, even take her for walks. But Callie was going to miss her. Stopping by for the occasional walk just wouldn't be the same.

Bella hadn't been the only guest at the vicarage in Notting Hill; Callie had been more than a bit surprised to find Triona in residence. Triona, just a week after her wedding! Though she'd been at the wedding, Callie didn't know Triona well—she knew her through Frances, and through Marco's friendship with Neville Stewart.

And the latter connection posed a potential problem. The ins and outs of the situation hadn't been explained to Callie, but it was pretty clear that Triona was in hiding and didn't want her new husband to know where she was. Could she, then, tell Marco that she'd seen her? She was sure she could trust him with confidential information, but was that putting him in too difficult a position with his friend Neville?

Callie had no great love for Neville Stewart, yet she could imagine that he must be frantic with worry over his wife's whereabouts.

Still, Callie told herself firmly, it wasn't her business.

Her other concern was closer to home and more immediate.

She and Marco were going to Serena's house. He'd said that Serena would be at work, that Chiara would be at home with her father.

Callie hoped he was right.

For some reason she was unable to fathom, Serena made her uncomfortable. She knew that she and Serena should get on like a house on fire, with all they had in common: they both loved Marco, for starters. And Serena's ill treatment at the hands of her husband Joe should have inspired not only pity but fellow-feeling, considering that Callie had been dumped by her fiancé Adam. The way Marco had always talked about his sister, with huge affection and respect, Callie had expected to hit it off wonderfully with her from their first meeting.

That hadn't happened. Serena was invariably courteous and hospitable, but Callie sensed no warmth there. Serena kept her distance.

'She doesn't like me,' Callie had said to Marco, more than once.

'Don't be ridiculous, *Cara mia*,' he always replied. 'You're just paranoid.'

Callie was sure she wasn't imagining it. Serena didn't like her. Was she just being protective of her younger brother, or was it the fact that Joe had seemed to take to Callie right away? Was it jealousy, pure and simple?

There was an even more disturbing corollary. Callie, who prided herself on seeing the best in just about everyone— even her difficult mother; even Adam's new bride, the lovely Pippa—admitted to herself, if not to Marco, that she didn't much like Serena either.

◇◇◇

Walking towards their meeting place, Mark had a sudden and profound instant of *déjà vu*. It was the same spot where they'd arranged to meet for their first date, though Callie hadn't wanted to call it that, and as he approached he could see that she was wearing the same cherry red cashmere jumper she'd worn that night.

Six months on, and so much had changed. Then she'd been an attractive woman whom he'd met only once and looked forward to getting to know better. Now she was the centre of his world.

She spotted him and her face lit up in a way that made his heart turn over in his chest. 'Marco!' she called, moving towards him.

'*Cara mia*.' He kissed her there on the street corner, in the middle of busy, anonymous London, as he'd not felt able to do in the church.

◇◇◇

A few minutes later, Chiara opened the door to them, fizzing with birthday excitement. 'Uncle Marco! Look! I've had my ears pierced!' She pulled her long black hair back to show him the little studs.

'Nice earrings,' he said.

She gave him a pitying look. 'These aren't the *real* earrings. They're just sleepers. Until the holes heal up. Isn't that right?' she appealed to Callie.

'That's right,' affirmed Callie. 'Your uncle Marco doesn't know about things like that.'

'And I'm going to get my hair cut,' Chiara went on. 'So you'll be able to see my ears better. Mum says I can. Dad's not very keen. He says he's old-fashioned, but he likes long hair.'

I'll bet he does, thought Mark sourly, hoping his distaste wasn't evident on his face as he imagined an endless procession of long-haired undergraduate girls moving through Joe di Stefano's life.

'How short are you going to cut it?' asked Callie. 'What sort of style?'

'A bob. Maybe kind of like yours.' Chiara put her hands at her chin-line with a chopping motion. 'I really want to have it like Jodee's, you know? Asymmetrical? And with some of it bleached blond? But Mum says definitely no to that.'

'I should think so, too, young lady,' Mark said with avuncular mock severity.

'But she looks so cool!' Then Chiara's expressive face went suddenly solemn. 'Her baby died, did you know that? Muffin? Poor Jodee.'

Callie caught his eye; Mark could see that she was thinking the same thing he was: this was definitely not the time to reveal his involvement with Jodee. 'I'd heard,' he said neutrally. 'It's very sad.'

'Cot death,' said Chiara. 'It happened to my friend at school's baby brother, last year. He was fine, and one morning there he was, dead. They never did know why.'

Mark looked at Callie, who was pressing her lips together. The last thing he wanted was to let her re-visit this afternoon's emotions, so he abruptly changed the subject. 'And you're a teenager now, *Nipotina*!'

Chiara grinned. 'So maybe you can stop calling me that. I'm not your *little* niece any longer, Uncle Marco.'

'Oh, you're very grown up,' he agreed.

She squinted her eyes at him suspiciously. 'Now you're making fun of me.'

'Would I do that?' He pressed a hand to his chest and tried to look innocent.

'Well, maybe not.' She gave him a spontaneous hug, and he rubbed the top of her head as he'd always done, realising how much taller she'd grown.

There was something bittersweet in the realisation. Mark had always treasured his relationship with Chiara, which was quite different from the relationship he had with her older sister Angelina. Mark had been a child himself—younger than Chiara was now—when Angelina was born; he wasn't at all interested in babies in those days, and regarded her as something of a nuisance, if not a rival for Serena's attention and affections. But by the time Chiara finally came along, after a string of failed pregnancies, he was sufficiently grown up to appreciate having a young niece, a *nipotina*. In his late teens by then, he'd been the right age to be a frequent babysitter; Serena had trusted him with Chiara and a strong bond had been forged from the start. She'd always adored her uncle, who was sufficiently younger than her parents to be 'cool'.

'So,' said Mark, 'what are the plans for the birthday?'

Chiara squirmed out of his arms. 'Family party tomorrow. Lunch. You're coming, aren't you?'

'Of course.'

'Then some of my friends are coming over later. Nonna's baking the cake, and I've asked Mum if she'll make pizza as well.'

'Sounds like fun.'

Chiara turned to Callie. 'Are you coming to lunch as well? I'd like it if you would.'

Callie shook her head. 'I wish I could. But Sunday's my busy day,' she said.

'Of course. Duh.' Chiara wacked herself on the side of the head with her open palm.

'But I'll be thinking about you.' Callie rummaged in her bag and handed Mark a wrapped square. 'Don't forget about this, Marco,' she said. 'The main reason we're here.'

Chiara produced a most un-grownup squeal. 'Oh, a prezzie!' She snatched it from his outstretched hand and ripped the paper off. 'Karma! Oh, Uncle Marco—it's just what I wanted!'

Well, Serena's suggestion had been right on the money, then. 'This album is *so* wicked. Mega. Have you listened to it?'

'No,' he admitted. 'I'm not really up on Karma.'

Another pitying look. 'She won "Junior Idol". Last year.'

'So I understand.'

Chiara consulted her watch. 'That reminds me—it's almost half-past six. Nearly time for it—for "Junior Idol".'

'Well, I guess we'd better be going then.' Mark looked at Callie, who nodded.

'Oh, you can't leave now! You've just got here, Uncle Marco. You have to stay and watch "Junior Idol" with us. Tonight's the semi-final!'

'With *us*?'

'Me and Dad.' Chiara went to the foot of the stairs and called up. 'Dad! It's almost time.'

Mark wouldn't have expected Joe to be a 'Junior Idol' fan. But then, he told himself bitterly, some of the contestants were probably pretty young girls. Young, as in junior. 'Why is it called "*Junior* Idol"?' he asked Chiara.

'They have to be under twenty-one.' She shook her head. 'I thought everyone knew that.'

The news conference was over. History. On the whole, Neville didn't think it had gone too badly.

The briefing room had been stuffed to its capacity; at the last minute they'd had to rig up a closed-circuit feed to an auxiliary room for the overflow. Neville himself might not have known— or cared—about Jodee and Chazz forty-eight hours ago, but he realised that he was clearly in the minority. Jodee, Chazz and Muffin were big news.

He'd read his statement, along the lines of what DCS Evans had suggested. He'd kept it vague, using the word 'inconclusive' more than once, leaving them—the police, the coroner, the CPS—room to manoeuvre as necessary in the future.

Of course the press hadn't allowed him to leave it at that. He'd been bombarded with questions—some of a frivolous nature, and some fairly tough ones. He'd handled them relatively well, all things considered.

Until that bloody woman Lilith Noone had stood up. Smiling, all sweetness and light. 'Exactly what,' she'd asked, 'do you mean by "inconclusive"?'

He'd taken a deep breath, tried to ignore his personal antipathy for the woman. 'I mean that we don't yet have enough information to draw any conclusions.'

'And why is that? You say that the post-mortem was "inconclusive". That must mean that there was something there to indicate that it wasn't a straightforward cot death. Could you comment on that, Detective Inspector? Is this death being treated as suspicious?'

'Cot deaths are seldom—if ever—straightforward, Miss Noone,' he'd snapped. 'Ask any doctor. If we knew what caused them to happen, there wouldn't be so many of them.'

Under the circumstances, it had been a good answer, and it had seemed to satisfy her. At least he hoped so. She'd sat down without further comment.

But Neville just couldn't help the nagging feeling that he'd not heard the last from Lilith Noone when it came to this case. She had a nasty way of getting her teeth into something and not letting go. Just like some bloody terrier.

Well, there wasn't anything he could do about it now.

And he wasn't going back to the Bettses' house. Not today. That would only inflame media speculation about the police's continued interest in Muffin Betts' death.

There was nothing for it. He couldn't avoid thinking about Triona any longer. It was, after all, their bloody one-week anniversary.

He was going to look for her. Unfortunately, from his starting point in Paddington, his flat in Shepherd's Bush was the opposite direction from hers in the City, but the traffic wasn't too bad, late on a Saturday afternoon. And he had the whole long evening ahead of him. He would head into the City first, and if she wasn't there he'd go back to Shepherd's Bush. That way, if his searching was in vain, and barring any further inspiration as to her whereabouts, he'd be home at the end. Close to all of his known and approved watering holes—all of those places where he could drown his sorrows, into the night, without having to get behind the wheel afterwards.

It wasn't that Neville was a natural pessimist, but he had a feeling that finding Triona was going to take more than a few hours. She obviously didn't want to be found.

Callie had known, before she ever met Joe di Stefano, about his infidelities. Marco had confided in her in the heat of his anger, immediately after confronting an unrepentant Joe. She'd dreaded meeting him, expecting a leering monster.

But Joe had been charming to her from the start, and not in a creepy, smarmy way. He'd been natural, funny, unforced. Joe had accepted her as Marco's significant other, and thus as part of the family—*la famiglia* Lombardi—in the same auxiliary capacity as himself.

It wasn't that she fancied him—not at all. Callie just couldn't help liking Joe, in spite of all that she knew about him. She enjoyed his company; he made her laugh.

So as Joe came down the stairs, though she could feel Marco tensing beside her, she smiled.

'Well, what a nice surprise,' Joe said. 'Marco and Callie.'

'We brought Chiara's birthday present,' Marco said stiffly.

'So I see.'

Chiara was dancing round and waving the CD in the air. 'Karma!' she squealed. 'I can't wait to listen to it!'

'Well, there's no time for that now,' her father reminded her.

'I know. I know.'

'Just time to get everything ready.' Joe smiled at Callie. 'Did Chiara tell you about our little Saturday evening ritual?'

'She said that you always watch "Junior Idol" together.'

'Oh, that's just part of the ritual. Then there's the food that goes with it. Food is a big element of ritual, don't you find? Especially in this family.'

Callie understood what he was saying. After all, she was part of an institution that had ritual at its heart: the ritual of the Mass, with bread and wine its central symbols. 'Bread and wine,' she said. 'Body and blood.'

'Exactly.' Joe nodded his approval.

'For us it's Pringles,' Chiara explained.

Marco looked horrified. 'Pringles?'

'Mum doesn't like me to have them. She says they're rubbish.'

'So they're our little secret, eh, *Principessa*?' Joe winked at his daughter. 'And the secret is part of the ritual, as well.'

Forbidden fruit, thought Callie. Chiara was learning the lesson young that forbidden fruit was often the sweetest. Was that really something a father should be teaching his daughter? She glanced at Marco, who was raising his eyebrows at this latest confirmation of Joe's character.

Chiara, perhaps belatedly sensing Marco's disapproval, appealed to her uncle. 'You won't tell Mum, will you?'

'Your secret's safe with me.' His voice was deliberately light, but Callie could tell that he was more bothered than he cared to let on.

'Good.' Chiara turned and headed towards the kitchen, adding over her shoulder, 'We have hot chocolate as well. Mum doesn't mind about that.'

'I think I'll pass on the hot chocolate and Pringles,' Marco said.

Chiara stopped. 'But you'll stay for "Junior Idol"?'

He looked at Callie for confirmation; she nodded. At that moment she would have just as soon have left, to enjoy the evening alone with Marco. But if this was what he wanted…

'We'll stay,' Marco conceded. 'For at least part of it.'

◇◇◇

Before the events of the past few days, Frances Cherry had never thought there would be any circumstances under which she would feel sorry for Neville Stewart, but she'd definitely changed her mind. He was a man to be pitied.

First of all, there was the distressing case he was involved in. A dead baby was the very worst thing to deal with; she knew that well from her work at the hospital. Frances had seen a great many deaths, many of them unexpected: death by accident, death by sudden illness. Somehow, despite the shock of loss, the survivors coped. The death of a baby, though, was different. No one expected it. And the poignancy of a tiny, vulnerable body, so much potential cut short…It affected people—and not just the parents—in profound ways which they sometimes never got over.

And then there were his marital problems.

Triona, she'd discovered, didn't want to talk about it. She seemed grateful to Frances and Graham for the refuge they'd provided, but Frances' efforts to get her to air her feelings had been rebuffed. She was keeping it all locked in, shut down.

She had joined them to watch the evening news, sitting without comment through the coverage of the latest natural disaster and the current political crisis in the Middle East. Then, after a few preliminary words of explanation from the newsreader, Neville Stewart had appeared on the screen, reading out a statement about Muffin Angel Betts' death.

Triona had simply got up and walked out of the room.

After the news, Frances and Graham moved to the kitchen to prepare dinner. Through their long marriage they had always shared kitchen duties; Graham enjoyed cooking more than Frances did, though his schedule as the vicar of a busy parish meant that she was more often than not the one who produced the meals. Saturday evenings were usually more relaxed for Graham—the sermon sorted, no meetings to attend—and he liked to do his spaghetti bolognese, with some help from Frances.

First she went to the corner of the kitchen to stroke Bella, who was sulking in her bed, missing Callie. 'Poor girl,' said Frances. 'You must be feeling abandoned.' She washed her hands and started on the salad while Graham chopped an onion.

'She's not the only one who's been abandoned,' said Graham. 'What about Neville Stewart?'

'Yes. I know.'

'Not that I like the man. After what he did to you.' Graham wielded the knife with particular ferocity, rattling the wooden cutting board.

'He was just doing his job,' she reminded him. 'He didn't take pleasure in it.'

Graham scooped the onion into the frying pan and stirred it into the mince. 'I suppose so. And he does love Triona. I'm sure of it.'

'I believe that he does.' Frances thought back to the wedding, just a week ago: how they had looked at each other—Neville and Triona—with such transparent happiness on their faces. 'She must know that. And she must realise how she's making him suffer.'

'Can't you talk to her, Fran?' Graham whacked a clove of garlic with the heel of his hand.

'I've tried. And tried. She just looks at me with that blank face and says that she doesn't want to discuss it.'

He discarded the papery skin of the garlic and minced the clove. 'She can't hide from him forever. Running away from your problems doesn't solve anything.'

'You know that. And I know that.' Frances smiled at her husband fondly. Their own marriage had not been without its problems—mostly in the early days, when he'd been priested but that option was not yet open to her, and her resentment had been unfairly directed at him as well as at the Church—but the things that had divided them over the years, the little wrangles over child-rearing and domestic responsibilities, seemed trivial in comparison to what Triona now faced. 'I think she has to decide now whether she wants to be married to him or not.'

'I think you're right, Fran.' Graham tossed the garlic into the frying pan and gave the mixture another stir. 'If she does want to be married to him, she has to accept that this is part of it—his job, I mean. And the fact that it will always have to come first.'

Frances made a face. 'I learned that a long time ago, as a vicar's wife.'

'Well, there's something in that,' he admitted. 'But how much more so for a policeman?'

'And if she can't accept it?'

'Well.' Graham put the wooden spoon down and gave her his full attention. 'I don't think, in all my years of ministry, I've ever counselled anyone to walk away from their marriage, from a commitment they've made in the sight of God, or even just in the sight of man. I've always told people that they had to work at it, and that it would be worth it in the end.'

'I feel a "but" coming on,' Frances guessed.

'But…' He smiled ruefully. 'In this case, Fran, I really do wonder whether they'd thought through what they were getting into before they did it. There was the baby on the way, and it was all so sudden. One minute she was complaining to you about what a bastard he was, and the next minute they were getting married.'

'They did wait a few months, to be fair,' Frances pointed out. 'And they've known each other for years.'

'Yes, yes.'

'And your mince is burning.'

Graham turned the flame down with one hand and grabbed the spoon with the other, stirring vigourously. 'That's what I get for trying to be pastoral while I'm cooking.'

'I do understand what you're saying,' Frances admitted. 'In spite of the baby, if they aren't prepared to work at the marriage and make the compromises they'll need to make, maybe it would be better for them to acknowledge that right now, before they do any more damage to each other. They're both such stubborn people,' she added. 'I do love Triona, but sometimes she makes me want to scream.'

The kitchen door swung open. 'Something smells divine,' said Triona.

'Onions and garlic,' Graham said, with a sideways glance at Frances even as he smiled in Triona's direction. 'My famous Saturday night spag bol.'

How much had Triona overheard?, Frances wondered. Well, perhaps it would be no bad thing if she *had* heard them.

'I'm ravenous,' Triona stated. 'When's dinner?'

Graham gave the contents of the frying pan another stir. 'Not for another thirty minutes or so.'

'Well, then, why don't I lay the table?' suggested Triona. 'Since I've landed myself on you, I might as well make myself useful.'

Callie allowed Joe to make her a cup of hot chocolate; she even guiltily ate a few Pringles, hoping that Marco wouldn't despise her for it.

They settled down in the lounge, Chiara taking the seat with the best view of the telly. Callie and Marco squeezed next to her on the sofa, while Joe made himself comfortable in a chair.

'Junior Idol' was a revelation to Callie, and not quite what she'd expected. In the first place, the quality of the singing was far better than the amateur, out-of-tune caterwauling she'd anticipated. But then, she reminded herself, this was the semi-final, and the worst singers would have been eliminated from the competition by now.

There were four young singers left; one would go home tonight and the other three would battle it out in the final next week. The first to perform was a young black girl—no older than about ten—called Taneesha, with amazing stage presence and a soulful, mature voice. Then came Raj, an Asian teenager who belted out a high-energy hip-hop number.

'He's so cute,' Chiara sighed.

Callie smiled at her, remembering all too well her own teen-age crushes on pop stars. 'Is he your favourite?'

'Well, I do like him,' the girl admitted. 'But I'm not voting for him to win, if that's what you mean. You have to wait to see *our* favourite. The one we want to win.'

The third contestant was a pretty, wispy blonde girl. 'Samantha,' Chiara announced. 'She's one of Dad's students. Isn't she, Dad?' she turned to her father for confirmation.

Joe nodded. 'That's right.'

'We hope she'll win. That would be so cool.'

Squeezed close to Marco on the sofa, once again Callie could feel the sudden increase of tension in his body. She glanced sideways at him; he pressed his lips together and shook his head. *Later*, his look told her.

Samantha sang a pop ballad, tunefully and in a pleasant if unremarkable voice. She did look amazing, though, in a shim-mering dress with artful slashes revealing glimpses of flesh as she moved, swaying with the music.

'She has sex appeal,' said Chiara, sounding very solemn and knowing.

Callie suppressed a giggle, but Marco stood up abruptly. 'We have to go now,' he said.

'But Samatha's still singing! You can't leave while she's singing!'

He reached out a hand and pulled Callie to her feet. 'We have a table booked at a restaurant. We'll be late if we don't go.'

Chiara's face crumpled, like the little girl she was trying so desperately to leave behind. 'You haven't even heard Tiger! And we have to ring up to vote for Samantha. All of us, to make sure she doesn't get eliminated.'

'Sorry, *Nipotina*.' Marco fished in his pocket and put a pound coin on the coffee table, next to the tube of Pringles. 'You can ring on our behalf if you like. I'll see you tomorrow, at your birthday lunch.'

'But, Uncle Marco…'

'Don't bother to get up.' Marco spoke stiffly in Joe's direction, without looking at him.

Joe shrugged, his eyes fixed on the telly as Samantha wiggled and shimmered from one side of the stage to the other. 'See you tomorrow.'

In a moment they were at the door, retrieving their coats on the way, and then they were out in the street, Marco practically dragging Callie towards the corner.

She halted, forcing him to stop as well. 'Marco! What is this all about?'

He turned to face her, his lips compressed, and when he finally spoke it was through clenched teeth. 'That…bastard.'

'Joe? Are you talking about Joe?'

'That…girl. That Samantha. She's the one.'

For a moment Callie had no idea what he was talking about. The *one*? The one they were voting for? Chiara had made that quite clear.

Then, as she looked up into Marco's tortured face, the penny dropped. It was the same expression he'd worn the night he spilled his heart out to her about Joe's infidelity—his betrayal of Serena with one of his students.

'I saw her, remember? In his office. He called her Sam. Her hair was a bit different, and she certainly wasn't dressed like that, but…it's the same girl.'

'You're sure.' It was a statement, not a question; Marco wouldn't be wrong about that sort of thing. He was a policeman, trained to observe faces.

'How could he expose his innocent young daughter to his… his lechery…like that? I mean, that woman—that *girl*—is his mistress!'

'Oh, Marco.'

'And Serena. Does *she* know? Or is that part of their little secret ritual? Keeping it from Mummy?' Marco's voice was raw.

'You won't tell her, will you?'

'God forbid.' He closed his eyes, shook his head. 'If Serena found out that he'd involved Chiara in his sordid little love affair, I wouldn't want to be around to see the consequences.'

Chapter Seven

Jane Stanford's so-far unsuccessful efforts to get pregnant made her abnormally sensitive to that condition in others. The fact that several young wives in the congregation were expecting babies served as a constant reminder to Jane of the age gap—and her own failure to conceive.

One of them, fairly new to the parish and unaware of the sacrosanct nature of Brian's Saturday day off, had rung the doorbell late in the afternoon. 'Oh, hello,' she'd said brightly to Jane. 'I was hoping to have a word with Father Brian. About the christening, you know,' she'd smiled, indicating her bulging middle, all the more evident because her coat wouldn't button over it. 'It won't be long now.'

Jane had not managed to be very gracious. 'It's the vicar's day off,' she'd said. 'He can't be disturbed. And,' she added tartly, 'it's customary to wait until after the birth before planning the baptism.'

After that, reminded that she must be getting close to the point in her cycle when she would ovulate, she'd gone to take her temperature and had discovered that it was up a notch, indicating that the time was right.

Brian was watching television—test match cricket from somewhere in the world where it was warmer than in England. He barely looked up as she came into the room.

'Brian, it's time to go upstairs,' she said coyly.

'Upstairs?'

'My temperature is up.'

He didn't stir. 'But Janey—it's…well, it's still daytime. And what if Callie came home?'

'Callie? What does it have to do with *her*?' Jane could hear the shrillness in her own voice.

'I'd be embarrassed if she came in and we were…you know.' He gave her a conciliatory smile. 'I'm sure a few hours won't make any difference. We can have an early night, if you like.'

Jane stalked out of the room without bothering to reply. She wasn't entirely convinced that Callie was the real reason for his reluctance, or whether he was using her as an excuse because he didn't want to miss the cricket; in either case, Jane was not amused.

She was even less amused a few minutes later when the phone rang. She went into the kitchen to answer it and was surprised to hear her son Charlie's voice. 'Hi, Mum,' he said, then with no further preliminaries, 'I've just seen your curate on the telly. On the news, no less.'

'On the news?' That was impossible. 'It must have been someone who looks like her,' Jane protested.

'It was her, all right.'

'But…what was it about? What has she done?'

Charlie laughed. 'I don't think she's *done* anything. Not in the way you mean. It was about that dead baby that everyone's so spun up about. Jodee and Chazz, you know? Watch it for yourself, Mum. On the BBC News channel. I'm certain it will be on again in half an hour or so.'

What on earth could Callie have to do with the dead baby? And why would it get her on the news?

Jane went back into the sitting room, and without asking Brian's permission, picked up the remote from the table in front of him and changed the channel.

'Hey,' he protested, focusing his full attention on her at last. 'What's going on? I was watching that!'

'You're not watching it any longer.' Jane settled down next to him on the sofa, keeping the remote firmly in her hand. 'We're going to watch the news.'

Brian folded his arms across his chest, sulkily, but he stayed. While they waited for the next cycle of news, Jane told him about Charlie's phone call.

After the weather, the newsreader gave out the headlines over clips of video footage. And there she was: Callie. In her clericals, going through a crowd of journalists into a tall, elegant house. Not identified by name, but there was no mistaking who it was.

The full story followed a few minutes later, after coverage of early spring floods in the West Country. 'Investigations continue into the death of Muffin Betts, the infant daughter of celebrities Jodee and Chazz Betts,' the newsreader said. 'The baby died yesterday morning, seemingly the victim of cot death.' The brief footage of Callie was repeated, panning back to show the house, then the scene shifted to the police station. 'In a news conference this afternoon, Detective Inspector Neville Stewart told the press that the post-mortem results were "inconclusive". He refused to confirm whether the death was being treated as suspicious.' A clip followed, in which the policeman read out a noncommittal statement. 'The Betts family,' the newsreader appended, 'were unavailable for comment.'

'But what was Callie doing there?' Brian mused, more thinking aloud than asking a question. 'Though I suppose it *is* in the parish.'

'Without consulting you, though? It's just not on.'

Brian reached for the remote and flipped back to the cricket. 'I'm sure there's a good explanation. I'll ask her when she comes in.'

There went their early night, thought Jane sourly. No one in this house would be going to bed before Callie got back and explained herself. Though with tomorrow being Sunday, surely she wouldn't be out late…

Thirteen. A teenager. No longer a child—a *bambino*, a *nipotina*. Chiara examined herself minutely in her bedroom mirror, as she had done the night before when she was still twelve. Did she look different? Had she changed?

There had been a time, long ago, when Chiara had thought that she would grow up overnight. One day she would be a child; the next morning she would wake up as an adult. Though she now realised it was a gradual process, something in her still expected some visible difference to mark the significant transition out of childhood.

The holes in her ears—they were new. Mum had taken her that afternoon to have them done. It had hurt, but only a little, and it was worth it. She pulled her hair back and twisted her head to examine the raw-looking punctures, with their little stud earrings, and remembered that she was supposed to dab them with alcohol to keep them from getting infected.

They'd given her a little bottle of alcohol, so she found some cotton buds and applied it to her ears, grimacing at the sting.

She *would* look different, she told herself, when she got her hair cut. It was a shame that Mum had run out of time this afternoon; Chiara had hoped to show off the new hairdo at her official birthday party tomorrow. Now it would probably be next Saturday before she was able to have it done.

Maybe in that time she'd be able to convince Mum to let her have it cut like Jodee's, though she doubted that Mum would ever agree to the bleached bit.

It was all right for Mum, Chiara thought glumly. Mum had beautiful hair—reddish-gold and wavy. Not like anyone else's in the family; she'd heard all the jokes about it, though Mum had explained that it was a throw-back to a Venetian ancestor. If only she'd inherited Mum's hair, instead of Dad's boring hair, dark and straight.

Chiara cleaned her teeth at her basin, put out the light, and scrambled into bed, then she switched on her bedside lamp and pulled a magazine from under her pillow.

It was the latest edition of *HotStuff*, bought with her pocket money. She would only allow herself to read a bit of it, as it had to last for a whole week until the next issue came out.

Once upon a time she'd read books when she went to bed. Even before that, Mum or Dad—or Uncle Marco—would read to her, fairy stories and babyish things like that. She'd loved it then, but now she'd outgrown make-believe. Stories were boring, compared to the activities of real-life celebrities.

She flipped through the magazine, sampling its delights: Karma at a London night-club in an outrageous frock, Kate snapped in a supermarket wearing low-slung jeans and sporting a new tattoo, Raj in a restaurant with an exotic-looking girl, Angie hauling her babies into an SUV. There was a feature story about Jodee, showing her in an expensive shop buying French designer baby clothes. That was so sad, considering what had happened since then.

After a few minutes, the excitements of the day caught up with her. Chiara's eyelids drooped; the magazine slipped from her fingers.

But she was wakened abruptly—it might have been five minutes later, or an hour or more—by one shouted word, sharp as a gunshot. 'Bastard.'

Her eyes flew open. It had come from her parents' room, next to hers. The voice had been her mother's.

There had been a time, a few months back, around Christmas, when shouting rows between her parents had wakened Chiara in the night more than once. Those weeks had been traumatic, upsetting, especially since up to that point Mum and Dad had always seemed to have such an easy, loving relationship. Not knowing where else to turn, Chiara had even spoken to Uncle Marco about it.

It had never been quite clear to her what the rowing was about. Usually it had come from another room, not their bedroom: loud enough to hear the anger, if not near enough to pick out what they were saying.

Then it had stopped, to be replaced by a chill politeness between them. It seemed to Chiara that sometimes they spoke to each other like strangers, not people who had shared a home for more than twenty years. In some ways it was worse than the rows, but at least it was quieter. And Chiara could ignore it if she really tried; she could pretend that things were the way they'd always been.

She blamed her mother. Mum had been the one who started the shouting, initiated the rows. It always sounded to Chiara like Dad was just defending himself.

And now that word. It was a bad word, one she'd be in big trouble if she ever used in their hearing, even now that she was no longer a child. Again Mum had started it. What could Dad have possibly done to deserve a word like that being fired at him?

'Keep your voice down,' Dad said. 'Do you want Chiara to hear?' It came through the wall clearly.

'Since when do you care about Chiara?' Mum's voice was bitter, if a bit quieter, and then she must have moved farther from the wall as her words faded into an indistinct stream of acrimony.

'That's not fair.'

'Fair?' The one word came through, then more muffled anger.

Dad was whispering now; Chiara couldn't make out what he was saying. Mum replied, her voice quietly venomous. Then her tone changed, penetrating the wall again. 'Do you take me for a fool?'

'Never that.' Dad sounded weary.

'If my parents find out…'

'Your parents. Spare me.'

'If Mamma and Pappa find out, so help me, Joe, I won't be responsible for what happens.'

Chiara could bear no more. She covered her ears with her hands, pressing hard to block the sound, screwed her eyes up tight, and buried her face in her pillow.

Callie got out of the taxi and approached the front door of the vicarage quietly; it was later than she'd intended to return, and by now—with any luck, anyway—Brian and Jane would have long since retired to bed.

But there was a light on in the front room, she realised as she slipped her key into the lock. That was not a good sign.

She really, really didn't want to talk to Brian—or Jane—tonight. She needed to be on her own, to re-live and savour the time she'd spent with Marco. Lovely, lovely Marco, with his warm brown eyes and his beautiful hair…

In spite of the rough start—Marco's anger at Joe, storming out of his house—it had been a good evening, and long overdue. They'd had a lovely meal at a rather upmarket bistro, where the service was good and the food excellent, and no one was rushing them to finish and vacate the table. Making a bottle of wine last through the evening, they'd talked and talked, catching up on everything that had happened in the days since they'd last been together.

Marco had wanted to see her safely home, but she'd persuaded him that it didn't make sense for him to go all the way to Bayswater with her when she couldn't even invite him in. So the hurried, public kiss at the taxi rank was the least satisfactory thing about the evening.

One of these days she'd make it up to him. One of these days…

She held her breath as she shut the door silently behind her and crept towards the stairs, feeling like a naughty teenager in danger of being caught after sneaking out for the night. But she hadn't *been* a naughty teenager, not ever: she'd been too afraid of disappointing her father and upsetting her mother. Peter had been the naughty one, though as far as she knew he'd never been caught out.

'Callie,' came Brian's voice from the sitting room. 'Could I have a word?'

She sighed and pushed the door open. 'I'm really sorry, Brian. I didn't mean to be so late,' she said sheepishly. 'You didn't need to wait up for me, you know.' Her apology was followed by an unexpected spurt of anger: she was a grown woman, after all, who shouldn't have to explain, let alone grovel.

Brian and Jane were sitting together on the sofa, as they'd been that afternoon when they'd watched the old movie. This time, though, the telly wasn't on.

A look passed between them and Brian spoke again. 'We saw you on the news tonight,' he said.

Oh, no—just what she'd been afraid of. Callie's momentary anger evaporated, replaced by defensiveness. She crossed her arms across her chest and waited.

It was Jane who spoke next. 'What were you doing at that house?'

Callie addressed her reply to Brian. 'It's in the parish. It was your day off. And they asked to see me.'

'What about?' he demanded.

She took a deep breath. 'About their baby's funeral.'

'I'm the parish priest,' said Brian. 'If they live in the parish they're entitled to have the funeral at the church, but I'm the one who will be taking it.'

'It was your day off,' Callie repeated, wondering whether she dared go on. 'And they specifically said they want me to take the funeral. I'm sorry, Brian, but they're the parents.'

'And Brian is the parish priest,' Jane interposed. 'How did they contact *you*, anyway?'

'My...um...friend Mark is their Family Liaison Officer.'

Jane's disapproval was visible. 'And he suggested that they should talk to you?'

'That's right.' Suddenly Callie's anger flared again. Why should she have to explain herself to Jane Stanford? Jane wasn't her boss. And she was just doing her job, dealing with people who had been bereaved in the most dreadful way imaginable. Petty matters of seniority and protocol seemed ridiculous in the face of what the Bettses had suffered. Brian should be *glad* that she was looking after their parishioners on his day off, rather than engaging in some stupid turf war, spurred on by his wife.

But she didn't want to say that, not at this moment. 'I'm going to bed now,' she said instead, turning and walking towards the door. 'If you want to discuss this further, we can do it in the morning. After church.'

◇◇◇

Mark's return home was also quiet, if not stealthy; he had no wish to disturb Geoff, awake or asleep, and was relieved to find his flatmate was nowhere in evidence.

He went to his room, flopped down on the bed, and pulled his mobile phone from his pocket. During the course of the evening it had vibrated, but he had chosen not to answer it; whatever it was about, he didn't want it to interrupt his dinner with Callie. After all, he told himself, it was Saturday night and he was off duty. The call was unlikely to involve a work emergency, or anything that couldn't wait for an hour or so. And surely the caller would have left a voicemail message.

The call, he saw, had been from Neville, and there *was* a message. Mark sighed and punched the button to listen to it.

'Nothing urgent, mate,' Neville said in a rather precise voice. Mark knew him well enough—from endless off-duty bachelor evenings at the pub—to recognise that Neville had been drinking, and probably rather a lot. He held his alcohol well, did Neville, and had a prodigious capacity for Guinness, but there were signs. Most people's speech grew slurred the more they drank; with Neville it was the opposite.

'Just wanted to let you know about the preliminary post-mortem report on Muffin.'

Mark wasn't sure he wanted to hear this just now, but he resisted the temptation to cut off the message and postpone listening to it until morning.

'Just between us, there were…indications…that something else was going on. Can't go into it now. Ring me tomorrow and I'll tell you about it. It's going to mean that you'll need to ask them some difficult questions. Ring me,' Neville repeated, adding, 'Sorry I didn't ring earlier, mate. It's been a bugger of a day.'

Mark frowned, his first reaction incomprehension and disbelief. Difficult questions? What on earth did that mean? He would have sworn to anyone who asked that Jodee and Chazz were above board, their grief genuine. That had been his gut feeling from the beginning, and even Mrs Betts' revelation that Muffin had been left alone hadn't shaken that. It had been a mistake, a one-off misunderstanding, not a deliberate abandonment. There was no pattern of neglect or abuse in that family. Apart from anything else, Jodee and Chazz weren't bright enough to dissemble convincingly about it. If they'd hurt Muffin, Mark was sure, they would have blurted it out immediately, or at least given themselves away within the first few minutes.

His second reaction was a purely selfish one. If difficult questions were to be asked, and by him, did that mean he'd have to do it tomorrow? Cancel his day off, miss Chiara's birthday party?

Maybe that wouldn't be such a bad thing. Sorry as he would be to miss it, disappointed as Chiara would be, it would at least remove him from yet another temptation to punch Joe's lights out.

Then he noticed that there was another voicemail message. From the di Stefanos' home phone number. Joe? Serena? But the call had come through before Serena would have been home from the restaurant. He pushed the button and put the phone back to his ear.

'Uncle Marco?' came Chiara's voice, whispering. 'I just wanted to let you know that Samantha is through to the final. Maybe it was our votes that did it. Isn't that brilliant? See you tomorrow,' she added, and made a kissing noise.

Mark smiled, in spite of himself.

When Lilith Noone awoke in the middle of the night, the first thing she realised was that she was not alone. Rolling over, she stifled a groan.

It had been one of those things. They'd met at the police news conference, where he'd squeezed into the chair next to her. She'd not run across him before, probably because he worked for one of the broadsheets and their paths were not likely to cross often. The Muffin Betts story, with its universal interest, had quite literally created strange bedfellows.

They'd both had stories to file, and quickly, after the press conference; the deadlines for the Sunday papers were early and there wasn't any time to waste. Lilith hadn't even had much time to think about the spin she was putting on her story. Just get it in: that was the priority, and she could work on fine-tuning and elaborating on it at her leisure for the Monday *Daily Globe*.

Hasty plans had been made for them to meet up later for a drink. One drink had turned to two, then they'd moved on to another venue for a few more, and finally, inevitably, they'd ended up at her flat. The flat was a mess as usual, but he hadn't really noticed. And it didn't much matter whether he did or not; she wouldn't be seeing him again.

He'd been a disappointment, she conceded to herself. A three-minute wonder, and that was being generous. Excessive alcohol hadn't helped his performance, though he probably wasn't much better at the best of times. It wasn't that she'd especially fancied him, either. It was more a matter of proving to herself that she could still pull a bloke if she wanted to.

Not that she'd wanted to all that much recently, and that in itself was a bit of a worry. Was she getting past it? Past that itch that needed to be satisfied?

She'd actually felt the itch that afternoon. Not for the sodden lump beside her, snoring now with his mouth open, but—improbably—when DI Neville Stewart had come into the room to read his statement. She'd suddenly been aware of him—not as her adversary, and someone who surely and quite justifiably hated her guts, but as an attractive, even sexy, bloke. For the first time she found herself wondering about him as a man. Was he married? Somehow she doubted it. With those looks, and that Irish charm to burn, he didn't seem the sort to tie himself down to one woman. Then he smoothed back his hair with his left hand and she saw the wedding ring.

Ah, well.

At that point she'd turned to the broadsheet bloke beside her and favoured him with a smile.

And here they were.

The second realisation followed on from this train of thought, but it was more gradual.

DI Neville Stewart.

She had scored a point against him, and that always pleased her. He'd been discomfited by her question, though he'd handled it fairly gracefully. Was it police-speak, or was he really holding something back from the press? She'd had a strong feeling, backed by years of experience as well as instinct, that he wasn't telling them everything.

Lilith Noone revelled in her reputation for being a thorn in the side of the police. She took every opportunity to go after them in print: pointing out their failures, decrying lack of action or information, hinting at cover-ups.

But...

In this case, if she attacked the police, what would she be saying? That they were concealing something about the death of baby Muffin? That what had appeared to be SIDS was...what?

It suddenly struck Lilith that to go down that path—the natural one for her—would bring her dangerously close to implying that Jodee and Chazz had something to hide.

And once she was on that path, others would follow. Questions would be asked, conclusions would be drawn. Speculation would run riot.

Public opinion could turn on Jodee and Chazz, as quickly as sympathy had arisen. Whether there was anything in it or not, overnight they could go from being the pitied darlings of the nation to the monsters who had done something to their baby.

She, Lilith Noone, would be responsible. Where would that leave her?

Outside of the charmed circle that she now inhabited as a family friend of Jodee and Chazz, certainly. No more exclusive interviews. No personal invitation to the funeral.

She had been about to walk into a trap of her own making. Lilith broke into a cold sweat as she realised how close she had come to forfeiting her favoured position.

It wouldn't happen. She had to be very careful to make sure that it didn't.

Writing her story for Monday's *Globe* would require all of her skill and cunning. But she could do it. Lilith was certain of that. Now that she knew what was at stake, she would step back from the edge of the abyss.

Sunday morning.

Mark stretched and hit the snooze button on the alarm. It was a luxury he allowed himself on his day off: an extra ten minutes in bed. Then he'd indulge in a long soak in the bath, instead of the quick shower he had on work days. Sometimes he would even have a cooked breakfast—but that was something he'd never admit to Mamma.

Mamma was old-fashioned about things like that. In the first place, cooked breakfasts were an English thing, a bad habit—in her opinion—he'd picked up in the police. And to eat anything at all, even a simple Italian breakfast of bread and fruit, on Sunday before Mass was anathema to Mamma.

Eleven o'clock Mass at the Italian Church, followed by a huge family lunch which more than made up for the lack of breakfast: that was the pattern for *la famiglia Lombardi*, and had been for all of Mark's life. In recent years, with his erratic work schedule, he hadn't always been able to take part in the weekly ritual, but it was still an ingrained part of him and he did it whenever he could.

The Italian Church in Clerkenwell was like a little slice of Italy; with its grand baroque architecture and its lavish furnishings—its wall paintings, statues and gilding, its mosaics and coloured marble—it was embellished within an inch of its life. And to Mark, it had always been synonymous with *church*. The only church he'd ever really known.

Certainly he had never even been inside an Anglican church. Not until very recently, when he'd begun slipping into little parish churches on his travels round London. How alien they seemed to him—the grey stone Victorian ones, with their quiet gothic piety, and the clean white Wren churches of the City. Alien, yet somehow appealing in their relative simplicity. He longed to attend a service in one, to see what it was like. For one who had lived his entire life in London, he was, he felt, woefully ignorant on the subject of the Church of England.

When visiting one church, he'd picked up and paid for a book at the bookstall: *What Anglicans Believe*. He'd been reading it, and was surprised to discover that Anglicans believed pretty much the same things he'd always been taught. He wasn't sure he believed all of them himself any more, but that wasn't really the point. For people to believe *anything* in this secular age was rather remarkable.

Mark hadn't discussed his flirtation with Anglicanism with anyone, not with Callie—and certainly not with Mamma.

One of these days, and soon, he would go to a service at Callie's church. Maybe on a Sunday when he knew she was preaching. He wouldn't tell her he was coming; perhaps he'd be able to slip in and sit at the back and listen to her sermon without her knowing he was there.

Soon, but not today. Today was Chiara's birthday, and Mass with *la famiglia* was compulsory.

After his extra ten minutes, Mark stretched again and got out of bed. Time for his bath.

It was only then that he remembered that he needed to ring Neville, to find out what was going on and learn whether he would have to alter his plans for the day. He picked up his mobile from the bedside table.

Before he could summon up Neville's number, the phone rang in his hand. Mark squinted at the caller ID: not Neville, as he might have expected, but Serena.

'Hello?'

'Marco.' Her voice was as calm as ever. 'I'm glad I caught you, before you left. There's a change of plan.'

Mark frowned. There was *never* a change of plan on Sunday. Unless…'Mamma's not ill, is she? Or Pappa?'

'No.' There was a fractional pause. 'It's Joe, Marco. He's... not well.'

'Joe!'

'He went out running first thing this morning. He's been doing that lately, nearly every day. And when he got back he was...dizzy, he said. Sick. Having a hard time breathing.'

'Heart attack?' Mark had seen a few of those in middle-aged men who suddenly took up rigourous physical exercise.

'That's what the paramedics think. I rang for them when he didn't seem to be getting any better.'

'And...?'

'They came straight away. We're on the way to hospital now. In the ambulance.'

'So you're with him. What about Chiara?'

'She was still in bed when we left. I didn't want to wake her. And I don't want to disturb Mamma yet. Could you go there now, Marco? Could you?' For the first time he detected emotion in her voice: on behalf of her daughter, not her husband.

'I'm on my way,' Mark said, reaching for last night's discarded trousers.

Chapter Eight

Though he'd downed a fair few pints of Guinness the night before, Neville was feeling as well as could be expected on Sunday morning. And his mind was perfectly clear, especially after a shower, a shave and a cup of strong instant coffee.

His search for Triona, at their respective flats, had been fruitless, but his subconscious reasoning powers had been hard at work and he'd waked in the middle of the night with the sort of crystal-clear revelation which occasionally manifested itself in his job—and had given him the reputation for being a good, intuitive detective.

Triona wasn't at her flat. Where would she have gone? Not to an hotel. The answer was bloody obvious, staring him in the face: she would be with a friend. And what friend more probable than Frances Cherry? Frances, the priest and professional shoulder-to-cry-on. Frances, who had attended Triona at the wedding.

Frances would also protect and shield Triona. Would she lie if he rang her and asked her straight out whether she knew where Triona was? That was an interesting question; as a priest, could she tell a deliberate falsehood? As a friend, would she betray a confidence?

At any rate, he hoped he wouldn't have to put her to the test.

He wouldn't ring. He would go to her house.

It was Sunday morning. With any luck, both Frances and her husband Graham would be in church. If he timed his visit right...

First, though, he had a phone call to make. Mark Lombardi hadn't returned his call, and although it wasn't urgent, it was fairly important for Mark to be fully in the picture, in case he felt compelled to check in on Jodee and Chazz at some point today.

Mark's phone was evidently switched off, Neville soon discovered. He left another message, made sure he looked as presentable as possible, and set off for the Central Line Tube station.

Shepherd's Bush is a large area, roughly triangular in shape, served by two Underground lines at some distance from each other. To the west is the Hammersmith and City Line, providing easy access to Paddington for Neville on those days when he didn't need to take a car into work, and it was at that end of Shepherd's Bush, near the Goldhawk Road, that Neville lived. The Central Line station, to the east across Shepherd's Bush Common, borders the much more upmarket Holland Park; as its name implies, that line leads into the centre of the City, via Notting Hill Gate and Oxford Street.

London was relatively quiet on Sunday morning, and the weather was mild, with a definite promise of spring in the air. By the time he'd crossed the common and reached the Tube station, Neville decided that he might as well walk the rest of the distance.

Graham Cherry's vicarage was to the north of Holland Park Avenue. Neville knew the way; he'd been there on a number of occasions in a professional capacity. As he approached, he was overwhelmed with a powerful sense of *déjà vu*, remembering the last time he'd been there. The weather had been autumnal that day; it was first thing in the morning, barely light, and he'd been there in the company of DS Sid Cowley to carry out an arrest.

The vicarage was set back from the pavement. Neville went through the wrought iron gate, walked up the short path to the door and rang the bell.

Nothing happened, not then and not after he'd rung a second time.

He experienced just a second or two of doubt. Had he been wrong, then?

No. She was there; he felt it in his bones. She just wasn't going to come to the door.

Well, he wouldn't give up so easily. Neville put his palm on the bell and held it down, hearing a muffled buzz from inside the vicarage. A dog started barking, tentatively at first and then more persistently.

He didn't remember that Frances Cherry had possessed a dog. Well, things could change in six months.

Could they ever.

Someone was coming. He heard footsteps approaching the door, a low voice speaking to the dog, the knob of the Yale lock being turned.

She stood behind the door, barefoot, her dressing gown falling from her shoulders. Obviously just awakened from sleep. Her hair was loose and tousled, and Neville had never seen her look more beautiful or fanciable. Desire shot through him like a spike of electricity. His hand fell from the bell. 'God,' he said tremulously. 'Triona.'

Triona pulled her dressing gown round her, crossing her arms over her chest, but she didn't shut the door in his face. 'Hello, Neville,' she said, her voice as unreadable as her expression, then after a moment added, 'I suppose you'd better come in.'

Mark let himself into Serena's house with his own key. There was no sign of Chiara.

In days gone by—and not so long ago, either—he would have thought nothing of going into Chiara's room without announcing himself. Now that she was thirteen, though, that seemed an unacceptable invasion of her privacy. He stood by her door, hesitating, and finally gave a tentative knock. 'Chiara?'

'Come in,' was the muffled reply.

Chiara was in bed, her dark hair all over the pillow and her eyes screwed shut.

'Sorry to wake you, sleeping beauty,' he said, feeling awkward. The room was almost the same as ever: pink walls, heaps of stuffed animals, though with the recent addition of a Karma poster blu-tacked over the bed. It was Chiara herself who was somehow different.

Her eyes opened in a squint. 'Uncle Marco! Where's Mum?'

'She's...not here. Your father—'

Chiara was out of bed in a bound, her face white with shock. 'She's killed him, hasn't she?' she blurted.

He stared at her, equally shocked. 'Why on earth would you say that?'

She lowered her head, averting her eyes. 'I had a bad dream. Never mind. Tell me.'

'He's had a heart attack. I'm afraid I don't know much more than that. They've taken him to hospital, and your mother has gone with him.' Mark watched his niece as she processed the information. 'I'm sure he'll be okay,' he added, though he had no basis for saying it other than the desire to reassure.

'You don't know that,' she challenged. 'He could...die.'

'The doctors won't let him die. He'll be in very good hands, you know. And your mother will make sure he gets the very best care.'

'Oh...Dad.' Chiara's voice broke, tears welling up. She sat down abruptly on the edge of the bed, as though her legs would no longer support her.

Mark perched beside her and put an arm round her shoulders. '*Nipotina*,' he murmured. 'Your dad will be fine. I promise.'

It said a great deal for her, he realised, that her concern was for her father rather than her ruined birthday celebrations.

And that reminded him that he was going to have to get in touch with Mamma, before she and Pappa left for church. She would be expecting to see them all there, and would have already started preparations for the birthday lunch.

Mamma might flap a bit at first, but she'd take it all in her stride and soon put herself in charge of the situation. Maybe, thought Mark, that was no bad thing. Dealing with families in trauma might be what he did for a living, but when it came to his own family, he was already feeling out of his depth.

Poor Serena, having to deal with something like this, out of the blue. Poor Chiara, having her birthday derailed. And her immediate assumption that her mother had killed her father—what was that about? Serena had assured Mark that she and Joe were keeping things as normal as possible at home for Chiara's sake; clearly that hadn't been as successful as she would like to believe. Chiara had obviously picked up on the underlying tension and it was coming out in her dreams.

And if Chiara knew, even at an instinctive level, what about Mamma? Mamma had sharp hearing and eyes like a hawk; nothing got past her. Mark had a feeling that if Serena thought Mamma was unaware of her problems with Joe, she was kidding herself.

He gave Chiara's shoulders a squeeze. 'I'll ring Nonna now, shall I?'

One black wall. The other walls were pale yellow, but the wall facing him was a shiny jet black. The colour of crows' wings, liquorice, Triona's hair. 'Who would paint a bedroom wall black?'

Neville didn't realise he'd said the words aloud until Triona answered him. 'Frances' daughter. Heather. This was her room. Frances said they keep meaning to repaint it, but haven't got round to it yet. I think,' she added, 'that she was a bit of a handful. Heather, that is.'

He rolled over to face her, running his hand down her side, lingering briefly on her breast and coming to rest on the bulge of her stomach. 'I hope our daughter doesn't get any ideas like that. If she wants to paint her room black I shall put my foot down.'

Triona's mouth curved into a smile. 'I don't believe that for a minute. You'll spoil her rotten. You'll give her whatever she wants.'

'If she looks like her mother, I'm afraid I will. How could I resist?'

Resistance was futile, and thank God for that.

She'd let him in—just to talk, she'd said. But instead of going into the drawing room or the kitchen she'd brought him to this room, the room where she'd been sleeping, in case Frances and Graham came home from church and interrupted them.

They hadn't done much talking. She hadn't even tried to stop him; she'd wanted it as much as he had. And now, by God, he was ready for more. He moved his hand.

Triona covered it with her own to halt its roving. 'Oh Neville,' she said with mock severity. 'This isn't always the answer, you know.'

'That depends on what the question is.' He kissed her shoulder. 'If the question is "what is the most bloody marvellous thing you can do with the woman you adore?"…'

'Don't be daft. Sentimentality doesn't suit you, Stewart.' But she was smiling as she said it, and she didn't try to stop his hand when he moved it again.

Half an hour later, dozing, he heard sounds which indicated they were no longer alone in the house: doors opening and closing, distant voices. Instinctively he pulled the sheet over himself.

Triona turned over. 'I suppose they're home. You'd better get dressed and get out of here.'

He laughed.

'I mean it,' she said. 'Maybe they'll be in the kitchen and won't see you go.'

Neville realised that she *did* mean it, but the very ridiculousness of the situation kept him from getting angry. 'For God's sake, Triona,' he said. 'I'm not some back-door lover-boy. I'm your husband. I refuse to sneak out like I have no right to be here.'

'Then go and wish Frances and Graham a good day before you leave.'

He sat up. 'I'm not going without you, Triona. You're packing your things and coming home with me.'

Triona tipped her head back and regarded him levelly. 'And where is "home", exactly?'

That brought him up short for a few seconds. 'I suppose I was thinking of my flat,' he admitted. 'But if you'd rather go to your flat, I'm happy with that as well.'

She didn't say a word, just looked at him, her lips pressed together.

'We'll go house-hunting this week,' Neville heard himself saying. 'Make the rounds of the estate agents. You don't have to go back to work for another week, and—'

'And you do, don't you?' she said tightly. 'The dead baby, remember? I saw you on the news last night.'

As if on cue, Neville's phone rang, somewhere amongst his discarded clothes.

The words of the Mass washed over Chiara; even the music, which she usually loved, didn't reach her today. Her eyes were fixed not on the priest at the altar but on the painting in the dome above the baldacchino: Jesus, his arms upraised, floating in the air above his disciples' heads as he ascended to heaven. Going to his father.

Usually Chiara said her dutiful prayers at the statue of Our Lady of Fatima, with her serene face and the oversized crown balanced improbably on her inclined head. Today, though, her prayers were all addressed to the ascendant figure in the dome. 'Jesus, don't let Dad die,' she said over and over again in her head, as though through repetition she would achieve a better result.

It had been Nonna's decision to go to church, in spite of everything. 'What better place to be?' she'd said. '*La chiesa.*' So they'd met there: Nonna and Nonno, Chiara and Uncle Marco. The others, Chiara was sure, were praying just as hard for Dad as she was.

A living nightmare—that's what it was. Dad sick, maybe dying. She'd thought that bad dream she'd had—Mum standing over Dad with a knife in her hand—was terrible enough, but this was worse. This was real. Dad might die. Really die.

'Jesus, don't let Dad die,' she said again, this time in a tiny whisper. Beside her, Uncle Marco gave her arm a little squeeze.

Neville rooted round in his clothes till he found his phone, punching the button to answer the call.

'Stewart? Hereward Rice here,' announced a crisp voice. The coroner.

Neville sat down on the bed. 'I thought you were away for the weekend, Dr Rice. In the country. With your wife.'

'I am. And my wife would kill me if she knew I was ringing you now. She's gone off bird-watching for an hour, and I've seen enough great-speckled-whatsits to last me a lifetime.'

'I can sympathise with that, Dr Rice.' Neville shot a look in the direction of Triona, who was calmly putting her clothes on, her back turned to him.

'So tell me. What the hell is going on?'

Neville played for time. 'What do you mean?'

'I made the mistake of switching on the news last night. I saw your news conference.

'And?'

'And what's all this "inconclusive" bollocks? Did they kill their baby, or didn't they?'

Hereward Rice was known for getting to the point, and he certainly wasn't letting his reputation down.

'Well,' said Neville, 'in a way, it's going to be up to you to say.'

'Explain yourself.'

'I don't think they *did* kill their baby, actually. But according to the preliminary p.m. report, someone shook Muffin Betts at some time in her life. Hard enough to cause a hairline fracture in her neck. It could have contributed to her death. Or maybe not.'

'And what makes you think the parents didn't do it, there and then?'

It was time, Neville decided, to come clean with the coroner. 'Well,' he said, 'In the first place, Dr Tompkins thought it had probably happened a few weeks ago. And I'm pretty sure they couldn't have done it right then, because…they were out of the house when she died. Everyone was. Muffin was alone. My FLO has had that from Mrs Betts, the baby's grandmother.'

'Christ almighty,' said Hereward Rice. 'Gross neglect, then.'

'I don't think so. The grandmother says it was accidental. The parents thought she was there and went out. She was mortified.'

'She *would* say that, wouldn't she?'

'She didn't have to tell him at all,' Neville pointed out. 'She brought it up. Volunteered the information.'

The coroner cleared his throat. 'Well, I'll tell you one thing, DI Stewart. There *will* be an inquest.'

'Yes, I thought you'd say that.'

'Opening tomorrow afternoon, so I hope you're free. I'll need a statement from you before I adjourn.'

'Tomorrow? That soon? Will it need to include…everything? We're still in the early stages of our investigation, you realise. And,' Neville added, 'there's a great deal of media interest in this case. I'm sure the press gallery will be packed.'

'Hmm. I'll give it some thought.' There was a brief pause. 'I think I hear my wife coming. I'll speak to you tomorrow morning, when I'm back at my desk.'

Triona had finished dressing; she stood with her arms crossed over her chest, looking at Neville as he ended the call. 'It sounds like you won't be free to go house-hunting tomorrow,' she said quietly.

'Well, maybe not tomorrow. But perhaps the next day.'

She narrowed her eyes at him. 'Get real, Neville.'

'Come back to my flat with me. We can talk about it later.'

'Later? After we've been to bed again, I suppose, and then you'll get another phone call and first thing you know you'll go haring off and leave me alone in that revolting flat? I don't think so.'

'You'd rather stay in a room with a black wall than come home with me?'

Triona took her time answering. 'I'm not coming home with you until you have a home to take me to.' Adding insult to injury, she came to him, pulled him to his feet, and kissed him full on the lips. 'I mean it, Neville,' she said, squirming away just as she had him panting for more. 'And that's that.'

To Mark's surprise, Chiara's birthday celebrations had gone ahead pretty much as planned, in spite of the absence of her parents.

Mamma sensibly pointed out that everything was in place, they all had to eat anyway, and it might serve to distract Chiara, just a little, from worrying about her father.

Admittedly, the family lunch was a flat affair, with just the four of them and so much that wasn't being said. Mamma made a determined effort to keep things cheerful and upbeat, but Chiara was not so easily deflected.

Serena came home from hospital and joined them before Chiara's friends were due to arrive. She seemed quite upbeat and positive about Joe's condition, though Mark suspected that much of it was for Chiara's benefit.

'Can I go and see him?' Chiara wanted to know.

'Not for a day or two,' Serena put her off. 'But he'll be back home in no time, I'm sure.'

Chiara so badly wanted to believe it that she questioned her mother no further, and later, when her friends came, she became positively manic, shrieking as she opened her presents and giggling with her chums over every silly remark in the inane, annoying way of young teenage girls in groups.

Things got so riotous during the eating of the birthday cake that Mark escaped to the kitchen to give his eardrums a rest. Serena was there before him, making coffee for the grown-ups.

'How can you stand it?' Mark asked. 'They're so shrill! It just cuts through me like a knife.'

'They'll grow out of it,' Serena said imperturbably. 'Angelina did. It's just something about being thirteen, fourteen. It brings out the worst in girls when they get together.'

'So you only have to put up with it for a few years.' A few years! What an unappealing prospect, Mark reflected as he helped Serena put the coffee cups on a tray.

'Well, it's better than having her in floods of tears because her dad is in hospital,' Serena pointed out.

Mark lowered his voice, though there was no one else to hear. 'How *is* he? Really?'

Serena shrugged. 'Holding his own, I think. There were some complications in the treatment.'

'What do you mean?'

'Well, in the first place, the ambulance took him to the Royal London, which is the main A&E for this area and has a specialist cardiac unit, but there were no beds available, so he had to be transferred to Paddington. They had a bed for him there, but they were really short-staffed today, unfortunately, so he won't be seen by a specialist until some time tomorrow at the earliest. They're doing what they can to keep him comfortable and stable.' She added, 'I didn't want to say any of that in front of Chiara. She's worried enough as it is.'

'So you don't really know…'

'The prognosis. No. Not yet.'

Mark's phone buzzed in his pocket. '*Scusa*,' he said to his sister, putting it to his ear. 'Hello?'

'Sergeant Lombardi?'

'Yes?'

'It's Brenda Betts. Chazz's mum, remember?'

'Yes, of course, Mrs Betts.'

She launched into a rather long soliloquy, giving him no chance to interject a word. 'Ever so sorry to trouble you on a Sunday. I wouldn't, you know, but you did give me your card and said I could ring any time I needed. And Jodee is that upset, like. Her mum rung, see. And some of her chums as well. They'd seen that detective on the telly. The one that was here, you know, the Irish one. And he said something about "inconclusive". Like, they don't know what happened. Like maybe it wasn't natural or something. Jodee's mum, she said it was like they thought Jodee and Chazz might of killed Muffin.'

With a sinking feeling, Mark remembered Neville's phone message. After all that had happened, he hadn't managed to get back to Neville and find out what it was about. 'I'm sure they don't think that,' he said, though he was by no means certain.

'Only, like I say, Jodee is beside herself, or I wouldn't ask. Chazz, too, of course. But do you think you could come round and talk to them, like? Tell them that nobody thinks they killed Muffin or nothing like that.'

Mark looked at the coffee cups on the tray, smelled the delicious richness of the coffee brewing on the hob. 'Yes, all right,' he said. 'I'll come.'

'Work,' he said to Serena's quizzical look as he pocketed the phone. I'm sorry, but I have to go.'

'Will you say goodbye to Chiara before you leave?'

He wasn't sure he was up to facing the teen screamers again. 'You can do it for me. Give her another birthday kiss on my behalf. And,' he added, 'keep me informed about Joe's progress. When you know anything.'

'Of course.'

As soon as he was out of the house, he retrieved his phone again and rang Neville; it was important that he had as much information as possible before he had to dispense comfort and reassurance to Jodee and Chazz.

But Neville wasn't answering; his phone went straight to voice-mail. Mark left a message and set off for Bayswater.

Callie had spent much of the day trying to keep out of Jane's way. After the morning service she'd informed Brian that she wouldn't be joining them for lunch at the vicarage; instead she'd rung Frances and snagged an invitation to the Cherrys', on the basis that she wanted to take Bella for a walk.

As she approached Frances' house, a man came out of the front door, passed through the gate, and turned in the opposite direction, towards Holland Park. Callie was sure it was Neville Stewart, but though she offered him a tentative smile he didn't speak or acknowledge her in any way.

A moment later Bella greeted her rapturously; Callie followed Frances into the kitchen to help with the vegetables, and a few minutes after that they were joined by Triona.

'I thought I saw Neville, just now, as I arrived,' Callie said. Frances looked enquiringly at Triona.

Triona nodded. 'Very likely. He stopped by for a chat.'

'You should have invited him to join us for lunch,' Frances said.

'He couldn't stay.' Triona didn't volunteer anything further; Callie could tell that Frances was dying to know more but didn't dare ask.

Through lunch Triona remained uncommunicative, causing a slightly strained atmosphere in spite of Graham's easy conversation, but anything, Callie told herself, was better than lunch with Jane and Brian.

She'd had her walk in Holland Park with Bella, enjoyed a cup of tea with Frances, then had returned to All Saints' in time for Evensong. Frances had provided her with a sandwich to take back for her evening meal, and had emphasised an open invitation to join them whenever she needed to get away from All Saints' vicarage. 'I'd ask you to stay here, of course,' Frances had said, 'but we have Triona in the guest room.'

'And I do need to be in the parish,' Callie admitted with regret. How much nicer it would be to stay at Frances', where she wouldn't have to be treading on eggshells all of the time.

After Evensong she'd gone straight to her room and switched her phone on, hoping that Marco might ring. Then she ate her sandwich and got involved on the internet doing some research for a future sermon.

She'd almost managed to forget the existence of Jane Stanford, when there was a knock on her door. 'Callie?' said Jane, in a voice heavy with disapproval. 'You have a visitor.'

'A visitor?'

'A man,' Jane announced. 'A Mr Lombardi. I've shown him into the sitting room.'

Callie's heart jumped. Why would Marco come here without letting her know? She could have arranged to meet him somewhere else if he'd rung her.

Allowing herself a few seconds for a quick glance in the mirror and a flick at her hair, she followed Jane down the stairs.

'Brian and I will be in the kitchen,' Jane said, ushering Callie into the room. 'Would either of you like coffee or tea?'

Callie shook her head. 'No, thanks.'

'A coffee would be lovely, Mrs Stanford,' said Marco in his most agreeable voice.

Instant, Callie mouthed at him, out of Jane's line of sight.

'Or could I change my mind and ask for a cup of tea?' he went on smoothly.

'Very well. I'll bring it through as soon as it's ready.'

Callie closed the door and went into Marco's arms. 'Mmm. To what do I owe this lovely surprise? Or to put it another way, have you lost your mind to venture into the lion's den like this?'

He kissed her. 'I just needed to see you, *Cara mia.*'

'You've come all this way without ringing? I did have my phone on.'

'I took a chance. I didn't want to give you the opportunity to make any excuses not to see me.'

'As if.' She raised her face for another kiss, then reluctantly disengaged from his arms, where she happily would have stayed for hours.

'Anyway, I was in the neighbourhood,' he said. 'Work.'

It took her a moment to realise what he meant. 'Oh—Jodee and Chazz?'

'That's right.'

'What's happened?'

'The news conference,' he stated. 'They heard about it from various busybodies, and got themselves into a real state about it. Jodee was practically hysterical at the idea that the police might think she killed her baby.'

Callie didn't understand. 'But…that's not what you…they… think, is it?'

'Well.' Marco took both her hands in his and squeezed them. 'The short answer is, I'm not really sure. *I* don't think they did,' he added quickly. 'And that's what I told them. But I've only just spoken to Neville. We were playing telephone tag, and…never mind. Anyway, I finally reached him, and he says that there were some unexpected findings in the post-mortem.'

'You can't really tell me, can you?'

'I shouldn't,' he agreed. 'Not now. But trust me. It doesn't look very good for them. I'm not sure what to do.'

'I know you'll do the right thing,' she said, meaning it; as far as she was concerned, Marco was honourable and good, and his instincts were sound. 'But if there's any way I can help—'

The door opened; Callie dropped Marco's hands and stepped back. 'Do you take sugar, Mr Lombardi?' Jane asked, poking her head into the room.

'No, thank you. And please call me Mark,' he added, with his most charming smile.

To Callie's amazement, Jane smiled back, and when she spoke her voice was noticeably warmer. 'It will be ready in a minute.' The door closed again.

Callie changed the subject. 'How was the birthday party?'

'Oh.' Marco looked stricken. 'You don't know. Sorry, *Cara mia*. I didn't have a chance to ring you.'

'What?'

'Family crisis. Joe had a heart attack this morning. He's in hospital.'

She stared at him, unbelieving. 'But we saw him last night! He was fine!'

'I know. I know. It was very sudden. He went out running, and when he got home, he collapsed.'

'Oh, poor Serena! Poor Chiara! How awful for all of them.'

He filled her in on the day's events: the subdued birthday lunch, Serena's report on Joe's condition, his own hurried departure. 'And then Jodee and Chazz to deal with. And talking to Neville. After all that, I just needed to see you.' The smile he gave her turned her insides to warm mush; Callie wished they were anywhere but the Stanfords' sitting room, with Jane bearing down on them carrying a mug of tea and a plate with two chocolate digestives.

'Thank you so much, Mrs Stanford,' Mark said. 'It's so kind of you. I've had a difficult day, and this is just what I need.'

She virtually simpered. 'Please, call me Jane. And you're very welcome.'

Chapter Nine

Chiara poked at her cereal with her spoon, stirred it, but didn't actually convey any of it to her mouth. She was suffering from a surfeit of birthday cake and pizza, as well as a deficiency of sleep. 'I don't want to go to school today, Mum,' she said. 'I don't feel well.'

Her mother shook her head. 'I'm not surprised that you don't feel well, you greedy girl—you must have eaten nearly two whole pizzas. But you have to go to school. I'm going to the hospital this morning, remember?'

As if she would forget. 'I want to go with you, Mum,' Chiara said promptly. 'I want to see Dad. I know he'd want me to come.'

'You can't have it both ways. If you're not well enough to go to school, how could you go to the hospital? Anyway,' her mother went on, 'it's too soon for you to see him. He'll be having tests and things today. They won't want extra people about.'

Extra people? Tears of hurt and frustration welled in Chiara's eyes. 'I'm not an extra person. I'm his daughter. I have as much right to be there as you do.'

Her mother sighed, and for a few seconds Chiara felt sorry for her. She looked tired—exhausted, in fact, with dark circles under her eyes. Chiara knew that she'd been up late, on the telephone; she'd heard her well into the night, talking probably to Angelina and maybe even to Dad's relatives in Italy.

But then Chiara hardened her heart. Mum was keeping her from seeing Dad. She was probably doing it because she was jealous of her relationship with Dad; all those evenings they'd spent together through the years while Mum was working at the restaurant had made them close, a real team, and Mum must resent that.

And then another realisation hit Chiara, so forcibly that she almost cried aloud.

It was Mum's fault that Dad was sick.

Heart attacks were caused by stress, weren't they? And what did Dad have to be stressed about, if not the way Mum talked to him when she thought no one could hear? Calling him bad names, saying horrible things to him. Everyone thought they were such a perfect, loving couple—Nonna and Nonno, Uncle Marco, Angelina. They just saw what Mum wanted them to see. Chiara was the only one who heard them at night, who knew the truth: that her mother had driven her father to a heart attack. She might have even done it on purpose.

And now she wouldn't let Chiara see him.

Chiara put her spoon down next to her cereal bowl and folded her arms across her chest. 'If you won't let me go to see Dad,' she said, 'I'll hate you for the rest of my life.'

Once again her mother sighed. She closed her eyes for a moment, pressed her fingers to her temples, then gave Chiara a thin smile. 'Well,' she said wearily, 'I suppose I'll just have to live with that, won't I?'

Neville was at his desk abnormally early on Monday morning, jotting down notes for his statement for the Muffin Betts inquest and waiting for DCS Evans to arrive in his office. The moment Evans reached his desk, Neville knew he would be alerted by Evans' admirable secretary Ursula.

Once upon a time, Evans' secretary had been a toothsome young woman called Denise. Neville, along with a number of other male officers, attached or single, had had rather a thing for Denise, whose physical assets were legendary—and entirely natural, not the result of the surgeon's art. But Evans had won her for himself, shedding a middle-aged wife in the process. Now that Denise was the second Mrs Evans, she had seen to it personally that her replacement as his secretary was no threat to that more exalted position. Ursula was plain-featured, flat-chested, and on the far side of fifty. She did, however, have an ill-concealed soft spot for Neville, and that was something he exploited to the full. He brought her flowers on her birthday and chocolates at Christmas, bought her occasional cups of tea in the canteen, and in return she warned him about Evans' moods, kept him up-to-date on his movements, and expedited his access to the great man.

Not surprisingly, Neville's mind was not really on Muffin Betts, and he found himself doodling a small but detailed draw-ing of Triona's breasts.

It really wouldn't do, he said to himself sternly. Triona's breasts were beautiful—as magnificent, in their own way, as Denise Evans', if rather less monumental—but thinking about them wasn't what he was being paid to do, and it wasn't getting him anywhere either.

He needed a plan of action, if he hoped to pry Triona out of Frances' vicarage. A battle plan, and allies in the fight.

But who would help him?

Frances, he thought suddenly. Frances was Triona's friend; she would want the best for her. And she didn't necessarily want her under her roof for the foreseeable future, either. Triona on her own was one thing; in a few months there would be a baby as well. Did Frances Cherry really want to convert that black-walled room into a nursery?

No, it would be in Frances' interest as well as his own if Triona were to see the light and come back to him. He needed to enlist her in his cause.

She might not have left for work yet. Even if she had, per-haps Graham would pick up the phone and he could talk to him, man-to-man. Surely Graham Cherry wasn't relishing the prospect of a squalling baby in his house, disturbing his sleep and his sermon-writing.

Neville threw down his pen and reached for the telephone directory.

It was Frances who answered.

'This is Neville Stewart,' he said. 'Is Triona with you now?'

There was a thoughtful pause on the other end of the phone. 'Yeees. But I'm not sure—'

'I'm not asking you to put her on,' he said quickly. 'I know she doesn't want to talk to me. It's you I'd like to speak to, really.'

'We're having breakfast.'

Good—she wasn't letting on to Triona who she was talking to. He was halfway there. 'Could I meet you later? At the hospital, maybe? I have to be out this afternoon, and could stop by to see you before that. Say eleven o'clock? In the cafe?'

'Well…'

'I'll buy you a cup of coffee,' he said. 'And I promise I won't bring my handcuffs.'

Frances laughed. 'All right, then.'

'And don't tell her,' Neville added.

'I can keep a secret,' said Frances. 'You should know that by now.'

Morning Prayer. Callie knelt beside Brian in their chancel stalls and said the General Confession with him. 'Almighty and most merciful Father, we have erred and strayed from thy ways like lost sheep.' The words were automatic, requiring no thought, coming as easily to her tongue as the Lord's Prayer or the Grace.

That left her free to pray the prayers of her heart: prayers on behalf of Marco's family.

She prayed for Joe's health and his recovery. She prayed for Serena and Chiara, for God's presence with them to comfort them through the times of uncertainty and worry. And she prayed for Marco, that he might come to terms with the anger towards Joe he carried in his heart and the guilt that must surely have followed it in the current circumstances.

There might not be anything practical she could do for the Lombardis and the di Stefanos, but she could pray. And that was something.

The service, attended by only a couple of people other than Brian and Callie, was over within thirty minutes. Brian shook the hands of the two congregational worshippers as they slipped out, then turned to Callie. 'Time for breakfast, then,' he said. 'Janey will have it ready for us.'

No chance of escape. 'All right,' Callie agreed, forcing a smile.

Jane had set out the cereal, made the toast, and was boiling the kettle as they came into the kitchen. 'My Janey,' said Brian proudly. 'She has the timing down to a fine art. She knows I like my breakfast as soon as I come in from Morning Prayer.'

It was the first time since theological college that anyone had made breakfast for Callie after Morning Prayer, or any other service for that matter, and it softened her feelings towards Jane considerably. There was much to be said for having a wife, she reflected as she tucked into her cereal; no wonder Brian was so uxorious.

'The marmalade is home-made,' Brian pointed out. 'Her own recipe. No one makes marmalade like Jane.'

'My mother's recipe, actually,' Jane clarified, scooting the jar along the table in Callie's direction. 'She's famous for it, in the WI.'

Callie spooned some onto her toast and took a bite. 'It's delicious.' She meant it. Her own mother's marmalade came from Waitrose and tasted nothing like this.

'Tea?' Jane wielded the stout brown pot over Callie's cup.

'I'd love some.'

It was like the Twilight Zone, Callie reflected, or *Men in Black*. Some strange creature had taken over Jane Stanford's body. It looked like Jane, it sounded like Jane, but it was a pleasant, hospitable creature, in place of the sour, grumpy one. Why had Brian not noticed?

'Your friend,' Jane said to Callie, when she'd poured Brian's tea and her own. 'Mark. He's delightful.'

'Yes…' she agreed cautiously.

'Why haven't you brought him round before?'

'Well…'

'He had to find his own way to us.' Jane looked up towards the calendar on the wall next to the telephone. 'We'll have to fix a date when he can come for a meal. Next Sunday, perhaps? For lunch?'

'He usually has Sunday lunch with his family,' Callie explained. 'In Clerkenwell.'

Jane raised an eyebrow. 'Family?'

'His parents. His sister and her family.'

'Oh, I see. I thought maybe he had…children, perhaps?'

'No. He's never been married. He's Italian,' Callie added. 'Italian families are very close, and the men tend to stay at home with their mothers for a long time.'

'And are none the worse for it, I'm sure.' Jane got up and looked more closely at the calendar. 'How about a Saturday evening, then? Maybe the Saturday after next?'

'I'll ask him,' Callie promised.

'And if he wants to visit you here at the vicarage, any time, that would be fine,' Jane added. 'After all, you're living here for the foreseeable future. We want you to feel like it's your home. Don't we, Brian?'

Brian nodded. 'Of course.'

'That's…very kind,' Callie managed.

What a turn-up for the books! Jane not only being pleasant, but giving her permission to entertain Marco at the vicarage. She suspected, though, that Jane's generosity on that point wouldn't extend to overnight stays in Callie's room. If it ever came to that, she thought ruefully.

Mark had been told by Neville that the inquest into Muffin Betts' death was to be opened on Monday afternoon. He knew full well that the proceedings at that point were a formality which the bereaved parents would be neither expected nor encouraged to attend, but they were certain to find out about it, before or after the fact, because of the press interest in the case. It was that consideration which impelled him to return to their Bayswater home on Monday morning.

He wanted them to hear it from him. And while he was at it, he would ask them the difficult questions that had to be asked, arising from the preliminary post-mortem findings. As far as Neville and the coroner were concerned, the questions could wait: it would be six weeks at least before the inquest was resumed and decisions were made about how to proceed in the handling of the case. But Mark knew that the longer he waited, the more difficult it would be for him. It would hang over his head, assuming increasing importance, affecting his dealings with the family. He might as well get it over with, then get on with rebuilding his relationship with Jodee, Chazz and Brenda Betts so that he could effectively support them through the funeral and the other ordeals yet to come.

Having a night to think about it and plan his strategy, Mark had decided that, tempting as it was to get it over with in one emotional session, it would be more useful to speak to each of them individually, the better to observe their reactions. And there might just be something one of them knew that they wouldn't feel comfortable saying in front of the others. Their responses were more likely to be honest if they didn't have to worry about what someone else would think.

First, though, he wanted to tell them about the inquest, and he felt that was probably best tackled rather informally, over coffee.

'I'll put the kettle on,' he said as soon as he arrived in the white sitting room with the huge plasma screen. There was still a remnant of the media circus at the front of the house, so the curtains remained drawn and the room was in half-light. Jodee, curled up on the large white leather sofa, was flicking through a magazine while Chazz sprawled on the floor, his attention fixed on the plasma screen. One of the Spiderman films was playing; Spidey was scaling a wall, evidently planning to rescue someone from the top of a tall building. Neither of the pair acknowledged Mark with more than a glance.

'You will not.' Brenda, who had let him into the house, blocked his access to the kitchen. 'That's my job.'

While she went to make the coffee, Mark perched on the smaller sofa and watched a few minutes of the film with Chazz. Spidey performed the rescue with aplomb, then moved on to his next adventure. No one in the room spoke.

Brenda came back with a tray. She shoved aside some magazines on the coffee table to make space for it. 'You take yours black, don't you?' she confirmed, handing a mug to Mark.

'Thanks.'

'White with three sugars for Chazz, and two sugars for Jodee.' Brenda smiled as she distributed them. Still there was no response from the couple themselves.

Mark cleared his throat. He'd worked with many bereaved people before, and was familiar with the varied manifestations of grief, from screaming rage to catatonic shock. Last night Jodee and Chazz had still been tearful, with Jodee verging on hysteria. Now they both seemed to have shut down. He wasn't sure whether that would make today's task easier or more difficult.

Jodee had put down her magazine and was watching as the scene changed and bumbling Peter Parker tried to declare his feelings to his dim-witted girlfriend.

'Do you mind if I turn this off?' Mark picked up the DVD remote and killed the film.

Jodee made a face, but Chazz shrugged. 'I've seen it like six hundred times.'

'There's just something I wanted to tell you. There's going to be an inquest.'

Jodee nodded. 'Me mum said, like. It was in that news conference.'

'Today,' Mark said. 'This afternoon.'

Brenda was the one who looked alarmed. 'Do Chazz and Jodee need to go? And what about me?'

'Oh, no,' he assured her hastily. 'None of you will be called on to give any evidence at this point. It's just a formality, what happens today. The coroner will open the inquest. The Senior Investigating Officer, DI Stewart, will make a statement—I think he'll just state the facts of the case. Then the coroner sets a date to continue the inquest, in about six weeks.'

Brenda put her mug down on the table. 'You mean it won't be all over after today?'

'I'm afraid not, Mrs Betts. There will be various test results that take time to get processed.' He left it at that; why upset them by mentioning toxicology, histology, virology and micro-biology—terrifying words, even if you didn't understand what they were about.

'I just want it to be over,' Brenda Betts said on a sigh.

'It won't never be over, like,' Chazz stated. 'Muffin's gone, and we'll never have her back.'

Brenda glanced at Chazz, then at Jodee. 'What about the funeral?' she asked Mark. 'Will they let us go ahead and, you know, bury her while they're doing all them tests?'

'I think so. Unless you want to order more tests yourself—'

'What would we want to go and do that for?' Brenda cut him off. 'Like Chazz says, she's gone. The way I see it, it don't really matter how.'

Mark somehow doubted that the coroner would see it quite that way. Nor DCS Evans for that matter, though they would surely both be delighted if it could be proved, this very minute, that Muffin Betts' death was clearly attributable to natural causes, with no further action to be taken.

He finished his coffee and set the mug down. 'I need to have a word with each of you, in private.'

If he'd expected to learn much from any of them, he was disappointed. Chazz, the first to accompany him into the kitchen, was polite but baffled. 'Shaken? You're trying to say that someone shook Muffin, like, hard enough to hurt her? But that's just daft. Jodee and me, we loved her. From the minute she was born, and before. We wouldn't of hurt her, not for nothing. And Mum, neither. She's my mum, remember? I know what she's like. When me and Di were growing up, she never laid a finger on neither of us. Never, even when we deserved a good hiding.'

It was the greatest number of words he'd ever had out of Chazz at one sitting, and he was inclined to believe him.

Jodee was equally adamant, if a bit more scathing. 'You're like joking me, right? Hurt Muffin? I'd sooner cut off me own right arm than hurt me baby.'

'And you don't remember ever asking anyone else to watch Muffin, even for a little while? A baby-sitter? A friend?'

'Why would we need to do that, when we have Bren? She's always here, like, and she loves…loved…Muffin as much as me and Chazz. Bren's brilliant. She wouldn't of hurt Muffin for the world.'

Predictably, Brenda stood up for both of them as well. 'They're young, yes. But they're not stupid. They wouldn't of done nothing like that. They thought the world of that baby, and that's the truth. She were their little princess. *Our* little princess. Anyway,' Brenda added, 'Muffin were a good baby. She didn't cry much. En't that why people shake babies sometimes, like, to stop them crying?'

'Yes, I believe that's right.'

'She were a good baby.' Brenda Betts repeated it, plaintively, as if begging him to believe her.

◇◇◇

Frances checked her watch and cut short her daily round of the wards: it was almost time to meet Neville Stewart in the cafe.

She was still feeling a bit ambivalent about meeting him, almost as if she were consorting with the enemy. Would Triona approve? Would she see it as a betrayal? But Frances told herself that, whatever his faults as a human being, he did love Triona. He deserved a chance to say whatever he wanted to say, and if Triona wouldn't listen to him, perhaps it was Frances' duty, as her friend, to hear him out. Anyway, he already knew where Triona was, so Frances was in no danger of giving away any secrets in that department.

Triona had been unforthcoming about his visit yesterday. She hadn't divulged how he'd found her, what he'd had to say, or whether they were any closer to getting back together. If Triona wouldn't confide in her, then maybe the only way forward was to talk to Neville and attempt to keep the lines of communication open. Even if Triona didn't see it that way.

Graham might not see it that way, either, Frances acknowledged to herself as she hurried along the corridors towards the cafe. He might think she was interfering where she had no right to do so, and tell her to mind her own business. Was that why she hadn't told him about Neville's call?

Well, it was too late for second guessing. Neville was waiting for her at the entrance to the cafe.

She greeted him a bit awkwardly; shaking hands seemed too formal for the husband of a friend, but it was hardly appropriate to exchange social kisses with someone who had once arrested you—and whose wife you were harbouring as a fugitive. So Frances settled for a nod and a smile.

'Coffee?' suggested Neville. 'Would you like something to eat? A sticky bun?'

'No, thanks. Just coffee.'

Frances found a vacant table while he joined the queue. The hospital cafe was a busy venue—a source of quick refreshment for the medical personnel and a place to kill time for visitors and day-patients. For Frances it was a convenient meeting-place as well; she thought about all the cups of coffee she'd consumed there over the years with various people, remembering especially her breakfast with Triona a few months ago, when she'd discovered Triona's pregnancy. Raw with emotion and sick as a dog, Triona had been much more willing to confide in her on that occasion. She'd told Frances the whole story of her relationship with Neville, going back nearly ten years.

With what Triona had told her that day, and the developments she had witnessed since then, it seemed to Frances that the two of them—Triona and Neville—lived their relationship on a more intense level than most people ever did. She didn't know how they managed to maintain that intensity; the very thought of it exhausted her.

Maybe that was much of the problem. They'd never allowed their feelings for each other to mellow into a comfortable sort of companionship. Everything was fraught, contentious. Passionate, in both the positive and negative sense: passionate love, equally passionate hate. It was in both their natures; if one of them had been like that it would have been bad enough, but putting them together was a recipe for stratospheric happiness and incendiary pain, a roller-coaster ride of emotion. Was it possible for them to settle down to being a normal family, with satisfying highs, moderate lows, and most of the time something between the two?

'I succumbed,' said Neville, sliding his tray onto the table. He'd bought himself a pecan danish. 'Breakfast was a long time ago. Would you like half of it?'

'No, thanks.' Frances took her coffee and waited for him to speak. After all, he was the one who had asked for this meeting.

He munched his way through the danish, washed it down with black coffee, then leaned back in his chair. 'Thanks for agreeing to see me,' he said.

She nodded, still waiting.

'I need your help,' he said bluntly, with no further preliminaries. 'I want Triona back. And she just won't listen to me.'

'What makes you think she'll listen to *me*?'

'You're her friend. She doesn't hate *you*.'

The poignant, self-deprecating way he said it tugged at Frances' heart-strings; for the first time she saw his vulnerability, and found herself liking him more than she'd ever been able to. 'Oh, Neville. She doesn't hate *you*, either,' she assured him.

'Sometimes it seems like she does. I can't seem to convince her that I really want our marriage to work. That I'll do whatever I have to do to make that happen.'

'Triona can be stubborn,' Frances said.

He sighed gustily. 'Don't I know it. That's the understatement of the millennium.' He looked into his coffee cup, as if he couldn't bear to make eye contact. 'I love her, Frances,' he said simply. 'More than anything in the world. It's taken me years to admit that. And now…well, I just can't face the thought of living without her. I've been there. I've done that. And I don't want to do it any more. I want her with me, for better and for worse.'

'I'll do what I can,' Frances heard herself saying. 'I'll try to talk to her.'

◇◇◇

Frances had gone back to work, and he'd better do the same, Neville told himself. He still hadn't composed his statement for the Betts inquest, and that was going to take some concentrated work and careful thought.

He wasn't sure whether his talk with Frances would bring any results, though he did feel that it had achieved one thing: she had warmed to him, for some reason. Maybe she'd seen how serious he was about his marriage; perhaps he'd convinced her of the depth of his love for Triona. Whatever it was, he felt he'd made some sort of breakthrough with her. She might not exactly be in his corner, but he was reasonably certain that at least she wouldn't side with Triona against him.

He'd made it nearly as far as the door of the hospital cafe when he heard his name called. 'Neville? Neville Stewart?'

Neville turned to see a young woman smiling at him. A young woman with spiky, carroty red hair and a ring in her nose. 'Willow,' he said, returning her smile.

'Buy me a coffee?' she suggested.

He was about to beg off, citing the pressures of work, then changed his mind. He liked her. In spite of her eccentric appearance she was sensible; she'd given him good advice in the past. 'Yes, why not?'

'I'll have a double latte,' she said. 'And a bacon roll, as long as you're buying.'

Once again he went through the line, then joined her at a table. 'So, Detective,' she said, giving him an ironic smile, 'what are you doing here? Arresting someone?'

'Meeting a friend. And I might ask you the same question, young lady.'

She pulled a face. 'Visiting. My boss at Planet Earth. She... well, it's just too boring. She fell off a ladder yesterday and ended up in hospital. She broke a few bones, might have a concussion. They're keeping her in for observation, so I thought I'd better come and see her. Bring her some grapes, that sort of thing.'

'Oh, I'm sorry,' he said perfunctorily.

'It's a bore. I'll have to work extra shifts until she gets better.'

Neville recalled that she had a job at a health food shop. Selling nuts and seeds and tofu, he imagined. That *would* be a bore.

He watched enviously as she tucked into the bacon roll. The pecan danish had taken the edge off his appetite, but the bacon smelled wonderful. 'Do you want some?' she asked. Without waiting for an answer, she pulled off the other end of the roll and handed it to him.

'Thanks.'

'I remembered, see. You're a man who likes his meat.'

How uncomplicated she was, thought Neville with a pang as he ate his share of the bacon roll. How refreshing and enjoyable to be with. She liked Irish music; she could hold her Guinness. If only things had been different...

'Did you take my advice?' Willow asked. 'That last time we met. I told you to go back to your girlfriend. Did you do it?'

'Yes,' he said, holding out his left hand to display the ring.

'Neville! You're married!'

'And I suppose I do have you to thank,' he admitted. 'You gave me the push I needed to go after her.'

'I'm glad I was good for something that night.' Willow grinned at him. 'Things could have been different, you know,' she added, echoing his thoughts. 'If you'd wanted me.'

'I *did* want you.'

'No, Neville,' she corrected him. 'You fancied me, maybe. Just a little. Like you've fancied lots of other girls. And broken a few of their hearts, I have no doubt. But there was only one woman you ever really wanted to be with. You know it's true.'

It *was* true. How wise she was. He nodded in acknowledgement. 'I didn't break *your* heart, did I?'

Willow laughed. 'You might have. But I didn't give you the chance. It was pretty clear to me that I would have been on to a loser.'

That was a relief. He would have hated to have that on his conscience.

'So—you're ecstatically happy?' she went on lightly. 'Revelling in married bliss? Happily ever after?'

'I wish.'

Suddenly Neville found himself telling her the whole story: the proposal, the pregnancy, the wedding. The honeymoon, disastrously curtailed. The brief reunion, Triona's ultimatum, his frustration. 'I just don't know what to do,' he concluded miserably. 'I've tried every bloody thing I can think of.'

Willow just looked at him, shaking her head. 'Oh, Neville,' she said. 'You really don't see it, do you?'

'What?'

'It's staring you in the face, man. She told you herself.'

What on earth was the woman going on about? He frowned at her, uncomprehending; she just laughed.

'Buy her a house, Neville. If you want her back, that's what you'll have to do. What could be simpler than that?'

Once he'd finished interviewing the Betts family, Mark decided that there was nothing to be gained by remaining. Chazz had returned to Spiderman and Jodee to her magazine, whilst Brenda was there to keep things ticking over on the domestic front. 'You could do some shopping for us,' Brenda suggested. 'We're running low on a few things.'

Chazz, it transpired, wanted pot noodles and Jodee needed a fresh injection of magazines. Sliced bread, milk, cornflakes, instant coffee and PG Tips were also in short supply, according to Brenda. She wrote down the list for Mark on the back of an envelope, into which she tucked two twenty-pound notes. 'You should be able to carry this much from the Tesco Express,' she said. 'If not, get a taxi. That's what I always do.'

'I'll be back as soon as I can,' Mark promised.

He waved to the few rather dispirited media people who clustered on the pavement in front of the house. They'd been waiting there for days, Mark realised, and as far as he knew the Bettses hadn't ventured out of the door even once. 'Will they be going to the inquest?' one cameraman asked him hopefully.

Mark shook his head. 'Don't get your hopes up, mate,' he said.

He knew the Tesco Express well; it was between the police station and Callie's flat, so he often stopped off there after work for a bottle of wine or some cooking supplies. It was also, he realised as he approached it, just a few streets from the hospital.

It was where they'd brought Joe yesterday. He really ought to stop in and see him, since he was so near. Serena would most likely be there; she could probably use some support.

But…he didn't really want to see Joe. Not sick in a hospital bed. Not at all, really. He would ring Serena later; he might even call by to see her at home or at the restaurant.

Would she be working later today? Monday wasn't usually a busy day at the restaurant, so he supposed that Mamma and Pappa could manage it between them, even if Serena wasn't able to make it. But what about Chiara? Maybe Serena would need him to keep an eye on her after school.

He really ought to find out what the situation was, and make the offer to look after Chiara. But he couldn't ring her, he realised: if she were at the hospital, she would have to switch off her phone.

Mark went round Tesco quickly, filling his basket and consulting the list. The magazines took the longest; there were so many to choose from, so in the end he selected one of each of the celebrity titles and anything else that had a picture of Jodee or Chazz on the cover. That made a heavy bundle. He went through the check-out and filled several carrier bags.

The Bettses could wait a few minutes for their supplies, he decided as he paid for the shopping with the money Brenda had given him. He would feel so guilty if, this close to the hospital, he didn't at least make the effort to find Serena. He might not locate her, but at least he would give it a try.

In the end it was much easier than he'd expected. Serena was standing outside of the hospital entrance, her phone in her hand, pushing buttons. When he was not much more than a few steps away from her, the phone in his pocket buzzed.

Ignoring it, he covered the distance between them. 'Serena,' he called.

She looked up at him, then down at the phone, puzzled. 'Marco. You came. How did you know?'

'Know *what*?'

'He didn't make it.' Serena's eyes were enormous, the pupils dilated. 'He didn't make it, Marco. He's dead. Joe is dead.'

Chapter Ten

'Buy her a house. What could be simpler than that?'

Bloody hell, Neville thought, walking back towards Paddington Green. Easy for Willow to say. But how on earth could he buy a house?

There was an estate agents' office ahead of him on the other side of the street. Impulsively he crossed over, dodging the traffic, and perused the offerings in the window.

A million, a million and a half. Two million. Five million.

It was cloud cuckoo-land.

Still, he thought. It wouldn't cost anything to ask. He pushed the door open and went in.

The receptionist was a girl so young she looked as if she ought to be playing with dolls' houses rather than selling real ones. 'Can I help you?' she enquired.

There was no reason Neville should have been intimidated by her, but he was; this world was so alien to him. 'Talk to someone about a house?' he mumbled.

She glanced over her shoulder. 'I believe Andrew is free,' she said, indicating the man at a nearby desk.

Andrew, a fresh-faced young man in a white shirt and colourful tie, was certainly free. He bounded forward to meet Neville halfway with a vigourous—if somewhat damp—hand-shake, then escorted him to his desk. 'Andrew Linton, at your service,' he said. 'How can I be of help to you, sir? Are you interested in buying or selling?'

'Well, both, I suppose, but—'

'Oh, excellent. Let me just take some details.' Andrew indicated a chair in front of his desk for Neville, then sat down behind a large flat computer screen. 'Name?'

'Neville Stewart. But—'

'Is that with an "e-w" or a "u"?' Andrew was evidently an efficient two-fingered typist, and had soon tapped in Neville's address, home phone, mobile, and e-mail. 'And is this the address of the property you're interested in selling, Mr Stewart?'

'Well, yes. If you can just give me some idea of what it might be worth…'

'I'll have to see it, of course,' Andrew said severely. 'Do a proper valuation.'

'Oh, I thought you might be able to tell me, roughly.'

He must have sensed Neville's disappointment, because he gave him a wink and a nod as he called up another screen. 'Well, let's see, Mr Stewart. How many bedrooms?'

'Two. But one of them is tiny,' he felt compelled to add. 'I just use it mostly to store rubbish.'

'One reception? One bath? Kitchen?'

'That's right.'

'Is it a kitchen/diner?' Andrew asked. 'Can you eat in it?'

'I *do* eat in it.' To call it a kitchen/diner might have been stretching the point a bit, but this was not the time to split hairs.

'And is the flat in reasonable order?'

That was a matter for some debate; Triona certainly wouldn't have said so. 'Revolting' was the word she'd used, if he remembered correctly. 'Well,' Neville admitted, 'it probably needs some decorating or something.'

'Cosmetic,' Andrew pronounced triumphantly. 'A lick of paint. Buyers can see past that. As long as it's structurally sound.'

'I'm sure it is.' He wasn't sure at all, but by now he was entering into the spirit of things.

'And the location? Close to local amenities?'

'Lots of local amenities,' Neville confirmed. Not least the pubs. 'There's the market—Shepherd's Bush market, and it's very near the Tube station.'

'Excellent,' said Andrew. He concentrated on the screen for a moment, tapping a few more keys, then smiled triumphantly. 'This is subject to personal valuation, of course. But I do think you might be able to get in the vicinity of a quarter of a million.'

'*Pounds*?' gasped Neville, astonished. He'd had the flat for nearly fifteen years; it had cost him next to nothing in those days and in all the intervening years he hadn't spent more than a few quid on fixing it up or maintaining it. His mortgage was negligible, so he was looking at a great deal of pure profit.

'We'd ask a bit more, of course. Maybe two seven five. But I think two fifty would be achievable.'

'Bloody hell.'

'That's only half the story, though,' Andrew reminded him. 'What sort of property were you looking to buy?'

'A house,' said Neville. 'A family house. Two bedrooms, minimum. Maybe three.'

Andrew frowned. 'You do realise that you won't be able to buy a house for that amount? Not in London. Are you in a position to take on a large mortgage?'

'There's another flat,' Neville said. 'I've recently married. My…wife…has a flat in the City.' It still seemed strange to him to think in terms of having a wife. 'If we sold that as well…'

'Oh, well.' Andrew smiled, relieved, and called up another screen. 'That makes a difference.'

Neville gave him the address. 'It's just a one-bedroom flat.' He wasn't sure how much of a mortgage Triona had on it. Probably not a large one, given the divorce settlement she'd had. 'It's very nice, though,' he added. 'Really well kept.'

'And centrally located in the City.' Andrew tapped away for a moment. 'Half a million, minimum. I'd put it on the market probably at six. Subject to personal valuation, of course.'

'Of course.'

Neville had never been outstanding at maths, but even he realised that he was looking at a rather tidy sum of money. 'So three-quarters of a million, maybe? For both of them?'

'That's right,' Andrew confirmed smugly. 'Possibly a bit more.'

'And can I buy a house in London for that?'

'Certainly. Not a mansion,' he cautioned. 'But a nice terraced house, maybe a semi. Depending on where you want to be, of course. North of the river?'

'Definitely. Somewhere not too far from here. And close to a Tube station for access to the City.' For Triona, assuming she would continue with her job.

'Notting Hill, perhaps,' Andrew suggested. 'Or maybe Maida Vale, if you want three bedrooms. I'm sure I can find something that ticks the boxes for you, Mr Stewart.' He put out his hand. 'Leave it with me.'

◇◇◇

'Tea,' said Mark. 'Sweet tea. Let's go to the cafe. We can talk there.'

Consciously or unconsciously, he slipped into professional mode. This was, after all, familiar territory. Yet the ground felt shaky under his feet.

Joe. Joe was dead. Impossible, unbelievable.

He'd seen enough people in shock to recognise the signs in himself.

Best to put it out of his mind, to forget that it was his own brother-in-law who was dead, his own sister who was bereaved. Best to treat this like part of his job.

'I don't like sweet tea,' said Serena.

'Neither do I. Lots of people don't, I've found. But it's the best thing.'

She raised her eyebrows, unbelieving. 'Isn't it an old wives' tale?'

'Trust me,' said Mark.

He followed the signs to a coffee shop just inside the main entrance to the hospital: an Italian chain coffee shop, he was pleased to see. 'I'd rather have a coffee,' Serena stated. 'Espresso. Double.'

Mark wasn't prepared to argue with her about it. 'All right.' He dropped his Tesco carrier bags at a table in a corner, as private as possible, and went to the counter to get coffee for both of them.

'Do you want to tell me about it?' he invited, when they'd had a few reviving sips. 'You were with him?'

Serena closed her eyes for a second or two. There were no tears, just a quiet statement of facts. 'I was there. It wasn't pleasant, Marco. He started having convulsions. His breathing was really rapid. I called for the nurse. She got the emergency team there. They worked on him for a long time. But…they couldn't save him. They did everything they could, but he died.'

'A second heart attack.' Mark knew that it often happened like that: a weakened heart succumbing some twenty-four hours after the first heart attack, in spite of being in hospital with the best medical care available. 'How awful for you.'

What a silly, inadequate thing to say, he thought as soon as it was out of his mouth. Awful wasn't the word. Serena had seen her husband die, and her life would never be the same.

'Did he have the last rites?' Mark asked to cover his self-disgust. He knew how important that would be to Serena, if not to Joe. And important to Mamma.

She nodded. 'The nurse sent for one of the Catholic chaplains. Paged him on his beeper. Father somebody—I can't remember. He was Polish. He came right away.'

Mark hoped the priest had been able to provide some spiritual comfort for Serena. 'Did you talk to him…after?'

Serena's laugh was without mirth. 'To be honest, his English wasn't very good. And his Italian was non-existent.'

An idea occurred to him. 'I could get someone to page Frances,' he said. 'Callie's friend—she's one of the chaplains here. I'm sure she'd come. She's C of E, of course, but she's very sensible and nice, and she'd be someone for you to talk to.'

'No.' One syllable, one word. Quiet, yet firm.

'Father Luigi, then. I'll ring him. He might come here. Or I'll take you to St. Peter's.'

Serena put a hand on his sleeve. 'Listen, Marco. I know you're trying to help, and I do appreciate that. But don't bother. Really. I don't need to talk to anyone.'

'But you *do*. You will. Maybe not this minute,' he acknowledged, reminding himself that she was still in deep shock. 'But there are so many things you'll have to think about, that you'll need help with. I'll do what I can, of course. Anything. And Mamma and Pappa...'

She shook her head. 'There's only one thing I'm worried about right now, and it's something I have to face on my own. No one else can do it for me.'

Mark waited, unable to imagine what she meant.

For the first time her voice faltered, just a little, and she closed her eyes. 'Oh, Marco. How am I going to tell Chiara?'

Monday, for Callie, was a day for doing parish visits. In her early days in the job she and Brian had gone together; now, more often than not, he left the visiting to her. She had a regular list of house-bound parishioners who appreciated receiving the Sacrament, and there were always people with special needs. For the most part, Callie enjoyed this part of her job: it seemed to her that ministry—in its truest sense—was all about dealing with individuals on a one-to-one basis. Usually she found it satisfying, if occasionally frustrating. Sometimes the frustration was with the people she was visiting, in all their human imperfection; more often it was with herself, for some perceived failure of empathy.

She was learning one truth the hard way: some people are more difficult to like than others. Much as she prided herself on seeing the best in people and meeting them where they were, Callie was discovering that with some of her parishioners it took a much greater effort than with others.

One of the difficult ones was Mildred Channing, an elderly widow who lived in one of the gracious squares off Sussex Gardens. She was on her own in a large house, with just a daily home help to see to her needs. Although she seemed to be in perfectly good health, Mildred Channing complained incessantly of her aches and pains. In fact, Callie had found, she complained about everything, from the late delivery of her post to the government's shocking policies on immigration to her children and grandchildren's failure to visit regularly. Although Callie offered sympathy on all complaints, when it came to the last one in particular she was in secret agreement with the children and grandchildren. Her own mother was bad enough; if she'd had the misfortune to be one of Mrs Channing's offspring, she would have stayed as far away as possible. Mildred Channing made Laura Anson seem like Mother of the Year by comparison.

Mrs Channing was prevented by her aches and pains from attending services at All Saints'; they didn't, however, seem to keep her away from the shops, and today her laments centred round the number of coloured people who had served on her when she'd gone out to do her shopping. 'I can't understand what they're saying,' she stated. 'Don't these shopkeepers realise how important it is for their employees to speak proper English?'

'Some of them *are* the shopkeepers,' Callie pointed out, thinking about the local Jamaican greengrocer and the Indian family who owned the newsagents'.

'That's even worse. In my day we never would have thought of such a thing as a foreign shopkeeper. There was a Welshman who had the butchers' shop when I was growing up, but that was as far as it went.'

Eventually Callie managed to escape, with a promise of returning next week. Her next call, on the opposite side of the square, was Hilary Dalton's house, but proximity was not the only reason for the order of the visits. Always a believer in delayed gratification, she preferred to get Mrs Channing out of the way, saving Hilary Dalton as a reward for her endurance—a welcome antidote to the negativity which surrounded Mildred Channing like a dark cloud.

Just about the only thing the two women had in common was living in the same square; beyond that, the contrast between them couldn't have been more pronounced. It started, for Callie, with their very houses. Where Mildred Channing's north-facing house was dark and gloomy, even on the brightest of days, Hilary Dalton's seemed suffused with light. Colourful paintings covered the walls, and the south-facing windows were unencumbered by heavy curtains, the deep sills populated with begonias and cyclamen in glazed pots.

Though she'd always felt comfortable in Hilary Dalton's presence, and enjoyed being with her, it had taken Callie several months to put together the pieces of her life story, not because Hilary was reticent but because she was unassuming and outward-looking. She was also, Callie came to understand, a woman who lived very much in the present rather than in the past. That, especially given the circumstances of her life, was a rare and beautiful gift.

Hilary Dalton was an artist—a painter. Back in the heady days of the 1960s, when London was the cultural centre of the world, a young Hilary and her equally young husband were at the heart of the vibrant art scene. She was considered promising while he was widely regarded as gifted, even a genius. But his burgeoning career and their happy marriage were cut short by a fatal accident, and Hilary was left a widow after less than a year of marriage.

To support herself, she had turned her hand to teaching art, becoming one of the most respected teachers in the field. And with her sunny personality she had drawn to herself a large circle of friends—by and large people as interesting, and as interested in life, as she was herself. The Bayswater house, bought with the proceeds of the sale of half of her husband's surviving paintings, had been a hub of London's artistic life for decades.

But an aggressive form of rheumatoid arthritis had curtailed Hilary Dalton's career. The painting had gone first, as her hands had been affected; she'd managed to carry on her teaching at the Slade as long as possible, years longer than anyone had predicted. Now, though, in her mid-sixties, she was in a wheelchair and her fingers were so badly deformed that she could barely hold a spoon, let alone a paint brush. For a while it had been feared that she would have to give up the house and go into sheltered accommodation. The remainder of her husband's canvases, kept back for a rainy day, had saved her from that fate: his reputation had grown through the years to virtually mythic proportions and they were now worth an almost obscene amount of money. The sale of just one of them, at a special auction, had brought in more than enough to install a lift in her house—from the ground floor to the open-plan reception room on the first floor to the bedrooms above and the airy studio at the top—and to fund any home care she might need for the rest of her life.

Through it all she had remained cheerful, upbeat, a joy to be around. Her friends had not deserted her either; it was rare for Callie to find her at home on her own.

Today was not an exception. The door was opened by a young woman whom Callie hadn't met before. She looked to be in her early twenties, with a lively face framed by long, straight honey-coloured hair held back with an Alice band. 'Hi,' she said, looking at the dog collar. 'You're the lady curate? Cool. Aunt Hil is expecting you. She's upstairs. Stairs or lift?'

Callie knew that she should take the stairs, but felt she deserved a bit of self-indulgence after her ordeal across the square. 'Lift, if you don't mind.'

'Great.'

They got in and the young woman pushed the button.

'You're Hilary's niece?'

The young woman laughed. 'Her god-daughter, actually. I've just always called her Aunt Hil. She and my mum are great friends. I've known her…well, all my life, obviously. I'm Victoria, by the way,' she added. 'Victoria Morpeach. You can call me Tori—everyone does. And you're the lady curate that I've heard so much about.'

'Callie,' she said, wondering what on earth Hilary Dalton might have told her.

'Aunt Hil really likes you. She says you're A Good Thing.'

'It's been my privilege to know her,' Callie said with sincerity.

'She's great, isn't she? I mean, she's not like an old person. When you're with her, you don't think about age at all.'

That was it exactly, Callie thought, impressed at Tori's insightfulness.

Hilary Dalton was waiting for them in the spacious, open room where she spent most of her days, sitting by the tall Georgian sash windows overlooking the square. Callie crossed to the wheelchair. 'I hope I'm not intruding,' she said, bending over to take one of the twisted hands. She gave it a gentle squeeze and felt the pressure returned. 'I can come another time, if it's not convenient.'

'Don't be silly. I was expecting you. Tori just dropped by a few minutes ago.'

'I was in the neighbourhood,' Tori confirmed.

'And took a chance that I'd be at home.' Hilary Dalton smiled at her god-daughter and they shared a laugh at the joke: Hilary was always at home.

'I'll put the kettle on, shall I?' Tori offered, flicking her hair over her shoulder.

'Good girl.'

Tori, her god-mother explained while she was out of the room, had recently got her degree in media studies and had embarked on her first job, as a production assistant for a television production company.

'That sounds interesting,' Callie said dutifully, though she had no idea what such a job would entail.

'She enjoys it, apparently.'

'I suppose she gets to meet lots of stars.'

Hilary laughed. 'That depends on what you mean by stars. These days they call them celebrities, and talent doesn't seem to enter into it a great deal. I must say, though,' she added, 'I enjoy watching her programmes more than I thought I would. It doesn't do to be too snobbish about these things. "All human life…", you know.'

When Tori returned, carefully balancing three mugs, she explained her job to Callie. She worked for Reality Bites, a production company specialising in reality television. 'We're the people who bring you "twentyfour/seven",' she said proudly.

'And "Dancing in the Jungle", "Celebrity Flight School", "Pet Swap", "Take my Teenager—Please"...'

Callie accepted a mug of what looked to be white coffee. 'What about "Junior Idol"?' she asked, since it was the only one she'd ever seen, even briefly.

'Yes, that's one of ours as well.' The words were accompanied by a proprietorial smile as Tori helped her god-mother to wrap her hands round her mug.

'What does your job involve?'

Tori blew on her coffee, then took a sip. 'Oh, I mostly conduct interviews and auditions. Prospective participants, you know. There are thousands and thousands of them, for every programme we do.'

'People really *want* to have their lives exposed on television?' Callie couldn't imagine anything worse.

'They're desperate for it. I mean, we have some people who turn up to try out for *everything*. They don't care what skill is involved, whether it's playing the kazoo, eating bugs, or having blazing rows in public. They just want to be celebrities. The extents they'd go to...'

'So you have to sort out the wheat from the chaff,' Callie said.

Tori nodded. 'The people who can play the kazoo from those who'd like you to believe that they can. It's not easy, I promise you. The lies people tell...'

'Do you use a lie detector?' Callie was only half-joking.

'It might come to that one day. I'm pretty good at spotting the out-and-out liars, before they get anywhere close to being selected. But I'm sure that some of them are good enough at it to slip through the net.' Tori laughed. 'I had one contestant recently who asked me what would happen if we found out they'd lied about something.'

Hilary leaned forward in her wheelchair. 'That's practically an admission, isn't it? What did you tell them?'

'Oh, I told her that it would depend on what they'd lied about. If it was just the sort of thing that women lie on their passports about—shaving a few kilos off their weight—then they wouldn't necessarily be disqualified. But we have to be very careful these days, with the industry watch-dogs and so forth. We have an accountability to the public.'

'Oh, there was all that kerfuffle about phone call-ins, wasn't there,' Callie remembered.

'Exactly.' Tori grinned. 'Well, it keeps my life interesting.'

Peter would have found this conversation fascinating; Callie told herself she'd have to remember to recount it to him. 'My brother watches all of those programmes,' she said. 'I'm sure he'd like to meet you.'

Tori widened her eyes. 'I'm sure I'd like to meet *him*. Is he available?'

'He's gay.'

'So are most of the blokes I work with.' Tori gave an exaggerated sigh. 'That, or already spoken for. Just my luck. The story of my life…'

'What about all of those thousands of men you interview and audition? There must be some eligible ones.'

'Oh, God.' Tori rolled her eyes. 'Who would want a relationship with a self-obsessed, fame-hungry celebrity wannabe? I'm not *that* desperate.'

'Point taken,' said Callie.

Mark Lombardi wasn't answering his phone. To be more precise, he evidently had it switched off, as every attempt Neville made to ring him went straight to voice mail.

No one at the station seemed to know where Mark was, either. He wasn't at his desk; no one could remember seeing him that morning. It wasn't like Mark, usually so conscientious, to disappear without making sure he could be reached if necessary.

Neville wanted to talk to him before the inquest. It wasn't essential that he do so, but the more he thought about it, the more important it seemed. He himself had seen Jodee, Chazz and Brenda Betts only briefly on that first day—when none of them were exactly coherent, let alone helpful –whereas Mark was the one who had spent hours with them. But Mark wasn't answering his phone, and that was that.

DCS Evans wasn't particularly helpful, either, when Neville finally managed to see him. 'Inconclusive,' he said. 'Just remember that word. After all, this is a coroner's court, not a press conference. You won't have to answer any awkward questions. Just stick to the facts, and remember "inconclusive".'

Eventually he rang the coroner, who was reassuring if brusque. 'No need to mention any specifics about the post-mortem,' Dr Rice said. 'You should know the drill by now. Names, dates, times. I'll adjourn as soon as you've said your piece. I've already pencilled the date in my diary—end of April.'

'Thanks,' said Neville.

'See you in court.'

He sat at his desk with a blank computer screen in front of him. 'Stick to the facts,' he told himself, repeating Evans' advice. What the coroner wanted from him was a concise chronology of the events. He'd done this sort of thing so many times before: who, what, where, when. The 'why' wasn't for him to speculate about. That would be dealt with at a later date, and by someone else.

The more Neville thought about it, the clearer it became to him that he was going to have to mention the fact that Muffin had been alone in the house when she died. It was actually part of the chronology: Jodee and Chazz had come home in the early hours of the morning and found a dead baby in her cot. It was a fact.

This wasn't like the post-mortem results, which could remain 'inconclusive' until the actual inquest, when all of the test results would be revealed, made public, interpreted. It had to be said at this point, and made part of the record. Whatever the consequences, he had to do it.

Lilith knew that the opening of the inquest into Muffin Betts' death would be a mere formality; she knew that Jodee and Chazz wouldn't be in attendance and that she could write an account of it without actually being present herself. She could, in fact, do what she usually did: send some underling to take notes, then write up the story as if she'd been there.

But in this case she wanted to be there herself, for a number of reasons. She wanted to be able to tell Jodee and Chazz that she'd gone, in case they ever asked. She wanted to get the flavour of the event so that she could accurately convey the atmosphere. And she wanted to hear the exact words of Neville Stewart's summary while she watched his body language and listened to the tone of his voice; that might help her to judge how truthful he was being, and intuit whether he was holding anything back.

She would allow plenty of time to get to Horseferry Road. First, though, she went to the ladies' room at the *Globe*'s offices to make herself presentable; Lilith was always conscious of the image she projected and wouldn't allow herself to go out in public looking less than her best.

While she was applying a fresh coat of lipstick her phone rang; she pulled it out of her bag and saw that the call was coming from the Bettses' home number.

'Oh, thank goodness,' said Brenda Betts when she answered. 'We need your help, Lilith.'

'My help?'

'That policeman. He hasn't half put the wind up round here.'

'That would be Neville Stewart,' Lilith guessed. 'DI Stewart.' It figured.

'No, not him. The other one.'

'DS Cowley,' said Lilith. Cowley was Neville Stewart's usual side-kick, and if such a thing were credible, he was an even nastier piece of work than his boss.

'No. The Italian one. DS Lombardi. Mark, he told us to call him.'

She didn't know him, though the name sounded vaguely familiar. Probably family liaison rather than investigating officer, Lilith concluded, making a mental note of the name.

'Our Chazz is that desperate for his pot noodles. I gave him the money—forty quid from my purse. And he's scarpered!'

Brenda Betts, usually so dependable and level-headed, was making no sense. She went on in the same vein for a few minutes before Lilith was able to unravel her tangled monologue and figure out what was going on.

'So what you're telling me is that you sent DS Lombardi out to do some shopping, and he hasn't come back.'

'That's what I said. And he en't answering his phone, neither. I've tried and tried.'

'Don't worry,' Lilith assured her. 'I'll get your shopping. It will be a bit later this afternoon, but I'll bring it as soon as I can.' She scrambled in her bag for her notebook and took down the list, item by item. 'Just ring and let me know if DS Lombardi shows up in the mean time. He's probably just been delayed.'

'Maybe he's decided he'd best not show his face round here again,' Brenda muttered darkly.

'What do you mean?'

Brenda told her. Absconding with the shopping money wasn't the only transgression DS Lombardi had committed against the Betts family that morning, or even the most heinous one. (Lilith loved words like heinous and horrific.) Again it took Lilith some time to put the picture together from Brenda's disjointed account.

DS Lombardi had interviewed each member of the family separately, but they'd compared notes afterwards. And to each one he had made the suggestion that Muffin had been violently shaken at some time before her death. They had all denied it, of course. It was daft. Mad.

'You're absolutely sure about that?' Lilith said, unable to believe what she'd heard.

Brenda was emphatic, almost belligerent. 'Positive. You don't think I'd make something like that up?'

'But why would he think such a thing?'

'He said it was that post-mortem.' Brenda choked. 'You know, when they cut people up and such. Somebody had shook her hard. That's what he said. Somebody shook our Muffin, and they think it was one of *us*.'

◇◇◇

Callie had been hoping for, and halfway expecting, a call from Marco all day. She'd tried to ring him once or twice and found that his phone was turned off. That in itself was a cause for mild worry; because of the nature of his job, he was almost always reachable.

So when her phone rang, as she walked back to Bayswater from Frances', where she'd seen Bella and had a cup of tea, she reached into her pocket for it eagerly.

It wasn't Marco, she saw on the display as she accepted the call.

Peter. 'Hi, Sis,' he said. 'Are you in the middle of something important? Or interesting?'

'No. But I'm on my way to church. It's nearly time for Evening Prayer.'

'Do you have plans for the evening?'

She'd been hoping that she would—hoping that Marco would suggest a meal out, or anything to get her away from the vicarage. That hadn't happened, and now she supposed it wasn't going to. 'No,' she admitted. 'No meetings or anything.'

'And no Marco?' Peter probed.

'It seems not.' She hoped she didn't sound as disappointed as she felt.

'Well, then, you definitely need cheering up. A night out with your brother should do the trick.'

It sounded a rather alarming prospect, given some of the things she knew he got up to, but infinitely preferable to an evening with Jane and Brian. 'Nothing too exciting, I hope,' she said. 'Keeping in mind my advanced age, and the dog collar.'

Peter laughed. 'I wasn't proposing to take you to a gay bar in Soho. I was thinking more along the lines of a noodle bar.'

'That sounds perfect. There's one not far from here that's meant to be good.'

'Sorted.' He gave a wicked chuckle. 'Shall I come and collect you at the vicarage? I haven't had the pleasure of meeting your delightful hostess.'

How had it happened that he'd avoided Jane up till now? He *had* been fairly reclusive during those days in December he'd stayed with Callie, she recalled. Was Peter really prepared for Jane? And more appositely, was Jane ready for the Peter experience? He was capable of being utterly charming, but…'Only if you promise to be on your best behaviour,' she said severely.

'When am I not?' he asked with arch innocence. 'I'll promise, if you'll promise to leave the dog collar at home.'

'I think that could be arranged.'

'Done deal,' Peter said. 'See you at seven.'

He was as good as his word. Charming to Jane and deferential to Brian, Peter stayed just long enough at the vicarage before whisking Callie away.

'What a dreary place,' he said as soon as they were out of earshot. 'How can you bear it, Sis?'

'I don't seem to have any choice at the moment.'

'I mean, that Dralon sofa. It's horrid. Sort of vomit-coloured. I think I'd be sick every time I laid eyes on it.'

'You *are* naughty,' she said, but with a smile that belied the severity of her voice.

They reached the noodle bar and sat on benches facing each other at one of the large communal tables. It was as well that they weren't in search of privacy, Callie reflected, though the restaurant wasn't overwhelmed with customers on a Monday evening.

'So,' she said after they'd perused the menus and placed their orders, 'what's the reason for this unexpected pleasure? Do you have something to tell me?' If he weren't so cheerful, she would have suspected that he was about to announce another break-up with Jason; with Peter's track-record, that was overdue.

He smiled at her across the table. 'Well, actually, I wanted to show something off.' Peter reached in his pocket and pulled out a flat black object. 'My new iPhone. Isn't it the coolest thing you've ever seen?'

'Didn't you just get a new phone a few months ago? One of those flip phones?'

'Well, yes,' Peter admitted. 'But I just couldn't resist one of these.' He pushed a button and showed her the touch screen. 'Gorgeous, isn't it?'

Callie shoved down an unworthy stab of envy. Her own phone was nearly three years old, bulky and old-fashioned by current standards. Decidedly uncool, with no internet access and only rudimentary texting capabilities. Not that she'd ever cracked the skill of texting: watching young people—on the Tube or just walking down the street—with their thumbs flying on tiny keyboards made her feel ancient and inadequate. One of these days, she kept telling herself, she was going to have to ask Peter to teach her to text properly.

'Anyway, Sis, I thought you might want my old phone.' He reached in his pocket again and brought out the flip phone, sliding it across the table towards her.

She resisted reaching for it. 'But it has your number.' The last thing she needed, or wanted, was to get Peter's phone calls. And to have to tell everyone that she'd changed her number.

'Don't you know anything about mobile phones?' he teased. 'All you need to do is swap the SIM card. I've already taken mine out. Just pop yours in, and as long as you're on the same carrier it should work just fine.'

'Can you do it for me?' She handed him her phone and watched as he switched it off, slid the back off and removed the tiny card.

'Chinese tea,' announced the waiter, at Callie's elbow. He poured from a fat pot into two handle-less cups and set the steaming cups in front of them. 'Your food come soon.'

'Lovely.' Callie waited for her tea to cool, while Peter blew on his and took a sip.

'Ouch! That's hot.' He made a face.

Typical, she thought fondly. Delayed gratification had never been part of her brother's vocabulary.

When he'd polished off the first cup and poured a second for himself, just about the time Callie ventured a sip, Peter resumed his labours with the phones. He took the back off the flip phone and carefully slotted the little card into place, then replaced the back. 'Now let's see if it works.'

Peter turned the phone on and watched the display. 'Yes, it's recognised the network. This should work just fine for you.' He handed it to her across the table.

'Thanks, Peter. I really appreciate it.' How generous he was, she said to herself. Impulsive, scatty and lot of other things, but generous to a fault.

The phone made an unexpected noise and she nearly dropped it. 'Oh! What does that mean?'

'It just means you have a message.' Peter took the phone back from her, flipped it open, and pushed a button. 'Voice mail. You've missed a call.'

Callie reached for the phone, put it to her ear, and heard Marco's voice. Her disappointment that she'd missed his call rapidly changed to shock and disbelief as she tried to take in what he was saying.

Her face must have reflected her emotions, because Peter demanded, 'What's the matter? Who is it?'

'Marco,' she said, staring across the table at her brother. 'His brother-in-law. Joe. He's dead!'

Chapter Eleven

Chiara had been having a wonderful dream. She was on stage on 'Junior Idol', singing a duet with Karma. Then Karma stepped back and left Chiara to carry on by herself, belting the song into the microphone. The audience went wild, chanting KEE-AR-AH, KEE-AR-AH at the tops of their voices. She had to sing even louder to be heard over the noise of the crowd.

She sang so hard, so loud that her throat hurt.

Her throat hurt.

Chiara struggled out of the dream into reality. There was still the trace of a smile on her face as she snatched at a remnant of the retreating dream, but her throat hurt. So did the rest of her face. Why did her face hurt?

It took her a moment to remember.

Dad.

Dad was dead.

She'd cried herself to sleep, and her subconscious, unable to deal with the horrendous reality of it, had wrapped her in a beautiful dream.

But now she was awake. And Dad was still dead.

Still dead, always dead. She was just beginning to grasp the finality of it. He wouldn't be alive tomorrow or the next day. Never again. Death wasn't a reversible state, like tonsillitis or a sprained ankle or a bad cold. Dead was forever.

Dad would never tuck her in again, or read to her at bedtime, or help her with her homework. He'd never watch 'Junior

Idol' with her on a Saturday night or share the guilty pleasure of Pringles and hot chocolate. He wouldn't be there to criticise her boyfriend, when she finally had one. He wouldn't walk down the aisle with her when she got married, or hold his grandchildren.

Dad was dead.

And Mum…

Mum hadn't even cried when she told Chiara.

'Your father didn't make it,' she'd said. Just like that. 'I'm really sorry, Chiara.'

Sorry?

She wasn't sorry at all, or she would have been crying. Crying like Chiara did, for hours after. Crying till her throat was raw and her eyes were sore and her face hurt. Crying till she felt sick and hollow and drained of tears, only the tears were still coming.

Chiara turned her face into her pillow—still damp—as the tears began again. 'She's a hard-hearted bitch,' she said aloud. It was something she'd heard in a movie once, and Mum would have a fit to hear her use a word like that. 'Hard-hearted bitch,' she repeated. The anger that the words engendered were the best defence yet against the pain. For a moment she almost felt a tiny bit better, and that made her even angrier. She buried her face in her pillow. 'Bitch, bitch, bitch,' Chiara cried. 'She's horrible and I hate her.'

Neville was in no rush to go to work on Tuesday morning. He was, quite frankly, feeling a bit cheesed off about the Betts case.

Had it really been necessary for him to be dragged back from his honeymoon? To put his private life in turmoil and his marriage in jeopardy?

Evans had made it sound so urgent, as if no one but Neville could deal with it.

But what, really, had he done? He'd seen Jodee and Chazz for a few minutes on Friday. He'd conducted the news conference on Saturday, and fielded a few phone calls. He'd prepared and delivered the summary for the opening of the inquest. And that was about it.

Sensitivity to the feelings of the bereaved parents was all very well, but where did that leave him as Senior Investigating Officer?

Why should he bother to rush in to his office? There was nothing for him to do there but bloody paperwork. Neville hated paperwork, and always postponed dealing with it until absolutely necessary.

Besides, he was technically still on his honeymoon. Even if he was without the companionship of his bride.

So when Andrew Linton rang, early, and suggested coming round to do his valuation of the flat, Neville didn't worry too much about being late for work. 'I'll be there in twenty minutes,' Andrew promised. 'The sooner we can put it on the market, the better.'

Twenty minutes wasn't much time to get the flat in order, but Neville made a stab at it. He threw the duvet over the bed, gathered up his dirty clothes and stuffed them in the wardrobe, then collected the coffee cups and other assorted crockery from around the flat and dumped them in the sink. That left him with enough time to squirt some air freshener in the bathroom and draw the shower curtain to hide the blackened grout round the bath.

All the while he was seeing his flat in an unaccustomed way, as if through someone else's eyes. It wasn't very nice, he admitted to himself. No wonder Triona wasn't that keen on living there.

Andrew was right on time. 'The location is great,' he enthused as he came into the flat. 'A real selling point, Mr Stewart.' Then he paused, looking round. 'Ah.'

'I did say it needed some work,' Neville reminded him defensively. 'Decorating and so forth. Cosmetic, you said.'

'Er…yes. Cosmetic.' He shook his head slightly as he followed Neville from the lounge into the kitchen, but his smile remained fixed and his enthusiasm seemed undimmed. 'Yes, the kitchen is a good size. *Nearly* a kitchen/diner. The units are a bit dated, but a new owner would probably want to gut it anyway.'

The bathroom gave him a bit more pause, especially after he peeked round the shower curtain. 'I think a new white suite would be in order. Avocado baths aren't very popular these days. And some better lighting, perhaps. It's a bit dark in here.'

'But I want to sell it,' Neville pointed out. 'You're not suggesting that I do those things before I put it on the market?'

'It depends on how much you want to realise from the sale. A little money spent fixing it up could mean a great deal more profit. People are swayed by those…cosmetic…factors, much as I try to tell them to look beyond the decor.'

'That's just silly. Everyone knows that when people move into a new place, they fix it up the way they want it anyway.' Though he hadn't, Neville admitted to himself. He was still living with the same tired decor he'd inherited all those years ago. Wood chip paper, shag pile carpets.

Andrew was adamant. 'I'm just saying that a lick of white paint would do wonders for this place and its saleability.'

'White? Don't you mean magnolia?'

'I said "white" in a general sort of way, but "magnolia" is out,' Andrew stated. 'And "stone" is in. More contemporary, and that's what people are looking for these days. Especially the sort of people we're trying to market this flat to. Young professionals.'

'I thought you were an estate agent,' Neville muttered. 'Not a bloody interior designer.'

Andrew looked hurt, but only for a moment. 'The marketing of properties is very sophisticated these days. And so are buyers. That's all I'm saying.' Then he grinned. 'I know! If you don't want to do any work here, we'll market it as a "retro gem". We might just find a buyer who's into seventies decor in a big way!'

Callie was on her way to Frances' to take Bella for a walk when her new phone rang in her bag. It took her a moment to realise what that strange noise was; the ring tone was unfamiliar to her. As she stopped and rummaged in her bag, she recognised the tune: 'I will survive'. Typical Peter, she thought. He hadn't showed her how to change the ring tone, but that one would definitely have to go.

She hoped it was Marco. Last night she'd managed to reach him, finally, and he'd seemed in deep shock. She'd told him that she would try to be available today if he needed her for anything.

But it wasn't Marco. Callie didn't recognise the number on the display, nor, when she'd managed to open the phone and accept the call, did she recognise the voice.

'Is this the Reverend Callie Anson?'

'Yes, that's right.'

'This is Sister Mary Catherine, the Headmistress of Regina Coeli School.'

Chiara's school. Callie had been there once, before Christmas, for the school's nativity play. It was a night she'd never forget: the first time Marco had introduced her to the Lombardi family, after having kept her away from them for months. The evening had gone remarkably well, considering the nervousness on all sides, and she'd liked Chiara from the start. Chiara, of all of them, had accepted her with no questions asked.

'Yes?' Why, she wondered, would Chiara's Headmistress be ringing her?

'This is a bit…irregular, you must understand, Miss Anson. But I think the circumstances warrant it.' Sister Mary Catherine went on to explain: Chiara di Stefano had come to school that day, having just lost her father. As was customary in instances of family bereavement, she'd been offered counselling, but she had refused. She didn't want to talk to Sister Mary Catherine, to the school's psychologist, to the chaplain or any of the priests attached to the school, or even to Father Luigi, her parish priest. The only person she wanted to talk to was Callie Anson. 'You're her uncle's girlfriend, she said?'

'Well, yes.'

'And a priest in the Church of England?'

'Still a deacon, actually,' Callie admitted.

'I did explain to Chiara that you aren't of our faith. She understands that. But she insisted. You're the one she wants to talk to, and that's that. Under the circumstances, I felt it was right to agree. Are you willing to come and spend a little time with her, at some point today?'

'Of course. I'll come straightaway, if that's all right.'

Callie took the Tube across London, then a bus, and found the school—in a quiet residential street in Islington—with no problem. After ringing the bell and being admitted, she was ushered to the Headmistress' office.

Sister Mary Catherine wasn't quite what she'd expected: she looked rather younger than her voice had suggested, and instead of a habit she was wearing a navy blue trouser suit and a white blouse, the large wooden cross hanging round her neck the only indication of her calling.

The nun greeted her cordially, though Callie had the feeling she was being sized up with care by someone who didn't miss much. 'Thank you so much for coming, Miss Anson,' she said. 'I'm very grateful.'

She took her to a small room off the school's chapel. 'This is where the priests vest before Mass,' she explained. 'It's a quiet place where you won't be disturbed.' A couple of chairs had been provided, with a box of tissues and a glass of water in readiness on the vestment chest. Sister Mary Catherine had seemingly thought of everything.

Callie waited there for a few minutes before Chiara was brought in. She tried to think about what she would say to the girl, but when she saw Chiara's face, blotchy with tears and pinched with misery, everything went out of her head but empathy. She covered the few steps between them in an instant and hugged her, allowing Chiara to cry for as long as she wanted.

Eventually, when not a few tissues had been used and discarded, Chiara took a sip of the water and sat on one of the chairs. 'You came,' she said, her voice raw. 'Thanks.'

'Of course I came.'

'I wasn't sure you would. Sister Mary Catherine said you're not of our faith.'

'We're all Christians, Chiara. We believe the same things about life…and death.'

That unleashed a fresh spate of tears, dabbed away almost angrily by Chiara. 'So are you going to say the same stuff that Sister Mary Catherine tried to tell me? That Dad is in a better place? Sitting on some cloud up in heaven?'

Callie's heart contracted with pity. 'No, I won't tell you that. It isn't what you want to hear, is it?'

'I don't want to hear…*anything*.' She crossed her arms across her chest, defensive. For a long moment she sat there in silence, not looking at Callie.

'Why *did* you want me to come?' Callie asked when the silence had stretched beyond her own comfort zone.

Chiara still didn't look at her. 'Because. You told me once. Your dad died.'

In an instant, Callie understood. 'Yes,' she said. 'He did.'

'And how did you feel?'

Callie chose her words carefully, but in the end they were honest words. 'It was the worst day of my life. I thought my life was over. I *wanted* it to be over. I didn't want to live in a world without my father.'

'Yes,' said Chiara fiercely, looking at her at last. 'That's it. That's how I feel. That's exactly how I feel.'

Of course she did: Callie had seen them together, Chiara and Joe. She'd recognised the bond that held them together. It had resonated with her, reminded her of the way she and her own father had been. How could she convey to Chiara what her life would be like from now on? How could she tell her that the pain would be almost unbearable for a very long while, but that eventually it would ease? That, though she would never stop missing him, in time there would be hours when she didn't even think about him? And that that forgetting would bring its own special torment, its own brand of guilt?

It probably, Callie realised, wasn't what Chiara wanted or needed to hear right now. She just needed to talk to someone who had experienced the same loss. It would be a long process, lasting years, and—God willing—Callie would be there with her every step of the way.

'No one else understands,' Chiara stated. 'Nonna—her dad died about a million years ago, so she wouldn't even remember what it's like. And Mum. Her dad is still alive!'

'But she's lost her husband,' Callie couldn't help reminding her. 'You're not the only one who's lost him, Chiara. Your mum must be feeling pretty much the same way you are right now. And I'm sure she understands how you feel.'

Chiara pressed her lips together and shook her head. 'She made me come to school. I didn't want to come.'

'Your mother?'

Scowling, the girl nodded. 'Yes. She made me come. She said it was the best thing, but I think she just wanted me out of her hair.'

'I'm sure she had your best interests at heart,' Callie said. 'There probably wasn't anything you could do at home, and here you could get some counselling.'

'And take my mind off the fact that my dad is dead. As if,' she said bitterly. 'School. Business as usual. Just carry on like noth-ing's happened. Like Mum. She'll probably go to work today.'

'Surely not.'

'I'll bet she will.' Chiara gulped, then went on all in a rush, as if the words were being torn out of her. 'She doesn't care that he's dead. It's her fault! Don't you see? She wanted him dead. She drove him to a heart attack. It's like she killed him, and she's glad he's dead!'

Callie stared at her, appalled. 'Oh, Chiara, sweetheart! That's not true.'

'It *is* true! She wanted him dead.' Chiara's hands went into fists, which she pounded on her knees to emphasise her next words. 'And I *hate* her. I hate her, I hate her, I hate her!'

◇◇◇

Lilith had seen the papers on Tuesday morning, so it was no surprise to her when she was called into Rob Gardiner-Smith's office.

Rob Gardiner-Smith was the editor of the *Daily Globe*. He was young—younger than Lilith, to her chagrin,—clever and ambitious. Educated at Eton and Oxbridge, he had a reputation for being a bully and was widely considered to be ruthless; consequently he was feared by both his competitors and his employees.

He had the papers spread on his desk, facing her, with the *Globe* squarely in the middle. 'All right, Lilith,' he said. 'Tell me what's wrong with this picture.'

'HOME ALONE' screamed one tabloid headline, while another had the single enormous word 'SHAME'. The other papers featured variations of the same, all accompanied by file photos of Jodee and Chazz in various states of undress and/or intoxication, staggering out of clubs or tossing down drinks.

Gardiner-Smith picked up one of the tabloids and began reading aloud. '"Shock revelations emerged from the opening of the inquest into the sudden death of the infant daughter of celeb couple Jodee and Chazz Betts. In his summary of the case, Senior Investigating Officer DI Neville Stewart revealed that at the moment tiny Muffin Angel Betts died, in the small hours of last Friday morning, her parents were out CLUBBING." Blah blah blah—more in that vein. I'll skip to the end.

'"The inquest was adjourned until the 25th of April, when Coroner Hereward Rice will ask the question: did Jodee and Chazz's irresponsible behaviour contribute to or even cause their daughter's death? Was this a case of Gross Neglect, or of Manslaughter?"'

'Bloody hell, Lilith.' He threw the paper down and picked up the *Globe*. 'It's not even our lead story. Bottom right-hand corner stuff: "Jodee and Chazz inquest Opened, Adjourned". What is this all about?'

'I don't choose the lead stories,' she said defensively. 'That's *your* job.'

It was the wrong thing to say. 'Jesus Christ, Lilith!' he exploded. 'You know exactly what I mean! You filed some weak-kneed little story about Jodee and Chazz being too upset to attend the inquest. No mention of any of this "Home Alone" stuff. Were you asleep during the inquest? Did you actually *go*?'

'Yes, I went. I heard what he said.'

'And this pathetic story was the best you could do?' He slapped it with the back of his hand. 'Give me strength.'

Lilith felt obliged to defend herself. 'I have a relationship of trust with Jodee and Chazz,' she explained. 'I didn't want to do anything to jeopardise that.'

He glared at her. 'And that excuses your criminally incompetent behaviour? I'm beginning to wonder whether you belong in this business at all, Lilith. In case you hadn't noticed, we play hardball. There's no place in tabloid journalism for sentimentality.'

That, thought Lilith, was unfair. There was plenty of place in tabloid journalism for sentimentality, when it suited their purposes. 'What about all those 'poor Jodee and Chazz' stories you wanted a few days ago?' she pointed out.

'Well, the tide has turned,' he stated, sweeping his hand across his desk to indicate the papers. 'The press is now baying for their blood, and the *Globe* has got to play catch-up. Quickly.' He fixed her with a challenging stare. 'You find something to give me for tomorrow, or we may have to consider your position.'

It hadn't even occurred to Mark that he might go to work on Tuesday. He rang the station first thing to tell them he was having a day off for personal reasons.

Serena needed him, and that took priority over his job.

He went to her house early. Mamma was there already, holding forth in the kitchen in spite of Serena's protests that she was perfectly capable of making coffee.

Chiara had left for school. 'I'm surprised,' said Mark. 'She told me last night that she didn't want to go.'

'She didn't,' Serena admitted. 'But what good would it do for her to stay at home? She'd just mope about and make herself feel worse. Better for her to keep busy. And at school they can provide her with some proper counselling.'

Mark was surprised, as well, to find that Serena's 'keep busy' philosophy extended to herself: she was planning to go to work in the evening. 'What's the point of staying at home?' she said. 'We still have to earn a living.'

Yesterday, at lunch time, they'd managed to cover for Serena at the restaurant; Pappa had taken over her front-of-house role. Last night they'd shut, for the first time ever, putting a sign on the door which said 'Closed due to family bereavement'. Mamma, in particular, had been needed at home, to make all the phone calls to the Italian relatives and to feed *la famiglia*. Serena was now insisting that Mamma and Pappa should open La Venezia at lunchtime today, while she and Mark took care of various arrangements, and that she would join them as usual in the evening.

'But what about Chiara?' asked Mark.

'You'll be here, Marco. Won't you?'

'Of course. If you want me to be.'

'And Angelina will be home by late this afternoon,' Serena added. 'Though I told her that there was no need to come just yet. I hate to have her interrupting her studies in the middle of term. And the funeral won't be till next week.'

Making funeral arrangements was one of the things on Serena's agenda for today. Mark had offered to go with her to the funeral director's. 'You can help me to choose a nice manly coffin,' Serena said.

It was a firm recommended by Father Luigi, located a bit too far away to walk. Mark insisted that they take a taxi, though Serena said she'd be happy to go by bus.

The dark-suited proprietor was waiting for them, suitably solemn if not quite lugubrious. 'Allow me to say, Mrs di Stefano, how very sorry I am about your husband's passing,' he greeted her.

Not all *that* sorry, Mark suspected cynically; without deaths— or passings, to be less bald about it—like Joe's, this bloke would be out of business. Well, at least he had a good line in professional patter.

'And this is…?'

'My brother, Marco Lombardi.'

'It's good to meet you both.' He inclined his head in a little bow. 'I'm Mr Silvestri, and I'm here to do all I can to make everything easier for you. Bereavement is a difficult time for people. They're seldom prepared for it, I find. Especially when one is… snatched away…in the prime of life, like your dear husband.' He led them to a desk, where the paperwork was already set out. 'If we can just take care of a bit of this first,' he said, 'then we can get on with choosing a suitable…erm…receptacle.'

Mr Silvestri helped Serena into a chair, leaving Mark to find a seat, then went behind the desk to his own chair. 'Now, Mrs di Stefano. The first question: burial or cremation?'

Serena shrugged. 'Burial, I suppose. I haven't really given it much thought.'

'Yes, yes. Quite understandable.' He put a tick in the appropriate box. 'I assume you'll want Father Luigi to take the funeral? At St Peter's?'

'Yes, of course. That's what Joe would have wanted.'

He made a note. 'And do you have a preference for the date?'

'Middle of next week? Wednesday, maybe?' She turned to Mark. 'I suppose we'll have to close La Venezia for the day, whatever day we choose.'

'I'll see what we can do,' said Mr Silvestri.

Serena turned back. 'Can't we set the date now? Could you ring Father Luigi and see if Wednesday is all right? We need to let the *famiglia* in Italy know as soon as possible so they can make travel arrangements.' She added, 'Joe's mother is too frail to travel, but several of his brothers and sisters want to come.'

Mr Silvestri put down his pen and rubbed his hands together apologetically. 'I'm afraid nothing can be set in stone until the post-mortem is concluded and the coroner releases the...remains.'

'Post-mortem?' Serena stared at him, then swivelled to look at Mark. 'What's this about?'

Mark raised his shoulders and his eyebrows; this was the first he'd heard of it. 'But a post-mortem shouldn't be necessary,' he said to neither of them in particular. 'Joe died in hospital, under medical supervision. Of a heart attack. There shouldn't be any difficulty about issuing a death certificate.'

The funeral director's hand fluttered to the knot of his sober tie. 'All I know is that when I rang the hospital to make arrangements to collect the remains, I was told that a post-mortem had been ordered.'

They were both looking at him, Mark realised. 'I'll get to the bottom of it,' he promised. 'I'll make a phone call or two and find out what's going on.'

Poor, poor Chiara, Callie thought as she headed for the bus stop. There couldn't be a worse age to lose your father than thirteen. Callie had been a young adult when her father died; how much more terrible at thirteen!

Thirteen was the worst age for *anything*, come to that. Callie remembered it all too vividly: awash with hormones, experiencing confusing body changes and bewildering mood swings. People telling you how lovely it was to be young and you knowing how wrong they were. Hating yourself—the child you'd been, the person you were becoming. Hating everyone else. Especially your mother.

She and her friends had despised their mothers. For hours on end they'd discussed it: how embarrassed they were by their mothers, by their uncool dress sense and their inconvenient standards, how they would have traded their own mother for anyone else's at the drop of a hat.

Surely there was more than a bit of that involved in Chiara's vehemence about Serena. She would have hated her whether Joe had died or not.

But it wasn't the whole story. Chiara had known more about the tension between her parents than the family thought—that much was clear. Had she, as a sensitive child, just picked up on the atmosphere, or did she know something specific?

And it wasn't just her mother that Chiara hated right now. She was also pretty angry with God.

God had let her father die. She'd prayed and prayed, every prayer she knew, from the very depths of her heart and soul. She'd begged God to save her father; she'd promised to be good for the rest of her life if he lived. But God hadn't listened to her. He'd let her father die.

All of that had emerged as Chiara poured her heart out to Callie. It was why she didn't want to talk to a priest or any of the professionally religious people at the school. They would just say it was God's will, but they wouldn't be able to explain why. And what use was that, any more than a God who didn't answer prayers?

Callie had been asked for not because of but in spite of her profession. She was there as a person who had lost her own father, not as a clergywoman. She understood that now, very well.

This was not the time to talk to Chiara about God. All the theology in the world wouldn't reach her now. Nothing about God watching his own son die, about his being with people through their pain, would mean anything to a girl who had set her heart against him.

For Callie herself it had been different. She'd had no faith before her father's death: no one to pray to, no concept of a personal God. It was Frances, the hospital chaplain who had been there at the bedside as his family had watched him die, who had introduced her to a strength outside herself and her own experience. Callie didn't know how she would have survived without that. The sense of being upheld, of not being alone in her terrible grief: it had saved her.

And eventually, God willing, it would save Chiara as well. Callie wasn't sure how, or when, but she would do all she could, whenever Chiara was ready to accept it.

Shortly after she reached the bus stop, her phone rang. This time she recognised the tune, though not the number displayed, and she managed to flip it open and accept the call without difficulty.

'This is Brenda. Brenda Betts,' said a tremulous voice. 'Remember? You came to talk about Muffin's funeral.'

'Yes, of course, Mrs Betts.' She'd given Brenda Betts her card, Callie recalled, recognising in her the only mature adult in the household. She'd told her to ring when they were ready to make more concrete plans, or if they needed her for anything else.

'Jodee's mum. She rung. The papers—they're full of terrible things about them. Saying as how they was out clubbing when Muffin died. Saying they was bad parents.'

Why, Callie wondered, was Brenda ringing *her*? Surely there wasn't anything she could do about it.

Brenda went on without stopping for breath. 'Our Chazz is that upset, and Jodee too, of course. I tried to ring that policeman, that Mark, who's meant to be helping us, but he en't answering. And Lilith. She'd write the truth, but she don't answer neither. I just didn't know where else to turn. We can't go out. But we just have to talk to someone, like.'

'All right,' said Callie.

'You'll come?'

Callie took a deep breath, thinking about Brian—and Jane—and the possible consequences. But she really had no choice: they were her parishioners, and they needed her. She'd just have to square it with Brian later. 'Yes,' she said. 'I'll come.'

Chapter Twelve

Lilith went to the ladies' room to refresh her make-up and think about what Rob Gardiner-Smith had said.

Could he be right? Was she losing it?

Had she really lost her killer instinct, the taste for blood, the 'going for the jugular' that had been her trademark for so long?

She'd heard what DI Stewart had said in his statement, recognised its potential as a story, and then she'd pulled back.

She was going soft.

Lilith stared at herself in the mirror, scarcely recognising the face she saw. Where was the confident Lilith Noone, the woman whose very name inspired fear in hearts across the United Kingdom?

Sentimentality. No one had ever accused her of that before.

She reminded herself of the explanation she'd given to her boss. Betraying the confidence of Jodee and Chazz would have consequences, severe repercussions. If they felt they couldn't trust her, she would lose her unique position and thus her competitive edge.

All of that was true.

But...

Lilith thought about Jodee and Chazz. Yes, they were in love with their own status as celebrities. They were self-absorbed and not terribly bright.

But their love for each other seemed genuine, and they had certainly loved their baby. Chazz was good to his mother—Brenda, who had been a rock through all of this, and who didn't deserve any more suffering than she'd already endured.

Lilith acknowledged to herself the shocking truth: she *liked* them. She liked them all: camera-courting Jodee, thick Chazz, managing Brenda. And she didn't believe that any of them had been responsible in any way for Muffin's death.

Their denials, when she'd taken the shopping round on Monday afternoon, had been unprompted, spontaneous and utterly credible.

And remarkably stupid, she reminded herself. They'd delivered themselves into her hands, given her the ammunition to destroy them completely. They knew she was a journalist, yet they'd told her something that at this point was known only to them and the police, and possibly the coroner. Something far more damaging than DI Stewart's revelation at the inquest. Something that, in one stroke, would save her job and confirm her reputation as the most feared, ruthless reporter in the business.

She didn't want to do it, Lilith admitted to herself. Sentimental it might be, but she didn't want to hurt them.

'No place in tabloid journalism for sentimentality,' he'd said. She repeated it to her image in the mirror, then reached for her phone with sudden resolve. She knew what she had to do.

Neville was on his way across London, into the City, where he'd agreed to meet Andrew Linton at Triona's flat. He felt vaguely guilty about it: the fact that he had a key did not necessarily mean that Triona had given him permission to put her flat on the market and sell it out from under her.

It wasn't to that point yet, he assuaged his conscience. All he was doing was getting a valuation. He needed to know how much money the flat might realise if he were to put his plan into action and win Triona back. No commitment had been made, no contract signed.

Andrew, eager as ever, was waiting for him at the entrance to the block of flats. 'I love this location,' he gushed. 'Brilliant.'

And his enthusiasm was undimmed after Neville wielded the key and took him inside. 'Oh,' he said, looking round, his eyelids fluttering and his mouth agape.

Neville had a sudden strong memory of a picture in a book he'd possessed as a child: Saint Francis receiving the Stigmata, with an upward gaze of supreme ecstasy as the blood spurted from his upturned palms. It had scared the bejesus out of Neville at the time; he'd had nightmares about that picture for years.

Andrew's palms were intact as he lifted them up, but his face wore that same look of concentrated rapture. 'Now *this* is just the sort of thing that young professionals are queueing up for. I have two or three dozen people on my books who are looking for a flat like this, in this area. We'll sell it in a day. It might even go to sealed bids.'

Sealed bids, Neville gathered, were like the Holy Grail to estate agents. 'How much?' he ventured.

'Oh, well over half a million,' Andrew stated. 'We'll achieve that with no problem. It might go as high as six, six fifty. In this condition…And it will show brilliantly,' he added.

Neville admitted to himself that Triona had done it up very well, and that she kept it immaculate. Minimalist, that was the word. White walls, with a couple of expensive modern oil paintings. No knick-nacks, no clutter. And she *did* employ a cleaner to keep it spotless and tidy.

'Oh, stainless steel,' Andrew enthused as he opened the door into the kitchen. 'And granite work-tops. Very nice indeed. Will she be leaving the appliances?'

Neville shrugged. 'I suppose so.' In for a penny, in for a pound.

'Excellent.' He moved across to the bedroom door as Neville's phone rang.

'Excuse me,' said Neville, reaching into his pocket for the phone.

Andrew waved his hand. 'Carry on. I'll just pop into the bedroom, if I may.'

'Go ahead.' Neville turned his attention to the phone. Mark Lombardi, the caller display informed him. Fine time to ring now, he thought with a flash of irritation. Before the opening of the inquest was when he'd needed him, not the day after.

'Mark!' he began. 'Where have you been, mate? I've been trying to get in touch with you for days!'

'My brother-in-law,' Mark said flatly. 'Joe. He died yesterday.'

'Oh, God. I didn't know.'

Mark didn't elaborate. 'Listen, Neville. I need your help.'

'My help?' He listened as Mark explained: the coroner had apparently ordered a post-mortem, and Mark wanted to discover why.

'You know the coroner, don't you?' Mark asked. 'Could you ring him and find out what's going on? It would be better coming from you than from me.'

'Hereward Rice, do you mean? But if Joe died in the City, that would be a different jurisdiction. A different coroner.'

'He *lived* in the City,' Mark explained. 'Clerkenwell. But he died in hospital. In Paddington.'

'So that puts him in Hereward's patch.' Oh, great, Neville said to himself. He thought he'd done with Hereward Rice for a while.

Mark was a good friend, though—probably the best he had—and it wasn't such a great favour to ask. 'Sure, mate,' he said. 'I'll see what I can find out, and I'll get back to you.'

Andrew returned from the bedroom with a clipboard, a space-age laser measuring device, a camera and a determined air. 'Right,' he said. 'I'll get these measurements done, take a few photos, and we can have it on the market by tomorrow.'

On her way to the Bettses' house, Callie stopped at a newsagents' and surveyed the headlines in the papers. It was bad: worse than she'd imagined. She perused a few of the stories until the proprietor began glaring in her direction. 'Thanks,' she said hastily, grabbing a bar of chocolate and taking it to the till. This, she thought, was likely to be her main meal today, the way things were going. No time to stop, even for a sandwich. And as for poor Bella...

Given the hysteria of the newspaper stories, she wasn't too surprised to see that the media watch at the Betts home had stepped up a notch or two. Once again she fought her way through the assembled photographers and cameramen; the door opened a crack and she slipped inside.

'Oh, thank you for coming,' said Brenda Betts. 'I didn't know where else to turn.'

'I'm glad to help, if I can.'

Brenda led her straight through to the kitchen. 'We can talk in here,' she said, putting the kettle on.

Callie sat at the kitchen table and watched her as she made the tea. Brenda Betts was an interesting woman: down-to-earth and unashamedly working class in her speech, her attitudes, her values. Yet she had the surface gloss that money brings, with her stylishly-cut hair and her expensive jewellery.

'I was disappointed in that policeman, that Mark,' Brenda stated. 'He left us high and dry. Said he'd do some shopping for us. Took my money and all. But he never came back. And he won't answer his phone, neither. Friend of yours, is he?' she added, looking at Callie.

Callie sprang to his defence. 'He's had a death in his family,' she explained. 'Very sudden and unexpected. I'm sure he didn't mean to abandon you like that.'

'Oh, well, then.' Brenda looked somewhat mollified.

'Do you need me to do some shopping for you?' Callie offered.

Brenda poured the tea into two sturdy mugs and put one in front of Callie. 'That's kind of you. But Lilith done it. She came round yesterday afternoon, as soon as she could. Chazz was getting that desperate for his pot noodles. Sugar?'

'No, thanks.'

Adding a generous spoonful to her own mug, Brenda sat down across from Callie. 'It's not true,' she said simply. 'All them terrible things the papers said.'

'You haven't actually seen the papers, have you?'

'No. But Jodee's mum couldn't wait to ring and tell her. The cow,' Brenda added. 'Fine mum she is. Read the stories out to her. "Home alone" and all that rubbish. Sent Jodee into hysterics, it did.'

'Where is she now?' Callie asked. 'Jodee?'

'I sent her off to bed—I reckoned that was the best place for her, till she calms down a bit. And Chazz,' she added. 'He don't say much, but he gets dead wound up. He's messing about with his Playstation, and that's what he does when he's really upset.'

It sounded to Callie as though Brenda was dealing with the situation perfectly well on her own; she wasn't sure why she had felt the need to ring her and get her involved.

As if reading her mind, Brenda admitted, 'I did feel a bit guilty ringing you. We're not church-goers, you know.'

'That doesn't matter,' Callie assured her. 'You live in the parish. Everyone in the parish is our responsibility.' It was one of the first lessons Brian had taught her, and she'd experienced it for herself, over and over again: people who couldn't be bothered with the Church for years on end always wanted it to be there for them when they needed it. For birth, marriage, and death, mostly, but sometimes for other things as well.

'Nothing against it, mind,' Brenda added. 'Just never had no time for it.' She said it matter-of-factly rather than defensively. 'I was a single mum, see. Not that I wasn't proper married, like, but Kev Betts wasn't cut out to be a dad. Soon as he found out it was twins, he scarpered. Said he couldn't stand one bawling baby, never mind two. And he never sent me tuppence, neither. I brought them twins up all on my own.'

Callie sensed that this personal history was a delaying tactic. Echoing Brenda's honesty, she decided to tackle the subject head-on. 'Why, exactly, *did* you want me to come?'

Brenda looked down into her mug. 'I wanted to talk to someone,' she admitted. 'Someone who wouldn't…go blabbing me business round the world, like.'

Callie began to understand: this wasn't what it had seemed to be at all. Jodee had been an excuse, and Brenda had rung her not because she couldn't reach anyone else, but precisely because of who—and what—Callie was.

'Anything you say to me is just between us,' Callie assured her.

'That's what I thought, like.' Still Brenda didn't look at her. 'All this palaver about Chazz and Jodee being out clubbing that night,' she said. 'Nobody's asked me where *I* was. Why I weren't at home with Muffin, like I should of been.'

Callie *had* wondered; the papers hadn't even mentioned Brenda. 'Do you want to tell me?' she prompted gently.

Resolutely keeping her eyes down, tracing the pattern of the tablecloth with her finger, Brenda told her.

His name was Eric. Brenda had met him several months ago, at the supermarket. His wife had died of cancer not long before; he'd asked Brenda's advice on buying washing powder. They'd talked, gone for a cup of coffee. He was lonely. They'd seen each other a few times after that, then more regularly. Usually they went out for a meal. She would tell Chazz and Jodee that she was going to see a friend. No names mentioned.

On the night in question, she'd gone to his place. She hadn't told anybody: she'd just gone. Things had progressed, and the upshot of it was that she didn't get home till morning. Under normal circumstances, no one would have even known she'd been out.

'It were the first time,' Brenda said, almost shyly. 'The first time I'd been with a man, since Kev Betts, all them years ago.'

And it had been wonderful, Callie could tell from the soft expression on Brenda's face. Her cheeks were pink; a smile played round her lips in spite of herself.

'You'll think I'm a silly old fool. All them years without a man. But when the twins were little, it just wouldn't of been right. And I just didn't have no time for it, anyway. Like I said about church. I worked all day, all the hours God gave, and at weekends there was the housework and the shopping and the washing and ironing. No time for nothing else. But he's lovely, is Eric.'

What Callie couldn't understand, immediately, was why Brenda had been so secretive about it. Why hadn't she just told Jodee and Chazz that she had a man in her life, and gone out with him openly? Surely they wouldn't have minded; they would have been pleased for her. After all, Brenda couldn't be more than fifty—still in the prime of her life. Why shouldn't she enjoy a full social life? A love life, come to that.

She had to ask. 'Why didn't you want Jodee and Chazz to know?'

Brenda's cheeks flamed from pink to red. 'I were…embarrassed, like,' she said softly. 'At first. And then time went on, and it got harder and harder. Made it seem like I was keeping it from them. But I *was* going to tell them. That night. Or that morning, when I come home. I'd made my mind up to tell them, straight out, about Eric.' Tears squeezed out of the corners of her eyes and ran down her flushed cheeks. 'I didn't have no chance, did I? Not that morning. And not since, neither. Now it's too late. I just can't tell them now.'

One of the things Lilith was good at—and one of the factors in her success as a journalist—was altering her persona, depending on the foibles of the person to whom she was talking. She always aimed to be a perfect mirror for their needs and personality quirks, playing up to their weaknesses and their vanities, telling them what they wanted to hear, rendering them desperate to talk to her—whether to set the record straight or to make themselves seem more important in the eyes of the world. People told Lilith things they'd no intention of revealing to a living soul, let alone a journalist. It was a sort of seduction, and it had always given her an enormous buzz when she pulled it off.

Often this process took place on the fly, without any opportunity for advance planning but relying on her acute instincts. When it was possible, though, Lilith liked to plot her strategy before an interview.

This was one such instance. It was too important to leave it to chance.

Hereward Rice had agreed to see her, so already she was over one major hurdle. Now she just had to figure out *why* he'd agreed, what he was hoping the outcome of the interview would be, and then shape her persona accordingly.

She'd never actually spoken to Hereward Rice, apart from asking a question or two at a press conference, but she'd observed him in action on a number of occasions. He was clearly a man with a larger-than-average quota of vanity and self-regard: that was evident in his carriage, his manner of speaking, and the way he presented himself, from his Savile Row suits to his crisply waving salt-and-pepper hair. And, if she wasn't mistaken, he had rather a weakness for the ladies; in court he often addressed women—especially young and pretty ones—with exaggerated courtesy, even gallantry.

That, then, should be the key to it. Play up to his ego and make him think she fancied him.

Lilith had enough time before the scheduled interview to stop at her flat and change clothes. A slightly shorter skirt, a sheerer blouse, higher heels. She mustn't overdo it, she realised: nothing too blatantly sexy or tartish. Just a discreet projection of classy femininity, with a hint of availability. She pulled a few tendrils of her blond hair out of the tidy French roll and arranged them round her face to look a bit more approachable.

'Oh, Hereward, my boy,' she said to herself in the mirror, after she'd refreshed her make-up and changed to a soft pink lipstick. 'You don't stand a chance.'

He was ready for her at the time set for the interview, in his office tucked at the back of the Coroner's Court. He seemed relaxed, in control of the situation.

'Miss Noone,' he said, rising from the chair behind his quite substantial desk and extending a hand. 'What can I do for you this afternoon?'

Lilith took her time. She shook his hand, accepted the seat he indicated. 'Thank you for seeing me,' she said demurely. 'I know how busy you must be.'

He nodded in acknowledgement of a simple truth, and Lilith realised in that instant that Dr Hereward Rice's vanity was more than skin deep: he knew himself to be an important man, and a powerful one.

'I was hoping you could clear something up for me,' she said. 'It's crucial to get all my facts right. I've come into possession of some information, and I'm hoping you can confirm it for me.'

'I'll help if I can, of course.' His voice was cautious, if courteous. 'Though you must realise, Miss Noone, that much of what comes across my desk is highly confidential.'

'It's about Muffin Betts.'

His eyebrows raised just a fraction. 'Anything that I'm at liberty to say about that case is already a matter of public record, Miss Noone.' *Don't waste my time*, the tone of his voice warned her.

'Yes, but…' Lilith cast her eyes down, then raised them again to meet his. 'This is difficult,' she said. 'People's reputations are at stake. I'm sure you'd be as horrified as I to see someone's reputation destroyed over a…misunderstanding. When it could be cleared up with a quiet word. From an anonymous, protected source.'

Hereward Rice's hand made an impatient gesture. 'What, exactly, are you asking me?'

She judged that it was time to get on with it, and put her question to him baldly, without elaboration. 'Is it true that the post-mortem on Muffin Betts showed that she had been shaken before her death?'

There was a quick intake of breath and the coroner leaned back in his chair. 'Where would you have heard such a thing, Miss Noone?'

'It's true, then?'

'I didn't say that. I asked where you'd heard it. None of the post-mortem results have been made public, and won't be until the inquest resumes.'

'The Bettses told me. Jodee and Chazz and Brenda. One of the police officers—their family liaison, I believe—was asking them questions about it. Or so they said.' Lilith played with one of the loose strands of hair and looked at him appealingly. 'They're not…educated people, you understand. They might have misunderstood, got entirely the wrong end of the stick. That's why I'm asking *you* for confirmation. For clarification, really.'

He cleared his throat and gave her an appraising look. 'You must realise that I can't possibly be quoted on this. Not officially.'

'Of course not. Not unless you want to be. I know how to protect my sources.'

'And you're definitely going to go to print with this story?'

'Journalism is a very competitive business,' she said. 'If I don't, someone else will.' Not strictly true, but it seemed to be working. She smiled at him appealingly. 'That's why I've come to you, Dr Rice. Straight to the source. To make sure I get it right, before anything makes it into print.'

'Well…' He tented his fingers together and considered them for a moment. 'In that case, Miss Noone, I can confirm the essence of your information. There were some…irregularities… that came to light in the post-mortem. A clear indication of prior shaking.'

Lilith had done her homework on the internet. 'Would that be subdural haematoma?'

'Neck fracture,' he said. 'Healed. That's how we know it didn't happen immediately before the child's death, but a few weeks previous.'

'But it's possible,' Lilith said carefully, 'that the injury actually caused Muffin's death?'

Hereward Rice smoothed back the crisp waves of his hair and replied with equal care. 'I would say it's possible, though by no means certain, that the injury contributed to, if not caused, her death. That's one of the things we'll be determining at the inquest, of course.'

The phone on his desk rang; Lilith frowned in frustration at the interruption as he reached for it.

'Excuse me a moment,' he said to her, then spoke into the phone. 'Hereward Rice.'

Lilith crossed her legs in a way she knew to be attractive, but realised he wasn't even looking. He turned his back to her as he carried on the conversation. 'DI Stewart? I didn't expect to be hearing from you again so soon.'

She uncrossed her legs and leaned forward, her attention truly caught. Perhaps, she told herself, this interruption would prove a useful one after all.

'Di Stefano? That's an intriguing one. What's your interest in it, exactly?' There was a pause; Lilith strained to hear the other side of the conversation, without success. 'Oh, I see,' Dr Rice said. 'Well, I'll tell you what I can. Mr di Stefano died yesterday in hospital. Evidently a heart attack—as you know, usually a death certificate would be issued without question for a hospital death like that. But one of the nurses who was looking after him thought there was something suspicious about it, and notified the doctor, who rang me. So I've ordered a post-mortem. As far as I'm aware, the family's been notified and it should be taking place some time today.' Another pause. 'Not at all. I'll have more information in a day or two. Probably nothing in it, but if there is, you'll be among the first to know. Professionally.' He gave a dry chuckle.

Hanging up, the coroner swung his chair back round to face her and rose to his feet. 'Sorry, Miss Noone,' he said. 'Now, before you go, do you mind if I ask *you* a question?'

She was being dismissed, Lilith realised. She'd taken up enough of his valuable time. 'Go ahead,' she invited as she stood. Would he be bold enough to ask for her phone number?

A smile tugged at the corner of his mouth. 'Do the Bettses deny that they shook their baby?'

Caught out, Lilith hesitated for just an instant; she didn't want to give anything away, but it seemed only fair to be honest with him after he'd played along with her. 'Absolutely. They all insist that they never did anything like that. Chazz, Jodee, Brenda. And,' she added for reasons she wasn't at all sure of, 'I believe them.'

His smile widened, displaying a number of even, white teeth and a hint of genuine humour. 'Well, then, Miss Noone,' he said. 'I can guarantee that, in six weeks' time, you and I will meet again at what should prove to be a most interesting inquest.'

◇◇◇

By the time Mark—sitting in Serena's kitchen, drinking coffee—heard back from Neville, Serena had had an official phone call from the coroner's office, informing her that a post-mortem was to be held that afternoon, and that she was entitled to have her own medical representative present. She declined the offer, and her request for clarification was met with bland bureaucratic language. The coroner's secretary could tell her no more than that a post-mortem had been ordered.

'But why?' she asked her brother. 'I still don't understand what this is all about. A heart attack is a heart attack. And it was a heart attack. I was there, remember?'

Neville's call provided little enlightenment. 'A nurse was suspicious about something,' Mark repeated to Serena cautiously. 'I suppose that's all it takes to set the wheels in motion. They have to be so careful these days to cover all the bases, tick all the boxes.'

Serena shrugged. 'Then I suppose it's nothing to get excited about. Just a formality. They'll find out it was simply a heart attack, and that will be that.'

'We won't even have to tell Mamma,' Mark thought aloud. 'Or the girls.'

The next phone call was from the Headmistress of Chiara's school. Serena took the cordless phone into an adjoining room, leaving Mark on his own for a few minutes. Returning, she avoided his look of enquiry.

'What was that about?' he pursued.

Serena compressed her lips. 'Evidently Chiara's not doing too well,' she said. 'I'll need to have a word with her when she gets home.'

Before that happened, though, Angelina arrived, letting herself into the house and coming through to the kitchen, where she dumped her bags, shed her coat, and went to give her mother a robust hug.

'My turn,' said Mark, opening his arms to her.

'Uncle Marco.' Her voice was a bit choked up, but the tears swimming in her eyes didn't spill over as they hugged.

'I'm so sorry about your dad,' Mark said.

'Me too.' Angelina disengaged herself, dabbed at her eyes with a tissue, and went to the range, reaching for the coffee pot and a mug.

At twenty, in her second year of university—reading law at Birmingham—Angelina was practically a grown-up. She'd always been a very different sort of girl from Chiara, inheriting her mother's more phlegmatic temperament. Now that Chiara was a teen-ager and even more emotional and unpredictable than usual, the contrast was marked. While Chiara was artistic and imaginative, Angelina was practical, down-to-earth. She would, Mark realised with gratitude, be a great asset to her mother during the next difficult days.

'You needn't have come till next week,' Serena said, echoing a conversation Mark knew they'd already had on the phone, but she didn't protest when Angelina started a fresh pot of coffee and began washing up the cups in the sink.

A few minutes later they heard the outside door slam. 'Chiara,' said Serena, waiting; Chiara, though, by-passed the kitchen without stopping and went straight up the stairs to her room, slamming that door as well.

Serena exchanged glances with Angelina, who raised her eyebrows.

'Would you like me to go up and get her?' Mark offered.

'No. I'll go.' Serena's voice was firm.

As soon as her mother had left the room, Angelina pulled out a chair and plopped down across from Mark at the kitchen table, cradling her cup of coffee. 'How is Mum doing?' she asked him. 'I mean, really?'

'She says she's okay.' That, he thought, was the most honest answer he could give. Serena was carrying on; she was doing what she needed to do. He had yet to see her shed a tear. But he had no idea what was actually going on inside her head. 'How are *you* doing?' he added. Angelina and her father had always been close, though there had been fireworks at Christmas when she'd brought home a boyfriend of whom Joe had vociferously disapproved. There had been more than a few tense moments between father and daughter; Joe had barely been civil to the young Chinese man.

'I'm not sure. I don't think it's actually sunk in,' Angelina confessed. 'It just feels weird. I keep telling myself he's dead, but I don't really believe it.' She looked round the kitchen. 'I keep expecting him to walk in, asking for coffee.'

Mark knew exactly what she meant, and his heart went out to his niece.

He made a stab at changing the subject. 'How is Li?'

Angelina shrugged. 'I suppose he's all right. He was the last time I saw him.' She took a sip of coffee. 'We're not together any more,' she added matter-of-factly.

'Oh! I'm sorry!' Mark meant it: he'd liked what he'd seen of Li, and had admired the way the young man had coped with the culture clash of being thrust into the middle of a voluble Italian family, some of whom were actively hostile towards him.

Surprisingly at the time, Mamma had not been one of them. Everyone had expected her to be upset about Angelina's relationship with Li—as upset as Joe—but she'd been philosophical about it. 'It won't last,' she'd said. 'They're too different. *Sono troppo diversi. Vedrete.* You'll see.' And she'd been right, Mark thought wryly.

'It's okay,' said Angelina. 'Really. We parted as friends.'

'He didn't…break your heart?' Mark asked awkwardly.

She laughed. 'God, no. To tell you the truth, Uncle Marco, Li's a nice bloke, but once we'd got over the novelty of sleeping together, we realised we didn't have that much in common.'

In spite of himself, Mark was shocked; he hoped it didn't show on his face. 'Oh,' he said.

Angelina leaned across the table and patted his arm in a kindly, almost patronising, way. 'Sorry, Uncle Marco,' she said. 'I keep forgetting you're one of *them*.'

'Them?'

'Their generation—Mum and Dad's. The ones that think people mate for life. Like swans.'

Mark wasn't sure whether to be insulted or flattered.

'Oh, don't get me wrong,' Angelina went on. 'I think Mum and Dad's marriage is…was…great. And it was wonderful to grow up in a family like that, with that kind of security. But my generation doesn't think that way. We don't expect relationships to last forever.'

'You don't?' He *was* shocked, and he didn't care if she knew it.

She shook her head. 'No way. We expect to have lots of different partners in our lifetime. And to put it crudely, the people I know at uni—my mates—wouldn't dream of buying something without sampling the merchandise first. It doesn't mean we don't have standards. Just that we're not necessarily looking for the same things our parents' generation think we are.'

Mark now knew what side of the generation gap he fell on; that was yet another shock. He was still mulling it over when Serena came back into the kitchen.

She was alone, and she wasn't smiling. 'Marco,' she said. 'We need to talk. Now.'

◇◇◇

Most of the clothes that Callie had hastily packed to bring with her to the vicarage had been worn. It was time to do some laundry, but she didn't really want to ask Jane to use her washing machine. She was bound to do something wrong—use too much washing powder, or get in the way while Jane was cooking supper. So she bundled up her dirty clothes and used towels, shoved them into a Tesco carrier bag, and went to a launderette. It was in the neighbourhood, in the parish; she walked by it nearly every day but had never had need to use it before.

The launderette was noisy, hot and unexpectedly full of people. There were students, single men—a good place to keep in mind if she ever needed to pick up a man, Callie told herself humorously—and foreign tourists, sorting through piles of pocket change to identify the coins they needed for the machines. No one she knew; none of the faithful of the parish. A place for transients.

She bought an over-priced miniature packet of washing powder, then found an empty washing machine, pushed in her bundle of laundry, and fed the machine with an extortionate number of pound coins.

Callie sat down on a plastic chair, shrugged out of her too-warm jacket, and watched her clothes go round. Round and round, wetly: slosh, thump, pause…slosh, thump, pause. Her mind emptied of everything but that rhythm. It was hypnotic, therapeutic. She didn't have to think about anything else—not about Chiara, or Brenda Betts, or Jane. Not even about Marco, and the fact that he hadn't rung her all day.

Slosh, thump, pause.

Dimly she became aware that a phone was ringing. Over the cacophony of the combined sloshes and thumpings of two dozen washing machines a tinny tune was playing: 'I will survive'.

It was *her* phone.

She reached for her handbag and managed to find the phone before it stopped its jaunty tune.

Marco, the display indicated. With fumbling fingers she flipped the phone open, covering her free ear with her other hand. 'Marco?'

'*Cara mia*? Where are you? It sounds like you're in an aeroplane hangar or something.'

'Launderette.' She said it quietly, then repeated it more loudly; a few heads turned. 'Just a sec,' she added. 'I'll go outside.'

Callie went out into the comparative quiet of the busy street. 'That's better. Oh, I'm so glad you've rung, Marco. I've been thinking about you all day. And about Serena and the family. How is Serena doing?'

There was a slight pause before Marco replied. 'So-so,' he said, then paused again. 'The thing is, *Cara mia*, she wasn't very happy. About you talking to Chiara.'

'What do you mean?'

'Chiara's at such a difficult age. She needs careful handling.' He said the words as though he'd memorised them.

Someone came out of the launderette and pushed past her on the pavement with their large bundle.

'But it's my job, Marco. It's what I'm trained to do. And,' Callie added, 'she asked for me. I couldn't let her down.'

'Serena said to tell you that it's a family matter, and that she would appreciate it if you didn't get involved.' Marco cleared his throat. 'I'm sorry, Callie.'

'But…'

'I'm sorry. Really sorry,' he repeated, adding, 'I'll ring you soon.' Then he hung up.

She closed the phone and stared at it for a moment, not quite taking in what she'd heard.

The traffic carried on, and the pedestrians rushed on their way, home to their suppers and their families. Suddenly chilled, Callie realised that she'd left her jacket inside and went back into the steamy, rackety launderette.

Her jacket was where she'd left it, on her chair. Her clothes continued to go round in their hypnotic rhythm.

But her bag wasn't where she'd last seen it, on the floor by the chair.

Her slouchy black shoulder bag, as indispensable to her as her right arm. The bag that held everything essential to her life, from her purse with her money, debit and credit cards to her diary to a spare pair of tights to her small prayer book.

She got down on her knees to look for it, convinced that it must have been kicked under the chair somehow.

Her bag was not there.

'My bag?' she said to the woman at the neighbouring machine. 'A black bag. Have you seen it?'

The woman shrugged, lifting her hands palms-up in a clear gesture of indifference.

Callie remembered the person—she wasn't even sure of the gender—who had pushed past her on the pavement. In a hurry to get out of the launderette.

'My bag,' said Callie, and burst into tears.

Chapter Thirteen

On his way to work in the mornings, Neville usually stopped at the newsagents' by the Tube station to pick up a newspaper or two, for reading material on the Tube and to keep up with what was going on in the world—not to mention what the papers were saying about the police in particular.

His choice of paper on Wednesday morning didn't require much deliberation. The headline on the front page of the *Daily Globe* was in letters at least three inches high: SHAKEN TO DEATH?

'Good God,' said Neville aloud, then swore savagely under his breath as he read the first few lines, beneath the prominent by-line of Lilith Noone.

'Tragic Muffin Betts may have died from being SHAKEN, this reporter has learned exclusively. The infant daughter of celeb couple Jodee and Chazz died last week in what appeared to be COT DEATH, but sources now confirm that —'

'Bloody woman!' Neville exploded, to the alarm of the woman at the till. 'Not you,' he assured her as he gave her a pound coin. 'Lilith Bloody Noone!' He slapped the paper with the flat of his hand. 'Where does she come up with this rubbish?'

'I don't know, I'm sure,' said the woman, handing back his change. 'But people seem to want to read it,' she added. 'We're nearly sold out of the *Globe* already. I've sent for extra copies.'

'Muck-raking, filth-spreading bloody woman,' he muttered.

And who, he asked himself as he read the story on the Tube, was her source? So few people knew anything about the post-mortem results. The pathologist himself, who'd shown him the x-rays. The coroner, probably the deputy coroner. DCS Evans. Mark Lombardi.

Surely Mark wouldn't have revealed anything to Lilith Noone? He would know better. Besides, Neville told himself, Mark had been tied up with other things. His brother-in-law's death. Neville hadn't even been able to reach him—how could Lilith Noone have tracked him down?

Ruling out Mark didn't leave many other options.

Evans would want to know. He'd insist on getting to the bottom of it. He'd probably, Neville realised, think that Neville himself could have been the source.

Well, he'd disabuse him of that notion if he so much as suggested it. The woman was trouble. Poison. He'd as soon talk to her as sup with the devil. And he didn't care who knew it.

Loss.

Callie woke on Wednesday morning, achingly hollow with the knowledge of it.

Her bag. Her *life*.

She hadn't felt so utterly empty since that horrible day when her fiancé Adam had told her he'd fallen in love with someone else. And before that, when her father died.

It was just a bag, but along with it had gone so many things she relied on.

How would she manage, for instance, without her diary? All of her appointments, meetings, places she had to be and things she had to do over the next months? Callie had a fairly good memory, but she relied on her diary to tell her where she was meant to be at any given time.

And the prayer book. That was important to her for other reasons. She used it, yes, on a daily basis—she'd read a Psalm or two when she was on the Tube with no other reading material, or use one of the prayers with a parishioner in hospital. The main reason she valued it, though, was for its associations: Frances had given it to her at her confirmation. Frances, who had brought her to faith—confirmation—and ultimately to her vocation— ordination. The little book had originally belonged to Frances' vicar father, who'd received it when he was confirmed, and he had, in turn, passed it on to Frances at her own confirmation. Since Frances' strong-minded daughter had refused to be con- firmed, Frances had given it to Callie. Her spiritual daughter, she said. The book was bound in leather, now a little rubbed round the edges, and its pages were of the sort of thin, expensive paper that you just didn't see any more.

And it was gone. Presumably forever.

When she'd arrived back at the vicarage without the bag, in tears, Jane had been unexpectedly sympathetic. She and Brian had offered practical advice: ring the bank, the credit card com- pany, the police.

All very matter-of-fact. The police had told her to go to the nearest police station in the morning to file a report.

'I wouldn't bother,' Brian said. 'They'll never catch him. Not if you can't give them a description.'

'I don't even know if it was a *him*,' Callie admitted.

But she would do as she was told.

Going to the police station: that was a strange thing. As she approached it, a forbiddingly utilitarian building protected by busy streets and a guard armed with a submachine gun, Callie realised that she'd only ever been inside it once—visiting the cells. It was where Marco worked—a familiar world to him—but to her it was alien and even frightening.

She might see Marco, Callie told herself. She wasn't sure she wanted to see him right now. She'd been trying hard *not* to think about Marco, ever since last night.

The armed guard didn't even turn his head to look at her as she sidled past, ready with an explanation of her mission. She was wearing a dog collar; he probably didn't think of her as a major threat to security.

'I'd like to report a theft,' she said to the person at the reception desk in the lobby, and after ten minutes in a waiting room she was ushered into a small office where a uniformed officer sat behind a desk. Twin towers of in-trays and out-trays held down either side of the desk. 'Yes?' sighed the young woman, beckoning to a chair. She would probably, Callie reckoned, rather be out on the street than stuck in this tiny, airless room without a window, surrounded by paperwork.

'My handbag was stolen,' said Callie, and with another sigh the WPC selected the appropriate piece of paper from one of the trays and pulled it in front of her, biro at the ready.

'Name?'

Callie supplied the necessary details, giving the vicarage as her address and providing her mobile number. She gave the date, time and location of the theft.

The WPC's eyes flicked over the dog collar. 'Now tell me what happened.'

'I was at the launderette, waiting for my load to finish. My phone rang. It was too noisy to hear anything, so I took the phone outside.'

'And left your bag behind?' The WPC rolled her eyes but refrained from stating the obvious.

'Yes. I know. It wasn't a very smart thing to do,' Callie said humbly. 'I didn't think.'

'Obviously.' She looked down at the form and made a note. 'And when you came back it was gone.'

'Yes.'

'So you didn't see the person who took it?'

'Sort of,' Callie said. 'Or at least the person who *probably* took it. They came out of the launderette while I was on the phone.'

'So you can provide a description?'

'No,' she apologised. 'I wasn't paying any attention, I'm afraid. I was…involved in the phone call. It was…important.'

She would *not* think about it. Not now.

'Well, then.' There wasn't much more to say, obviously. The WPC scribbled a few additional words, then shoved the paper across the desk towards Callie, proffering the biro. 'Sign here, Reverend Anson.'

Callie signed. The WPC tore off the back copy of the triplicate form and handed it to her.

'We have your details. We'll be in touch if anything turns up.' *Not bloody likely*, her body language said, as she stuck the form into the appropriate tray on the opposite side of the desk.

'Thank you,' said Callie, backing towards the door. The WPC didn't even look up.

Back in the waiting room, Callie retraced her steps to the entrance lobby, folding up the paper and putting it in her jacket pocket. She felt almost naked without her bag; she'd have to go out later and buy a new one.

There was a familiar-looking figure crossing the lobby. Not Marco, but Neville Stewart, a newspaper tucked under his arm and an intent expression on his face. Heading towards the lift.

'Neville?' she said tentatively. 'DI Stewart?'

He stopped and turned his head, focussing for a second without seeming to register who she was.

'Callie,' she supplied. 'Callie Anson.'

'Callie, of course! Mark's Callie.'

She nodded, though she wasn't so sure about that any more. She wasn't going to go there; she wasn't going to think about that.

Neville Stewart smiled at her, and for the first time she saw how charming he could be if he set his mind to it. 'Sorry—I was a million miles away. If you're looking for Mark, I'm not sure whether he's here or not. He's had some time off—family bereavement. But I'm sure you know all about that.'

'Yes,' she said. 'That's not why I'm here. My bag was stolen.'

'Oh, bad luck.'

'It was just a bag,' she heard herself saying. Callie could see that his eyes flicked towards the lift. 'I won't keep you,' she added. 'I'm sure you're busy.'

'Yes. Good to see you.' He was already on his way. 'I hope we catch the bastard who stole your bag,' he said over his shoulder.

Just a bag. That was all it was. So why were Callie's eyes prickling with tears yet again?

◇◇◇

Mark was of two minds about going to work on Wednesday. On the one hand, if there was a chance that Serena needed him, that he could be useful to her, he didn't want to let her down. But he didn't think that she *did* need him particularly: Angelina and Mamma were there for the practicalities, and perhaps it would be better for him to save his time off for the days around the funeral, when members of the Italian *famiglia* would descend. Besides, all of the plans that had yet to be made were on hold until the formality of the post-mortem was out of the way. Mark would ring the coroner's office today to find out the status of that; he could do it from work. If the coroner was satisfied by the post-mortem results and agreed to release the body, they could set a date for the funeral and start sorting out the details.

He rang Serena first thing, and she was emphatic about it. 'Go to work, Marco,' she said. 'There's no reason for you not to. I'll be working today myself.'

So that was that. He really should check in with Jodee and Chazz and Brenda, apologise to them for his sudden disappearance. In fact, he realised with horror, he still had Brenda's shopping; the Tesco bags were piled in the corner of his bedroom. Things had developed so rapidly that he'd never had the chance to deliver it to her. The milk was *not* going to be in good shape; he'd have to replace it before he went.

He had been seriously derelict in his job there, he admitted to himself. But what else could he have done? Serena's need had been more important than cornflakes and pot noodles. Surely Brenda would understand that.

Callie. His thoughts returned to her, circled round her, as they inevitably did; she was never far from his mind. Now, though, those thoughts were too painful to contemplate.

He knew her so well. Her voice on the phone had conveyed shock, hurt. She must be feeling betrayed. By him, the man who loved her.

How could he possibly make it better? He hadn't meant to hurt her, though he could see how she could have taken it that way.

What *had* he done?

He wasn't equal to sorting it out. Not now. He just couldn't ring her and risk her hanging up on him. He would go to work, and with any luck he'd keep busy enough that he wouldn't have time to think about her…and what he'd done.

◇◇◇

Neville had a quick conversation with DCS Evans' secretary, the admirable Ursula, who told him that the great man was tied up with urgent matters—an important phone call, evidently—but promised to let him know when Evans was available. 'There are a few things I need to discuss with him,' Neville told her.

When his phone rang, though, it was Andrew Linton. Everything was in readiness: the property details were completed in draft and the agency agreement contracts had been drawn up to authorise Andrew to show and sell the flats. All he needed now was for Neville to pop in, check the details, and sign the contracts. 'I have a viewing scheduled for this afternoon,' Andrew told him proudly. 'One definite viewing, and two tentative. And I've pulled out a few property details for you to take a look at. Terraced houses that fit your criteria.'

Neville looked at his watch. 'Yes, all right. I'll come right now,' he decided. Andrew's office was no more than a ten-minute walk; he could get there and be back before Evans was off the phone.

But he'd barely made it out of the building and across the street when his mobile rang. 'He's finished his phone call,' Ursula reported. 'How quickly can you get up here?'

'Change of plans,' Neville said. 'Half an hour, maybe? I'll ring you before I come to see if he's still free.'

'No,' said Ursula. 'You don't understand. He wants to see *you*. Right now.'

'Oh, God. I'm on my way.' Neville changed direction, nearly causing an accident on the pavement, and headed back across the street to the station. He took the lift straight up to Evans' floor; it wasn't a good idea to keep Evans waiting, he'd learned a long time ago.

'Any idea what it's about?' he asked Ursula.

She shrugged. 'He's been talking to Hereward Rice. That's all I can tell you.' She buzzed through. 'DI Stewart is here, Sir.'

'Send him in.'

Neville opened the door into the inner sanctum and found Evans behind his desk. He meant business, then: no preliminaries, no small talk. Neville's heart sank. What on earth could this be about?

'Sit down, man,' said Evans, gesturing to a hard wooden chair.

He sat; he waited.

'Joe di Stefano,' said Evans. 'I understand you've been making enquiries?'

This wasn't at all what Neville had expected, it caught him off guard. 'Yes, Sir. He's…he was…Mark Lombardi's brother-in-law.'

'So I gather.' Evans frowned, lowering his caterpillar eyebrows.

Wrong-footed, Neville stumbled on. 'He died of a heart attack. Mark asked me to find out why a post-mortem had been ordered.' Had Hereward Rice rung Evans to complain? He couldn't understand why: he'd only been asking for information, not trying to interfere in any way.

'Well, the post-mortem has taken place,' Evans informed him, the sing-song Welsh rhythm of his voice more pronounced than usual. 'And though Joe di Stefano did die of a heart attack, it was only in the most technical sense.'

'What do you mean?'

'Heart attack was the cause of death. But it wasn't a natural heart attack.' Evans put his elbows on his desk and glared impatiently at Neville.

'Sir?'

'Do I have to spell it out for you, man?' With a gusty sigh, Evans delivered the punch line. 'Joe di Stefano didn't die naturally at all. He was murdered.'

A new bag. Callie focussed her thoughts on that.

Fortunately, her cheque book hadn't been in the stolen bag: she seldom used it these days, as a debit card was much more convenient. Quite a few shops no longer even accepted cheques, she'd noticed, and you couldn't use a cheque to get money from a cash machine.

But you could use it to get money out of a bank in the traditional way. There was, Callie knew, a branch of her bank close to Paddington Station, so she headed there when she'd left the police station. Though she'd already reported the theft to the bank by phone, at the teller window she checked her current account balance to make sure that no one had been using her debit card, then cashed a cheque, stuffing the money into her pocket.

Callie recalled seeing a bag shop in Paddington Station, targeted at travellers and tourists. These days the station resembled an airport terminal, with all the shopping and eating options provided for people in transit: no longer just a newsagent and a place to grab a bar of chocolate, but full-fledged boutiques and restaurants.

She found the bag shop and discovered that it was targeted at *wealthy* travellers; the price tags were as hefty as her old bag when it was fully loaded. Still, she told herself, a good bag was an investment, not a throw-away fashion statement. She'd had the old black one for five or six years at least, and would have kept it even longer if it hadn't been forcibly removed from her life. If you pro-rated the cost out over the amount of use…

A quick survey of the shop revealed a bag quite similar to the old one, and Callie had just about steeled herself to its price tag when she spotted a red leather bag that was the stuff of dreams: soft as butter, impossibly expensive. Its colour was not a blatant pillar-box red or an orangey tomato red, but the red of sweet, ripe cherries. After checking the price tag with a grimace of pain, Callie reached out an involuntary finger to stroke it.

Her sigh of longing was audible; a middle-aged woman who was browsing nearby caught her eye. 'I think you should buy it,' she said in an American accent. 'It's beautiful.'

'Yes, it's beautiful. But I should probably get the black one. It's more practical. Safer, if you know what I mean.' Her hand went to her clerical collar.

'Safer, yes.' The woman gave a rich laugh. 'I don't know about you, my dear, but sometimes I think "safe" is over-rated. Quite frankly, I don't always want to play it safe. Life is too short.'

Callie looked into the woman's warm brown eyes and saw a lifetime of wisdom there. 'You're right,' she said, and reached—with reckless resolve—for her chequebook.

◇◇◇

Neville stared at the Detective Chief Superintendent. 'Murdered?'

'Unless he committed suicide in a particularly bizarre way. And that doesn't seem very likely to me.'

'But…how?'

Evans pulled a notepad towards him and consulted it. 'Ethylene glycol poisoning,' he read out, adding, 'That's anti-freeze, to you and me.'

Neville still couldn't take it in. How on earth did that square with a heart attack?

'According to Dr Rice, di Stefano ingested a quantity of anti-freeze, which brought on coronary failure—cardiovascular collapse, he said. It doesn't take much, apparently,' Evans went on. 'An ounce or two of the stuff can be fatal.'

'How can they tell that's what he had?'

'Easily, it would seem. If they're looking for it.' Again Evans checked his notepad. 'Some sort of crystals in the kidneys. A dead give-away, so to speak.' He allowed himself an ironic smile.

'So…someone gave Joe di Stefano anti-freeze to drink?'

'Now you're getting it. Rice says there's no doubt about it. Murder. He'll be opening an inquest as soon as it can be arranged.'

Neville was still processing the 'm' word. 'But who?'

Evans put the palms of his hands on his desk and hunched forward slightly, fixing Neville with a purposeful stare. 'That, DI Stewart, is what you're going to find out.'

'Me? But there's the Betts baby case,' he protested. 'I'm SIO. I came back from my honeymoon to do it.' Neville knew it was feeble: that very morning he'd just been about to suggest to Evans that his time could be better spent.

'On hold,' Evans said crisply. 'You've done what you can with that one, and nothing else will happen until the inquest resumes. No, the thing that concerns me more is Mark Lombardi. You're friends, I understand?'

'Well, yes. Yes, we are,' Neville said, seeing a possible escape. That must be why he was so reluctant, he realised: Mark was a good mate.

'But you're a professional. That won't stand in the way of your dealing with this case properly. Will it?' Evans raised his eyebrows and waited for an answer.

Neville sighed. 'No, Sir.'

'You'll need to talk to Lombardi first, of course. Where is he?'

'I have no idea,' Neville admitted. 'He might be with the Betts family.'

Evans glowered, his brows lowering '*Might* be? I thought you were SIO on that case. Or so you've just reminded me.'

'Well, yes, Sir.'

'Find Lombardi, wherever he is,' Evans ordered him. 'Pull him off. You can talk to him, of course, and find out everything you can about di Stefano, but as of right now, DS Lombardi is on leave. I don't want him involved in our enquiries in any way.'

He nodded. 'The Betts family. Will they need a new FLO?'

Evans shook his head. 'I shouldn't think so. This di Stefano business should be cleared up before the Betts inquest resumes.' *It had better be*, his gaze said.

Resigned, Neville stood up. 'Well, I suppose I'd best be getting on with it, then.'

'Talk to Dr Rice yourself, if you want to,' Evans suggested, genial now. 'He'll give you the technical low-down, maybe tell you where you should start looking.'

'Yes, Sir.'

'You'll want to use DS Cowley, of course.'

Sid Cowley, his sergeant. He'd been avoiding Sid—with surprising success—since his precipitate return from honeymoon. Before Neville's wedding, Sid, the perpetual and enthusiastic bachelor, had been scathing about the institution of matrimony in general and Neville's embrace of it in particular. He'd warned Neville, over and over, that he was making a big mistake. Now he would be unbearably full of himself. Crowing. *I told you so.* He might not say it in so many words, but it would be written all over his smug face.

Neville wished he had the nerve to ask Evans if he could have a different sergeant. But he couldn't avoid Sid Cowley forever. He would have to face him sooner or later; it may as well be today. 'Yes, Sir,' he said. 'I'll find him.'

'Keep me informed,' Evans instructed. 'I'll be looking for results quite quickly on this one, Stewart.'

'Yes, Sir.'

Neville didn't look back as he left the office; to Ursula's quizzical glance he responded with a shrug and a shake of his head.

◇◇◇

Frances was doing a routine round of the wards when her pager went off, with the message that she should go to her office.

She was surprised to see Callie waiting for her there. 'I hope I haven't interrupted anything important,' Callie said, as Frances gave her a hug. 'I was nearby, and thought I'd drop in to see you.'

'I'm overdue for a break, as a matter of fact,' Frances assured her.

Callie looked a bit peaky, she observed. In need, perhaps, of sustenance. 'Do you have time for some lunch?' Frances suggested, glancing at her watch.

'Definitely.'

'Nice bag,' said Frances. 'Is it new?'

'Brand new. I'll tell you about it over lunch.'

'I love the colour. You can get away with it.' Frances tried not to sound envious; with her red hair, she would never dare.

They headed for the cafe and went through the queue. Frances selected a salad, while Callie asked for a jacket potato with tuna mayo. It was a bit early for lunch, so they didn't have any trouble finding a table.

'All right,' Frances prompted. 'Tell me about the bag. Was it a gift?' Maybe, she thought, Callie's extravagant brother had bought it for her; it was obviously expensive, and she couldn't imagine Callie spending that much money on herself, certainly not as long as there was any life left in the black bag Callie had been carrying as long as Frances had known her.

'I bought it,' Callie confessed. 'And I'm already wondering whether I was mad to do it. But I did need a new one.' She told her, then, about the theft of her old stalwart.

'But that's dreadful!'

Callie sighed. 'It wasn't the bag so much, or even the inconvenience of having to make all the phone calls and go to the police. It was the things I can't replace.' She hesitated, looking miserable. 'I just hate to tell you, Fran. The prayer book was in it. The one you gave me. I've always carried it with me, and now it's...gone. I'm so sorry.'

Frances felt a stab of regret, quickly masked with a brisk shake of her head. 'It doesn't matter,' she said. 'I'll get you another one.'

'But that book meant something to me. And to you.' Tears welled in Callie's eyes.

'Things,' Frances said firmly. 'Possessions. "Treasures on earth". We must never let them possess *us*.'

'That's what I tell myself. But I can't help it.' Callie fumbled in her pocket for a tissue and dabbed at her eyes.

At least, thought Frances, it explained why she hadn't heard from Callie in more than a day. She'd been expecting Callie to call round and take Bella for a walk; now she knew there was a good reason why it hadn't happened.

Suddenly the trickle of Callie's tears turned into a flood. 'It was just a bag,' she sobbed. 'Just a book.'

Frances looked on with concern, sure with the instinct of a priest that there was more to it than that. 'There's something else, isn't there?' she probed. 'Tell me, Callie.'

Mark had expected that by now, five days after the tragedy, the media circus in front of the Bettses' townhouse would have dwindled. If anything, though, the numbers had increased, and there was a buzz of expectancy, even excitement, as he pushed his way through them to the front door.

He was taken aback to find Brenda Betts in a state of anger—and mightily relieved that it wasn't directed at him. He wouldn't have been all that surprised if it had been, after his dereliction of duty. But he seemed to have been forgiven for that.

Over the past days he'd seen Brenda in the grip of a variety of emotions: shock, raw grief, bewilderment, contrition, protective mother-love, defensiveness. This was the first time he'd seen her truly angry.

Ignoring his apologies and his proffered Tesco bags, she waved a tabloid newspaper at him. 'Have you seen this? The *Globe*?'

'No,' Mark admitted. Catching up on tabloid gossip was the last thing on his mind that morning.

'Jodee's mum rang, of course. Spiteful cow. I just couldn't believe it, not even when she read out every word. So I rang our Di and she brought it round, like. Had to get through that lot out there, and her photo will probably be in tomorrow's papers. "Baby killer's sister"!'

'What?' He wasn't following her at all, so he took the paper from her and glanced at the headline, then read through the story.

It was an appalling piece of sensationalist journalism—exactly what he would have expected from Lilith Noone and the *Globe*—but the facts were essentially correct, and that horrified Mark. So few people knew about the post-mortem findings. Did she think that he'd been the one who'd spilled the beans?

'Disloyalty,' Brenda spat, her arms flailing. 'When you think someone's on your side, and then they stab you in the back… People like that are dirt. Hanging's too good for them.'

'Mrs Betts, I didn't talk to the press,' Mark assured her. 'They didn't get this from me. I haven't discussed it with a soul.'

'I know that.' She gave him a scathing look. 'It was that Lilith Noone.'

'Yes, but…someone talked to her. This information…it's highly classified. Not many people…'

Brenda's arms dropped to her side. 'We thought she were our friend, like,' she said simply, the anger seemingly drained out of her. 'We trusted her.'

In an instant Mark understood: Brenda Betts herself, presumably along with Jodee and Chazz, had told Lilith Noone about the post-mortem x-rays. The sheer daft naivety of it stunned him into silence.

'We told her about them questions you asked us, if anybody shook Muffin. We was upset—I admit it. She were all sympathetic. Butter wouldn't melt, like. I never thought she'd do this to us.'

No wonder the feeding frenzy on the other side of the door had stepped up. This was going to get worse before it got better, Mark realised. And there wasn't much he could do about it.

Maybe a press statement. If he helped the Bettses to draft a statement, denying the allegations of shaking and asking to be left alone, and read it out to the gathered media…

It wouldn't satisfy them, and they wouldn't go away. Mark knew that. But it was something to do, something to distract Brenda for a short time.

She put the kettle on and made instant coffee, then they sat at the kitchen table with Mark's notebook. 'The Betts family deny…' he said as he wrote. 'Should we say "absolutely" deny?'

Brenda nodded. 'Yeah. That's good.'

Mark's phone rang, and taking it from his pocket he saw that it was Neville. Reluctantly he went out into the corridor to answer it, aware that he should have kept Neville informed of his whereabouts without being asked. 'Listen, Nev, I'm at the Bettses' house,' he said pre-emptively. 'I should have rung. They're pretty spun up about Lilith Noone. I suppose you've seen the *Globe*—'

Neville cut him off. 'Never mind about that.' He paused, then produced the words that were a horribly prophetic echo of Serena, the day before. 'Mark, mate,' he said. 'We have to talk. Now.'

Chapter Fourteen

Acting on a tip from the duty sergeant, Neville tracked Sid Cowley down in the forlorn little outside yard at the back of the station where smokers congregated. Knowing the extent of Sid's nicotine addiction, Neville reckoned he probably spent a fair amount of time there, now that the entire station was off-limits for smokers. That would explain why it had been so easy to avoid him over the past few days.

In the end, though, Sid Cowley didn't say a word. Not 'I told you so' or anything like it. Neville couldn't even detect a smirk, suppressed or not.

No, Sid greeted him without comment, and seemed happy to see him. 'I hope you have something we can get our teeth into, Guv,' he said. 'Things have been dead dull round here without you.'

'We're going to Clerkenwell.'

'Clerkenwell's a bit out of our patch,' Cowley observed.

'Isn't it just,' agreed Neville. 'But the bloke died in hospital down the road, so that makes him ours.'

Neville filled the sergeant in as he drove across town. 'Mark Lombardi's brother-in-law, which could be a bit awkward,' he said.

Mark hadn't taken the news well: either the fact that Joe di Stefano had been murdered, which he'd refused to believe, or his own suspension from work, which he had strenuously protested. 'Evans,' Neville had told him. 'Nothing to do with me, mate. I'm just passing along the word from on high.'

Mark had, though, told him where he could find the widow—at the family restaurant—and had said that he would meet them there.

'As long as you don't say anything to her before we get there,' Neville had warned him. 'I want to tell her myself.' It was essential that he be able to see her face when he told Serena di Stefano that her husband had been murdered.

'Not that I think she did it,' he said to Cowley, thinking aloud. 'Not necessarily.'

'But it usually is the wife, isn't it, Guv? Or someone in the immediate family. In cases like this. Poison and so forth.' Sid nodded sagely. 'Grieving widows—I never trust 'em.'

That said, Neville reflected, from what he had observed Cowley rather liked grieving widows, especially young and pretty ones. They seemed to bring out what little gallantry the man possessed.

'Mind if I have a fag?' Cowley asked.

Neville shrugged. As an ex-smoker himself, he was vociferously anti-smoking, but he was not actually averse to a bit of second-hand smoke from time to time. 'Kill yourself if you must. As long as you hold it out of the window,' he warned: theoretically the police car was an extension of the work-place and smoking was therefore prohibited. If they brought the car back stinking of stale tobacco, he would be the one who'd have to answer for it.

'Bloody fascists,' Cowley grumbled, rolling the window down. As they were pretty much stuck in slow-moving traffic on Oxford Street, hemmed in on all sides by red buses, that let in the exhaust fumes. 'Bloody diesel fumes are more likely to kill me than fags,' he added.

They arrived at La Venezia at the end of the lunch hour, just as the 'closed' sign was going up at the entrance, and managed to find a place to park on the street right in front of the restaurant, newly vacated by the last customer.

'Good timing,' said Neville, locking the car.

Cowley dropped what was left of his latest fag on the pavement and ground it out with his heel. 'Show time, then,' he said, with some relish—obviously looking forward to this more than Neville was.

Mark met them at the door and escorted them to a small private dining room, furnished with one long table and about a dozen chairs. 'I'll get Serena,' he said. 'There's no need for Mamma to know about this—it would upset her too much. She's in the kitchen, clearing up. And Pappa's helping.'

Neville forbore to say that Mr and Mrs Lombardi—Mamma and Pappa—would have to be questioned at some point as well; no member of the family was going to escape. And that included Mark.

But Serena was definitely the first order of business. The grieving widow, in Sid Cowley's parlance.

Mark brought her in and performed the introductions, almost as though he were the host at a posh dinner party. 'Detective Inspector Stewart, Detective Sergeant Cowley. My sister, Serena di Stefano.'

Neville nodded awkwardly at her and was aware that Sid was staring. She wasn't at all what he'd expected: not dark like Mark, but golden-haired and quite beautiful.

She regarded them levelly. 'How can I help you, gentlemen?'

'Mrs di Stefano,' Neville said, wanting to get it over with, 'there's no gentle way to say this. I'm sorry to have to tell you that your husband's death wasn't from natural causes—he was murdered.'

Her eyes widened. 'Joe? That's absurd. I was with him when he died. It was a heart attack.'

'A heart attack brought on by ethylene glycol poisoning.'

She frowned. 'Don't be ridiculous. Joe wasn't poisoned.' Turning to Mark, she said, 'Tell them, Marco. I don't know whose idea of a joke this is, but I don't find it very funny.'

Mark looked uncomfortable, glancing between his sister and Neville. 'They say the post-mortem results have confirmed it,' he told her.

'Ethylene glycol,' Neville repeated. 'Better known as anti-freeze. Do you keep anti-freeze in your home, Mrs di Stefano?

Or here, at your business? I believe it's used in industrial refrigeration units.'

'Certainly not!'

He'd talked to Hereward Rice, as Evans had suggested, and had even spent a few minutes on the internet checking the facts. Anti-freeze, it seems, has a sweet taste, not at all unpleasant, and can be administered rather easily by mixing it with various beverages. 'Did your husband drink anything before he was… taken ill?' He asked. 'To your knowledge?'

'No. Just…I don't know.'

'Was he taken ill at home? Or somewhere else?'

'At home,' she stated. 'He'd just come in from his run.'

Neville glanced at Cowley, who had taken out his notebook and was dutifully jotting it down.

'His breathing was funny,' Serena di Stefano went on. 'Ragged. He said he felt sick. Then he…collapsed. He was unconscious. I rang 999 straightaway.'

'And the paramedics came?'

'Yes. They said it was a heart attack. A heart attack.' She repeated it like a mantra. 'They took him to hospital. He died the next day. Another heart attack, and I was with him.'

'So you were with him when he had *both* heart attacks,' Sid Cowley chipped in for the first time.

She gave him a filthy look. 'I wasn't pouring poison—anti-freeze, or whatever—down his throat, if that's what you mean, sergeant.'

Neville interposed. 'Could you tell me who else was in the house when your husband was taken ill?'

'Just my daughter. Chiara. She's twel—thirteen,' Serena stated. 'And she didn't poison her father, either,' she added sarcastically. 'She adored him.'

'There wasn't a row or anything?' Cowley asked, unabashed. 'Teen-age stuff? I know that teen-aged girls can be funny.'

Neville hoped Sid wasn't going to tell one of his stories about his sister: they were without number, and all equally boring. Neville didn't like to think how many of them he'd endured over the years, from her first unsuitable boyfriend to her protracted and painful experiences in childbirth.

He thought that Serena di Stefano hesitated for a micro-second before she said, 'No. Not with her father. As I said, she adored him.'

'I'm afraid we'll need to talk to Chiara,' Neville said apologetically.

'She's just a child.' Her voice was sharp, protective.

'Serena can be with her when you talk to her, can't she?' Mark interposed.

'Of course.' Neville shot him a grateful look. 'And I'm afraid we'll have to search your home, Mrs di Stefano,' he added. 'I hope you understand.'

'You won't find anything,' she stated, defiant. 'You can search all you like. You won't find anything.'

Now came the hard part, the part he'd been dreading. 'Would you like to sit down, Mrs di Stefano?' he suggested, pulling out one of the chairs from round the table.

'No,' she said, but she sat anyway, as if aware that something unpleasant was about to unfold.

'You know I have to ask you this. How was your relationship with your husband?'

'I loved him,' she said simply, not at all defensive now. 'We were married for twenty-two years.'

'And you didn't have any problems?' Neville thought, unbid-den, about Triona, and realised what a stupid question it was. How could anyone be married for longer than about five minutes and not have problems? Let alone twenty-two years. 'More than normal, anyway,' he amended.

Serena turned and looked at Mark; he gave her a little nod and put a hand on her shoulder. She sat for a moment, scarcely moving a muscle, then spoke quietly. 'He was having an affair,' she said. 'With one of his students. We rowed about it when I found out, a few months ago. I was…hurt. I felt betrayed.' She raised her chin and her eyes met Neville's. 'But I loved Joe. Always. Even when he hurt me.'

Neville waited. Bloody hell, he thought. Why didn't Mark tell me?

'Inspector Stewart,' she said, enunciating carefully, 'Let me make one thing very clear. I did not kill my husband.'

Lilith felt as if she was floating on a cloud of happiness.

Her work day had begun with a summons into the boss' office, but it couldn't have been more different than the day before.

'You've played a blinder,' Rob Gardiner-Smith said with relish. 'Your story's blown the competition out of the water. I knew you could do it.'

Mixed metaphors, thought Lilith, even as she allowed herself to smile in acknowledgement. And hadn't he changed his tune?

'We had to go back for an extra print run,' Gardiner-Smith exulted. 'It's selling like hot-cakes.'

He'd given her an assignment for the day: while the rest of the tabloids were playing catch-up, she was to re-write and amplify the 'shaken to death' story for tomorrow's front page, and do another story for the inside centrefold. That was to be a retrospective on Jodee and Chazz, into which they'd drop lots of photos. 'A recap of the whole story,' he said. '"The rise and fall of a celebrity couple" sort of thing.' And, he'd added, when she'd finished that, Lilith was to go home and put her feet up. 'You've earned a few hours off.'

She'd knocked off the two stories—it hadn't taken her very long—and had left the *Globe* offices before midday. On her way home she'd stopped for lunch. She'd considered going to an elegant little bistro, but in the end she chose a much more down-market cafe, where the patrons were more likely to be discussing subjects close to her heart. Indeed, from the snatches of conversation she could overhear all round her as she tucked into her fry-up, Jodee and Chazz were the topic of the day. 'Who would of thought they could of done that? It's unnatural.' 'Poor

little mite, that Muffin. I always did worry about her, you know.'
'I never trusted that Jodee. She looks hard.'

At home she indulged in a prolonged bubble bath, ignoring
the phone when it rang, getting out only when the water cooled.
She wrapped herself in a fluffy towel, deliciously warm from the
heated towel rail, then swapped it for her cosiest dressing gown.

Time to check her phone messages.

The first one was from Addie McLean, editor of *HotStuff* magazine. 'Ring me,' she said succinctly, and added her number.

The second one surprised her, if only because, in her experience, he was so taciturn. 'It's Chazz,' the voice said. 'Mum's
that upset. Couldn't trust herself to ring, could she? And
Jodee—you've broke her heart, like. She can't stop crying. We
thought you was our friend, like.' There was a pause, as if he were
considering his next words, then he spoke softly but precisely.
'I hope you're happy, you effin' bitch.'

Taking a quick, temporary leave of Serena, Mark caught up with
Neville and Cowley at their car.

'You won't need to drive,' he said. 'The house is just round
the corner. I'd leave the car where it is.'

'Thanks,' said Neville. He wasn't smiling as he re-locked the
car. 'Any reason why you didn't tell me about the affair?'

'She needed to tell you herself,' Mark said defensively.

'It would have helped if I'd known.'

Mark recognised the truth of that, even as he tried to explain.
'I knew she'd tell you. And if she didn't...well, of course I would
have.'

'Is there anything else you haven't told me?' Neville crossed
his arms and looked at him.

'The girl. I can give you her name.' Mark didn't understand
why, a few minutes ago, when Neville had asked Serena for the
girl's name, she'd said she didn't know. Had she really blotted
it so successfully from her mind? She had certainly known it at
one time.

Cowley got out his notebook and waited.

'It's Samantha,' Mark said.

'That narrows it down,' Neville said sarcastically.

Mark prodded at his memory, thinking back to when Serena had first told him. 'I believe her surname is Winter.'

'We'll ask at the university. I'm sure we'll be able to track her down.'

'You can find her more easily than that,' Mark suddenly recalled. '"Junior Idol". She's one of the contestants.'

That elicited an instant reaction from Cowley. 'Bloody hell! Samantha!'

Neville turned and stared at him. 'You're not a "Junior Idol" fan, Sid?'

'I do watch it now and then,' Cowley muttered, as an improbable flush crept up from his neck.

'I would have thought you'd have better things to do on a Saturday night.' Neville grinned, seeming to enjoy the sergeant's discomfiture.

'Samantha,' Cowley repeated, ignoring him. 'Guv, she's hot. I mean really hot.'

'Your point being?'

'This di Stefano bloke. He was…what? Forty-four, forty-five? How would an old bloke like that pull a hottie like Samantha?'

Neville glared at him; Mark knew him well enough to realise what that was about. Neville, as he drew dangerously close to the dreaded age of forty, was very sensitive about the issue of age, especially with the not-yet-thirty Sid Cowley. 'There's no accounting for taste,' Neville said coldly. 'I believe there are some girls who even fancy *you*, Sid.'

'Quite a few, as a matter of fact.' Cowley gave a smug smile, confident of his own attractiveness. 'Let me have a go at Samantha, Guv. I'll show you how it's done.'

Neville raised his eyebrows. *Over my dead body*, his expression said.

Mark brought the subject back to his real purpose in following Neville to the car. 'There's something else I wanted to mention,' he said. 'The girls. Chiara and Angelina. I realise you have to talk to them, but…be careful, please. They don't know anything about their dad's affair. About the problems between their parents. Neither do Mamma and Pappa. Serena's done everything possible to keep them all from finding out. She's just carried on as normal with Joe. For the sake of the family.' He didn't know how she'd done it, as a matter of fact. He—her brother—was the only one who was aware of what was going on. The only person she could talk to.

But now—now that Joe was dead—would it be possible to keep her secret? Murder: it had a way of laying things bare, of dredging up things that had been long submerged in the deep waters of secrecy.

Mark didn't particularly care about protecting Joe, in death. It was too late for that, and Joe had made his own bed. But he cared deeply about protecting Serena—and perhaps even more about protecting the two innocent girls who thought that their father had been a good and honourable man, faithful to a marriage that was as near as possible to being perfect.

'If there's any way you can keep them from finding out…' he pleaded.

Neville stared at him. 'That might not be possible. A man's been murdered. We have to find out who killed him. And other people might get hurt.' He reached out a hand and touched Mark on the arm, not without a certain gentleness. 'You know that as well as anyone, mate.'

Lilith knew she shouldn't have been surprised by Chazz's phone message, and in one way she wasn't. His reaction was predictable, even understandable. What surprised her more was her own reaction.

She was quite frankly shaken by his venom. It took the shine off her day of triumph; it let the air out of her balloon of euphoria.

And it made her think about the dilemma she'd been firmly pushing out of her mind all day.

What was she going to do now?

Now that she'd killed the goose that laid the golden eggs, now that she'd burnt her bridges, and now that she had churned out the definitive re-hash of the story of Jodee and Chazz—from its literally steamy beginnings to its tragic down-spiral—there was nothing else to say.

Yes, the other papers were, as Rob Gardiner-Smith described it, now playing catch-up. But when the next chapters in the story unfolded—the funeral, the resumption of the inquest— they would all be on an even playing field. No advantages for Lilith any more. Nothing but her cunning and her journalistic skills to fall back on.

And the free-lance story Addie McLean had commissioned for *HotStuff* magazine? The insider account of Muffin's funeral? Toast.

Dejected, she picked up the phone and dialled Addie McLean's number. She might as well get it over with.

'Thanks for returning my call,' Addie McLean said. 'I wanted to congratulate you on your story. "Shaken to Death?"—it was dynamite.'

'Thanks,' Lilith acknowledged, then pre-empted what she was sure was coming next. 'But about the inside story on the funeral—I don't think I'll be able to do it.'

Addie McLean gave a dry laugh. 'I shouldn't imagine so.'

'I'm sorry to let you down.'

'Never mind about that.' She made a dismissive noise, blowing it off. 'Small potatoes. That's not why I wanted to talk to you, Lilith.'

'It's not?'

'No. I was really impressed by your gutsiness. You went for it, no holds barred. And as I read that article, I realised that your talents are wasted in tabloid journalism—even on a paper as sleazy as the *Globe*.'

'They are?' She couldn't figure out whether she was meant to be flattered or insulted by that.

'You've got balls, Lilith,' Addie McLean declared, in a way that left no doubt she was paying her a massive compliment. 'The kind of balls we need at *HotStuff.*' She paused, and when Lilith didn't say anything she went on. 'What I'm saying is that I'm offering you a job. Full time, on the staff. If you want it. And what ever Gardiner-Smith is paying you, we'll beat it. Can't say fairer than that.'

Now he knew for sure why he'd been so reluctant to take on this case, Neville realised. It was going to be messy. No matter how carefully he handled it, Mark wasn't going to be happy. Mixing work and friendship was a recipe for disaster.

How could he possibly do a thorough job, ask all the questions he needed to ask, without letting those girls know that their adored father was something other than they thought him to be?

It was inevitable. Murder didn't allow people to hang on to illusions. And the truth often hurt.

But he could at least delay the inevitable by a few minutes. He would give Serena di Stefano a chance to get home and prepare her daughters for the arrival of the police.

Neville stopped on the pavement before he got to the di Stefano house and switched his phone on. He had turned it off so it wouldn't interrupt their interview with Mrs di Stefano; now he could make use of the hiatus to put some things in motion. 'Go ahead and have a fag,' he said to Cowley. 'You know you want to.'

Cowley lit up with alacrity while Neville rang the officer in charge of the Scene of Crime team. 'We'll need a thorough search of the house,' he explained. 'I'll meet the SOCOs there. We'll be looking for ethylene glycol, and anything else that's relevant. And we'll need to search his office, as well,' he added. 'At the university. Computer, diary, papers.'

His phone beeped at him: a missed call. 'Damn,' said Neville, accessing the voice mail.

'Mr Stewart? This is Andrew Linton,' said a plaintive voice. 'I've been trying to reach you. You haven't signed the papers, and I have three people who want to view your flat this afternoon. I've arranged the viewings for half-past three, four o'clock, and half past. If you can't meet them at the flat, could you at least drop off the keys at the office? I'll be waiting to hear from you.'

Neville looked at his watch: nearly four o'clock. 'Bloody hell,' he said. Andrew's office was at the other end of all the Oxford Street traffic they'd fought through to get here, now undoubtedly even worse as it headed into rush hour. Why hadn't he thought to stop off on their way to Clerkenwell?

Well, there was nothing he could do about it now.

And there was one more phone call he needed to make.

If ever there was a family that required the most sensitive and discreet of family liaison officers, it was the di Stefanos. 'Yolanda Fish,' he said aloud as he found the number.

◇◇◇

Sharing a quick cup of coffee with her husband in the police station canteen was a simple pleasure, but one which DC Yolanda Fish genuinely savoured. It was one of the bonuses of her second career as a Family Liaison Officer: seeing more of Eli, when their schedules coincided and they both happened to be in the station at the same time.

Their marriage was a rarity, in Yolanda's experience—a union of many years' duration and truly happy. They were more that just lovers: they were best friends as well. The only shadow over the marriage, the thing which kept it from being perfect, was the tragedy of childlessness. Much as they'd tried, they'd not had children, and for one with as deep a maternal craving as Yolanda possessed, that was tragedy indeed. She had compensated for the lack in the choice of her first career: as a midwife, she had brought many hundreds of babies into the world.

Then, after the Stephen Lawrence inquiry, which had recommended the recruiting of liaison officers from the minority community, she had been encouraged by Eli to change careers. Different as this job was from midwifery, she enjoyed it very much and found it provided an equally satisfying outlet for her nurturing skills. She was demonstrably good at it, and consequently much in demand, especially when the family in question included children.

'What are you going to make for supper tonight, doll?' Eli asked. In the division of labours in their household, Eli left the cooking to her. Fortunately Yolanda didn't mind; she enjoyed cooking when she had the time to do it properly.

Yolanda consulted her watch. 'If I get out of here on time, I'll pick up a chicken at the supermarket.'

'Tell you what, doll. How about I take you out for a meal? That new Thai restaurant, maybe?'

'You're on,' she agreed.

'Did I tell you how hot you're looking today?' Eli reached across the table and playfully tweaked one of her many little braids.

'All right, now I'm suspicious. Just exactly what are you after, Eli Fish?' She shook her head, making the braids dance. 'Bribing me with Thai food and dishing out compliments—what's up with you?'

'You malign me, doll. I'm hurt.' Eli put his hand over his heart melodramatically. 'Aren't I allowed to spoil you a bit?'

'Or maybe you're feeling guilty,' Yolanda suggested. 'I saw the way you looked at that new WPC. Have you been flirting with her or something?'

They both knew she was teasing; Eli had a well-deserved reputation as the most uxorious of men, who never looked at another woman. If he did look at them, it was only to compare them unfavourably with his wife. 'That skinny little thing?' he scoffed. 'Not an ounce of meat on her bones.'

Yolanda wasn't fat, but she was statuesque: tall, broad-hipped, full-breasted. That, she knew, was the way Eli liked her. Womanly, he called it. And she liked him just the way he was as well—large-framed, with a shiny shaved head and a trim moustache.

She'd put her phone on the table; they both jumped slightly when it rang. Eli frowned as Yolanda reached for it.

'Yolanda? It's Neville Stewart. I hope you didn't have any plans for this evening.' He filled her in; she scribbled the information on a paper serviette.

'Sorry, babe. No Thai tonight,' she said to Eli when she'd finished. The look of disappointment on his face made her feel just a bit guilty, but she couldn't help the little thrill of excitement that always accompanied a new assignment.

'No worries, doll,' he grinned. 'I guess I could always take that WPC out instead. Fatten her up a bit, you know?'

◇◇◇

By the time Neville drove back across town, rush hour was long since over. Red buses still plied Oxford Street in their numbers, but at least the traffic wasn't bumper-to-bumper.

It had started to rain, which was bad news for Sid Cowley. Every time he put his fag out of the window it fizzled out; eventually he gave up and sat in bad-tempered silence.

Neville tried to draw him out. 'Quite an evening, eh, Sid?'

'I suppose.' He turned a packet of fags round in his hands, shook one out, then put it back in again.

'What did you make of her? Mark's sister?'

Cowley shrugged. 'A cool customer, I thought. Bit of a cold fish.'

Neville agreed: for someone who had just been told that her husband had been murdered, she was remarkably composed. No hysteria, just consistent denials. Admittedly she'd had a couple of days to get used to the fact that her husband was dead, but…

'That Angelina,' Cowley volunteered. 'Phoar.'

'A pretty girl,' Neville concurred. Not yet beautiful, in his opinion. She was like a younger version of her mother, with as yet just the promise of her mother's beauty.

Did that mean he was really getting old, to prefer the mature charms of Serena to her daughter's youthful freshness? God help him.

He was a married man, he reminded himself. He shouldn't be thinking about either one of them in that way. Leave that to Sid…

Sid, to give him credit, had been the one who had found it. The bottle—almost certainly the murder weapon. While the

SOCOs had scurried round looking in cupboards and under beds, Sid had spotted it.

It had been in plain sight, in the house's small entrance hall. There was a table at the foot of the stairs to collect keys, post, and daily detritus, and on it, amongst the other things, was a bottle—a Lucozade bottle, the sort athletes and runners used to keep themselves hydrated. Sid had unscrewed the top and sniffed it. 'Lucozade,' he said. 'Just like it says on the tin. But isn't there something else as well?'

Neville took it from him and gave a sniff. Anti-freeze—he'd swear it.

The SOCOs had bagged it up and taken it away for analysis, but Neville would bet a week's wages that it was the murder weapon.

An elegant way to kill someone, he admitted to himself with sneaking admiration. Someone who went running every morning, anyway. Just pour out a bit of the Lucozade and replace it with anti-freeze. The taste wouldn't be very noticeable, and by the time the runner had taken a few slugs, it would be too late. An ounce or two of anti-freeze could be fatal.

And unless the killer left fingerprints all over the bottle— which hardly seemed likely, in a crime so beautifully planned—it would be almost impossible to catch him. Or her. Anyone could have done it, then ditched the tell-tale bottle of anti-freeze in any kerbside bin or skip in town. Well in advance, even, knowing that sooner or later…

But the fact was that the wife was far and away the best suspect. She knew her husband's habits; she would have had access to his supply of Lucozade. And she had motive. The classic motive, the old favourite. The green-eyed monster.

'Do you think she did it, Sid?' Neville asked.

'Angelina? But she wasn't even at home. She's been away at uni in Birmingham since after Christmas.'

Still thinking about Angelina, Neville realised, bemused. While his own ruminations had ranged far beyond, Sid was still fantasizing about that girl.

'I meant her mother,' he explained. 'The grieving widow, as you put it.'

Cowley shrugged. 'I'd lay money on it. She didn't seem very grieving to me. And she had the best reason to do it, if he was shagging Samantha Winter. The lucky bugger,' he added.

'Lucky? Sid, he's *dead*!'

'Oh, well, yeah. But at least he must have died happy.' He grinned.

Neville dropped the sergeant off at the police station, where he'd left his car.

'See you in the morning, Guv,' Cowley said, sounding eager rather than jaded.

He must be looking forward to interviewing the dead man's mistress, Neville realised. That wasn't going to happen: he was determined not to let Sid Cowley within a mile of Samantha Winter. There were plenty of other things he could send his keen young sergeant to follow up on. But he didn't have the heart to tell him that now, Neville decided: he'd let Sid enjoy his wet dreams of Samantha for one night. 'I'll be in touch,' he said cryptically.

Unable to face the Tube journey, and knowing that he'd need the police car in the morning, Neville drove it home to Shepherd's Bush, and miraculously found a place to park it on the street.

He climbed the stairs, let himself into the flat, and resisted the temptation to collapse on the sofa: if he did that, he'd never get up again. He was knackered, and he was hungry; he couldn't remember the last meal he'd eaten.

But he didn't possess the energy even to scramble an egg. Neville poured himself a bowl of cornflakes and ate them quickly, standing up.

God, he missed Triona: the thought came unbidden to his mind. He didn't want to think about her. Not now. But if she'd been here, waiting for him...

Not allowing himself to mull over the wisdom of it, he picked up his phone and rang her mobile number.

There was no answer.

Of course not.

But when it went to voice mail, instead of hanging up, he left a message.

'It's me. I'm thinking about you,' he said quietly. 'I miss you. I…I love you.'

Callie got into her pyjamas, cleaned her teeth, washed her face, and applied some moisturiser, then switched off the overhead light and climbed into bed. Inevitably she rolled into the crevasse in the middle, where she curled up under the covers.

She missed Bella, that warm little black-and-white body who snuggled against her so comfortingly when Callie was in need of a cuddle.

Callie closed her eyes and listened to the rain slapping against the window. The sound was hypnotic, even soothing, and Callie hoped it would soon lull her to sleep. Sleep, where she could escape from the memory of what she'd done.

She had told Frances.

Even now she couldn't believe she'd done it. She'd told Frances about Marco's phone call, asking her to stay clear of the di Stefanos. Under Frances' gentle probing, she'd confessed the hurt she'd been bottling up, trying not to think about.

She'd cried, as well: not just a few trickles but hot, scalding tears, mourning for a relationship she'd thought was so strong, so promising. 'He said he loved me,' she wept. 'How could he do that if he really did? How could he shut me out like that?'

'His sister's put him in a difficult position,' Frances pointed out. 'Right in the middle.'

'Yes, but he chose *her*. He's taken her side.'

That was what really hurt: when confronted with a choice, Marco had sided with Serena.

His bloody family, Callie told herself savagely. Always his family. She should have known it would be like that, from the beginning.

She should have run a mile, as soon as he'd told her about *la famiglia*—Mamma and Pappa and beloved Serena. The very fact that it had taken him so many months to get round to introducing her to them…

It should have been a warning. But by then she'd already started falling in love with him.

She'd been on the rebound, she reminded herself. Deeply hurt when Adam broke their engagement, she'd fallen for the first man who'd come along and shown some interest in her.

Just her luck that it was Marco, an Italian man who was still tied to his mamma's apron strings, who dropped everything and ran whenever his sister needed him.

Yes, he was undeniably gorgeous. Yes, he was funny and sweet and thoughtful. Yes, he made her insides turn to jelly when he kissed her. Yes, he said he loved her.

But they weren't engaged. He hadn't asked her to marry him. There was nothing formal between them. Nothing but the love, the warmth, the wanting to be together…

Maybe, Callie told herself sternly, there in the dark in the middle of the world's most uncomfortable bed, it was for the best. Best that they broke it off now, before they were in any deeper.

His family would always come first. When push came to shove, he would always choose them over her. And she didn't need that.

He said he'd ring. He hadn't rung.

The wind picked up; the rain increased in intensity.

Eventually, emotionally exhausted, Callie cried herself to sleep.

Chapter Fifteen

First thing on Thursday morning, Neville made the necessary phone calls. He rang the TV network which aired 'Junior Idol'; they referred him to Reality Bites, the production company. Eventually tracking down the producer of the show, Neville explained that he needed to interview Samantha Winter on an urgent police matter.

'Good Lord,' said the producer in a stunned voice. 'What's she done? Drugs? Drink driving? Bloody hell! Not before the final!'

'Nothing like that,' Neville assured him.

'Can't it wait till next week?'

'I'm afraid not.'

'But she's in rehearsals all day,' the man protested. 'It's only two days till the final!'

Neville put on his sternest official police voice. 'I'm investigating a homicide, sir. Miss Winter is an important witness, and it's essential that I interview her today.'

'Oh, well,' the producer said weakly. 'If you go to the studio, you might be able to catch her between rehearsals. I'd appreciate it if you tried not to upset her too much,' he added. 'Not so close to the final.'

'Heaven forbid that a murder investigation should stand in the way of the "Junior Idol" final,' Neville muttered to himself when he'd obtained directions to the studio and instructions about getting through security.

Then he made another phone call, imparting the bad news to Sid Cowley. 'I have an important assignment for you, Sid,' he said. 'Go to the university. To di Stefano's office, to his department. Talk to as many people as you can—colleagues, staff, secretaries, students. Get a feel for what they thought of him. Try to find out—without giving anything away—if people knew about him and Samantha Winter. Or him and anyone else, for that matter,' added Neville. 'If he was sleeping with one of his students, how likely is it that she was the only one? He's probably been shagging pretty girls for years—Mark seemed to think so. Track them down. Talk to them.'

'But…what about Samantha, Guv?' Cowley protested. 'Isn't it important to interview her?'

'Don't you worry your pretty little head about that, Sid.' Neville gave a dry chuckle. 'I'll deal with Samantha.'

First, though, he had to deal with Andrew Linton.

He drove the police car to Paddington and pulled up on a double yellow just outside of the estate agents' office. The traffic wardens wouldn't dare ticket a police car, and he intended to be quick about it.

The secretary waved him through to Andrew's desk.

'Mr Stewart!' said Andrew, rising from his chair. 'I've been trying to get in touch! Didn't you get my messages?'

'Sorry. Urgent police business. A murder to investigate.'

Mollified, Andrew subsided into the chair. He spread out the papers on his desk and began to explain them. 'This is the sole agency agreement. That means—'

'Never mind.' Neville got out his pen and scribbled a signature on each document, then dropped his spare set of keys on the desk.

'Don't you want to check the draft details?' Andrew flapped them at him.

'I trust you,' Neville assured him. 'I've got to run,' he added. 'Keep in touch.'

◇◇◇

After Morning Prayer, Callie made her excuses to Brian: she just couldn't face breakfast at the vicarage, though she didn't tell him that. She didn't have much of an appetite anyway, and the thought of munching cornflakes under Jane's beady eye was less than appealing.

The rain had recently stopped, leaving London looking new-washed and fresh, and there was a promise of spring in the mild temperatures which followed the rain. Callie thought she might go to Frances' and take Bella for a walk, but first she wanted to stop at the newsagents' to check out the latest coverage of the Bettses.

Most of the papers—all of the tabloids—had front-page stories on variations of 'shaken to death'. A banner at the top of the *Daily Globe* said 'Inside: Exclusive. Jodee and Chazz - The Whole Story', by Lilith Noone'.

Callie bought a copy and took it into the nearest Starbucks, where, baffled by the proliferation of choices, she ordered something at random—a regular house blend latte—and settled down in an armchair to read her newspaper. She was, she realised, probably one of the few people in the United Kingdom whose knowledge of Jodee and Chazz—up until a few days ago—was limited to recognition of their names and their faces. She felt this put her at a real disadvantage in her dealings with them, and was thankful to the *Globe* for giving her an opportunity to catch up with things it might be helpful for her to know about them.

It was a centrefold story, liberally illustrated with photos.

'A little over a year ago,' she read, 'Jodee Fuller was working as a nail technician at a beauty salon in Newcastle, specialising in nail extensions and French manicures. After growing up in Lamesley, a village to the the south of the River Tyne, Jodee left her home and family behind at the age of sixteen, attracted by the bright lights of the city. With her went her boyfriend from school, Darren Shotton, who works as a garage mechanic. They shared a small one-bedroom flat in Newcastle for nearly four years.

'In an exclusive interview last summer, while Jodee was in the "twentyfour/seven" house, Darren talked about their relationship. "Jodee's a right fit lass," he said. "She's brilliant—a real goer. Always up for it, whether it's drinking, dancing, partying, shagging. We was cracking together. But I always knew it couldn't last—me and her. She was too big for Lamesley. She was too big for Newcastle. All she could ever talk about was going to London, being rich and famous. Getting on 'twentyfour/seven' was, like, destiny. I wish her well, but I miss her." Darren has since moved back to Lamesley.

'In contrast, removal man Chazz Betts auditioned for "twentyfour/seven" on the urging of his mates—"for a laugh, like". London born and bred, Chazz lived with his mother Brenda on a Westbourne Green council estate. His father abandoned the family when Chazz and his twin sister were babies, and his mother worked as a cleaner to support the family. But handsome Chazz captured the imagination of the nation, who voted in their millions to make him the winner of "twentyfour/seven", at the same time that he captured the love of Jodee Fuller.

'Now, wildly rich from prize money, product endorsements and modelling jobs, Chazz and Jodee share a posh house in tony Bayswater. A perfect couple, you might think.

'But behind the perfection, behind the wealth, there is a story of heartbreak and tragedy…'

Callie skipped across to a sidebar story about Jodee's best friend in Newcastle, a hairdresser called Kim who had been responsible for the famous bi-coloured, asymmetrical bob. 'She wanted something that would set her apart, like,' Kim was quoted. 'And I think it did, if I say it myself. But once she got famous, she forgot about all her mates up north. I haven't heard from her since the wedding. I hope she's happy.' The story was accompanied by dramatic before-and-after photos: Jodee with forgettable dishwater blonde tresses hanging lankly to her shoulders, and Jodee as she was now, instantly recognisable.

Callie's phone rang and she reached for her new bag.

The number was one she didn't recognise—from another mobile, she noted as she answered it. 'Hello?'

'Callie?' said a whispered voice. 'It's Chiara.'

Oh, no. She hadn't prepared herself for this; hadn't decided what she'd say in case Chiara rang her. 'Oh…hi,' she managed.

'I've borrowed my friend's phone,' Chiara added. 'Mum won't let me have one. She says I'm too young. But I need to see you.'

'I'm not sure…'

Chiara cut over her. 'I'm allowed out of school at lunch time. Could you meet me by the school gates?'

Deciding that honesty was the best approach, Callie took a deep breath. 'Listen, Chiara. Your mother doesn't want me to talk to you.'

'I know that.' Chiara snorted impatiently. 'She told me. You're not of our faith, and all that rubbish.'

'Don't you think you should respect your mother's wishes? You could ask to see your priest.'

'You don't understand.' Chiara gulped, sounding on the edge of tears. 'I *have* to talk to you. Everything's changed now. Dad's not just *dead*. He was murdered.'

'*What?*'

'The police were here. They wouldn't tell me why, but I know what that means. Someone killed him, Callie.'

◇◇◇

It took Neville nearly an hour to drive to the 'Junior Idol' studio, on the suburban fringes of north London. He didn't mind the drive or the solitude; it gave him the opportunity to reflect on the strangeness of this case. It was, he reckoned, extremely unlikely that it would ever be solved. Unless they found a half-empty bottle of anti-freeze in someone's possession, covered with fingerprints, there was little chance they'd be able to tie the poisoning to anyone.

Well, he would go through the motions and do the best he could.

This, at least, would be a diversion.

The studio complex was tucked behind heavy security gates. Neville showed his warrant card and was eventually waved through, with directions to the building he wanted, then he left the car in a vast car park and went through the security routine yet again at the door.

He asked for the producer of 'Junior Idol', but after much shaking of heads and conferring he was eventually handed over into the care of a production assistant. His keeper was a willowy young man in tight black jeans and a black 'Junior Idol' tee shirt, from whom Neville was unsurprised to receive a limp-wristed handshake. Neville didn't usually trust stereotypes, but every once in a while, he thought, amused, they proved themselves true.

'I'm Tarquin,' said the young man, without apology or even a trace of irony.

'DI Stewart. And I need to talk to Samantha Winter. I'm investigating a homicide,' he added.

'Oooh, Sam never killed anyone?' It was a question rather than a statement; Tarquin's eyelids fluttered in excitement.

'She's a material witness. An important one.'

Tarquin's brow creased. 'This isn't going to get into the papers, is it?'

'I sincerely hope not,' Neville assured him.

'Well, you can't talk to her right now.' The young man consulted a clipboard, shaking his head. 'She's rehearsing. She'll probably be finished in...oh, say, twenty minutes. Then she'll go to her dressing room for a break. I suppose you can talk to her then. If you must.'

Fortunately Neville wasn't in a hurry. 'Is there somewhere I can wait?'

'Well, I can get you a cup of coffee and find you a seat somewhere. Or,' Tarquin added, 'if you like, you could slip into the studio and watch for a bit.'

'Watch the rehearsal?' Why not? thought Neville. This was a world with which he was totally unfamiliar. Why not soak up a bit of the atmosphere? Besides, it would give him something to tell Sid Cowley about. Rub it in a bit, if he was feeling particularly sadistic. 'Yes, all right,' he agreed.

Tarquin put a finger to his lips. 'Quiet, then,' he whispered. 'Quiet as a mouse.' He led Neville down a corridor and opened a door, then beckoned him to follow into the darkness beyond.

It was a large studio—much larger than Neville had expected, more like a theatre than an intimate rehearsal space, with a stage and a great deal of fixed seating.

And the noise! A group of musicians, heavily amplified, flanked the stage and whaled away at their instruments, while a young woman in the centre sang into a microphone.

Tarquin touched Neville's arm—Neville tried not to flinch—and guided him to a seat in the back row. It was difficult to see; the stage was illuminated with overhead lights and spotlights, but the rest of the vast room was in darkness. Neville groped his way into his designated seat, and was rather relieved to realise that Tarquin wasn't planning to remain with him. The young man leaned over and breathed, rather than whispered, into his ear. 'Enjoy. I'll come back for you.'

Enjoy. Neville intended to do just that with this welcome break from routine. He was willing to bet that Sid Cowley wouldn't be the only one of his colleagues to be jealous of this opportunity to enter, if just for a few minutes, a world that most people saw only from the outside.

He wasn't actually a fan of pop music; Neville's passion was for traditional Irish music, with occasional forays into jazz. He didn't recognise the song Samantha was singing, but could tell she was singing it well. Her voice, he reckoned, was a good one, if not truly great: she had a broad range, swooping effortlessly from high notes to low ones, and a pure tone, without vibrato. She sold the song well, too, strutting across the stage with a sassy bounce and then staring soulfully out across the dark, empty chairs.

And as for her appearance…

That was something Neville did feel competent to pass judgement on, as a long-time connoisseur of female beauty. And in that arena, Samantha was truly astonishing. She was, in his expert opinion, breathtakingly lovely. Creamy skin, huge eyes, a tumble of blond hair, and a figure to match, clad in low-slung tight jeans and a midriff-baring top. God, she was gorgeous. Neville didn't care whether she could sing or not: he could have sat there and watched her for hours.

But after she'd been through the song a few more times, and stood centre stage for comments from her vocal coach, Samantha disappeared from view. A moment later Tarquin was back at Neville's elbow. 'Come with me,' he beckoned.

Neville followed him through a maze of endless corridors. 'You haven't told her, have you? Why I'm here?'

'No worries. I've watched enough cop shows.'

They reached a door with Samantha's name on it and Tarquin gave a tap.

'Yes?' called a voice from within.

'Sam, it's Tarquin. I've brought someone to talk to you.'

'Come in, then.'

Tarquin nodded at him to open the door before slipping away.

She was rather artfully arranged on a chaise longue, a glass of water in one hand while the other hand played with her hair. Looking up at Neville, she gave him a beguiling smile and gestured to a chair. 'I'm Samantha,' she said. 'What's your name? And what paper are you with?'

Neville took his time replying, partly for effect and partly so he could just look at her.

Up close, he could see that a measure of her beauty was attributable to artifice—the expertise of her makeup people. But she was still a stunning example of female pulchritude, and he wondered about the question Sid Cowley had posed: what had she seen in the middle-aged Joe di Stefano?

'I'm Detective Inspector Neville Stewart,' he said at last. 'With the Metropolitan Police.'

She frowned. 'Not a journalist?'

'No.' Neville sat down. 'I'd like to ask you a few questions, Miss Winter.'

'Sam. Everyone calls me Sam.' She'd seemingly recovered from her surprise and smiled at him prettily.

'Sam. Are you aware that your…professor, Mr Joe di Stefano, is dead?'

She bit her lip. 'I'd heard that. It's a shame. Very sad.'

Not exactly the reaction he would have expected from a bereaved lover, Neville observed. Maybe she was a good actress as well as a talented singer. He plunged ahead. 'I need to ask you about your relationship with Mr di Stefano. Or was he Dr di Stefano?'

For a moment she just stared at him. 'You're sure you're not from the press? You're not going to sell them my story?'

He took out his warrant card and showed it to her.

Samantha was silent for another few seconds, then gave a small shrug. 'I suppose enough people knew about it,' she said. 'It wasn't a very well-kept secret. We were a bit careless. Even his wife knew.'

'So you confirm that you and Joe di Stefano were…lovers.'

'There's no point denying it. But,' she added, 'it was over. Weeks ago.'

That made sense: with the press avidly watching the "Junior Idol" contestants, they'd probably had to cool it when the show began. 'Which one of you broke it off?' he asked.

'I did. It had run its course. And I'd met someone else.' Samantha smiled to herself.

'And who is that, Miss…Sam?'

Her smile disappeared. 'That's none of your business.' She narrowed her eyes and stared at him. 'What is this all about, Inspector? Why are you asking me these questions? I didn't do anything illegal. Stupid, maybe, but not illegal. I slept with Joe di Stefano for a while, then broke it off, and now he's dead. End of story.'

'Not quite the end of the story,' Neville said evenly. 'Joe di Stefano was murdered.'

'Jesus.' Her eyes widened; she pursed her lips into an O and exhaled in a long breath. 'But…I thought it was a heart attack. That's what I was told.'

'Poison.' Neville decided not to elaborate; it was best if the exact details weren't made public just yet. 'So you can see why I have to talk to everyone who knew him…as well as you did.'

Samantha took a sip of her water, put the glass down on a nearby table, then leaned back in the chaise, twirling her hair round her finger. 'No one knew him as well as I did. Not for those few months, anyway.'

Neville didn't understand it. 'But…why? I mean, why would *you*…?'

'He listened,' she said simply. 'Joe di Stefano may not have been much to look at, but he was a good listener. He had this way of…' She stopped, then gave him a wry smile. 'That, and he was great in bed.'

Unexpectedly embarrassed by her candour, Neville looked down at his hands and twisted his wedding ring. It was *not* like him to react like this. But then he didn't usually interview women as stunning as Samantha Winter. There was something intimidating about that combination of beauty and frankness.

'So in case you think I killed him,' she said calmly, 'you can see that I didn't have any reason to. We were finished, I was with someone else. If anyone was upset about it, it was Joe, not me.' Samantha reached for her water glass and took another sip. 'I think you should be talking to his wife. If anyone had a good reason to kill him, it was his wife.'

Neville was inclined to agree with her, but he wasn't going to let her off so easily. Her new boyfriend, whoever he was, might have been jealous of her previous lover, and…'I'm going to ask you again,' he said. 'I'd like the name of the person you're currently…with.'

'You won't tell the press?' She gave him a coy smile.

He was getting tired of this. 'Not bloody likely.'

'It's one of the production assistants. Tarquin. Tarquin James.'

Now it was his turn to gasp in astonishment. 'Not…*that* Tarquin?'

She laughed. 'You should see your face, Inspector.'

'But he's…'

'What? A poofter? A screaming queen? I can assure you he's not.' She tossed her head and ran her hands through her hair. 'Tarquin loves to camp it up. So no one will suspect a thing. But believe me, it's all an act.' Samantha smiled knowingly, not an innocent young girl but a woman of the world. 'I can quote you chapter and verse, if you like. I can tell you what he did to me last night at the hotel. Or what he did in this dressing room, earlier this morning.'

'No,' said Neville, getting up. 'That won't be necessary.'

'It wouldn't surprise me if she done it, our Jodee. Shook that baby, I mean. She's always had a nasty temper, that girl.'

Lilith sighed as she sat at her desk, reading the competition— one of the other tabloids. Predictable, that's what it was: going to Jodee's poisonous mother for a quote. She wondered how much they'd had to pay the grasping bitch to accuse her own daughter of lethal child abuse.

Probably not all that much, if experience was anything to go by. The one time Lilith had talked to Debs Fuller she'd offered her a few hundred pounds, and it had been snatched with alacrity. Maybe, though, Debs had got greedier since then.

That had been back last summer, when Jodee was still in the 'twentyfour/seven' house. Lilith had taken the train all the way to Newcastle—the ends of the known universe, as far as she was concerned—for the interviews with Jodee's boyfriend and mother. She'd felt like asking Rob for hazard pay, considering what she'd had to put up with. Not just the interminable train journey, but what followed. The tiny council house reeked of tobacco, and everything in it, from the beat-up furniture to the woodchip-papered walls to the cheap curtains, was yellow with nicotine. If that wasn't a clear cautionary message about the evils of smoking, Lilith didn't know what was.

And in the midst of the fug of smoke, puffing away, sat Debs Fuller. Mutton dressed as lamb: jeans that had been cut off just below the crotch, a disastrously drooping tube top, sequinned spike-heeled shoes. Not yet forty, though her smoke-aged skin, tanned as old leather, made her look closer to sixty. At her side was the latest in a string of live-in toy-boy 'partners'. Probably out of his teens, but certainly not out of his twenties. Tattooed, pierced, pasty. Inarticulate to the point of total silence, which was undoubtedly a blessing. Craig, maybe, or was it Carl? Lilith didn't remember, and it didn't matter. He was probably history already, replaced by another of his interchangeable tribe.

All Debs Fuller had wanted to do was slag off her daughter—in language far riper than the current article indicated—and take the money.

Lilith forced herself, now, to read on. 'Jodee's temper—that's why I weren't sorry when she left. I had my own baby to think of. Jodee's little sister.'

She snorted. The only reason Debs had been glad to have Jodee—a free babysitter—out of the house was because of the boyfriend. Carl, Craig or whomever it had been at that time. Debs didn't like the competition from her younger, prettier daughter.

Well, she'd come into her own now, had Debs, now that the tide of public opinion had turned so firmly against her daughter. She'd better make some money out of it while she could. In a few weeks Jodee and Chazz, currently public enemies numbers one and two, suspected child abusers if not baby killers, would be yesterday's news. In a year's time they'd be forgotten altogether. 'Jodee—wasn't she the one with the funny hair?'

That's what bothered Lilith about the job offer from *HotStuff*. Yes, it would be tremendous fun to write about celebrities, to knock them down a peg or two whenever possible. But the world of celebrity was essentially meaningless. There was such an element of arbitrariness in it: Jodee hadn't discovered a cure for cancer; Chazz hadn't found the answer to global warming. Neither was a poet, a theologian, a philanthropist. Neither, quite frankly, possessed anything even close to an average allocation of brain cells. They'd both been in the right place at the right time, and that was all one could say for why they were famous and someone else wasn't. If they'd been Mr and Mrs Joe Bloggs, and had shaken their baby until its toothless gums rattled, no one would have known and few would have cared.

As well as being arbitrary, celebrity was so transient, so ephemeral. Great romances came and went, winners became losers and losers became nobodies. The public was so fickle, and so insatiable.

And at the end of the day it amounted to…nothing. Precisely that. Conjecture, gossip, rumour. Outright lies, if that was what was called for and you could get away with it. Hard facts had no place in the world of *HotStuff.*

Yes, Lilith liked to stir things a bit—she admitted it to herself. She loved the thrill of the chase. She enjoyed making an impact, having her name known and feared. She wasn't even averse to pandering to the British public's appetite for scandal.

But she was a journalist, first and foremost. Not a gossip-monger.

Admittedly, the *Daily Globe* wasn't the *Telegraph,* august and above reproach. Yet Lilith believed—though she was aware some would disagree—that they were on the same side of the invisible line which divided both from *HotStuff.* It was a fine line, not easily defined—and it wasn't just the difference between newspapers and magazines. There was more to it than that: a difference of intent.

If Lilith had to define her ambitions for her career, if she were to project herself five years into the future…

She realised, with a bit of a shock, that she would rather be working for the *Telegraph* than for *HotStuff.* She was firmly on that side of the line.

And yet…

What fun it would be to work for Aggie McLean. To throw caution to the winds, to get down and dirty. The money wouldn't go amiss, either. She might be able to move out of Earl's Court, to somewhere more upmarket. She'd meet interesting people. Interesting men, even.

The phone on her desk rang: the office phone, not her mobile. She picked it up. 'Lilith Noone.'

'Is this really Lilith Noone?' said a breathless voice.

'It is. Last time I looked.'

'Thank God. I kept saying I wanted the organ grinder, not the monkey. I thought they'd never put me through.'

'And this is…?'

'I work at the "Junior Idol" studio. And I have some information I thought might interest you.'

More celebrity gossip, Lilith thought, suppressing a sigh. One of the finalists probably had an unsightly spot on the end of their nose, two days before the final—shock, horror. But she reached for her notepad nonetheless. 'Yes?'

'A policeman was here this morning. Detective Inspector Stewart.'

Lilith's heartbeat quickened; as far as she knew, DI Neville Stewart hadn't yet stooped to investigating unsightly facial blemishes. 'And?'

'He insisted on interviewing one of the finalists. Samantha Winter. He said she was an important material witness in a murder case. I thought you'd like to know.'

'Thanks,' said Lilith, smiling. 'Thank you very much. Now, if you could…'

But her mysterious informant had already rung off.

Joe's death: murder? Callie didn't believe it. But Chiara evidently believed it, and that was the important thing.

She couldn't *not* go, Callie told herself as she made the bus journey to Islington. Chiara needed her, and that had to come above all other considerations.

And she hadn't given any promises to Marco that she wouldn't see Chiara.

He'd made it clear what Serena's wishes were in the matter. But he hadn't asked her to promise to honour them.

If there'd been any chance of salvaging her relationship with Marco, she realised, this would probably sink it, once and for all. As soon as he found out that she'd defied Serena's edict, he'd never speak to her again.

This was, Callie reckoned, a pastoral matter: something she had to square with herself, and then deal with the consequences. There would be times in her ministry when she had to do things that other people wouldn't like, and this was one of them. Whatever it cost her personally, she couldn't abandon Chiara.

Chiara was waiting for her at the school gates: standing alone, looking so forlorn that Callie had to resist an urge to give her a big comforting hug.

'Thanks,' said Chiara, with a watery smile. 'Thanks for coming.'

'You're sure you're allowed to do this? To come out of school?'

'In Year Eight we're allowed to go out at dinner time. Sometimes we go down to the chippy—me and my friends. Or to one of the fast food places. Or we just eat crisps and go shopping.'

Callie could imagine—a gaggle of uniformed girls cutting a swathe through the neighbourhood, giggling and leaving a litter of empty crisp packets in their wake. 'Where would you like to go now?' she asked.

'Somewhere quiet. Where we can sit and talk.'

'Didn't I come past a sort of ice-cream shop?' Callie recalled. 'Round the corner and down the road?'

'That would be perfect.'

It was the kind of place Callie remembered being taken to as a child, for a special treat—with formica counters and little individual tables. When given a choice, Callie had always asked for a Knickerbocker Glory, mostly because it sounded so splendid. She loved saying the name: 'I'll have a Knickerbocker Glory, please.'

One such instance was as clear in her mind as if it had happened last week. Her mother had protested. 'You won't be able to finish it, Caroline. You never do. It's so wasteful. Why don't you just have a dish of ice cream with chocolate sauce?'

'Let the girl have what she wants, Laura,' her father had intervened.

'I'll eat it all. I promise.' And she had—every last bite of ice cream, fruit, jelly, syrup, nuts and whipped cream—though she'd had to force it down towards the end, and later that day she'd been sick. Horribly sick.

After that, Knickerbocker Glories had never appealed to her in quite the same way again.

'What would you like?' she asked after Chiara had studied the printed menu card at their table for a few minutes.

'I believe I'd like a Knickerbocker Glory,' Chiara decided. 'If that's all right.'

Callie smiled. 'Good choice. And I'll have a dish of ice cream. With chocolate sauce.'

She placed the order at the counter, then returned to the table.

'Mum probably wouldn't let me order a Knickerbocker Glory,' Chiara confessed.

'It's a great deal of ice cream. And all of the other bits as well.'

Chiara sighed. 'Mum would be furious if she knew I was here. With you.'

'Yes, I know.'

'Did she tell you not to talk to me?' Chiara gave her a shrewd look.

Callie's eyes prickled at the unwelcome memory. 'Indirectly. I got the message.'

'She told me not to talk to *you*. But I don't care,' Chiara added fiercely. 'She can't tell me what to do. And I'm glad you didn't listen to her, either.'

Callie knew she'd never be able to make Chiara understand that it wasn't that straightforward. She wasn't just defying Serena, or taking sides with Chiara against her mother. It was so much more complicated than that. 'I care about you,' she said simply. That was the best she could do.

'I'm glad *someone* does.' Chiara leaned back in her chair and folded her arms across her chest. 'Mum doesn't.'

'That's not true. Your mother loves you,' Callie said. 'And there's Angelina, and your Nonna and Nonno, and Uncle Marco…'

Chiara clearly wasn't having it; she changed the subject. 'Angelina's come home,' she said. 'Yesterday.'

'Oh, that's good.'

'She's broken up with her boyfriend. Li. She told me. I was surprised,' Chiara confessed. 'I thought she loved him.'

Callie bit her lip. 'Sometimes,' she said, 'even when people love each other, things just don't work out.' She swallowed hard; there was a painful lump in her throat.

'You mean like Mum and Dad?'

It was a welcome relief that the ice cream arrived at that moment, before Callie had to answer. The Knickerbocker Glory was an awesome concoction, crowned with not just a biscuit fan stuck into the whipped cream but a little paper umbrella as well.

'Wow,' said Chiara, and picked up the long-handled spoon. But she wasn't going to let Callie get away without answering her question. 'Like Mum and Dad?' she repeated.

Callie scooped up a spoonful of ice cream and dunked it in chocolate sauce, taking her time. 'Your parents stayed together. No matter what bad things happened between them—and you can't know that; no one can—they stayed together.'

'Maybe.' Chiara put down her spoon and pushed the tall glass away from her, untouched. 'I'm not really very hungry.'

'What do you mean, maybe?'

Chiara didn't look at her; she stared down at the table. 'You remember I told you, a few days ago, that I thought Mum had been responsible for Dad's death? That she drove him to a heart attack by the way she treated him? I don't think that any more.'

'I remember. I know you were in shock when you said it, and I'm glad you've realised that it was—'

'No,' Chiara interrupted her fiercely. 'No. You don't under-stand what I'm saying.' She turned her face in Callie's direction, and her expression was enough to stop the spoon halfway to Callie's mouth. 'I don't think that any more because now I know that Dad was murdered. Now I think that Mum killed him. Not just by accident, or by being hateful to him. I think she really, *really* killed him.'

Chapter Sixteen

Instead of going to the hospital cafe for lunch, Frances ate a sandwich at her desk, relishing a few moments of solitude. Her morning had been tiring and highly emotional: she'd been with a young man as he died after a road accident, then had had to deal with his understandably distraught mother, who had expected her to come up with answers for the unanswerable questions. 'Why my son? How could a loving God take away my son, in the prime of his life, when he had so much to live for? How can you believe in a God who could do that?'

There were no answers. Only more questions.

And after the past twenty-four hours, Frances felt she was qualified to hang out her shingle as a relationship counsellor—or at the very least an agony aunt.

It had started with Callie, pouring out her heart about her relationship with Mark. Admittedly, Frances had prompted her to confide in her, and she knew that it had cost Callie a great deal to do so: up till that point, Callie had seemingly managed to escape from thinking about it, but putting it into words had made it concrete, unavoidable.

And again, Frances had no easy answers for her. She could merely listen and act as a sounding-board for the things Callie already knew. The only advice she'd offered had been, 'Don't give up on it yet. If you really love him, you can work it out. Don't do anything hasty, or say anything you'll regret.'

Easy to say, when you had a good, stable marriage. She could only imagine Callie's pain, facing the prospect of life without the man she'd come to love.

Her other experience, at breakfast this morning, had been a happier one. Triona had been smiling as she sipped her coffee.

'I've been thinking,' Triona said. 'And I think I've been awfully hard on Neville.'

Frances had been of that opinion all along, but she didn't say that. 'He means well,' she said. 'And he does love you. Very much. I'm sure of it.'

'It's his bloody job,' admitted Triona. 'I hate it. I hate the way he's at their beck and call, day and night. How can we have a decent life together if I never know when I'm going to see him?'

'That's the way it is. Not everyone can work nine to five,' Frances pointed out. 'Someone has to do that job, just like someone has to be the doctor who's called out in the middle of the night to save a life.' Or a priest who was called out to hold a dying person's hand, she added to herself.

'That's what I keep telling myself. And I know he loves his job.'

'And he's good at it,' Frances reminded her. 'Most of the time. When he's not arresting innocent people.'

That brought a wry laugh from Triona. 'I suppose I'll just have to get used to it,' she said, almost to herself. 'Cut him a bit of slack.'

Frances couldn't help wondering what had brought about this change of mind. Ever since her heart-to-heart with Neville she'd been looking for an opportunity to have this conversation, but any attempt she'd made had been rebuffed. Now Triona had actually brought up the subject herself. 'I'm glad,' Frances said. 'I think you can make each other happy, if you give it a chance.' They would also almost certainly make each other miserable at least half of the time, but she didn't mention that. 'And there's the baby,' she added.

Triona smiled again, stroking her belly with both hands. 'Yes, there's that. He—or she—deserves a dad.'

'So…what are you going to do?'

'Well, the first thing is to get out of your hair,' Triona stated. 'I've abused your hospitality long enough.'

'Not at all.'

'Oh, absolutely. The reason I came here was so Neville wouldn't find me, remember? But he tracked me down days ago, and I've stayed on anyway. I suppose,' she confessed, 'I've just enjoyed being pampered a bit, and having some company.'

'You're welcome to stay as long as you like. You know that.'

'I'll go back to my flat. Probably this afternoon,' Triona said. 'Then I'll ring Neville, and we can start talking things through.'

So that, Frances fervently hoped, was that.

Now her thoughts returned to Callie.

Tomorrow was Callie's day off, she knew. Callie wouldn't want to spend it at the vicarage, and in her current frame of mind she certainly didn't need to inflict her mother on herself.

It would be good if they could spend a bit of time together. Frances usually didn't work on Friday mornings; she was owed plenty of time from the extra hours she'd put in and could easily take the afternoon off as well.

In her lingerie drawer at home, Frances had a voucher for a 'Pamper Day for Two' at a day spa in Chelsea. It had been a Christmas gift from Graham—a generous and thoughtful gift for a chronically over-worked wife who didn't get to spend as much time with her friends as she liked. While she had understood and appreciated the impulse behind the gift, Frances had been so busy since Christmas that she hadn't even thought about redeeming it.

This, she decided, was the time. She and Callie could soak in a whirlpool bath, have facials, get manicures and pedicures. A girly day, with no churchy shop talk allowed.

Bliss.

Frances reached for the phone.

Driving back into London, Neville brooded on what had just happened at the 'Junior Idol' studio. It wasn't something that he experienced very often: the feeling that he'd been bested. That bloody girl had toyed with him, manipulated him, taken the mickey. And she'd enjoyed every minute of it.

It shouldn't have happened. He was the one in control, asking the questions. But she'd twisted him round her elegant little finger. In short, she had humiliated him.

He was only glad—fervently—that Cowley hadn't been there to see it. He would never have lived it down.

Not that Cowley would have fared any better at the hands of that ruthless little bitch, Neville told himself.

It was just a shame that he didn't have a good reason to arrest her and teach her a little lesson. She might not be so ready to take the piss if she were locked up in a cell for a day or two. But she'd been quite right in saying that she would have had nothing to gain by killing Joe di Stefano, a discarded lover. He was out of her life, ancient history, not even worth thinking about. She'd moved on: to fame, fortune and Tarquin. Tarquin, the simpering little fop.

What if, Neville asked himself, trying hard to put her in the frame, Joe di Stefano had threatened Samantha that he would go public about their affair? It was the sort of thing Lilith Noone and her ilk would have a field day with: '"Junior Idol" star had it off with professor'. But at the end of the day, though it might have embarrassed her a little to be linked with an unglamorous middle-aged man, it was all about publicity. And wasn't there a saying that there was no such thing as bad publicity?

Besides, di Stefano had surely been as anxious as she to keep it all quiet, if nothing else for the sake of his family. He would have had nothing to gain from going public about it, and it would have broken his daughters' hearts. Whatever you could say about Joe di Stefano, Neville was convinced, from what he knew of the man, that he'd loved his daughters.

No, he would have to look elsewhere for Joe di Stefano's killer. More the pity.

He wondered what Cowley had turned up at the university. Probably nothing that would switch their focus away from the family.

At the end of the day, Neville told himself, Serena di Stefano was almost certainly the one they were looking for. Much as Mark Lombardi might disagree, in his eagerness to protect her, she was the person who'd had the best reasons to want di Stefano dead. How humiliating it must have been for her to know that—beautiful as she was herself—her husband preferred a younger model. And she'd been bending over backwards to keep it from the family. Bottling up her hostility and hurt, revealing her feelings only to her brother. Not surprising that she'd cracked. Seeing him going out jogging every morning to keep in shape for his mistress…

And there was the opportunity, right there. The Lucozade bottle. Unscrew the top, empty a bit out, fill it up with antifreeze—readily available at any auto supply shop or even at the supermarket.

Problem solved.

She was such a cool customer. She could have done it, just like that. No tears shed, just a problem solved.

But how could they prove it?

And however it played out, this was going to tear a family apart. That was unavoidable, inevitable.

Driving past a McDonald's, Neville realised, suddenly, that he was hungry. He turned into the car park on impulse and went in, queued up, and ordered a bacon-and-cheese quarter-pounder with fries.

He was trying to tear open a packet of tomato ketchup when his phone rang.

'Neville Stewart,' he answered.

'Mr Stewart, this is Andrew. Andrew Linton.' Andrew sounded even more ebullient than usual.

'Yes?'

' I managed to reschedule those viewings from yesterday. And we have two offers!'

'Offers?'

'To buy your flat! The first couple this morning—they loved it so much that they offered the asking price. On the spot. Two six-nine nine-fifty.'

'Wow,' said Neville, scribbling the number on his serviette to help him visualise it better. 'Great.'

'And then the next people. I told them we had an asking-price offer on the table, so they put in an offer of two seventy.'

Two hundred and seventy thousand pounds. Unbelievable.

'So I went back to the first couple. They really want it, Mr Stewart. Really. It ticked all their boxes. They upped their offer to two seven-five. Best and final, off the market today, completion within eight weeks.'

Whatever that meant in plain English. 'You think I should take it?'

'They're cash buyers, Mr Stewart,' Andrew said, as close to reproachful as Neville had ever heard him. 'No chain. You'd be mad not to take it.'

'I'll be guided by you, then. Tell them we have a deal.'

'Brilliant! Brilliant.' He paused for breath, then went on. 'And your wife's flat. I have a huge amount of interest from people on my books, like I said. So I'm scheduling an open house tomorrow afternoon. Sealed bids at the end of the day.'

'That's…excellent.' Neville felt almost dizzy with the speed of it.

'So you'll be needing a new property soon. I've pulled a few details out for you to look at. I've left them at your flat, to save you a trip into the office.'

'Thanks,' said Neville. 'I'll be in touch.'

Callie was horrified at Chiara's readiness to believe her mother was capable of murder. Still unconvinced that Joe's death had been anything other than natural, she wished she could ring Marco and ask him what was going on. Now that she'd expressly defied his wishes and talked to Chiara, though, she knew that wasn't possible.

Frances' phone call, inviting her to spend her day off at a spa, provided a welcome distraction and gave her something to look forward to.

But today wasn't over yet, and as she rode the bus back across town from Islington, Callie pondered something that had been bothering her since she'd read the *Globe* story about Jodee and Chazz. It had made her think back over her conversations with Brenda, and given her the glimmer of an idea about what might have happened to Muffin. Little more than an instinct, an intuition...

It was none of her business, Callie told herself. Her involvement with the Betts family was pastoral, not investigative. That was the police's job.

Yet when the bus terminated at Oxford Circus, before switching to the Tube, Callie bought a bunch of spring flowers from a street seller. And when she came out of the Tube station at Lancaster Gate, instead of heading for the vicarage she turned towards the Bettses' house. She fought her way through the photographers: still there, still waiting. For a moment Callie felt sorry for them. How many days had they been there besieging the house, with no one of interest coming out or going in? Were they there on the basis that sooner or later one of the Bettses would have to show their face?

Brenda opened the door a crack to let her in. 'We wasn't expecting you,' she said.

'It's such a beautiful day,' Callie said, handing her the flowers. 'I thought if you couldn't go out and enjoy the spring, I'd bring a bit of it in to you.'

'How kind.' Brenda smiled at her. 'I'll find something to put them in. Would you like a cuppa?'

'That would be lovely.'

Callie followed Brenda to the kitchen and watched while she arranged the flowers in a vase. 'I was wondering something,' she said. 'Do you mind if I ask you a question?'

'Course not.'

'When was the last time you saw your husband? Kev?'

Brenda scowled. 'I thought I told you. When I were in hospital with the twins. I ain't laid eyes on Kev Betts since that day. And good riddance to bad rubbish,' she added.

'So he's never come here, to this house?'

'He'd know better than to show his face here,' Brenda stated. 'Though I must admit, I wouldn't of put it past him to come sniffing round, once our Chazz got famous. And rich. But if he so much as tried it, I'd send him packing so fast he'd wonder what hit him. He never had no use for us when Chazz needed a dad. Now Chazz don't have no use for *him*. Chazz would say the same, if you asked him.'

It was the answer Callie had more or less expected. But she wasn't finished yet, and she had her chance to resume her enquiries a short while later, after they'd joined Jodee and Chazz in the white sitting room. Brenda went back to the kitchen to top up the tea pot, and Chazz—evidently bored—sloped off to another part of the house to commune with his Playstation.

This was, Callie realised, the first time she'd ever been alone with Jodee. She knew that it wouldn't last long—Brenda would soon be back—so she decided to tackle her head-on. Subtlety would probably be wasted on Jodee, in any case.

'Have you ever met Chazz's father?' Callie asked, attempting to sound casual.

Jodee paled visibly; her eyes widened. 'How'd you know?' she gasped.

So she'd been right. 'He came here, didn't he?'

'Oh, God.' Jodee emitted a long, drawn-out sigh. 'I swear I didn't mean to, like, lie about it. I just didn't want to, like, hurt Chazz. Or Bren.'

Callie reached over and touched Jodee's arm. 'Tell me what happened.'

Jodee closed her eyes. 'It were a few weeks ago, like. Chazz were out. So were Bren, though she didn't say she were going. I were looking for Bren to like keep an eye on Muffin—I had a photo shoot to go to. Then he, like, rang the doorbell.'

'So you weren't expecting him.'

'Course not. Out of the bloody blue, it was. I thought he were a salesman or something—he didn't look like no journalist. I told him to bugger off, I didn't need no kitchen cloths or nothing like that.'

It was, thought Callie, as if Jodee had re-lived this in her mind for days, as if she'd rehearsed it, waiting for a chance to tell someone.

'And then he said he were Chazz's dad. Kev.' Jodee slumped in her chair, her eyes still shut. 'I could see it, like. Looked like Chazz, he did, only old. Nice smile, just like Chazz. That's why I didn't slam the door in his face.'

'What else did he say?' Callie prompted her.

'He said I were even prettier than I looked on the telly.' Jodee smiled in spite of herself, and her hand went to her hair.

So vanity was the way to her heart, realised Callie without surprise. Kev Betts must really be a smooth operator—first charming his way into Brenda's knickers, all those years ago, then getting round Jodee with glib compliments.

'Then he said he wanted to see Muffin. Just once, he said. His own grandbabby, like. His flesh and blood.' She sighed again, deeply. 'And I thought it were only right. I admit I did, like. He's her granddad, when all's said and done. Blood's thicker than water.'

'Even if Brenda and Chazz wouldn't have wanted it.'

'They didn't have to know, did they? I didn't think it would do no harm, and what they didn't know wouldn't hurt them.' She gave Callie a defensive, sideways look. 'Then I said I had to like go out. I were going to take Muffin with me, since Bren weren't about.'

Callie held her breath, listening for Brenda's return, praying to be granted just a few more minutes.

'Then he—Kev—said he'd stay with her. Do each other a big favour, he said, like. He could get to know his granddaughter while I were out.' Jodee squeezed her eyes shut; big tears trickled from the corners. 'I were only gone an hour. No more. She were sleeping when I left, and she were sleeping when I got back. He said she'd been good as gold. But now I think, like…'

Callie could imagine the scenario that must have played over and over in Jodee's head over the last few days, like an unstoppable horror movie: Muffin waking from sleep and crying for food or because her nappy was wet. Kev Betts trying to stop her crying… Kev Betts, who—according to Brenda—couldn't stand bawling babies, not meaning to hurt her, only trying to make the crying stop.

Brenda's footsteps were coming down the corridor, almost to the door.

'Don't tell Bren!' Jodee whispered frantically, dashing away her tears. 'And for God's sake, don't tell Chazz!'

Lilith's first port of call was the Metropolitan Police's web site. She navigated to the page where the Met's press bureau posted sterile—and, in her opinion, badly written—news releases about cases in progress.

Di Stefano—that was the name Hereward Rice had mentioned, in that conversation she'd overheard. As she typed the name into the search engine, Lilith congratulated herself on her good memory. A nurse had been suspicious: that's what he'd said. Evidently with good reason.

'Poisoning Investigation Launched' was the headline.

Lilith clicked on it and read the story.

'Detectives are investigating the death of Guiseppe "Joe" di Stefano, of Clerkenwell. Dr di Stefano, a professor of sociology at the University of London, died in St Mary's Hospital, Paddington after being admitted with a suspected heart attack.

'A post-mortem examination was carried out, and the cause of death was found to be ethylene glycol poisoning. An inquest has been scheduled for Friday.

'The death is being treated as suspicious. Police are anxious to talk to anyone who might have information about Dr di Stefano. Contact DI Neville Stewart…'

Nothing to indicate that it had anything to do with Samantha Winter or Lilith's anonymous tipster. What would connect a university professor with a glamorous 'Junior Idol' contestant?

On the other hand, how many murder cases would Neville Stewart be working on at any given time? It wasn't likely that he'd have more than one.

Leaving the Met's dry prose behind, Lilith went to the official 'Junior Idol' web site. There the prose was anything but dry.

She clicked on the photo of Samantha Winter—posing with her head tilted provocatively, surrounded by a cloud of golden hair—and was taken to her bio page.

'Twenty-year-old Samantha has brains as well as beauty,' enthused the bio. 'Before being selected as a contestant on "Junior Idol", Samantha was a student at the University of London, reading sociology. Now Samantha has her sights set on a career in the music business.'

'Bingo,' Lilith whispered gleefully, highly pleased with herself.

Next she googled 'ethylene glycol' and was directed to Wikipedia, where amongst the incomprehensible chemical formulae and scientific jargon a word jumped out. 'Anti-freeze.'

'Bloody hell,' said Lilith aloud. 'He was poisoned with anti-freeze!'

This was going to be an interesting one, she reckoned, smiling to herself.

Neville had been summoned to Evan's lair, but before he went upstairs he rang Sid Cowley to find out what his sergeant had turned up.

'Not much, to be honest, Guv,' Cowley admitted. 'He was a well-respected bloke. His colleagues liked him. No professional jealousy or anything like that. His students liked him, as well. I haven't found anyone who will admit to shagging him, or can tell me anyone else who did. Though,' he added, 'several people seemed to know about Samantha. Sounds like they weren't all that discreet.'

From his own dealings with her, Neville could guess which one of them might have been responsible for indiscreet behaviour. The little bitch, he thought, grimacing.

'What everyone does say,' Cowley went on, 'is that I need to talk to a Miss Harwood. Departmental secretary. Went off sick the day di Stefano died and no one's seen her since. Apparently she was quite fond of him.'

'Fond of him? What's that supposed to mean?'

'I'm not sure, Guv. But I think you should try to talk to her.'

'Right.' Neville made a note of it; it was best to tie up all the loose ends.

'How was Samantha?' Cowley asked, his voice wistful.

'Oh, just peachy.' Neville's mouth twisted into a cynical smile. 'You would have loved her, Sid. Just your cup of tea.'

'Thanks, Guv. Thanks a lot.'

Neville did a not-very-creditable Kenneth Williams impression. 'Oooh, Mr Grumpy.'

Cowley told him, succinctly, where to go, then hung up.

Now it was time to go and get kicked by DCS Evans.

'No arrest yet?' Evans greeted him from behind his desk.

'No, Sir.'

Fortunately Evans seemed to be in a pretty good mood, more interested in information-gathering than apportioning blame. 'Tell me what you've discovered,' he invited, waving Neville into a chair.

'Well, Sir, Mr di Stefano—or *Dr* di Stefano, I should say— was having an affair with one of his students, and his wife found out about it. Things must have been pretty tense between them. Even Mark admits it.'

'So she's your chief suspect? The wife?'

'Has to be,' Neville confirmed. 'There doesn't seem to be anyone else in the picture at the moment.'

'What about the mistress?'

He shook his head regretfully. 'I wish I could say yes—she's a real piece of work, that one—but she didn't have the motive. It was over between them, and she just wants to put it all behind her and forget that it ever happened.'

'She's the one who broke it off?' Evans asked shrewdly.

'Apparently so.'

Evans rested his elbows on his desk and templed his fingers together. 'What if he wouldn't let her forget?'

'Blackmail, you mean, Sir?'

'An old-fashioned word, but…yes. Is that possible?'

Neville repeated what he'd worked through himself. 'He wouldn't have wanted it to get out. It would have hurt his family too much, and I don't believe he would have been happy about that. Two young daughters,' he added.

'Well, then. Suicide?' Evans suggested. 'Say he's really cut up by this girl ditching him. Would he kill himself?'

'It would be a hell of a way to top yourself, Sir. Like you said yesterday.' Anti-freeze in your own Lucozade? There had to be easier methods of self-destruction. 'What would be the point of doing it like that?'

'To put the blame on his wife,' Evans stated. 'This is a clever boyo we're talking about, right? PhD? Say he wants to do himself in, and get one over on his wife at the same time.'

Neville shook his head. 'I can't see it.'

'So we're back to the wife. No other family members in the frame?'

'Apparently,' Neville said with a faint pang of disloyalty, 'the only other person who knew about the affair was Mark Lombardi. Her brother. The parents didn't know, and neither did the daughters. Mrs di Stefano bent over backwards to keep it from them, Mark said.'

Evans raised his caterpillar eyebrows and looked at him, waiting.

'I just don't think Mark would have done anything like that, Sir. He loves his sister, but—'

'They're Italians, for God's sake,' Evans pointed out. 'Hot-blooded. The honour of the family, and all that. There's a history of it.'

That one was worthy of Sid Cowley, and Neville was appalled. 'We're not talking about the Mafia!' If they were going to descend to racial stereotyping, he could point out a few things about the Welsh; he bit his tongue to keep himself from chanting a childhood slur, 'Paddy was a Welshman, Paddy was a thief…'

'All right, then. The wife,' Evans conceded.

'The trouble is, Sir,' Neville admitted, 'there just doesn't seem to be any evidence. No bottle of anti-freeze, nothing to incriminate her. The SOCOs tore the house apart and they didn't find anything. Nothing but the doctored Lucozade bottle, with his prints on it.'

'Hmm.' Evans sat for a moment, seemingly deep in thought. 'Here's a little something for you to ponder before you go to sleep tonight, Inspector.'

Neville didn't like that sound of that. 'Yes, Sir?'

'If she did it, why didn't she get rid of the Lucozade bottle? Why leave it sitting there for us to find?'

◇◇◇

On her way back to the vicarage, Callie had a phone call from a number she didn't recognise.

'Miss Anson?' said a vaguely familiar Cockney voice. 'It's Derek Long. The roofer.'

'Oh, yes.' It seemed a lifetime ago since he'd sat on her sofa, drinking highly sugared tea and cheerfully consigning her to living at the vicarage. But it had been, she calculated, exactly one week.

'I 'ave some good news for you. I fink it's good, anyway.'

'Yes?'

'I've spoke to your insurance company. Everyfink's in order. And I've 'ad a cancellation, next week. Some cove decided to use another roofer. So I can fit you in, like. Next week. I can start on Monday.'

'Oh, that's wonderful! How long will it take, then?'

'A week. Ten days. Depends on the wevver, like.'

'I'll pray for good weather,' Callie told him, trying to make it sound like she was joking.

A week! Within a fortnight she could be back home. Back where she belonged, and Bella with her.

And wouldn't Jane be pleased?

Callie smiled for what seemed the first time in days.

But her smile didn't last, as she quickly remembered what she'd been pondering before her phone rang.

Jodee.

What on earth was she going to do with the information Jodee had given her?

What Jodee had told her—it hadn't been a formal confession, in either the legal or the theological sense. Callie didn't feel she was bound to any sort of confidentiality, apart from Jodee's plea not to tell Brenda or Chazz. In other circumstances, Callie told herself with a pang, she'd have confided in Marco. He would have known what to do.

Now that wasn't an option.

She couldn't just sit on the information; it was too important for that. But she wouldn't feel right in passing it along without Jodee's permission. At the end of the day, the decision had to be Jodee's.

That didn't mean that Callie couldn't push her in the right direction.

With sudden resolve, she rang Jodee's mobile—the private number she'd been given on her first visit.

'Listen, Jodee,' she said, when she'd ascertained that Jodee wasn't in a position to be overheard. 'I've been thinking about what you told me.'

'Yeah,' Jodee admitted. 'Me, too.'

'I know you don't want Chazz and Brenda to find out,' she said. 'But right now everyone out there thinks that one of you killed Muffin. You don't want that, do you?'

Jodee's answer was emphatic. 'No!'

'Then don't you see that you have to tell the police?'

'I…can't,' Jodee whispered. 'I just can't do it. It was different, like, telling you. But not the police. Not me. I can't.'

'Not even for Muffin?' It wasn't playing fair, Callie realised, but extreme measures were called for.

Jodee burst into tears. 'Muffin!' she wailed.

Callie sighed. 'Do you want me to do it?'

'Would you?,' Jodee sobbed. 'Oh, I'd be ever so grateful. Do it for me. For Muffin. Tell them.'

That was that, then.

Callie remembered the friendly way Neville Stewart had greeted her at the police station. He was, after all, the Senior Investigating Officer on the Betts case. A word with him would undoubtedly be the best thing. He would know exactly how to handle it from there.

Her phone was still in her hand. Callie rang the police station—she still had the number in her phone from the other day—and asked for DI Neville Stewart.

'He's in a meeting,' she was told after a short delay. 'Can I take a message?'

'Ask him to ring Callie,' she said. 'Tell him it's important.'

If she had poisoned her husband, why hadn't Serena di Stefano got rid of the Lucozade bottle?

Neville didn't wait till the time Evans had suggested—before he went to sleep—to ponder the question. He thought about it as he took the stairs back down to his office.

It was a good question, he admitted.

But there were some possible answers. Maybe she was confident that the police would never be involved—that the heart attack scenario would hold up without any questions being asked. Perhaps it was a clever double-bluff, with her counting on them to reach the conclusion that if she'd left it, she must be innocent. Or maybe she'd just forgot. Been careless. Maybe—

His phone rang, and his heart skipped a beat when he saw that it was Triona. He stopped in the stairwell to take the call.

'Hi,' she said. 'I got your message last night. It was…sweet. Thanks.'

'I meant it,' Neville said.

After a pause, Triona spoke again. 'I was wondering if you were free this evening.'

'Absolutely free. I can come and collect you, and—'

'I fancy a middle eastern meal,' she cut across him. 'I've been craving hummus for days. Are you interested?'

'Interested? Triona, you don't know how—'

'There's that restaurant in Notting Hill, or Bayswater. Westbourne Grove. Remember, we ate there once?'

He remembered. 'Shall I come and collect you?' he repeated. 'Say, seven o'clock?'

'I think it's better if we meet there.' She paused again, and this time he waited for her to clarify herself. 'Listen, Neville. I'm not making any promises. But I do think it's about time for us to talk. And I do mean *talk,*' she added wryly. 'Not just go to bed, like that last time we were supposed to be talking.'

'Whatever you say. I want to make it work.'

'Well, we'll see.'

He felt he had to say it again. 'I love you, Triona.'

'Don't go soft on me, Stewart. It's unnerving.' But she had a smile in her voice. 'Seven o'clock, then.'

'Yes!' he shouted as he heard the click that signified she'd hung up.

Fortunately there was no one else in the stairwell as he clattered down, grinning like an idiot.

He would win her back—he was sure of it. He'd tell her about selling his flat, and...

No, he decided in the next instant. He wouldn't tell her. He'd wait till it was all sorted, then surprise her with a *faît accompli*.

Back in his office, he threw himself into his chair with a happy sigh.

On top of all the clutter on his desk was a pink post-it: a phone message slip, of recent vintage.

'Call Cowley,' it said. 'Important.'

'Oh, God,' he said aloud.

He punched the speed-dial on his phone. 'Sid?' he said. 'What's up?'

'Nothing. Nothing new, Guv,' said a slightly puzzled-sounding Sid Cowley.

'Then why did you leave a message to call you?'

'I didn't.'

'Okay, then. Have it your way.' Neville rang off; this was, he supposed, Sid's juvenile way of getting back at him for the 'Mr Grumpy' comment.

He scrunched the pink post-it into a ball and lobbed it at his rubbish bin.

Sid could play all the childish games he wanted. Neville wasn't going to let it get to him.

He had a date. With his wife.

◇◇◇

To Jane's surprise, the first cheque to compensate the Stanfords for accommodating Callie had arrived in the morning's post. She hadn't expected the insurance company to be quite so prompt—or so generous.

It had put her in a good mood, and sent her to the shops feeling rather generous herself.

So dinner that night was something above the ordinary: her special chicken casserole and dumplings, made not with Tesco Value chicken but with a lovely, plump free-range bird from the butcher shop. And there was trifle for pudding, an even rarer treat; much as Brian enjoyed puddings, and none more so than Jane's trifle, they were usually reserved for Sunday lunch. If they had pudding at all during the week, it would be tinned fruit or at best a dish of ice cream.

Tonight, though, Jane felt like pushing the boat out. And it was worth it. Brian was appreciative—vocally so—and though Callie didn't seem to have much of an appetite, she made a point of telling Jane how delicious everything was.

Brian pushed himself back from the table with regret. 'Lovely meal, Janey,' he said. 'I'd have seconds on the trifle, but I'd be late for my meeting.'

'Meeting?' Jane didn't remember him mentioning a meeting.

'School governors,' he said. 'I'm sure I told you.'

So he would be gone for the evening, and Callie would undoubtedly make some excuse to retreat to her room, or go out herself. Jane didn't really feel like spending the next few hours on her own.

'Would you like to watch a film?' she asked Callie almost shyly, expecting to be rebuffed. 'I have a DVD of *All About Eve*. Bette Davis, you know. Charlie gave it to me for Christmas.'

It seemed to Jane that Callie hesitated for a micro-second, before smiling at her. 'That sounds nice,' she said. 'I don't much fancy being on my own this evening.'

Jane started clearing the table, and Callie pitched in to help with the washing up.

'I'll be out tomorrow,' Callie said. 'My friend Frances—she's invited me to go to a spa. For a "Pamper Day", no less.'

Jane suppressed a niggle of envy. It wasn't just the pamper day she envied—it was the comfortable way Callie spoke about her friend.

Friends hadn't been much a part of Jane's life—not since her school days—and it wasn't until the boys had left home that she'd begun to realise what she might have missed. She'd always, at least in the last few years, thought of the twins as her best friends. But the boys were…gone.

It wasn't easy, as a vicar's wife, to have close friends: getting too intimate with people in the parish was neither advisable nor suitable for a variety of reasons, and it was difficult to meet other people—women—who might become friends. How nice it would be to have someone she could accompany to a spa—or even just have a cup of tea with. Was it too late for her?

To her surprise, Jane enjoyed the evening. The film was wonderful, and Callie was a good, if quiet, companion. Maybe, Jane told herself as they shared a cup of cocoa after the movie, she had misjudged Callie.

Before going off to her room, Callie thanked her. 'I needed the distraction,' she said. 'Thanks for inviting me. And I have some good news for you,' she added, smiling. 'You won't have to put up with me for much longer—not nearly as long as you thought.' She went on to tell her that the roof repairs would begin the following week, and be completed a week or so after that.

Jane had expected to feel delighted at the news. To get rid of Callie, to have their house back to themselves…It was what she wanted.

Didn't she?

Why, then, did she feel unsettled by the prospect?

Chapter Seventeen

Waking on Friday morning, Mark spent some time convincing himself that he should get out of bed. To be honest, he couldn't come up with any convincing reason why he should.

He was a man without a function.

No job to go to—that was forbidden to him.

Yesterday morning it had seemed a more attractive prospect, rather like an unexpected holiday. He could have a bit of a lie-in, wait till Geoff had left for work and take his time in the shower.

But the novelty had already worn off, and he wondered how he was going to fill the hours of the day.

Yolanda Fish. There she was, looking after his family the way he'd so often looked after other people's families. How strange it was to watch her in action, intensely aware of what she was doing. By virtue of his position in the family he was involved—he had to be. He should be the one doing that job. Yet he was barred from it, forced to remain detached from the vital functions of a Family Liaison Officer. Too close to the situation. Neither here nor there.

Serena didn't even need him. Maybe she never had. Now, though, with Yolanda Fish there, and Angelina at home to take up the slack, he was definitely surplus to requirements.

And Callie.

Today, he knew, was Callie's day off. With him not working, it would have been a wonderful opportunity to have spent the day with her. Yesterday had been a beautiful day, and today was supposed to be equally spring-like. They could have taken a long walk in Hyde Park; they could have gone to the zoo in Regents Park, for that matter. They might have had a picnic. Or they could have gone to a film or a play or a concert. They might have cooked an elaborate meal together—here at the flat, while Geoff was at work—and eaten the lot, or invited someone to share it with them. Peter, or Frances and Graham.

Just to spend a full day with her would have been bliss, whatever they did.

But he'd blown it. Comprehensively and spectacularly.

Callie would never speak to him again: he was sure of it.

And he couldn't bear it.

Just a few days away from Callie had convinced him more surely than ever that he didn't want to spend his life without her.

She made him feel whole, gave his life meaning. Being with her made him happy; being away from her made him miserable.

How could he have thrown it all away? In just a minute or two, he'd wounded her and destroyed any chance they'd had of a future together.

And for what? *La famiglia*. Serena, and her insistence that she knew what was best for her daughter. In his heart, Mark didn't even agree with her: he didn't see any reason why Callie shouldn't talk to Chiara, if that was what Chiara wanted.

It wasn't as if, he told himself, Serena was doing an outstanding job in dealing with Chiara.

Realising he was getting dangerously close to disloyalty to his sister, Mark tried to push the thought away. Chiara was at a difficult age; Serena was coping the best she could. They were both grieving, trying to come to terms with a loss that was almost too great to comprehend.

But the thought wouldn't be completely banished. Serena's treatment of Chiara, at the moment, was bordering on the insensitive.

And was Serena really grieving that much? It was hard to tell. Mark was accustomed to her character: her stoicism, her suppression of emotion, the impression she gave that nothing touched her. But he was also experienced in dealing with people who had been bereaved, and Serena's behaviour didn't fit in with any models he was familiar with. He hadn't seen her shed a tear—not at any point.

Hating himself, for the first time Mark allowed himself a moment of doubt. Was it possible—remotely possible—that Serena had solved the problem of Joe with an ounce or two of anti-freeze?

He knew that was what Neville would be thinking, and he could understand why, even as he denied it in his own heart. Serena wasn't a murderer. She couldn't be.

But then…who?

Not his problem. Not professionally, anyway.

The phone rang, forcing him out of bed to answer it.

'Marco?'

'*Buon giorno,* Mamma.'

'Marco, are you busy today?' she asked. 'Could you come to the restaurant? We could use your help.'

'*Certo*, Mamma.'

At least, he thought gratefully, someone needed him.

In contrast to his friend Mark, Neville woke an extremely happy man, his wife beside him.

She was deeply, soundly asleep, a smile on her face and her hair loose on the pillow.

They *had* talked. They had. Over an extended meal of mezze, and no alcohol, they had been honest with each other—possibly for the first time—about what they expected of each other and their marriage. Neville had learned, to his surprise, that Triona disliked his job and felt threatened by it. And he'd spoken honestly about his fear of commitment and what a huge step it was for him to give his heart to her so completely. He'd admitted that the responsibilities of fatherhood terrified him, but that he felt he was coming to terms with it, and by the time the baby arrived, he would be more than ready.

They would give it a go, they'd agreed. Not just for the sake of their baby, but for themselves. They recognised that it wouldn't be easy, yet they both felt it would be worth the effort. After all, they loved each other.

And there was the sex: undeniably important for both of them, and something that would always, for better or for worse, be a big part of their relationship. They'd admitted that, and then—their appetite for it sharpened—they'd come back to his flat and made love, deliciously, into the night.

Squinting at the bedside clock with one eye, Neville realised that he hadn't set the alarm, and was going to be shockingly late for work. With regret he abandoned his initial idea of waking Triona and making love to her again; instead he decided—as a good husband should—to let her sleep on as long as she wanted and needed to. He kissed her lightly, and when she didn't respond he slipped out of bed, retrieved his scattered clothes and went for a quick shower.

Yes, he would be late. But there were, Neville told himself, more important things than work.

He had his wife back, and he was determined to keep her.

Even before she got to work, Lilith was feeling frustrated.

She'd stopped by the newsagent's near the Earl's Court Tube station to pick up a copy of the *Globe* to read on her journey, fully expecting a front page by-line beneath a headline reading something along the lines of 'Sizzling Samantha Questioned in Anti-Freeze Murder'.

Instead the lead story was about the weather. 'Spring Has Sprung?' it said.

By the time she reached the office, her frustration had morphed into anger. She didn't stop at her desk, but went straight to the editor's office, knocking sharply on the door.

'Come in.'

Lilith waved the paper at Rob Gardiner-Smith. 'What do you call this?'

'I call it today's paper,' he replied with a sardonic smile. 'What do you call it?'

'I call it rubbish! "London had a taste of spring yesterday, along with most of the country." What happened to my story about Samantha? I thought you were going to run it on the front page.'

He pushed his chair back from his desk and looked up at her, shaking his head. 'Change of plan.'

'But why? It's a fabulous story. No one else has it.'

'Exactly.' He picked up a pencil and tapped his cheek with it. 'That's why we can afford to wait a day or two to run it.'

She still didn't understand. 'Why?' she repeated. 'Why wait?'

'Let me put it this way, Lilith. I ran it by our legal people, and they advised waiting. They'd like you to do some more digging, provide a bit of corroboration. Facts, Lilith. Not speculation. Anonymous tips are all very well, but they don't give us much to fall back on from a legal point of view.'

Lilith snorted. 'Since when does the *Globe* worry about facts?'

'Since last year, when we ran a story about one of the "Junior Idol" contestants, Luke de Brun, and claimed he was a drug addict,' he said bluntly. 'Remember? We got taken to the cleaner in the courts on that one. They dropped Luke from the programme, so he sued both us and the producers. After he won damages, the producers sued us as well. I don't want that happening again. When it comes to "Junior Idol", I'm not prepared to take chances.'

'But Luke de Brun *is* a drug addict,' Lilith pointed out. 'Everyone knows that.'

Rob Gardiner-Smith gave an exaggerated sigh and rolled his eyes. 'Of course the bastard's an effing drug addict. But that's not the point, dear girl, as you know very well.'

'What exactly *is* the point?'

'The point is that we couldn't *prove* it. Any more than you can prove that Samantha was involved in this anti-freeze murder. Unless you can get the police to confirm that she was questioned…'

As if Neville Stewart would do any such thing, Lilith fumed to herself. And Samantha Winter wasn't likely to admit it, either. Even if she could get through to her to ask.

She would have to find some way round it. That story was too good to die a premature death. Or, worse yet, to be picked up by another paper.

There had to be a way.

Neville usually tried not to pre-judge the people he interviewed, but he had unconsciously built up a mental picture of Miss Rosemary Harwood, the university departmental secretary, as a sort of a version of Evans' secretary Ursula: middle-aged, plain, shapeless. Probably hopelessly in love with her boss—though that was something one would never say of Ursula, whose perspective on Evans was mercilessly clear-sighted.

With that picture in his head, during his journey he worked out a scenario in which the smitten secretary, insanely jealous of her beloved's affair with a young and beautiful woman, decides that if she can't have him, no one will. Seeing the Lucozade bottle on his desk, she nips out and buys a bottle of anti-freeze…

It wasn't impossible.

Approaching Miss Harwood's house in Ladbroke Square, Notting Hill, Neville wondered whether Ursula lived somewhere like this: genteel terraced houses facing onto a huge, park-like green. He'd never thought about Ursula having a home before.

This was lovely—just the sort of place he'd like to live himself, Neville thought. Conveniently located in the heart of the city, close to a couple of Tube stations, yet overlooking green grass as far as the eye could see. The trees were still leafless, of course, but in a few weeks' time this would be lush with vegetation.

He located the house, in the middle of a long line of period terraces—white on the ground floor, greyish brick above.

He'd rung ahead to tell her he was coming, in case she'd decided to go in to work that morning, so she was waiting for him, answering the doorbell within a few seconds.

'Miss Harwood?' Neville said. 'I'm Detective Inspector Stewart.'

'Please come in.'

She was nothing like Ursula, of course. Rosemary Harwood was older—well over sixty, surely—and as willowy as Ursula was solid. She had a fine-boned face, high-cheekboned, and translucent skin that would be the envy of many a young woman. Her hair, pure white, was swept up and coiled elaborately on her head. Her clothing, too, was nothing like Ursula's sensible plaid skirts and twin sets; she wore a pair of loosely-cut dark trousers and a soft pink polo-neck tunic which looked like cashmere.

The interior of the house was as unexpected as its owner. No trace of period features remained in the open-plan sitting room which comprised most of the ground floor. The walls were the colour of clotted cream, the floors were stripped wood, and there were French doors leading to a back garden, letting in light from the south. 'What a lovely house,' Neville said involuntarily.

She smiled, transforming her rather austere face. 'I'm glad you like it.' Gesturing him into a chair, she went on, 'Now, Inspector. I imagine you'd like a cup of coffee?'

'That would be very nice.'

In what seemed little more than a few seconds, she reappeared with a tray containing a cafetière, two cups, milk jug and sugar bowl, and a plate of thin shortbread biscuits. She slid it onto the glass coffee table and waited for the coffee to brew. 'You're here to ask me about Dr di Stefano, I imagine,' she said.

'Yes, that's right. I understand that you…knew him well.'

Rosemary Harwood smiled. 'You could say that. We went back a very long way. More than twenty years, if you can believe it.'

'Twenty years!'

She seemed to be doing a sum in her head. 'About twenty-seven years, actually. He was just eighteen or so when we met—an undergraduate.'

'And you were…?'

'Oh, I was doing the same job I'm still doing. Departmental secretary in the sociology department. Frightening, isn't it? How time gets away from you, and the years just whizz by?'

Neville didn't want to get side-tracked down that path. 'So you knew Joe di Stefano when he was a student.'

'Just over from Italy,' she confirmed. 'His English wasn't very good in those days. He used to ask me for help when he didn't understand certain words. Now, of course, you wouldn't know he wasn't native-born.'

'I never met Dr di Stefano,' Neville reminded her.

'Oh, how silly of me.' Rosemary Harwood blinked back a few tears, the first sign he'd seen of emotion. She leaned over and pressed down on the plunger of the cafetière.

'So he spent his entire career at the university?' Neville asked quickly.

She swallowed, then answered. 'That's right, Inspector. He was an undergraduate, then a graduate student, then became a lecturer, and moved up from there. He'd planned to go back to Italy, initially,' she added. 'When he'd finished his studies. But of course he married, and that changed things.'

Neville could imagine: no chance that Serena would leave her family—and the family business—to follow her husband back to the ancestral homeland. She and Mark were London-born, with no desire to leave the place of their birth. Instead, Joe had been sucked into the Lombardi family and had put down new roots.

'And how did you feel when he married?' Neville asked.

Rosemary Harwood stared at him for a moment. 'I was happy for him, of course. Surely you're not suggesting that I was interested in him romantically?'

Neville back-pedalled furiously. 'No, of course not.'

'Because that would be…silly. I was old enough to be his mother, Inspector. We were friends, for many years. I felt protective of him, especially as he had no family in this country to begin with. And as I never had children myself...'

He understood: if anything, Joe di Stefano had been a child-substitute for Miss Harwood, not a longed-for lover. 'Yes, I see,' he said. 'So you were upset when Dr di Stefano...died.'

The tears welled up again as she handed him a cup of coffee. 'Help yourself to milk and sugar,' she invited before addressing his question. 'Yes, I was upset. Terribly upset. I'd known him so long, you see. And it was a sort of...I suppose you could say it was a wake-up call,' she said.

Neville wasn't sure what she meant. 'A wake-up call?'

'Life is too short,' she said simply. 'We put off doing the things we want to do, and the years slip by, and suddenly...'

'It's too late,' he said, without meaning to.

'Exactly, Inspector. So I've decided not to wait any longer to do the things I want to do.'

'And that would be...?'

'I've always wanted to live by the sea,' she said, stirring a bit of milk into her coffee. 'In a little cottage, very close to the sea, where I could potter along the beach and spend my days painting water-colours.' She smiled, looking into the distance as though she were picturing it in her mind. 'So I'm going to do it,' she added resolutely. 'I'm going to retire from the university, sell my house, and move to the seaside.'

'You're going to sell this house?'

She must have picked up something of the excitement in his voice, because Rosemary Harwood re-focused her attention on him. 'Why? Do you want to buy it?'

'I do,' he said, and meant it. 'I'd very much like to buy your house, Miss Harwood.'

◇◇◇

'Graham is a prince among men,' Callie sighed, leaning back into the whirlpool jets. 'What a brilliant gift this was.'

'This is just the beginning,' Frances said. 'Lots more to come.'

'Mmm.'

Frances plucked the strap of her swimming costume. 'This is looking decidedly tired,' she stated. 'I think I need a new one.'

'Mmm.' Callie didn't even open her eyes.

'What do you think?'

Callie forced her eyes open a crack. It looked fine to her, but that evidently wasn't what Frances wanted to hear. 'I think you could use a new one,' she said obediently. 'It's loose on you. You must have lost weight.'

'Liar.' Frances splashed some water in her direction. 'Did I tell you that Graham and I are thinking about going to the States this summer?'

'I don't think you've mentioned it. To see Heather?'

Frances smiled. 'Yes. She says she wants us to come.'

'Where, exactly?'

'She and Zack are living in California.'

The less said about Zack the better, Callie judged. Frances had made a real effort to accept her new son-in-law, but he wasn't the mate Frances would have chosen for her only child. Approaching sixty, Zack had grey plaits…and a vasectomy. Callie knew how much Frances had looked forward to having grandchildren one day; now that probably wasn't going to happen. Not unless Zack obliged them by dying in the not-too-distant future, leaving Heather to re-marry while she was still in her childbearing years. 'Sounds like a nice trip,' she said neutrally.

The water bubbled along her spine; she shifted a few inches to direct a jet at her tight shoulders. 'Do you know what one of the nicest things about today is?' she asked, heedlessly ungrammatical. 'Apart from spending time with my best friend, of course.'

'What's that?'

'The only decision I have to make,' Callie said on a sigh, 'is what colour to have my nails painted.'

Calm down, Neville told himself. Maybe the rest of the house is totally unsuitable.

'Would you like to see the rest of the house?' Rosemary Harwood asked him. 'If you're serious, that is.'

'I'm serious,' he assured her. 'My wife is expecting a baby. We really need to find a proper house, before the baby comes. And the location here—it just couldn't be better.'

'It's not the sea,' she said with a smile. 'But if one has to live in London, Ladbroke Square is as good a view as any. It's almost like living in parkland.'

'Close to Paddington for me,' Neville said, 'and the Central Line Tube for my wife. It's perfect.'

After showing him the modern kitchen/diner, she took him upstairs, and it was just as delightful as the ground floor: three bedrooms on two floors, a large family bathroom, and an ensuite.

'It's always been too large for me, really,' Miss Harwood said, almost apologetically. 'It was my family home, you see. I've lived here all my life. When my parents died, I thought about selling it and buying something smaller. But I didn't want to leave Ladbroke Square. So I modernised it instead. Gutted the place, got rid of all the fireplaces and the Victoriana my mother loved so much. Opened it up, took up the carpets, stripped the floors. I did quite a bit of the work myself, in the evenings.'

A woman of many talents, clearly.

'It's beautiful,' said Neville. Clean, bright rooms, overlooking the parkland in the front and the south-facing garden at the back. Triona would adore it. 'I'd love to buy it. If I can afford it,' he added, with belated dismay.

'I'm sure we can come to some arrangement,' Miss Harwood said. 'After all, if I don't have to go through an estate agent, a private sale would save me quite a bit of money.' She smiled at him. 'And I'd love to think of a family living here again.'

They went downstairs to finish their coffee. Neville's head was spinning: was this really too good to be true? There had to be a catch somewhere.

With difficulty, he turned his thoughts back to Joe di Stefano and the derailed interview. There were still questions he needed to put to Rosemary Harwood.

'Did you ever see a bottle of Lucozade in Dr di Stefano's office?' he asked.

She looked puzzled at the question. 'Well, yes,' she said. 'Quite often, on his desk. Sometimes he'd go out running during his lunch hour. Recently, that was. Within the last six months or so.'

The next one was tricker; he phrased the question as delicately as he could. 'Were you aware of a relationship he had with a young woman called Samantha Winter?'

Miss Harwood pressed her lips together. 'Yes,' she said.

There was a moment of silence. 'And you didn't approve?' he prodded.

'Certainly not. It was most…unsuitable,' she said crisply. 'He was a married man. And she was a student. Too young for him, even if he didn't already have a wife.'

'Did you say anything to Dr di Stefano about it?'

'Many times.' She sniffed. 'He knew I didn't approve. But he was absolutely besotted by the girl. He wouldn't listen to anyone. He was…reckless. Even when his wife found out, he didn't break it off.'

'So his wife knew.'

'Yes, he told me she'd found out. He didn't like hurting her. He wasn't a cruel man,' she said earnestly. 'But as I said, he was besotted.'

There was another delicate question to be posed. 'She wasn't the first, though, was she? I mean, there had been other students in the past.'

Rosemary Harwood raised her eyebrows. 'Why would you think that, Inspector?'

'I just assumed…'

'That if there'd been one, there were a whole string of them? Not at all,' she stated. 'Until that little…Samantha,' she checked herself, 'came into his life, he never even thought of going astray. He was a faithful husband. He loved his wife. I'd stake my life on that.'

Well, well, thought Neville. If that was indeed the case, he'd be willing to bet that Samantha was the one who had initiated the affair, as well as breaking it off.

'But the…relationship…was over before he died?' Neville continued.

'It ended a month or two ago,' she confirmed. 'He was devastated. I've never seen a man more cut up. I'm sure he tried to hide it from his family, but he didn't hide it from me.' For a moment she gazed off into the distance with a thoughtful expression. 'You haven't told me why the police are interested in Joe di Stefano's death,' she said at last. 'I'd been given to understand that he died of a heart attack. A natural death. Would I be right in thinking that you suspect he somehow committed suicide?'

'Let's just say that we're keeping our options open.' Maybe, Neville told himself, he'd been too hasty in ruling out suicide. A horrible way to go, but if the man were that low…

◇◇◇

It was undoubtedly the most unusual—and possibly the most difficult—police case Yolanda had ever worked on.

In the first place, she just couldn't make Serena di Stefano out. Although she usually had an excellent instinct for people, when it came to Serena that instinct failed her. If Neville Stewart were to ask her for her reading on Serena—and she had no doubt that he would ask, sooner or later—she wouldn't know what to say. Reserved and unemotional? In denial? Guilty? She didn't know.

And she was desperately worried about Chiara. The girl was on the edge, not knowing where to turn. It had taken some time for Yolanda to get Chiara to trust her. Finally, last night, she'd gone to Chiara's room to chat, and had broken through the wall of defence the girl had erected round herself. That, though, brought with it another problem. Chiara had told her, with every evidence of total sincerity, that she believed her mother had killed her father.

What was Yolanda supposed to do with that? She would have to tell Neville, of course. The fact that Chiara believed it didn't necessarily make it true, but it was pretty damning all the same.

In addition, there was the issue of Mark Lombardi. He'd been hanging round like a wet weekend, miserable and not too bothered who knew it. Yolanda could understand it: putting herself in his shoes, she realised how difficult it must be for him to stand by and watch her do his job. She wouldn't have liked it any better than he did. At least today he was out of the way— helping out at the restaurant, she'd been told.

And Angelina was all right, thought Yolanda gratefully. She liked Angelina: she was sensible and down-to-earth, not in the least moody, and didn't mind pitching in to help out where she was needed. Today Angelina was tackling the huge pile of condolence cards and letters that had flooded in over the past few days, writing personal answers to each one on behalf of her mother and the family, while Yolanda addressed the envelopes.

'I'm glad Uncle Marco's not here today,' Angelina confided in between letters. 'He's like a bear with a sore head.'

'Everyone's a bit tense,' Yolanda said in his defence.

'But it's not like Uncle Marco to be like that. Do you know what I think?'

'What, then?'

'I think he has love troubles,' Angelina stated. 'His girlfriend Callie. I expected her to be round here this week, giving moral support and all that. But when I asked Uncle Marco why she wasn't here, he said she was busy.'

'Maybe she *is* busy.'

'Hmph.' Angelina grunted sceptically. 'Maybe *you* could talk to him, Yolanda. Tell him to sort it out, or get over it. He wouldn't take it from a kid like me, but *you* can tell him.'

'Maybe I will,' said Yolanda. 'Maybe I will.'

Chapter Eighteen

Callie's state of unthinking bliss lasted through the whirlpool, the facial and the tasty lunch they were served. She even managed to get through the manicure without engaging her brain beyond the vital matter of choice of varnish colour—dusty rose, in the end. But as she and Frances sat side by side having their pedicures, she thought about Chiara, and her mellow mood evaporated.

'Do you mind if I tell you something?' she asked Frances.

'Tell me whatever you like.'

'I saw Chiara di Stefano yesterday. In spite of the fact that her mother didn't want me to.'

Frances turned to look at her. 'Was that wise?'

'No, of course it wasn't wise. But I had to do it.' What if Frances thought she'd done the wrong thing? Maybe she shouldn't have told her.

She needn't have worried; Frances was smiling. 'I knew you'd make a good priest,' she said.

'I'm not a priest yet,' Callie felt compelled to point out, though she was greatly heartened by Frances' words.

'But you'll be a good one. Sometimes ministry means making tough decisions like that.'

Callie contemplated her pristinely pink fingernails. How long would it be before they were chipped and unsightly? 'She's a really mixed-up girl,' she said. 'Chiara. I'm worried about her, Fran. She actually told me that she thinks her mother killed her father.'

'But didn't he die of a heart attack?'

'Apparently the police have been making enquiries. Chiara's put two and two together and got five.'

Frances gave an understanding sigh. 'And you can't ask Mark about it.'

'No.' Callie swallowed. 'I haven't heard from him. I suppose that's that.'

'I didn't want to ask,' Frances admitted.

And Callie didn't want to think about Marco. Not now. 'I just don't know what to do about Chiara,' she said quickly. 'She needs help. Professional help. I'm not sure how long I'll be able to be of any use to her, especially if her mother finds out.'

'Hmm.' Frances was silent for a moment, then spoke. 'Have you thought about talking to her parish priest?'

'Her parish priest?'

'At the Italian church. I'm sure he'd want to know about what's going on. And maybe he could have a word with Serena.'

Callie remembered his name. 'Father Luigi.'

'That's right,' Frances confirmed. 'Father Luigi. I've run across him once or twice at ecumenical things. He seems quite a reasonable man, from what I've seen of him. It would be good to get him on your side.'

How wise Frances was, Callie thought gratefully. And how lucky she was to have Frances for a friend. She would never have thought of it herself. But then, Frances did have years more experience.

'Thanks,' she said. 'That's a brilliant idea. I'll go to see him. Maybe later today.'

The time for relaxation was over. Callie couldn't wait for the technician to finish with her toenails so she could get on with what she needed to do.

◇◇◇

The suicide scenario still seemed rather far-fetched to Neville, but he wanted to have a word with the pathologist before ruling it out.

Back at his desk, he rang Dr Tompkins.

'Can it wait?' Tompkins said tersely. 'I'm in the middle of a post-mortem.'

'Just a quick question,' Neville assured him. 'Joe di Stefano. Is it possible that he killed himself?'

There was a pause of a few seconds on the other end of the phone. 'From a clinical point of view, it's certainly possible. He could have deliberately ingested the ethylene glycol. How was it administered? Do we know?'

'We found anti-freeze in his Lucozade bottle. The lab has confirmed it.' Neville had the report on his desk, along with other findings from the SOCOs' search of the di Stefano residence. 'His prints were on the bottle,' he added. 'No other prints.'

'Well, then. He could have done it. But it's not a very tidy way to kill oneself. A bit painful, and prolonged. I wouldn't do it, myself.'

Neville was tempted to ask Dr Tompkins how he *would* choose to kill himself, should he be so inclined, but didn't think the doctor would see the humour in it.

'Thanks,' said Neville. 'Thanks for your time. I appreciate it.'

Maybe Hereward Rice could shed some light.

His call to the coroner's office was put through with little delay.

'Dr Rice,' he said, 'in your experience, have you ever known anyone to kill themselves with anti-freeze?'

'Not that I recall. It could be done, of course.' Hereward Rice paused. 'You're talking about di Stefano, aren't you? I have the papers here. It will be interesting to hear what you have to say at the inquest.'

'Has it been scheduled?' Neville asked.

'You're joking, right?'

Neville could feel his heart sinking towards his proverbial boots. 'Um…remind me.'

'This afternoon, DI Stewart. Three o'clock. You're giving a statement, remember?'

Neville had absolutely no recollection that the subject had ever been discussed in anything but the vaguest of terms. He started shuffling papers on his desk, looking for his diary, and found a piece of paper on which someone else had printed in large letters: 'di Stefano inquest. Friday 3 p.m. Statement needed.'

Cowley's writing, he thought. The little toe-rag. Hadn't even bothered to tell him.

'Dr di Stefano died on Monday. It's Friday today,' Hereward Rice said with exaggerated patience. 'The family would like to plan a funeral. Some time before the last trump. I don't think that's an unreasonable expectation, do you?'

'No, of course not.'

'Then I'll see you in court at three,' said Dr Rice.

Neville slammed the phone down. 'Bloody hell,' he sputtered. He'd better get busy: he had a statement to write.

And he would deal with Cowley later.

It was unusual, but Yolanda didn't see any way she could prevent it: Mark Lombardi had declared his intention of accompanying her to the opening of the inquest, representing the family's interests. It was Serena's wish that he go in her place.

Perhaps it wouldn't be a bad thing, she reflected. It would give her a chance to spend some time with him in a non-threatening way. Maybe she could break through his resentment and be of some positive help to him.

Though she would usually have driven the car, she let him do it.

'I know this must be difficult for you,' she said, trying not to sound patronising.

Mark was noncommittal. 'Mm.'

'I'd hate it, if I were you.'

'It's not much fun,' he admitted. 'I feel…surplus to requirements. Pretty useless, to be honest.'

'But you're helping Serena by going to the inquest,' Yolanda pointed out. 'And you helped your mother at the restaurant earlier.'

Mark shook his head. 'They didn't really need me. Mamma just asked me to give me something to do. I'm sure of that.'

Taking a deep breath, Yolanda plunged in. 'Maybe this weekend you can spend some time with your girlfriend,' she said, as innocently as she could manage.

He kept his eyes on the road, but she could feel the tension radiating from him. 'Probably not,' he said.

'Oh, is she away?'

'No.'

Yolanda waited. Sometimes, she'd found, that was the best way. Once you'd asked the question and got the ball rolling, patience was often the thing required.

They'd travelled a good distance before Mark spoke again, sounding strained. 'I did a really stupid thing,' he said. '*Molto stupido.*'

'Oh?'

It was like a dam collapsing then, as it all poured out: how he'd passed on a message from Serena and thus put himself between his sister and his girlfriend. 'I didn't think it would come out sounding like that,' he said. 'I suppose I didn't think, full stop. Stupid, stupid. I'm sure she'll never speak to me again.'

'And how does that make you feel?' Yolanda asked quietly.

'Unbearably awful. First of all because I've hurt her, and secondly because I love her. I don't want to lose her.'

'And right now is when you need her the most,' Yolanda pointed out, thinking about how often Eli had been there for her when she'd been down, and what a difference it made.

'I do,' Mark admitted, as though it was the first time that had occurred to him.

'Well, I don't think it's too late. Not at all,' Yolanda said. 'You love her, right?'

'Very much.'

'And she loves you?'

'I think so. She says she does.'

'Then what are you waiting for?'

'I don't know,' said Mark miserably.

She shook her head so hard her braids bounced. It was a good thing all men weren't as backward as Mark Lombardi, she said to herself. What was the matter with him? He was a good-looking man, in that Italian way; he was intelligent, and he had a kind heart. Yet here he was, at his age—over thirty, he had to be—an unreconstructed mamma's boy and more concerned with what his sister thought of him than he was with winning his woman and keeping her happy. Were all Italians like that? Thank God that West Indians weren't.

It was going to be difficult—she had no illusions about that. He was going to have to make some changes in his life, in his priorities. He was going to have to grow up a bit. But he could do it if he really wanted to. Yolanda knew him well enough to believe that he had it in him.

'You go to that girl,' she said in her bossiest West Indian voice—the one Eli pretended to hate. 'You tell her you love her. You hear me, boy?'

'I hear you.'

'If you don't,' she went on, 'you'll be sorry for the rest of your life. And what's worse, Yolanda's gonna come and give you a smack the side of your head that'll make your teeth rattle.'

A smile tugged at the corner of his mouth.

Well, thought Yolanda, that was something. She'd managed to get half a smile out of him. It was a start.

◇◇◇

Lilith had her brain wave after lunchtime.

She'd been round and round the problem, looking at it from every conceivable angle. How could she get more information about the di Stefano case, short of ringing the family and asking them straight out? They weren't any more likely to talk to her than Neville Stewart was.

She went back to the Met web site, hoping for something additional, and realised it had been there all along.

'An inquest has been scheduled for Friday,' the news release said.

Today.

It was a mixed blessing, of course. She wouldn't be the only journalist at the inquest. Even if no one else had any suspicions that there was mileage in this case, it would be covered as a matter of routine. If something sensational were to come out, everyone would know about it.

But there was always a chance that she would pick up something that could lead to other things.

She rang the coroner's office and asked for confirmation of the time, hoping she wasn't too late already.

Three o'clock.

Lilith would be there.

◇◇◇

It would have to do. The statement wasn't very polished, but Neville had run out of time. He read it through, quickly, to make sure he'd covered the important points, then thought about how he was going to get to the coroner's court. The Tube would be the quickest way, he judged. On a Friday afternoon he could so easily get stuck in traffic if he took a car. Edgware Road to Baker Street, then change to the Jubilee…

He was just about to go down the steps into the Tube station when his mobile rang.

Triona, he saw.

But there was no time to stop and chat. He had to concentrate on getting to court on time. 'Listen, I'll catch up with you later,' he said, without preliminaries.

'Neville Stewart, what the hell is going on?' she demanded in a terrifyingly quiet, yet intense, voice.

He stopped in his tracks. 'What do you mean?'

'I had a nice lie-in, tidied up your pig-sty of a flat, then came back to my flat. And what do you think I found?'

'I don't kn—'

Oh, God. He *did* know. Andrew Linton, eager as a puppy, and any number of prospective City-dwellers, clamouring to buy her flat.

Neville sagged against the nearest wall, blocking the path of others who were in a hurry to get to the Underground. 'Triona, I can explain,' he said weakly.

'This had better be good.'

He looked at his watch. 'Listen, Triona. I really, *really* don't have time right now. Where are you?'

'I've locked myself in my loo. They're getting angry out there because they can't get in. I can hear them buzzing, like killer bees.'

Oh, God.

'Go back to my flat,' he said. 'I'll be there as soon as I can. And I promise you I can explain everything.'

Mark had attended an uncounted number of inquests in a professional capacity, providing moral support to bereaved family members. How odd, then, it felt to him to be sitting there with Yolanda beside him, in a totally different role.

Yet, in a peculiar way, he was no less detached from the proceedings than when the deceased was a total stranger to him. The 'Dr Giuseppe di Stefano' the coroner was talking about didn't connect in Mark's head with Joe.

Mark listened, unmoved, as Neville read out his statement. This, too, was a part of the ritual very familiar to him. In Mark's experience, Neville was usually quite good at delivering a concise summary of the facts of a case, couched in police-speak. Today, though, he seemed distracted and almost ill-prepared. He glanced at the coroner and concluded abruptly. 'Laboratory tests have confirmed the presence of ethylene glycol in Dr di Stefano's Lucozade bottle. The police's enquiries are continuing.'

Hereward Rice looked back at him, shrugged, and delivered the expected words: the inquest would now be adjourned until the end of April, pending further police enquiries. In the mean time, he was directing that the body be released to the family.

It was then that it hit Mark, as it hadn't hit him before.

Joe was dead. Joe, who had been a part of his life since his childhood. Joe, whom Serena had adored and who had made her so happy for more than twenty years. Joe, who had been such a good father to Angelina and then Chiara, cherishing them and lavishing more than the average father's amount of attention on them.

Mark had been so angry with Joe—deservedly, he was certain—in the last few months that he'd lost sight of all of the good years. Now Joe would never have a chance to put things right, to repent the way he'd hurt Serena and atone for his sins. It was too late for Joe. Too late for all of them.

As Yolanda turned to him in surprised consternation, Mark took out his handkerchief and sobbed: wracking, unmanly tears. Tears for Joe, tears for Serena, tears for Angelina and Chiara. Tears for himself.

◇◇◇

As soon as the inquest had been adjourned, Lilith left the press area and positioned herself by the exit, hoping for a chance to speak to Neville Stewart: it was just possible that she could catch him off-guard and get something out of him.

And pigs might fly.

Once again, as he'd been delivering his statement, she had looked at him in that strange new way, aware of him as an attractive man. How fanciable he was: she wondered why it had taken her so long to see it. The set of his shoulders in his tweed jacket; the tousled hair, as though he'd just got out of bed; the greenish-blue Irish eyes, crinkled at the corners; the lovely mobile mouth, just made for…

Stop it, she told herself sternly.

Spotting him as he approached the door, she took a step forward.

But Neville Stewart didn't even look at her. Instead he focused his attention on the man who was standing next to her.

'You!' he said contemptuously. 'What are you doing here, then? Come to look out for the interests of your precious Samantha? Did you want to make sure I wasn't going to spill the beans about her? Well, no worries, mate. She has quite enough publicity already without me adding to it.'

Then he brushed past Lilith, close enough for her to smell his spicy aftershave, and sprinted in the direction of the Underground station.

Catching her breath, Lilith turned to the man who had been the target for DI Stewart's contempt. He was young and willowy, clad in skin-tight black jeans and a leather jacket. Camp as Christmas, she said to herself, while giving him a smile. 'What did you do to deserve that?' she said in what she hoped was a convincingly commiserating voice.

The young man shrugged.

'I'm Lilith,' she said. 'Lilith Noone.'

'Ah.' He smiled. 'I'm Tarquin.'

'I don't know about you, but I'm thirsty. Can I buy you a drink, Tarquin?'

His smile turned into a grin. 'That's an offer I can't refuse.'

She was waiting for him at his flat, and the expression on her face would have stopped a basilisk in its tracks. Neville took a step towards her, then stopped, outstretched arms dropping to his sides.

'I can explain.' The words came out on a plaintive sigh.

'Jesus God, Stewart. You've pulled some stunts in your time, but this takes the biscuit.' She crossed her arms across her chest, above the little bulge that was their baby. 'I'm listening.'

'Last week. You said you wouldn't come home with me till I had a home to take you to. And that's a direct quote,' he pointed out.

'And how does that relate to me coming home to my flat—*my* flat—to find it full of people opening my wardrobes and peering into my loo? Turning on the water in my power shower and examining the contents of my fridge? Excuse me, but somehow I'm missing the connection.'

'I wanted to find you a house. Like you said, Triona. Like you wanted. But I realised that we'd have to sell both our flats first.'

She waited; he went on.

'I talked to an estate agent. Andrew. He said—'

'That annoyingly yappy little bloke, like an inbred Jack Russell on uppers?'

Neville grinned at the perfect description, heartened at the indication that she could at least see some humour in the situation. 'That's the one.' He pressed his advantage. 'Yes, he's annoying. But he knows his business. He's already sold my flat. And by the end of the day he will have sold yours as well.'

She stared at him. 'And you were going to tell me…when, exactly?'

'I wanted to surprise you.' He stretched his hands out to her, palms upward. 'Honest to God, Triona. I just wanted to surprise you.'

'Well, you've done that, all right.' Her mouth, pressed together, started to twitch; she gasped, then sputtered, covering her face with her hands, doubling over at the waist.

'Are you all right? Triona, are you all right?' Neville covered the distance between them, terrified in that instant that she was about to lose the baby.

Triona pushed him away. 'You eejit!' she gasped. 'You great clot!'

She was laughing, he realised belatedly. Laughing as he'd never heard her laugh before. Gustily, almost hysterically. Tears ran from her eyes; she had to grope her way to the sofa to sit down, and still she laughed.

It was contagious, of course. His laughter started with relief and progressed to an hysteria equal to hers.

She thought it was funny. She wasn't going to kill him, or divorce him. Neville collapsed next to her on the sofa and howled with mirth.

Later, after they'd gone to bed and made love with an intensity somehow fuelled by the laughter, before he fell into a deep sleep, Neville remembered something. He hadn't told her the best part: he hadn't told her about the house he'd found to buy for her.

She was already snoring.

He would tell her in the morning.

◇◇◇

There was a pub just down and across the road from the coroner's court; Lilith had sought refreshment there in the past.

'It's a bit early to start drinking,' Tarquin demurred, looking at his watch, but he didn't object when Lilith returned to their table with a bottle of white wine and two glasses.

While waiting at the bar she had been overtaken by an intuition that verged on certainty. Thinking back to the tip-off call from her mysterious informant, she was almost sure that she recognised the voice.

The bartender had opened the bottle, so all she had to do was pour. 'Cheers,' she said, lifting her glass in Tarquin's direction, and he did the same.

'Ooh, lovely,' he said after his first sip. 'I do like a nice Chardonnay.'

She hadn't skimped on it; it *was* a decent bottle of wine.

No point being flirtatious with this one. Even if she'd fancied him—and he was far too young for that, as well as being not even remotely her type—it was obvious that she would have been wasting her breath, barking up the wrong tree. The train was never going to stop at that station. 'Tell me, Tarquin. What do you do?'

He took another sip of wine, put the glass down on the table, and pulled open his leather jacket with a dramatic little flourish. His tee shirt was emblazoned with the words 'Junior Idol'. 'Production assistant,' he said, his narrow chest swelling with pride.

'Oh, my!' Lilith widened her eyes, hoping she looked suitably impressed. 'What an interesting job!'

He nodded. 'I couldn't ask for a better one.'

'You get to work with all of those celebrities. And things must be getting exciting, with the final coming up. Tomorrow, isn't it?'

'That's right. I'm practically run off my feet at the moment.'

Which begged the question of what he was doing in a pub, drinking Chardonnay, after having attended an inquest at the coroner's court.

Time to cut this little game short, Lilith decided; time to put her cards on the table. If she was going to get her story written for tomorrow's paper, she needed to get her skates on.

'You rang me, didn't you?' she asked him bluntly. 'And it wasn't any accident that you were standing beside me outside of the court.'

Tarquin looked at her for a moment, then shrugged. 'It's a fair cop.'

'So what is this all about?'

'After I rang you, I was sure there would be a story in the *Globe* today. But there wasn't anything. So I thought maybe you'd be here, at the inquest. And here you are,' he added.

Lilith wasn't complaining, though she still didn't understand. 'But…why?'

'Publicity, innit? The more people who see Sam's name in the paper, the better. Just think about it.' He tapped his head with one finger. 'All the people who read the *Globe*. If even a fraction of them picked up the phone and voted for her because they'd seen her name on the front page of the *Globe*, she'd win "Junior Idol" for sure, hands down. I'm just doing my job.' He fixed her with an accusing glare. 'So why haven't you done *yours*?'

Callie had never been to the Italian church before; though she had the address, she almost walked past it. Unlike any Anglican church she'd ever seen, it wasn't surrounded by any sort of church yard, or even an open space, but was flush with the pavement, attached to the buildings on either side. Admittedly it stood a storey higher than the flanking buildings, but that wasn't immediately evident from the pavement. She hesitated outside, then went through one of the twin rounded arches and into the church.

The interior was darkened, but not empty: she could hear the murmur of voices some distance away. A sign just inside of the door told her what was going on: 'Stazioni della Via Crucis: Venerdì alla Quaresima, 6 p.m.'.

Between the smidgeon of Italian that she could understand, and her knowledge of the Church, she figured it out. Stations of the Cross. Fridays in Lent.

Callie crept into a pew at the back of the church and waited.

The stations were fixed at intervals along the walls; the worshippers were moving anti-clockwise round the church, stopping at each station for a prayer in Italian.

After the relaxing treatments Callie had enjoyed that day, the unintelligibly musical words acted as a soporific. She closed her eyes—just to listen, she told herself—and drifted off.

She woke with a start at the sound of her name at close range. The lights were on and someone was standing over her, peering into her face. 'Callie?' repeated the voice she'd first thought was part of her dream. 'What are you doing here?'

It was, Callie realised with dismay, just about the last person she wanted to see: Grazia Lombardi. Marco's mother. If she'd known Mrs Lombardi was here as part of the praying group, she wouldn't have stayed.

Callie blinked. 'Oh. Oh, I'm sorry. I must have dozed off. I was waiting for Father Luigi.'

'Does he expect you?'

How silly of her not to have rung ahead, Callie told herself. But she'd come straight from the spa, hoping to catch him. 'No,' she admitted.

'He's gone to *la sagrestia*. To change from his robes. He'll be back soon.' Grazia Lombardi sat down in the pew in front of Callie and twisted round to face her.

So there was no escape, short of being rude.

'We haven't seen you for a few days,' Mrs Lombardi stated.

'Well…no.'

'I thought you would come. To support Marco in our family's loss.'

The implied criticism—unjust as it was—was too much for Callie; tears stung her eyes. 'I'm…I'm sorry,' she said.

Grazia Lombardi leaned closer. 'Is something wrong? With you and Marco?'

How could she answer that? 'We haven't spoken for a few days,' she evaded.

'Something is wrong.' Mrs Lombardi nodded, frowning. 'I knew it. Tell me, if you can.'

Well, thought Callie, what did she have to lose? She took a deep breath. 'It was to do with Chiara,' she began. 'She asked to see me, to talk about her father's death. I went to her school, and we talked.'

'That's good. I'm glad she talked to you. I did not know. I'm worried about Chiara,' Mrs Lombardi added, in a confidential voice. 'I came tonight, before *i stazioni*, to speak to Father Luigi about her.'

Thank goodness at least one member of the family was concerned about Chiara, Callie said to herself. It gave her the courage to continue. 'Serena didn't like it, though,' she said. 'She had Marco ring me and tell me to stay away.'

Mrs Lombardi drew back, her dark eyes wide with surprise. 'Ah. So that is what happened.' She shook her head. 'My daughter. Sometimes she is not so *intelligente*—clever, yes?'

'I'm sure Serena does what she thinks is best for her family,' Callie stated, determined to be fair.

'What is best? Yes, she tries, I believe. But sometimes she is foolish. Like with Chiara.' Grazia Lombardi looked over her shoulder, as if making sure she wouldn't be overheard, then lowered her voice. 'She tried to keep it from us—her pappa and me—that she and Joe were having *i problemi*. Does she think we are *stupido*? Does she think, *veramente*, we would not know?'

Serena would be mortified, Callie thought, with a touch of guilty gratification. 'I suppose she didn't want to worry or upset you,' she said in restitution.

'Marco. He knew, didn't he?' Grazia asked. 'And he told you.'

'Yes,' Callie admitted.

Mrs Lombardi's next words were more in the nature of thinking aloud. 'I do not know anything about their problems—just that there were some. Maybe I don't want to know. Joe is dead now, I don't think it matters any more.'

But it *did* matter. Callie wanted to tell her that, and found that she couldn't. It certainly wasn't up to her to spill Serena's carefully kept secrets. And perhaps it would make things worse, especially for the girls. Instead she said, 'I don't think Serena likes me very much.'

Marco would have denied it, but Mrs Lombardi did no such thing. She reached over and patted Callie's cheek. 'No, of course she doesn't. She is *molto geloso* of you and Marco. He's always been special to her. If I had been able to have more *bambini* it would have been different. But there are just the two of them.'

Callie did understand about the special sister/brother rela-tionship, but it was beyond her to comprehend the jealousy. Part of loving Peter was wanting him to be happy, in whatever way—and with whomever—he could find happiness.

'And now,' Grazia said, sadly, 'she has managed to come between you and Marco. You must not let her do that.'

'What can I do?' It was a rhetorical question, not a plea for help.

Marco's mother, though, was a practical person. 'Do you love Marco?' she asked bluntly.

Callie, not trusting her voice, nodded.

'I thought so. And Marco loves you, I believe. You make him happy. *Felice.* Now he is not happy. And that makes me sad.'

A tear escaped and trickled down Callie's cheek.

'It makes you sad, too. Ah, *povero* Callie.' Grazia Lombardi got up, came round to Callie's pew, wiped the tear away with her finger, then took Callie's face between her hands and kissed her on both cheeks. 'Leave it with me,' she said. '*Corragio. Abbi fede.* Have faith, my dear.'

And then she was gone.

Chapter Nineteen

On Saturdays, Brian's day off, Callie had the responsibility of taking Morning Prayer by herself. She frequently had to rush to get there on time, but that was primarily a function of how late she'd been up the night before, on her own day off.

This week, getting up early wasn't a problem. She'd had an early night, and in spite of the mediaeval torture device that was the vicarage guest bed, she'd slept soundly, still feeling relaxed from her 'pamper day'; she woke naturally before seven, without the aid of her alarm.

Secure in the knowledge that Brian and Jane would be enjoying a lie-in, Callie allowed herself the luxury of a bubble bath rather than a hurried shower.

Soaking in the fragrant bubbles, she allowed herself to think back to her encounters in the Italian church—the almost surreal conversation with Marco's mother, a wise woman if ever there was one, then her talk with Father Luigi.

The Italian priest had treated her like a colleague, not—as she'd feared—like an interfering busy-body. He was reassuringly on top of the situation with Chiara, and not at all averse to Callie's own involvement. It was true that he hadn't yet spoken to Chiara herself—she was still refusing to talk to him—but he was happy that she'd sought out Callie, and encouraged Callie to keep the lines of communication open. And he was planning to talk to Serena as soon as possible. 'I can't push it, you understand,' he'd said. 'Not just yet. But as soon as the funeral is over, I'll be working to facilitate healing in that relationship.'

So Callie was cautiously optimistic—if not about herself and Marco, at least about Chiara and Serena. As long as nothing else horrible happened, and if Chiara could be persuaded to give up this nonsense about her father being murdered…

When she'd dressed, Callie still had a few minutes to spare, and was about to ring Frances to confirm her plans to stop by in the morning and give Bella a long walk, when her mobile rang.

It was Frances. 'Hope I didn't wake you,' Frances said.

'Not at all. I was just about to ring *you*, as it happens. I'd like to come round this morning and collect Bella for a walk, if it's all right with you.'

'Yes. Fine. I'll be here.' Frances went on, 'Listen, Callie. I rang you for a reason. I think you need to go out and get a copy of the *Daily Globe* this morning. There's a story on the front page that will interest you.'

Oh, no, Callie thought. Not something else about Jodee and Chazz? Why couldn't the wretched press just leave them alone to mourn their baby in peace? 'All right,' she said. 'But why would you be reading the *Daily Globe*? It doesn't seem like your sort of paper, somehow.'

'It's not,' Frances confirmed succinctly.

'Then why…'

'Don't even ask.' Frances rang off, leaving Callie intrigued and curious.

◇◇◇

A growling stomach woke Neville; he tried to remember the last time he'd eaten, and realised he'd grabbed a sandwich after he'd interviewed Rosemary Harwood. A long time ago.

And if he was hungry, he thought, Triona would be even more so: she had to eat for two, and it was unlikely that she'd eaten any more recently than he had.

He eased himself out of bed, found his dressing gown, and went in search of something to eat.

The last visit he'd paid to a supermarket had been in the remote past—before the wedding. Ancient history. Since then he'd bought a few things at the corner shop, but even that hadn't happened very recently. He still had a few eggs on hand that were probably not dangerously past their sell-by date, and a loaf of bread that was beginning to go a bit green round the edges.

Neville examined the bread and found a couple of interior slices which would do if he pinched the mouldy spots off. He bunged those in the toaster while he scrambled up the eggs and put the kettle on. It would have to be instant coffee, black, as there was no milk.

Once they were settled in their new home, he told himself, he would turn over a new leaf. He would make regular visits to the supermarket, not expecting Triona to do it. He would learn to cook in a less haphazard way. He would transform himself into a domestic god.

Their new home. That reminded him that he'd switched his phone off when he got back yesterday. He went and got it, then listened to the messages.

Needless to say, more than one of them were from Andrew. 'The open house has been a huge success,' he said. 'Though I'm a bit concerned about Mrs Stewart. She didn't seem totally on board with this. Ring me.' Then, 'I have eight sealed bids. Ring me.' Finally, 'I've opened the bids, Mr Stewart. They're all well over the asking price. Ring me and we can discuss who's in the best position to proceed. And have you had a chance to look at those details I left for you?'

Grinning, Neville went back to the kitchen to find the eggs were rather over-cooked. He scraped them out of the pan onto the spotty toast, dividing them between two plates, made the coffee, and put the lot onto a tray which he carried through to the bedroom.

Triona was sitting up in bed, the duvet tucked demurely round her. 'The smell of the coffee woke me,' she said. 'I'm starving.'

'It's not very inspiring, but it's the best I could do.'

'It looks bloody marvellous to me.'

'And you,' said Neville, 'look bloody marvellous to *me*.'

'Food first, Stewart.' Triona took the tray from him, settled it on her lap, and tucked in.

Callie made a dash for the newsagent's before Morning Prayer, and had a few minutes to sit at the back of the church and read the front-page story.

Not Jodee and Chazz. Much worse.

'"Idol" Sexy Sam Questioned in Anti-Freeze Murder,' screamed the headline. The by-line, of course, was Lilith Noone.

'Sexy Samantha Winter, one of the competitors in tonight's "Junior Idol" final, has been questioned by the police in connection with a grisly murder, this reporter has learned exclusively.

'Giuseppe di Stefano, known as "Joe", died on Monday in St Mary's Hospital, Paddington. It was initially thought that he died of a heart attack, but a nurse's suspicions led to a post-mortem, where it was discovered that di Stefano was poisoned with ANTI-FREEZE.

'Yesterday an inquest was opened into di Stefano's death by HM Coroner Hereward Rice. Detective Inspector Neville Stewart, the Senior Investigating Officer, read out a statement in which he revealed that di Stefano was given the anti-freeze in a bottle of Lucozade. The inquest has been adjourned until April.

'Di Stefano, aged 44, was a professor of sociology at the University of London. Samantha Winter was reading sociology at that university until she was picked from thousands of aspiring singers under the age of twenty-one to compete in "Junior Idol". The top-rated programme concludes tonight, and sizzling Sam is a hot favourite to take this year's "Junior Idol" crown. Bookmakers are currently giving odds of 6/4 for blond stunner Sam, 20, to win over fellow finalists Taneesha and Raj. Last year's winner, Karma, went on to a lucrative recording contract and is currently at number one in the charts.

'Police questioned Sam at the "Junior Idol" studios on Thursday, sources have revealed.

'Reality Bites, who produce "Junior Idol", the Metropolitan Police, and the di Stefano family were unavailable for comment.'

◇◇◇

It hadn't taken them long to polish off their breakfast.

'That's better.' Triona sighed happily and took a gulp of coffee, emptying her mug. 'The coffee is foul. Can I have another cup?'

Neville jumped off the bed and bowed at the waist. 'Refills on foul coffee, coming right up. Would you like seconds on mouldy toast as well?'

'I'll give that a miss, if you don't mind.'

He returned a few minutes later with two fresh mugs of coffee. 'And I have news for you, as well,' he announced. 'Andrew left several messages last night. Eight people want to give you in excess of six hundred thousand pounds for your flat. Isn't that brilliant? All you have to do is decide which one you want to sell it to.'

Triona reached for the mug. 'Aren't you forgetting something?'

'What's that?'

'One little detail, Stewart. Just exactly where are we supposed to live, now that you've sold both our flats out from under us and made us homeless?'

'Oh, didn't I mention that?' Neville contrived to look innocent. 'I've found us the perfect house.'

'*What?*'

'A nice terrace in Notting Hill,' he said, grinning. 'Ladbroke Square. Three bedrooms. Private sale, practically signed and sealed. I promise you, Triona—you'll love it.'

She set the mug down on the bedside table and threw back the duvet. 'Then why are we wasting time drinking foul coffee?' she demanded.

Neville took that as an invitation, and a welcome one at that, given the alluring sight of flesh that the displaced duvet had been concealing. He slipped out of his dressing gown and into bed. 'I thought you'd never ask,' he said. 'Not that I need asking.'

'Forget about it!' She gave him a shove that sent him sprawling onto the floor. 'I want to see my new house. This morning. Right now!'

Joe really had been murdered. Callie couldn't take it in. She hadn't believed Chiara; she'd told herself that the police's involvement must be routine.

But who? And why?

And poor, poor Chiara. Callie hoped, fervently, that Chiara wouldn't see the *Globe*—that somehow the family would manage to keep it from her. She hoped that the scurrilous implications of Lilith's story wouldn't go any further, and wouldn't have to impinge on a young girl's feelings about her adored father.

She went into her stall in the church and opened the prayer book that resided there. Fortunately, considering her state of mind, this was one of the mornings when no one else had turned up for the service, not even the dim young man who hardly ever missed a day. It was such a beautiful morning; presumably every one else had better things to do with it than attend Morning Prayer at All Saints' Church.

So although Callie read the words of the Office aloud, her mind was engaged elsewhere. When it came time for the prayers, she prayed fervently for Chiara, and for all of the di Stefano family. For poor Joe, whose life had been taken from him in a cruel and deliberate way. 'Rest eternal grant unto him, O Lord, and let light perpetual shine upon him,' she prayed. 'May he rest in peace, and rise in glory.'

The time-honoured words brought some measure of comfort to her, as they were intended to do. She wondered, not for the first time, how people who had no faith managed to cope with bereavement and loss.

It wasn't easy, even with faith. There was no simple way to get through it—only the promise of God that he would not desert his people in their pain.

She got to the end of the service, concluding with the words set for Morning Prayer during Lent: 'May God our Redeemer show us compassion and love. Amen.'

Amen, Callie echoed in her heart, finding a crumpled tissue in her cassock pocket and dabbing her eyes.

Time to go back to the vicarage. With any luck, she could just drop off her cassock in her room and slip out to Frances', without having to make any complicated explanations to Brian or Jane.

It was only as she approached the back of the church, though, that Callie realised she wasn't alone in the building. There was a dark shape in one of the back pews, reading the copy of the *Globe* that she'd left there before the service.

He looked up, dropped the paper, and stepped out into the aisle, blocking her way.

'Hello, *Cara mia*,' said Marco.

'You rat-bag,' said Triona, fondly, as they walked along Holland Park Avenue towards Notting Hill. 'When were you going to tell me about the house?'

'I really was going to tell you this morning,' Neville assured her.

'And what if I hate it?'

'You won't.'

'It's right on Ladbroke Square Gardens?'

'Facing it. Great views. And the sprog will have a brilliant place to play.'

Triona patted her bump, smiling. 'The sprog thanks you for your consideration.'

'Miss Harwood grew up in the house,' Neville told her. 'She says it's a wonderful family home.'

'And it's practically just round the corner from Frances and Graham,' Triona added. 'That will be nice.'

Neville wasn't quite as keen on that as Triona was; the next thing he knew, he reflected, she'd be talking about going to church. Having the baby christened as an Anglican.

'That reminds me,' Triona said. 'I think I left my dressing gown hanging on the back of their bathroom door. Maybe we can drop by and retrieve it when we've seen the house.'

'Yes, all right,' he agreed.

He'd rung ahead; Rosemary Harwood was ready for them with coffee that was a great improvement over his earlier efforts, and another plate of her delicious shortbread biscuits.

But first there was a tour of the house, and he was quietly overjoyed to see the expression of delight on Triona's face; it only increased as they went from room to room. She didn't say much, yet her smile said it all.

As they drank coffee, making small talk, her eyes roved round the open-plan sitting room, exploring each corner. Her head twisted towards the kitchen, then towards the staircase. Rosemary Harwood must have noticed it as well; after a pause in the conversation she said 'Would you like to explore the house on your own, my dear?'

'Oh, yes,' Triona said eagerly. 'Yes, I'd love to.'

She got to her feet as nimbly as she could with her expanding waistline and changed centre of gravity.

'I think she approves,' Neville said, smiling, when Triona had disappeared up the stairs.

'I'm so glad.' Miss Harwood sounded sincere.

He could still scarcely believe it. 'And you're absolutely sure you want to sell us your house? I'd hate for her to get her hopes up…'

'Don't worry,' said Rosemary Harwood, who had clearly taken to Triona. 'I can't think of anyone I'd rather have in my house. I can tell that it will be in good hands.'

'If we could be in by the time the baby arrives…' he said, almost thinking aloud.

'That shouldn't be a problem. All I have to do now is find my cottage by the sea.'

Neville settled back in the comfortable chair, content to wait for Triona. But Miss Harwood evidently had had a hidden agenda in urging Triona to explore upstairs. 'There was something I wanted to mention to you, Detective Inspector,' she said.

His feeling of well-being evaporated abruptly with the use of his title. 'Yes?'

'About Miss Winter. Samantha. I said that her…liaison… with Dr di Stefano had ended a month or more ago. But I should have mentioned that I saw her recently. Just over a week ago, I think it was. Thursday or Friday.'

'Where was that?'

She put her head to one side, thoughtfully. 'In his office. She came to see him. It was the lunch-hour, so there weren't many people about. But when I got back from my lunch, the door of his office was closed. I could hear raised voices. Hers, his. Then she came out, slammed the door, and walked past my desk, without so much as a word.'

'What?' Neville stared at her.

'I didn't mention it to him,' she added. 'I could see he was upset, and I didn't think there was any point winding him up further.'

'So that was the last time you saw her,' Neville said slowly.

'No, actually.' Rosemary Harwood looked off into the distance. 'She came back later that afternoon. Dr di Stefano was giving a lecture, so I told her he wasn't in his office. But she said she'd left something in there and needed to fetch it. I didn't stop her.' She turned her eyes back towards Neville, frowning. 'Should I have stopped her?'

Frances was surprised when she opened the door to find not just Callie, as she'd expected, but Callie and Mark.

To Frances' practised eye, Callie seemed a bit nervous, and so did Mark: nervous with each other, rather than with her. 'I hope you don't mind,' Callie said. 'We'd like to take Bella for a walk.'

Bella duly appeared, and was gratifyingly enthusiastic to see both of them. 'Well, so much for me,' Frances said drily. 'I'm just the one who's been feeding her for the past week.'

Callie and Mark were both on the floor with Bella, receiving slurpy kisses.

'Would you like something to drink first?' Frances asked. 'Coffee? Or even some breakfast? I've just finished giving Graham his Saturday fry-up, so it wouldn't be any trouble. The frying pan's still warm.'

'I haven't eaten anything,' Callie admitted.

'Well, then. Come on through and I'll make you some breakfast.'

Mark stayed on the floor with Bella for a few minutes, which gave Frances a brief opportunity to query Callie in the kitchen. 'What's going on?' she whispered.

Callie lifted her shoulders. 'I'm not sure yet,' she said quietly, looking over her shoulder towards the door. 'He turned up at the church after Morning Prayer. He said he thought we needed to talk. So I invited him to come with me, to walk Bella. But on our way over, all we talked about was Joe. Oh, Fran—it's horrible! I can't believe he really was murdered!'

'Mark's confirmed it, then? It's not just a fantasy by Lilith Noone?'

'Oh, it's true, all right. They've launched a full investigation, with Neville Stewart in charge. And Marco's been put on leave until they solve the case. It's awful for him.'

Frances could see that. 'I assume they're looking at the family first? Serena?'

'Yes. And of course Marco doesn't think Serena could have done it.' Again Callie glanced towards the door. 'But what I want to know, Fran, is how you happened to find out about the article in the *Globe*. Very mysterious.'

She should have known she'd have to admit it, sooner or later. Frances made a wry face at her friend. 'It's Graham,' she said. 'His guilty little secret.'

'That he reads the *Daily Globe*?'

'No,' said Frances. 'That he's a secret "Junior Idol" addict! I can't tear him away from it on a Saturday night. And he's got a real thing about Samantha. I think he's even rung up to vote for her once or twice.'

'Good grief,' said Callie, with feeling.

'So when he went along to the newsagent's to get his papers this morning, he saw the headline on the *Globe* and couldn't help buying it.' Frances put a finger to her lips. 'But for heaven's sake, don't say anything. He'd kill me if he knew I'd told you.'

Neville wasn't keen to make the stop at Frances', as he was anxious to follow up on what Rosemary Harwood had revealed to him, but since it was so close he couldn't very well say no to Triona. He was determined, though, to refuse offers of hospitality and to get away as quickly as possible.

It didn't quite work out that way.

Triona explained her errand to Frances, and was waved upstairs to search out the missing garment. 'Come on through to the kitchen,' Frances said to Neville. 'Breakfast is on offer, if you'd like some.'

She turned and walked away so he followed her, stopping in his tracks in the doorway as he saw who was sitting at the table, tucking into a cooked breakfast. Mark Lombardi, with his girlfriend Callie.

'Hi there, mate,' Neville said, hoping he didn't sound as awkward as he felt.

Mark, his mouth full of sausage, nodded.

Frances gestured at the frying pan. 'I can give you eggs, sausages, bacon, and tomatoes. And toast, of course. The mushrooms are gone, I'm afraid.'

'I love mushrooms,' Callie apologised, her fork poised over a plate of mushrooms on toast.

He wanted to say no. He wanted to turn around and leave. But his treacherous stomach betrayed him, his mouth watering like Pavlov's dog at the very words 'egg', 'sausages' and 'bacon'. 'All right, then,' he said, pulling out a chair.

Callie looked at him quizzically. 'Did you get my message? I left it a couple of days ago, but you didn't ring back.'

'Message? No.'

'They said they'd make sure you got it. I said it was important.'

'A phone message?' Something tickled the back of his mind. 'Important? What was the message, exactly?'

'I just asked her—the woman who answered the phone, that is—to tell you to ring Callie.'

Then he remembered the pink post-it—the one he'd lobbed at the rubbish bin—and the penny dropped. 'Callie!' he said. 'The dozy cow wrote "Cowley" on the message slip. My sergeant, you know. He denied making the call, and I thought he was just trying to wind me up.'

Callie looked confused, then said, 'Oh…I see. Callie—Cowley. Must have been a bad line.'

'So what did you want to tell me? What was important?'

She looked at Mark, then at Frances' back as she laboured at the cooker. 'It's about Jodee and Chazz,' she said.

So it was confidential, then, if she didn't want her boyfriend or her friend to hear. 'Can we use the front room for a minute?' he asked Frances, casting a regretful glance at his breakfast in the making.

'Of course,' said Frances. 'This will be ready for you when you get back.'

Callie was admirably concise as she told him about a conversation she'd had with Jodee—a conversation in which Jodee admitted that Muffin had been left alone with Chazz's father for something like an hour. More than enough time for the damage to the baby's fragile head and spinal cord to be done.

'Thank you,' Neville said, genuinely grateful. If the di Stefano case were still as clear as mud, this meant that they might be able to tidy up the loose ends of the Betts case before the resumption of the inquest.

As Callie returned to her breakfast, Neville made a quick call on his mobile. 'Sid?' he said. 'I have a little job for you.'

'But Guv, I'm—

'I don't care what you're doing right now, or who you're doing it with. I need for you to track down a Kevin Betts. Last known address, London. Look in the phone book. When you've found him, let me know, and have him brought in. I'd like to have a few words with Mr Betts.'

◇◇◇

Mark hadn't had an appetite earlier that morning, especially after Mamma'd had a go at him, but now he found himself devouring the breakfast that Frances had put in front of him, just barely restraining himself from picking up the plate and licking it.

He watched Neville doing the same, silently and with concentration. When Neville had finished, and Triona had been supplied with toast and coffee, Mark chose his moment to speak. 'Have you seen today's *Globe*?' he asked Neville.

'No. Do I need to?'

'Yes, I think you do.' He looked at Callie, who pulled the tabloid out of her bag and handed it across the table to Neville.

'Bloody hell,' were his first words. 'That damned, bloody, interfering woman. If you reverends will please excuse my French.' He read through the story while Mark watched his face.

Neville wasn't very good at hiding his emotions, particularly when it came to anger. He was, Mark saw, furious.

'Who told her?' he demanded, obviously not expecting an answer from the people round Frances' kitchen table. 'Who are her sources? If I find them, I'll murder them myself.'

'Is she—Samantha—a suspect?' Mark asked. 'Or is Lilith Noone just making a mountain out of a molehill?'

Neville stared across the table at Mark, his lips pressed together. For a moment he was silent, seemingly debating with himself. 'I don't know,' he said at last. 'I thought that she couldn't have done it. I thought she was just pissing me about for fun. But this morning I've learned something that might just change everything I thought about this case.'

Callie spoke. 'Can you tell us?'

Again a moment of silence, then Neville said abruptly, 'What the hell,' flinging his hand out in a gesture of abandon.

What he told them was that Samantha Winter, who had ended her affair with Joe some weeks before, had had the opportunity to murder him. A reliable witness had overheard a row, and had seen Samantha in circumstances that were not incompatible with her having administered the fatal poison to Joe.

'So what you're saying,' Mark simplified, 'is that Samantha could have done it.'

Neville nodded. 'That certainly seems entirely possible, from what I've just been told. But what I can't seem to get my head round is the motive. *Why* would she poison him? As she told me, she'd broken it off with him at least a month before, and she already had a new boyfriend.'

'Blackmail,' Callie said promptly. 'What if he was blackmailing her? To get her back? You said there had been a row?'

'But there are plenty of other fish in the sea,' Mark said bitterly. 'I'm sure that he'd already found someone else. Some other pretty undergraduate.'

Neville turned to Mark first. 'That's what I thought. But my source...she said that Dr di Stefano—Joe—really loved Samantha. That she was the only one, ever—the only affair— and he was devastated when she broke it off. She was sure of it. "Besotted" was the word she used.'

Mark felt as if he'd just been kicked in the stomach. All of his preconceptions about Joe over the past few months—he'd just assumed that the fling with Samantha was part of a selfish pattern of behaviour. Having his cake and eating it, over and over again. Not a one-off. Not something genuine, that had caused Joe pain. Not real love, challenging a lifetime of fidelity and loyalty, but a heedless, ego-driven expression of his disregard for the vows he'd made to Serena.

Had he been wrong, then?

If Joe had really loved Samantha, that changed everything. Mark wasn't sure why it should make such a difference, but it did.

Neville had turned to Callie. 'I thought about blackmail,' he said. 'He might have threatened to make their affair public, unless she came back to him.'

'He wouldn't have wanted it to be public, though,' Callie pointed out immediately. 'It would have devastated his family. Chiara—I just can't imagine that he would have wanted that.'

'No. That's what I thought.' Neville picked up his fork and tapped it on his empty plate. 'And besides, she wouldn't have that much to lose if he did go public. That's why I decided that she couldn't have done it. No motive. Now, though…I just don't know.'

◇◇◇

There was something nagging at the back of Callie's brain. Tantalisingly close, yet just beyond her grasp. Something…

'What if you looked at it in a slightly different way?' she said slowly, working through it in her head.

Neville raised his eyebrows. 'What do you mean?'

'Samantha. Say it doesn't have to do with him threatening to tell about their affair?'

'Then what?'

She was getting there. She could almost… 'I've never met Samantha,' Callie said. 'I've only seen her on the telly. So I could be way off base. You've met her, though, Neville. What would you say is the thing that drives Samantha? The most important thing in her life?'

'Apart from herself, that is? Fame,' Neville said promptly. 'Celebrity. She wants to win "Junior Idol". She wants to be a household name.'

'So what if…it has to do with that? What if Joe somehow threatened that goal? Would she kill him to keep that from happening?'

Neville replied without hesitation. 'She would.'

'Fame,' Callie repeated to herself, trying to jog her memory. 'Celebrity. "Junior Idol". Tori Morpeach. Hilary Dalton's god-daughter, who worked for Reality Bites. They just want to be celebrities,' she'd said. 'The extents they'd go to…' And then, 'The lies people tell…'

'What if,' Callie said, 'She'd lied about something to get on "Junior Idol"? And Joe found out about it?'

Triona spoke for the first time, sarcastically. 'You mean like saying she had talent?'

Neville ignored his wife's comment. 'What could get you disqualified from "Junior Idol"?'

Callie thought back to the conversation with Tori Morpeach. 'I had one contestant recently who asked me what would happen if we found out they'd lied about something,' Tori had said.

'Lying. About something important,' she stated.

'But what could be that important in qualifying for "Junior Idol"?' Frances chipped in.

'What if she'd been working in a strip club to pay her university fees?' Neville hypothesised wildly. 'Lap dancing? Or in porn films, having it off with a herd of sheep? Or what if she'd been banned from driving for running down a little old lady in a zebra crossing after tossing back a dozen tequila slammers?'

'Any of those things would just add to her mystique,' Frances disagreed. 'Publicity is publicity, good or bad, for someone like her. The legend of Samantha.'

'It's right here in front of us.' Mark leaned forward, an expression on his face like—Callie thought—Moses coming down off the mountain with his stone tablets. Glowing with certainty. 'Age.' He jabbed his finger at the front page of the *Globe*, which Neville had flung contemptuously on the table. 'Under the age of twenty-one. It says it right here.'

◇◇◇

'It also says that Samantha is twenty,' Neville pointed out, then his jaw sagged as the implications sank in. 'Good God,' he said, weakly.

What if she'd lied about her age—claimed she was a year, or even a few months, younger? Was that the sort of thing she would have confessed to her lover, then regretted? 'But age is a matter of public record,' he said. 'Surely if she'd lied about her age to get on "Junior Idol", lots of people would know about it. Parents, family, friends.'

'But only a desperate lover would threaten to use it to get her thrown out of the competition,' Mark stated.

Callie was pulling a phone out of her bag. 'I'd like to make a couple of calls,' she said. 'Just to verify something.'

She left the room for a few minutes; they all just sat there, looking at each other, until she returned with a triumphant grin.

'I've spoken to Victoria Morpeach, whose god-mother is one of my parishioners. Tori works for the company that makes "Junior Idol", amongst other things. And she's confirmed that when Samantha Winter auditioned, she asked what would happen if the producers found out that a contestant had lied about something.'

'Why would an innocent person even ask a question like that?' Mark demanded.

Neville's question was more direct. 'And what did Miss Morpeach tell her?'

'She told her,' Callie said, 'that if it was a matter that affected the contestant's eligibility, they would be dropped from the competition.'

'So it would behove her that the producers not find out,' Neville said thoughtfully, stroking his chin. 'But this is all speculation, plausible as it is. Now it's time for *me* to make a phone call.'

He went back into the vicarage's front room and speed-dialled Sid Cowley again.

'Guv, I was just going to ring you,' Cowley said, his voice smug. 'We've got Betts. I ran his name through the system—didn't even have to look in the phone book. He's in the nick in Hackney. Got picked up a couple of days ago, flogging cut-price fags round the pubs. Said they fell off the back of a lorry, of course. Couldn't make bail, so he's not going anywhere for a while. You can talk to him whenever you want.'

'Good job,' Neville said, though he knew it was really down to good luck rather than good police work. 'Just as well you've cracked it, because I have another little job for you.'

Cowley groaned. 'Give me a break, Guv. It's Saturday.'

'This has to do with your own favourite Idol, Samantha.'

'I saw the *Globe*,' Cowley said, sounding more eager. 'You want me to go and talk to her, Guv? See if I can get anything more out of her?'

'You wish. No, Sid, I'd like a few facts checked. First, take a look at her bio on the "Junior Idol" web site—I'm sure you have it book-marked,' he added snidely. 'See what it says for date of birth. And place of birth, if it gives that. Then cross-check it with the General Register Office. I want to know exactly when and where she was born.'

'She's twenty, Guv,' Cowley told him. 'Everyone knows that.'

'We'll see,' said Neville.

Chapter Twenty

Neville had rushed off; Triona had stayed behind to drink coffee with Frances.

Bella was dancing round the door, clearly ready for her walk. 'Shall we take her to the park?' Callie suggested to Mark.

That was why he'd come, and what he wanted to do. But he realised, suddenly, that there was something else that he needed to do first. Something that couldn't wait. 'Can you hold on for an hour or so?' he pleaded. 'I wouldn't ask you if it weren't important. I'll be back as soon as I can—I promise.'

'All right,' Callie agreed. 'I can join the girly coffee morning. Bella will just have to cross her legs.'

The Tube journey across town was slower than he would have liked, with all of the Saturday shoppers heading to Oxford Street. By the time he got to Clerkenwell he realised that there was no point going to the di Stefano house; instead he went straight to La Venezia.

It was too early for the first of the lunch-time crowd. Mark found Serena checking the diary for bookings and putting 'Reserved' signs on the appropriate tables. 'I'd like to have a word,' he said. 'In the private dining room, if that's all right.'

She shook her head. 'After lunch, Marco. Come back later.'

'Now.' He said it so firmly that she looked up from what she was doing, startled.

'But there's a party of eight due in…' She checked her watch. '…Quarter of an hour.'

'Pappa can deal with it. And this won't take long, I hope.'

Serena shrugged and followed him.

He'd been thinking, on the cross-town journey, about what he was going to say to her. It would be premature to tell her that Neville thought he'd solved Joe's murder, but there were other things that needed to be said.

'I'm worried about Chiara,' he said bluntly, as soon as Serena had closed the door behind her.

'She's having a difficult time,' Serena admitted. 'But we'll get through it. It's partly her age, you know.'

'She blames you for her dad's death.'

Serena gave a mirthless laugh. 'So do your friends in the police, evidently. Is that what this is about?'

'You know it's about a lot more than that.' Mark pulled out a chair and sat down; Serena continued to stand. 'It's about you…and Joe. And what that situation has done to the family, and to Chiara.'

'And *you* know,' she said, 'that I've done my utmost to keep it all from them. From the girls and *i genitori*.'

'You've dumped it all on me instead.' Mark tried to keep the bitterness out of his voice. 'Which I wouldn't mind, except that I don't think you've been totally honest with me.'

She looked surprised at that. 'What do you mean, Marco?'

'You led me to believe that Joe had had a string of affairs over the years.'

'And?' she challenged.

'It's not true, is it?'

Serena's reply didn't answer his question. 'What difference does it make?'

'It makes all the difference! I've been hating Joe for months because I thought—you let me think—that he was a serial philanderer. And you've known all along that it was just the one affair.'

She didn't deny it. 'He was unfaithful to me. To our marriage vows. What difference does it make if it was once, or a hundred times?'

Mark could see how Serena would feel that way, as a betrayed wife, but to him—as a man—the difference was vast. Joe hadn't set out to deceive Serena, systematically and repeatedly. He had been broad-sided by feelings he couldn't control. His actions hadn't been exemplary or even excusable, but he had tried to do his best by his family.

Why, then, had Serena as much as told him that Samantha was just the latest in a series of infidelities? Because she wanted him to believe it? Because she couldn't, or didn't want to, deal with the truth? But why?

'Wouldn't it have been worse?' Mark asked aloud. 'If there had been lots of girls, wouldn't it have been worse?'

'Is that what you think?' Serena leaned her back against the door and narrowed her eyes at him. 'It would have been bad, yes. To think that I couldn't…satisfy him. That he had to go else-where for his physical needs. But this wasn't like that, Marco.'

'No,' said Mark. 'He loved her.'

Serena's eyes widened. For a moment she stood there, staring at her brother, then she crumpled into the nearest chair.

'Serena!' He jumped up and went to her side.

'He loved her!' Serena's voice rose in pitch. 'Don't you see, Marco? He would have left me. Left *us*. For her. She bewitched him, that *puttana*. I wasn't enough for him. After all those years together, suddenly I wasn't enough.' She pounded her fist on the table. 'The bastard! And then he goes and dies on me, and what am I supposed to do?'

For the first time since Joe's death, Mark witnessed his sister's tears. They started as a trickle; the trickle soon became a flood.

Mark knelt by her chair and put his arms around her, his anger towards her evaporating.

It had been a long afternoon. Neville didn't believe Sid Cowley when he rang to tell him that the General Register Office had, in fact, moved, and was proving difficult to track down. Yes, they had a web site. No, they weren't answering their phone on a Saturday afternoon.

While a grumbling Cowley dealt with the dilemma, Neville took advantage of the lull in the proceedings to cross London and pay a visit to the Hackney police station, where the helpful custody sergeant fixed him up with an interview room, set up the recording equipment, and brought Kevin Betts through from the cells.

Kev, Neville was interested to see, resembled Chazz in his wiry build, and provided a rather sobering hint of what his son might look like in another twenty-five or thirty years: receding hairline, weatherbeaten face. Then again, Chazz had the money to keep the years from taking their toll in quite that way. Kev's three-day growth of beard in no way resembled Chazz's designer stubble, and with Chazz's contract promoting a famous men's fragrance, it would be surprising if he ever smelled like Kev did now, probably not even back when he was working as a removal man.

'Would you like to have your solicitor present, Mr Betts?' asked the custody sergeant.

'No need. I'm not saying nothing.' Kev sat down, leaned back, and folded his arms across his chest, glaring truculently at Neville. 'Them fags fell off the back of a lorry. End of story.'

Neville smiled. 'I see. Was it by any chance a French lorry?'

Kev Betts looked at him with suspicion, as if sensing a trap. 'Might of been,' he said cautiously. 'I didn't get a butcher's at the number plate, like.'

'Well, that would certainly explain the French writing on the fag packets.'

It was a shot in the dark, but it clearly hit home. Kev exercised his right to remain silent.

Neville sighed, tired of the game. 'Listen, mate,' he said. 'I'm frankly not interested where or how you choose to spend your days off. If you want to take a little trip on a ferry, I don't give a toss. I'm just here for a friendly chat.'

At that, Kev seemed to relax.

'By the way, what sort of work do you do?'

'I'm in the building trade,' Kev said. 'A bit o' this and a bit o' that, you know?'

That probably wouldn't amount to a very steady income, then. But Neville wanted to steer the conversation—such as it was—away from the touchy subject of money, and the implication that Kev would need to supplement his income by illegal means.

After a quick look round to make sure that the custody sergeant was well out of the way, Neville fished in his pocket and brought out a packet of fags, picked up on his way for this very purpose. He opened it and held it out to Kev Betts.

'Thanks, mate.' Kev gave him a conspiratorial grin as he expertly fingered one out of the packet. 'Decent of you. These new laws—it's like a bleedin' police state. If you'll pardon the expression.' He chuckled, pleased with his own wit.

He was going to have to smoke one himself, Neville realised, just so Kev wouldn't think of it as bait. Ah, well, the things he did for his job. This one was for justice: justice for baby Muffin. He struck a match and lit both cigarettes, then waited while Kev sucked deeply and exhaled.

'You have a family?' Neville asked, as casually as he could.

'A brother. We work together, like. We're good mates, as well. Go down the pub together and all that.'

'No wife or kids?' It had been a while since Neville had smoked a cigarette; he savoured the taste of the first lungful.

Kev shrugged. 'Technically. I have a wife. We split up years ago, but there weren't never no point in getting a divorce. We never got round to it. And kids—yeah. You might of heard of my son. Chazz. He was on that "twentyfour/seven" on the telly. Won, and all. Good-looking lad, if I say it myself.'

Neville tried to look impressed. 'You must be very proud of him.'

'Yeah, well.' Kev turned his head and dragged on his cigarette. 'To tell you the truth, mate, I ain't been much of a dad to Chazz and his sister. I ain't proud of it, but that's just the way it is.'

'Raising kids is tough,' Neville sympathised. 'My wife—she's expecting our first in a few months. And I have to tell you that it scares the hell out of me.' In his head he apologised to Triona, though there was more than a grain of truth in it. As far as he'd come in the last few months, he still had a way to go, and he knew it.

'I know where you're coming from.' Kev's words were heartfelt. 'Bren and me, we got married on account of the baby on the way. Then it turned out to be twins. Jesus. One, I might of managed, but not two.'

'Bad luck,' Neville said. 'Must have been a shock.'

'God—I ain't thought about that day in a long time. Day of the bleedin' Royal Wedding, wasn't it? I was working when Bren went to hospital, and afterwards I couldn't hardly get there for all the people in the streets. And then when I get there, Bren tells me it's twins, and she's naming them Charles and Diana, because of the flippin' wedding. That near finished me off, then and there—saying she was giving my kids toffee-nosed names like that.'

Well, I'll be, thought Neville.

'Then the nurse brings 'em in and hands 'em to me. Screamin' their heads off, both of them. Like they was being tortured or something. Little red things, ugly as sin. And screamin' like they'd never stop.'

Neville tapped some ash into a styrofoam cup. 'What did you do?'

'Handed 'em right back. "I'm outta here," I said to Bren. Straight out, I said it. "I told you I'd stand by you and the baby, but I never counted on two, and I just can't do it. A man can only take so much." And I ain't never seen her again, not from that day to this.'

'And your kids?' Neville asked. 'You haven't seen them, either?'

Kev rubbed his chin with his hand; it made a rasping sound. 'Nah,' he said.

'But Chazz—he must have quite a lot of money,' Neville pointed out.

That produced a scowl from Kev. 'I wouldn't ask him for no money. That wouldn't be right.' He smoked in silence for a moment, then said reflectively. 'I did want to see my grand-daughter, though. His baby, Muffin. After I seen her photo in a newspaper. I thought she looked like me, a bit. I wanted to see her, just once.'

'And did you?'

Kev had reached the end of his fag; he smoked it down to the last half-inch, holding it carefully between thumb and forefinger, then stubbed it out on the table. Judging from the ancient burn-marks, he wasn't the first one to use that particular table as an ash tray. 'Yeah,' he said. 'Yeah, I did.'

◇◇◇

It was as perfect a day as early spring ever provided, with temperatures so mild that a jacket was scarcely required. Though the trees had yet to clothe themselves in green, pink and white blossom was much in evidence, and daffodils showed their yellow faces in flower beds everywhere. Crocuses—white, purple, lilac and yellow—dotted the grass, opening to the sun.

Callie and Marco, with Bella on the lead, strolled round Holland Park: it was not too far from Frances' house, and there was ample space to give Bella a good long walk.

'I wonder if Samantha *did* lie about her age,' Callie said. 'There's no proof as yet, but it makes sense of everything.'

Marco raised his hand. 'I don't want to talk about it,' he said. 'Not now. Let Neville get on with it. If there's anything to be found, he'll find it.'

'What do you want to talk about, then?'

'Us.' Marco stopped, forcing Callie to stop as well. Bella's lead grew taut as the cocker spaniel carried on, then she turned round and trotted back to them with a quizzical look, wagging her tail.

Callie waited, looking not at him but at the cherry tree which flaunted pink blossom at the side of the path.

'First of all,' Marco said, 'I want to apologise. What I said to you about Chiara—it was totally out of line. You were doing your job, thinking of her welfare, and I had no right to try to interfere with that.'

'You were just carrying out orders,' Callie said with a weak smile.

'I shouldn't have done that. I was wrong.'

Well, she thought. At least he recognised that. But was there any hope that things would be different another time? His loyalty to Serena was unshakeable, and Serena would always do everything in her power to exploit it. 'So you want us to…carry on seeing each other, like before?' she said.

'Not exactly.'

Perhaps it *was* unrealistic, after what had happened. She would try to pretend it didn't hurt, though she was sure she would break down later. 'All right, then,' Callie said bravely. 'I suppose we should acknowledge it now, and be realistic about it. Your family will always come first with you, and that's…just the way it is.'

'You don't understand,' said Marco.

Callie turned her head to look at him. 'But I do. You love your family. That's…a good thing. And I don't want to be the one who puts you in the middle, between me and them.'

'I want you to be my family, *Cara mia,*' he said. 'You and Bella.'

Callie swallowed hard as Marco took her free hand, then went down on one knee. 'This isn't the way I planned it,' he apologised. 'I've dreamed about taking you to Venice, and asking you in a gondola. I don't even have a ring. But I have to do this now. So you'll know I mean it.' He raised his eyes to meet hers. 'Callie Anson, will you marry me?'

Bella jumped on him, licking his face and knocking him off balance. He rolled over and landed under the cherry tree.

Ridiculous as he looked, Callie couldn't help grinning. Marco laughed out loud, lying on his back with an ecstatic dog on top of him, her feathery tail flailing away.

'I suppose Bella's answered for both of us,' Callie said.

'I'd like you to answer for yourself, if you don't mind.'

She reached out a hand to help him to his feet. 'Then yes, Marco. Yes, please.'

◇◇◇

Eventually some high-level phone calls had produced the result that Neville had been half-expecting—and hoping for. The date of birth claimed by Samantha Winter on the 'Junior Idol' web site was not corroborated by her birth certificate, as held by the General Register Office. She had in fact been born six months earlier, which meant that she had passed the milestone of twenty-one years some two months ago.

In spite of Sid Cowley's pleas, Neville left him behind in favour of a WPC when he repeated the drive to the suburban 'Junior Idol' studios. She was a star-struck young woman, over-joyed at the prospect of entering into that Holy of Holies, and she chattered all the way about the relative merits of the finalists. Not a great improvement on Sid, then, Neville thought glumly. But he tuned her out and thought about Kev Betts.

Kev had admitted it, in the end. It had taken another fag and some delicate probing, but Kev had admitted it, and the act of doing so had seemed to come as something of a relief to him.

He hadn't meant to shake her. Everything had been fine at first: Jodee had gone; Muffin had slept. When she woke up, though, she wouldn't stop crying. He'd held her, jiggled her, talked to her, begged her to stop. Finally, desperate, he'd shaken her. 'Not that hard,' he insisted. 'Just till she stopped. It couldn't of hurt her none. She was fine by the time her mum come back. Sleeping again, like there'd never been no peep out of her.'

He didn't know, Neville realised suddenly. Kev Betts might have seen the newspaper coverage of the inquest, the 'Home Alone' headlines. But by the time 'Home Alone' had been superseded by 'Shaken to Death', Kev had been banged up in Hackney nick. He had no idea that his actions might have been indirectly—or even directly—responsible for Muffin's death.

Well, he had the confession on tape, and they had Kev in custody. Now it was up to the coroner and the CPS to decide, in the light of the rest of the post-mortem test results, whether Kev Betts would be up on a charge of involuntary manslaughter—maybe even murder.

What Neville wasn't expecting was the huge tail-back as they approached the studio. 'Must be the studio audience for tonight,' burbled the WPC. 'Those lucky people. Some of them win the tickets in competitions. Some of them just have the right connections. I don't know anyone who could afford to buy a ticket. I think they sell for about five hundred pounds.'

Eventually they reached the gates, where security was carefully checking each and every ticket—hence the tail-back.

'Tickets?' asked a uniformed man.

Neville showed him his warrant card.

'Oh, we didn't realise you would come straightaway,' the man said.

'I beg your pardon?'

'About the counterfeit tickets. We only reported them about an hour ago. This is good service, it is.'

Neville didn't bother to disabuse him. He drove through the gates and pulled the car up in a disabled parking space near the entrance of the building where he'd gone the last time.

'Look at that!' said the WPC, pointing to a huge crowd of cameras and other media types gathered round the entrance.

The press corps and paparazzi must have deserted their fruitless watch at the Betts house and moved their operations here, Neville realised. He wondered how much of it was in response to this morning's *Globe* story and to what extent it would have happened anyway. 'Ignore them,' Neville instructed her, keeping his eyes straight ahead and marching through the double doors with her following behind.

Inside he bulldozed his way through security, waving his warrant card like a talisman. 'But sir—you don't know where you're going,' one of the uniformed phalanx protested.

'Oh, yes I do.'

'But you can't go that way. That's where the dressing rooms are.'

'Exactly.' Neville tried to recall the circuitous route on which he'd been guided by Tarquin, and had almost made it to the door that said 'Samantha' when he was overtaken by Tarquin himself.

'They called me,' Tarquin said breathlessly. 'Security. They said some man with a warrant card had pushed his way through. And it's *you*.'

'It's me, all right.'

'You can't go in there. Sam's in makeup.'

'I think I'll be able to deal with the shock,' Neville said. 'Though I'm not sure about my young colleague, here.'

'But…' Tarquin sputtered as Neville pushed the door open.

She was in the chair, having the final touches applied to her flawless face. Samantha's brow lowered when she saw Neville.

'Don't do that,' chided the makeup artist. 'You'll ruin everything if you frown.'

'Can't you see I'm busy?' snapped Samantha in Neville's direction.

'I'll wait.' Neville sat down on the chaise longe and patted the space beside him; the WPC sank onto it with an awestruck sigh.

Eventually the makeup artist finished, and Sam got out of the chair, fluffing her hair and checking the results in the mirror. She nodded to the makeup artist to go, then turned to confront Neville.

'How dare you barge in here?' she said, though the dramatic effect or her words was spoiled by her determination not to frown. 'I said everything I have to say to you the other day. Just go away and leave me alone. I'm going on stage in less than an hour.'

Neville smiled. 'Ah, but it's not that simple. Things have changed a bit since Thursday, Miss Winter.'

She tossed her head. 'I don't see how.'

He reached into his pocket and produced a bit of paper. 'Miss Winter. I believe this is your birth certificate?'

Her eyes widened, and she hesitated for just a second before replying, but her voice was still aggressive. 'So?'

'So the date on this birth certificate does not quite tally with the one on the official "Junior Idol" web site,' he pointed out, still smiling.

'Big deal.' She shrugged. 'Women lie about their age all the time. It's not a hanging offence.'

'But it's a bit more serious than that, isn't it? Would you like me to show this to the producers of this programme? I'm sure they're in the building.'

'No!' she said, taking an involuntary step towards him.

'Now we're getting somewhere.'

She dropped gracefully into the makeup chair and glared at him, no longer bothering to preserve her perfectly smooth brow. 'What do you want?' she demanded.

'I want you to tell me why you went to Joe di Stefano's office last week.'

'That nosy old cow,' Samantha glowered. 'I should have known she'd have her ear pressed against the door.'

'From what I hear, you were talking loud enough that she didn't have to do that.'

'He wanted me back,' she said, sneering. 'He was pathetic. He said he loved me, more than anything. He said he was willing to leave his wife and family for me, if only I'd come back to him. As if I would! As if I'd want that pathetic middle-aged man.'

'And you told him that.'

'He still wouldn't believe me.' Samantha spun the chair around so that she was facing the mirror.

'So what did you do?'

'I…left,' she said, looking into her own eyes.

'But you went back.' When she didn't reply, Neville continued, 'The secretary saw you. She'll testify to it. And then,' he added, deliberately and ambiguously, 'there's the little matter of fingerprints.'

Samantha recoiled. 'But I—' She clamped her mouth shut.

'You were wearing gloves? Is that what you were about to say?' he guessed. The oldest trick in the book, and she'd fallen for it—almost.

Still she didn't turn round, glaring into the mirror.

'I suppose you felt that he left you no choice.'

Her expression changed; a whole spectrum of emotions played across her face. 'He said he'd tell,' she murmured, so softly that Neville had to lean forward to pick up the words.

'About the birth certificate,' he prompted.

'Yes. He knew. I'd told him. Pillow talk, you know.' Samantha gave herself a cynical smile in the mirror. 'I'd only found out myself, not that long before. My parents lied to me. They didn't want me to know that they had to get married. Bun in the oven. So they just changed my birthday. As far as anyone else knew, I was born in July, not in January. But I'd told him, so I had to kill him.'

As simple as that, thought Neville. 'Why anti-freeze?' he asked. 'Not a very nice way to kill someone.'

'I'd seen it on the telly. Someone finished off his wife that way, putting it in a glass of wine. It's easy to buy, and obviously it works quite well. Seeing the Lucozade bottle on his desk gave me the idea.'

The cold-hearted bitch, he said to himself. That beautiful face masked the black soul of a narcissistic sociopath.

She stood up. 'Are you going to let me go on tonight? Are you going to let me sing?'

'No. I'm taking you to the police station, where you'll be cautioned and charged.'

Samantha spun round to face him. 'Tell me something. Are there many photographers out there?'

The WPC answered—the first word she'd spoken. 'Hundreds,' she said.

Neville didn't fancy running that gauntlet himself. 'We can try to get you out by the back, if you like,' he offered.

She laughed. 'You don't get it, do you, Detective?' She ran her fingers through her hair to fluff it up, examined the results in the mirror, then held her wrists out to Neville. 'Cuff me,' she said.

'I don't think that's necessary, Miss Winter.'

'But *I* do. And it's front door or nothing.'

The WPC produced a set of handcuffs and clicked them in place.

Samantha Winter tossed her head and moved towards her dressing room door. 'I might not be the winner of "Junior Idol",' she said defiantly. 'But at least I'm going to be famous.'